tell us we're

*Home*

*Also by*

MARINA BUDHOS

*Ask Me No Questions*

# tell us we're

# *Home*

## MARINA BUDHOS

ATHENEUM BOOKS FOR YOUNG READERS

*New York   London   Toronto   Sydney*

ATHENEUM BOOKS FOR YOUNG READERS
An imprint of Simon & Schuster Children's Publishing Division
1230 Avenue of the Americas, New York, New York 10020
ATHENEUM BOOKS FOR YOUNG READERS is a registered trademark of
Simon & Schuster, Inc.
For information about special discounts for bulk purchases, please contact Simon & Schuster Special Sales at 1-866-506-1949 or business@simonandschuster.com.
The Simon & Schuster Speakers Bureau can bring authors to your live event. For more information or to book an event, contact the Simon & Schuster Speakers Bureau at 1-866-248-3049 or visit our website at www.simonspeakers.com.
Also available in an Atheneum Books for Young Readers hardcover edition.
Book design by Lauren Rille
The text for this book is set in Perpetua.
Manufactured in the United States of America
First Atheneum Books for Young Readers paperback edition May 2011
10  9  8  7  6  5  4  3  2  1
The Library of Congress has cataloged the hardcover edition as follows:
Budhos, Marina Tamar.
Tell us we're home / Marina Budhos. — 1st ed.
p. cm.
Summary: Three immigrant girls from different parts of the world meet and become close friends in a small New Jersey town where their mothers have found domestic work, but their relationships are tested when one girl's mother is accused of stealing a precious heirloom.
ISBN 978-1-4169-0352-9 (hc)
[1. Friendship—Fiction. 2. Immigrants—Fiction. 3. Social classes—Fiction.
4. Household employees—Fiction. 5. Mothers and daughters—Fiction.
6. New Jersey—Fiction.] I. Title. II. Title: Tell us we are home.
PZ7.B8827Tel 2010
[Fic]—dc22
2009027386
ISBN 978-1-4424-2128-8 (pbk)
ISBN 978-1-4424-0610-0 (eBook)

*To Ginee Seo*

*Chapter 1*

Meadowbrook, New Jersey, looks like it's right out of an old-time postcard. It has a big town hall, with huge columns and a neat border of red tulips. There's a quaint little Main Street, its wrought-iron lampposts twined with evergreen sprigs at Christmas; a big green park, where the kids trace ice-skating loops on the frozen pond.

The town is nestled in a valley, and on one side is a steep incline that thrusts up into the ravine, where some of the expensive modern houses are perched like wood and glass boxes. On the other side the larger homes slowly give way to two-family houses and apartments on gritty Haley Avenue and to the big box stores of Route 12. More and more, shiny new condos have sprung up in the open gaps of land, a grove of pale brick McMansions standing where an old horse stable used to be.

Halfway up the hill, in the old section of town, is Mrs. Abigail Harmon's house. It isn't much of a house, as far as Meadowbrook houses go. More it's a cottage, with a steep gabled roof and low exposed beams. The garden is a froth of eccentric tastes: pinwheels and tangled raspberry bushes, a crumbling slate wall and herb garden with chipped zigzagging paths.

Mrs. Harmon inherited the place from her mother, who'd been born in the pink-wallpaper nursery, and whose grandfather once owned the hundred acres of farmland that makes up what is Meadowbrook today.

Around the time Mrs. Harmon was born, her family's apple orchard was sold off to build the train station. Nowadays, when the early train draws up, a stream of women, mostly from the Caribbean or Latin America, step down in their rubber-soled shoes, cradling their Dunkin' Donuts coffees, and make their way to the pretty clapboard houses. A few minutes later, up and down the streets, comes a chiming of voices, good-byes, slammed doors, cars backing down driveways, mothers and fathers rushing across town with their briefcases and still-wet hair to catch the next train to the city.

It was one of those not-quite-spring days, weak sun slanting through the drafty windows, and Mrs. Lal, the housekeeper at Mrs. Harmon's place, was giving the vacuum one last firm push on the bedroom floor. Mrs. Lal stood tall at nearly six feet, black hair cropped short and stylish, showing her broad neck and shoulders. Mothers liked her because she gave them a tidy sense of everything in its place: children in bed by seven o'clock, no whining, no peas left behind on the plates.

Downstairs, Mrs. Lal's daughter, Jaya, was sitting at the big table in the kitchen. She was supposed to be memorizing the periodic table. Really she was trying to work up the nerve to tell her mother about the middle school spring dance.

"Jaya!"

Jaya's mother stood in the kitchen doorway, holding up three colored markers. "Jaya Lal, you have something against putting the tops on things?"

"Sorry."

"How many times I have to tell you? This isn't your house. You can't just go mooning around like it's yours. What's Mrs. Harmon going to think of the way I'm raising you!"

"Okay, okay."

In fact, what Jaya liked about Mrs. Harmon's house was that she could treat it like hers. She didn't have to say hello. Or good-bye. Mrs. Harmon just assumed she'd walk in if she felt like it. Of all her mother's bosses, Mrs. Harmon was the only one who seemed to want Jaya there—she encouraged it. *Make yourself at home. I've got too many rooms as it is.* Jaya would spread out her homework at the nicked pine table or help herself to what was in the refrigerator, even though half the time the milk was well past its expiration date.

As Mrs. Lal was turning away, Jaya called out softly, "Mama?"

"Yes?"

Jaya hesitated. Shoved into her backpack was a bright pink flyer saying SPRING DANCE EXTRAVAGANZA! Quietly she handed the sheet to her mother, watching Mrs. Lal's brow furrow while she read it. Usually Jaya didn't bother showing her mother any of the permission slips for ski trips or overnights to Washington, D.C. She just threw them into the garbage. Even if there was some kind of disclaimer in tiny print at the bottom that the school would pay for those "in need." No way was she going to sign up for that.

"It's a really big deal." Her voice quivered. "Me and my friends, we wanted to go."

Her mother's mouth made a tight line.

"And . . . I thought maybe I could get a new dress?"

"What's wrong with that blue dress you bought last year?"

"That was last year."

Silence fell as her mother kept standing in the doorway, the flyer clutched in her hand. Jaya could hear her mother go on: *Don't you be like those American kids. So spoiled. Wasteful. Designer clothes and doing drugs and bad things. I take care of them all the time. They show no respect for their parents. They run the house.*

"Mama—"

"Jaya!" Her mother was using the Keep Your Voice Down, This Is Not Your House and Where Did You Learn to Talk That Way voice.

"About the dress?"

"Next year you get your work permit and you can have a job and buy yourself dresses and whatnot. Jolene from church told me her daughter got a good job at the Home Depot."

*Oh, great.* Jaya imagined herself wearing an orange apron and standing around giving advice on garden shears to all the dads in Meadowbrook. Was there nowhere she could hide who she was? Did everyone have to know how much they needed money? Why couldn't she just be casual, like all those other kids, who sauntered into the cafeteria with a new pair of hundred-twenty-dollar sneakers, as if it were nothing?

"And what about your homework?"

Jaya's face burned.

"Is that a drawing?" She pointed to a quick sketch Jaya had started with her markers. Mrs. Lal didn't approve of Jaya's artwork, even if Jaya's father had been an artist. *Keep your eye on your science,* she would often say. *That's what will get you a job.*

"Now go and see if there's anything that Mrs. Harmon needs."

"Yeah, sure."

Shoving the flyer into her bag, she thought about the dance again, how all the kids got to dress up and spin across the polished parquet floor under a ceiling of balloons, the golf course lit up just for them. It reminded her of her father: how back in Trinidad, they would wake up early and go to the tourist part of town.

Before Jaya opened the front door, she paused in the hall, looking over to the living room, where Mrs. Lal was now tidying. She felt a whiff of sadness watching her mother punch the sofa pillows, just a little too hard.

Sundays in Port of Spain, while her mother studied her nursing books, Jaya used to accompany her father to the beach, where he would set up his easel by one of the resorts and paint, and sometimes sell his work to the tourists. She would lean against his legs, digging her toes into the hot white sand, watching the foamy surf curl and break on the shore. Not far away was an octagonal restaurant, where she could hear the *tap-tap* melody of a steel band, men and women dancing under Chinese lanterns that shivered in the breeze.

Then her father began to complain of stomach troubles and went into the hospital for tests. As he grew sicker, his hands trembled and he could barely hold up the brush; he still lugged his easel to the beach, but it became harder for him to work for long stretches. His figures became more ghostly, as if he didn't have the energy to fill them in. At the end, he would lie in bed with a board propped across his knees and try to draw, but most of the time he fell asleep before he was done.

After Jaya's father died, her mother began to say, *Your parents, Jaya, we're unfinished business.* That's because she never completed nursing school and her father never finished engineering school—or his life.

Whenever her mother said those words, Jaya felt she was the unfinished one, like one of her father's drawings, with its spindly lines, all that unfilled space. By the time her father passed away, she was nothing, just pure air and sadness.

Mrs. Harmon was standing next to a garden bed, two sacks of new planting soil slumped on the top step of the porch. "Oh, there you are!" she called. "You think you can help me with this?" She held up a lattice basket filled with drooping black-eyed Susans. "I'm getting an early start."

"Sure," Jaya answered.

Usually, on the good-weather days like today, Mrs. Harmon

was bent over her flower beds, dressed in her usual khakis and a worn work shirt, a straw hat with a beaded string tied around her chin.

Crouching down, Jaya helped Mrs. Harmon dig a hole, plant the flowers, and sprinkle mulch on top. Jaya noticed—not for the first time—how much Mrs. Harmon's hands trembled and her eyes watered.

"Why so glum?" Mrs. Harmon asked.

Jaya shrugged. "My mother won't buy me a dress for the school dance." She added, "She never buys me anything I want. No new art supplies. Not even a set of markers."

Mrs. Harmon laughed. "What a dictator."

Jaya pushed her trowel hard into the ground. "It isn't fair. She's always bossing me around."

"That's what mothers do. Although in my case, it was my husband who did the bossing." Mrs. Harmon didn't have any children of her own.

"Yeah. Well. She does it too much." Jaya lifted a black-eyed Susan from the basket. She was surprised by the bitter rush of tears in her eyes.

"She is trying to do what's best for you."

*Best for you.* Jaya hated that phrase. "Yeah, but why does she have to bug me so much?" Even saying the words aloud sounded funny, like the American kids at school.

"You're right. She's a real monster." She pointed at Jaya's hole. "Watch. You need to fill that in more."

Then she went back to planting, carefully scooping out holes, untangling a stalk from the bunch, patting the dirt smooth.

When Mrs. Harmon stood, she lost her balance, her fingers groping the air like claws. Jaya steadied her, shocked at how thin Mrs. Harmon's arm was, how she could feel the bone through her skin.

"Oh, dear," Mrs. Harmon said, sighing. "That's been happening a bit too much lately." Jaya noticed that her words came out a little slow and slurred. She also looked odd. Her straw hat had toppled off and hung by its string down her back. Her white hair was snared into a wild nest. And she looked especially puzzled. "Where are my gloves?" she asked.

Jaya pointed. "You're wearing them."

Mrs. Harmon gave her a hollow look and staggered up the path.

Recently Jaya and her mother had noticed that Mrs. Harmon had become more absentminded. "A little soft in the head" was the way Mrs. Lal put it. Mrs. Harmon would forget her keys, the route to the supermarket. Jaya's mother had taken to brewing tea with licorice and ginger, the way she did in Trinidad when old folks started losing their memory.

As Mrs. Harmon headed back to the house, Jaya thought about what her mother always said: *If it weren't for that lady, we wouldn't even be here in the first place.*

Jaya's mother was a practical woman. When Mrs. Lal and Jaya first came to the United States from Port of Spain, she quickly assessed her options. Nursing school was too expensive. So they'd lived in a tiny apartment in Newark with three dead-bolt locks, while Mrs. Lal signed up with a home aide agency, putting aside fifty dollars a week to send to Jaya's grandmother back in Trinidad.

One day Mrs. Lal picked Jaya up from school and put them on a New Jersey Transit train that went to a town with a sweet all-American name. It was the most impulsive thing she had ever done, for Mrs. Lal was not an impulsive woman.

To Jaya, Meadowbrook looked like a different country: pretty shingle houses with porches and neatly tended walks and gardens. In the parks they saw lots of West Indian women pushing the strollers or wiping juice spills. Sure enough, Mrs. Lal went to the community bulletin board at the library, where they met a tiny woman with silver hair wearing thick rubber boots, peering at the notices.

"Are you looking for work?" the old woman asked.

"Are you looking for someone?" Mrs. Lal asked back.

Mrs. Harmon didn't have a lot of money to pay, but her needs were simple: a small laundry load and someone to empty the refrigerator and make sure the house was tolerably clean.

Something about her appealed to Mrs. Lal. She reminded her of the old people in Trinidad. She was thrifty and spare. She saved plastic bags, kept old yogurt containers stacked in the larder. She used a woodstove in the living room, and if it got too cold, she put rolled-up towels against the door cracks. Inside her rooms were Windsor chairs with the polish rubbed off their arms, and all kinds of funny antiques: porcelain-head dolls slumped in a small wicker rocking chair, even a framed embroidery sampler done by some great-great-aunt during the Civil War.

"A real American," Mrs. Lal teased. "Blue blood, with all those old things."

"Nonsense," Mrs. Harmon replied, waving her hand. "Pack rat, more like."

Soon after Jaya's mother began working for Mrs. Harmon twice a week, word got around that Mrs. Lal was a good bet. She did three days babysitting for the Siler twins, a Saturday morning cleaning job for the Meisners, and a few others too.

But it was Mrs. Harmon's place that felt most like home. Jaya would come upon her mother and Mrs. Harmon sitting in the kitchen, swapping recipes and chatting. When Mrs. Harmon had indigestion, Mrs. Lal would bring her stalks of aloe from the Caribbean market that she boiled in an old pot. "You are a dear," the old woman would say gratefully. Jaya would sit down too, the three of them blowing on their tea mugs and laughing. It was the closest she had come to belonging since they'd come here.

"It's a sign," Jaya's mother liked to say of that day they'd run into Mrs. Harmon, her eyes shining. "We were meant to be here."

Ten minutes later Mrs. Harmon was back again, only this time she was agitated. "I don't understand it. I can't find them."

"Your gloves?"

She stared at Jaya. "Is that what I was looking for?" She rubbed her eyes, blinking.

Jaya had always been impressed with Mrs. Harmon's eyes. They were an astoundingly bright blue, the color of the Caribbean, and big. It wasn't hard to see the little girl that Jaya had seen in the old grainy photographs that were staggered up the wall along Mrs. Harmon's stairs—the wispy white-blond hair, the girl in a starched pinafore standing next to an old-fashioned wheelbarrow.

"I think so."

"I'm just not sure." Mrs. Harmon touched her temple lightly. "There are these spots in my head."

She went off again, her gait a little more crooked. Inside the house, Jaya heard a loud metallic crash.

Throwing down her spade, Jaya raced through the garden and into the kitchen, where she found Mrs. Harmon leaning against the table. Something was weird: Mrs. Harmon's face drooped, as if the skin on her cheek were made of putty sliding off her jawbone. Her lips moved thickly around her words. She tried blowing out a few sounds, but it was like a children's noisy toy, the battery wearing down.

"Oh—" Mrs. Harmon drawled. The next words were more of a gargling noise.

She touched her mouth and practiced a few more sentences. But some circuit had come disconnected, as if her brain couldn't tell her mouth what to do. "Call . . ." she struggled out. ". . . mother." That seemed to knock the breath out of her.

Jaya rushed upstairs to the bedroom, where she found her mother looping the vacuum hose onto its hook, and pulled her down the stairs.

Jaya was amazed at her mother's efficiency, all the little important things she knew. How she led Mrs. Harmon by the wrist, even as her right foot was dragging on the floor, and laid her gently on the sofa. How she checked her pulse, probed her lids.

"Don't panic. Just lie right there. I believe you're having a stroke. But you're going to be all right, darlin'."

Mrs. Harmon nodded, her blue eyes wide and frightened.

Then Mrs. Lal hurried into the kitchen, called 911, and very firmly gave them the instructions. "Vitals okay. Her heart is racing a little. But she needs an ambulance right away."

Jaya stood a few feet away, unable to keep her eyes off Mrs. Harmon's arm, which hung, limp, off the sofa edge.

"Jaya!"

Jaya could not move. Her insides felt like crumbling chalk, trickling through the soles of her feet.

Her mother came to her, putting a firm hand on each shoulder. "I need you now. No spacing out. I'll go to the hospital, but you need to stay here and close up the house. Do you hear me?"

Jaya trembled. Mrs. Harmon's body was very still now.

"Jaya!"

Jaya reeled back, as if struck. She knew she couldn't be as calm and brave as her mother wanted her to be. She could hear her mother telling her sternly, *Jaya, we don't have time to be cowards in this life. Not the life that was handed to us, a widow mother and a daughter. We got to be strong.*

After a few minutes an ambulance came shrieking up the driveway, its red lights cascading across the walls. Jaya could hear the scratchy whine of a walkie-talkie, a metallic thump as a stretcher was lowered down. The sound shook right through her.

An instant later the front door banged shut and the ambulance was gone, its siren piercing the air.

*Call your friends,* Jaya told herself. But she couldn't move. She could only stand on the bare floorboards, listening to wind scour the windowpanes.

*Chapter 2*

Revolution.

Lola Svetloski was sitting in Mr. Cohen's social studies class, dreaming of revolution. Battle plans. Marches. It was weird, she knew. But Lola loved to read about huge, cataclysmic change. About worlds turning upside down. The French Revolution. So gory and glorious, rivers of blood on the Paris streets. And then her favorite: the American Revolution. George Washington, Mr. Genius Strategist, with that bland, wide face, who elected not to be a tyrant.

*Wake up!* Lola wanted to shout now. But she knew if she opened her mouth, the other girls would gaze at her, with their sparkly green glitter eyes, their perfect tanned arms, as if she were an alien on the planet. Not even a girl. Just a bigmouth history freak. History was fine for doing the assignments, or for raising your GPA so you could get into a good college, which is what it was all about, anyway. If you were going to get excited about something, at least make it English, where you could recite love poems, or memorize Sylvia Plath. But history?

Now Mr. Cohen wrote on the board, in big block letters: **DEMOCRACY. CONSTITUTION. INDIVIDUAL RIGHTS.**

"Can you tell me, what were the central principles of the Declaration of Independence?" he asked.

Lola's hand shot up. "Life, liberty, and the pursuit of happiness," she called out, not even waiting for him to call on her.

"Exactly." Mr. Cohen grinned. "So what does the 'pursuit of happiness' mean?"

"I can spend as much as I want at the mall and no one should complain," Rachel Meisner offered.

"Except your parents," Mr. Cohen replied.

The whole class burst into laughter. Lola looked at Rachel, annoyed that she could be so jokey with a teacher, like they were friends. She always rolled her eyes when Lola spoke up, as if to say, *Oh, please. Don't be such a brownnosing know-it-all.*

There was something different about kids like Rachel. It was an air they carried, a casual, I-don't-care-and-besides-you-know-I'm-smart-enough attitude that the teachers just ate up. If something happened to them, or a teacher was mean or unfair, they knew a grown-up would come marching through the doors and stand up for them. For Lola, the message from her parents was different: Go to school and don't make trouble. Except Lola just didn't listen; she was always piping up.

"Okay," Mr. Cohen continued, "we'll be finishing up our year with the Founders' Project. That means conducting a reenactment of the American Revolution, acting out its principles and conflicts."

"Cool!" Dana Robbins flipped back her hair from her shoulders. She was starring in the end-of-year play, *Grease*.

"Wait. This isn't about how well you perform, but how you research. You'll have to research a figure in history and give me an argument about their role."

A few of the kids in the class looked discouraged. Clearly they'd thought the project was going to be a breeze.

"And don't just give me the usual stuff. Paul Revere woke up houses. You have to discover something new that you didn't know before."

"Do girls get to be guys?"

"Absolutely. We're bending gender here, all the way."

A wave of giggles erupted.

Lola was already scribbling in her notebook as the bell rang. This would be her chance. She'd do an amazing presentation. Dig out the real thing. Something spectacular, nothing phony. Make a real discovery about the revolution. Show those stupid girls, she thought.

Rachel and her friends were hurrying down the corridor and outside. "Oh my god, guys. You have to see the stuff my mom just got in!" Rachel's mother owned Vamps and Vixens, a funky clothing shop where a beaded wristband cost more than Lola's lunch money for a whole week.

Now she found herself pausing before an old case with trophies and photos of the lacrosse and baseball teams. Something about this place gave Lola a snug, safe feeling. She grew up in a village in Slovakia, and she knew all about history and crumbling old walls. But this was different. This was a history that she could be a part of. When she and her family first moved from a cramped apartment in the Bronx, Lola used to spend time at the local history room at the county library. A nice man used to help her, pulling out flat steel drawers that held land deeds and marriage certificates, the corners pockmarked with water stains. That, she knew, was way past nerdy. It was just plain queer. But that's what she loved. Old wedding invitations. A boy's satin baseball ribbon. To touch something simple—even a girl's embroidery hoop—was to feel the magic dust of history, of real Americans buried in cemeteries with slanted stones, the ones whose blood and skin and genes gave them a right to be here. And she, Lola, running her fingers along moth-eaten lace, was rubbing some of that belonging into herself, too.

Lola pressed her face against the dusty glass and stared at the faded black-and-white photographs of boys lined up in their padded uniforms, the girls in their pleated skirts. *I'm going to be one of you,* she thought.

Green Valley Garden Apartments sat right on the edge of town, not far from the strip malls on Route 12. Lying in bed at night, Lola could hear the constant hum of cars. Everybody else in school lived in houses that they owned, and even the complex Lola's family lived in had a pretend feel of big brick colonial houses, with front pillars. But the porch really opened to a wall of tiny mailboxes and buzzers, and the walls were so thin she could hear their neighbors arguing about who forgot to turn off the tap water. Most of the residents came from somewhere else: there was the man from Ghana next door, who worked as a taxi dispatcher, and a group of Ecuadorians, who did construction. She always knew they were back from their day because the water pressure went suddenly low as they each took a shower, and their spattered pants soon hung on the clothesline. Summers the evening sky turned raw and the haze from Route 12 hung like a smudge of cigar smoke. Her father presided from his folding chair in the courtyard.

As she unlocked the front door, Lola was hit with the stale smell of cigarette smoke. The blinds were drawn, newspapers scattered on the floor, mail dumped by the telephone. She could just make out the top of her father's head, and his feet—socks in rubber sandals—propped up on the coffee table. Her stomach went sour. She hated coming home to this.

"Papa?" Lola called.

He grunted.

"I hear your knees are bothering you."

"Bad." He rubbed his kneecap. He didn't even move off the couch. "Lola, today you do the meat."

*Yeah, what else is new?* she thought, dropping her knapsack. To cook was humiliating for her father. Unlike all those Meadowbrook fathers with their Williams-Sonoma aprons and Grill Master barbecues.

Mr. Svetloski shrugged and turned back to the TV. He was watching the Russian news. Hard to believe that her father, in his stained white undershirt stretched over his belly, actually knew five languages. He'd been brilliant at school, her grandmother said, the only boy who left the village to become a civil engineer, building bridges and roads.

A lot of good that did, Lola thought now. The first year in America he went to job interviews while working with a Russian construction company. But nothing ever came of it. His license wasn't good, or his accent too thick. For a while he was a doorman in Fort Lee, but complained about the hours and the snooty residents, especially those Koreans. And so it was her mother—the one who never even graduated from high school and whose English was lousy—who went out and found work. First it was serving food in a school cafeteria in the Bronx, then it was cleaning houses, and finally she landed a solid housekeeping job with the Vitales.

Sitting on the counter were sausages wrapped in newspaper, their juices dripping off the edge. Next to them were sliced onions and a chopped-open cabbage head. Her father had given up on the cooking halfway. He did that a lot these days. All over the apartment were his unfinished projects: a bookcase with only one shelf fastened; a set of broken blinds, so they eventually put sheets up on the windows.

Too often Lola found herself staring at sausages leaking on a counter, a sink full of dirty dishes, and bills that would send her mother's blood pressure through the roof. Now she sorted through the mail and found a letter from her mother's doctor. There were numbers on her latest blood sugar report, and a note scrawled across the top. "Please make an appointment as soon as possible."

"Lola!" Her father called from the living room. "Lola, bring me another ashtray."

Lola threw down the rag. *I am not doing this. I'm not covering for him. Not anymore.* She would walk out of this dirty kitchen, right past his fat cloud of disgusting cigarette smoke, out the door, to anywhere, out onto Route 12 with the trucks bearing down on her like giant silver Minotaurs and her legs shaking from the wind whipping past. She'd walk all the way to the county library and not call anyone, and dig into real archives and come up with the most amazing presentation, to show up those girls.

Lola didn't hear the phone until the fourth ring. She picked it up. Her mother was on the other end, her voice a weary rasp from too many cigarettes. "How is everything over there? Your father go out today? You were good at school?" Her mother always asked those same questions, though she didn't seem to expect an answer.

"Yeah."

"What about dinner?"

"What about it?"

There was silence. This happened more and more these days, her mother's disapproving quiet. *This country spoiling your mouth,* Mrs. Svetloski chided. *You sound like rotting fish, nothing good, just flopping around with stinking words. Big waste.*

Lola sighed to herself, pushing the damp rag back and

forth. If she walked out now, it would be her mother who would come home, tired from taking care of someone else's house, and then she'd have to make dinner all over again.

"It isn't fair. Papa didn't cook," she finally answered. "He said his knees hurt."

"Who said anything about fair? You respect your father, Lola. One thing we know, where we come from, we know how to respect. Your father, he look up to his father. You do the same."

She hoped she wouldn't launch into that old story of how her grandfather fell down in the wheat fields one day, and Lola's father carried the old man on his back for twenty kilometers, to the nearest doctor. From then on, every week, even though he had to help with the farm and study, he did the same, back and forth on those stony roads, the old man slumped over his shoulders.

What happened to that hero with the strong back and arms? she wondered as she hung up the phone. Where did he go?

"Lola, you got my ashtray?"

She picked up a glass bowl. "Yes, Papa," she sighed. "I'm coming."

Change, revolution, was so hard. Lola just felt tired and achy, like an old person. But tomorrow, definitely. She would do something different.

*Chapter 3*

Maria was sitting cross-legged on the grass at Grove Field, watching the white boys play sports. Their bodies seemed made of light. They spiraled, they ducked, they flew. Maria was supposed to be watching her cousin Renaldo play soccer with his friends. But her eyes kept drifting to the other side of the field, where the lacrosse players were expertly wielding their sticks. And the real angels—the Ultimate Frisbee boys—twirling, spinning, shooting from behind their backs, showing their perfect elbows and wrists.

A shout pulled Maria from her thoughts, and she looked up to see Renaldo hurl himself across the field, trying to stop their stray soccer ball. Renaldo watched over her like a brother, since she had no one else but her mother. Most days he worked for a landscaping company, except for times like this, when all the Spanish-speaking guys—the Mexicans and Ecuadorians and Dominicans and Costa Ricans—came from the surrounding towns and brought their coolers, their plastic goalie nets, and played hard and good, sweat flying off their shiny brown legs. Sometimes the old men came too, with their folding chairs and their portable radios and checker sets, the girlfriends and wives dancing merengue as the sun set behind town hall.

Now she saw a clump of boys gathering. One of the lacrosse boys in a red and white uniform was holding the soccer ball against his hip, while another was yelling. Renaldo was in there too, and even from here she could see his body tense.

"I told you, get this ball off the field," the other boy said.

"What are you talking about?"

"You heard me."

"It's a park. Anybody can come here and play."

"Get that ball out of here."

Renaldo grabbed it from him. "No need to be like that, man. This place is for everyone."

"You got that wrong. This is a field for teams. You hear?"

"I don't think so, man. This is a park. For everyone."

Maria's stomach hurt. What Renaldo said was true. It was a public park. But everyone also knew Grove Field was where the high school teams came for extra practice, since some of the school fields were out of commission while the new Astroturf was being installed, and the lacrosse and Ultimate Frisbee teams had first dibs here.

"Yeah," one of the boys said. "What is this, Union City? We going to have a Puerto Rican Day parade here?"

Renaldo's group hunched their shoulders, spit in the dirt, and cursed.

Maria looked at her cousin: a vein on his neck was throbbing, and his hands had curled into fists. Maria knew that when Renaldo got angry, his English left him, and he could easily slug some guy.

*Don't,* she thought.

"Hey." One of the Ultimate Frisbee boys shouldered his way in, between the lacrosse players and Renaldo. Turning to her cousin, he said, "*No hay una problema.* My guys can move to the lawn by town hall."

Maria listened, amazed. He spoke Spanish! Just like that! In and out, almost Spanglish.

Renaldo didn't seem pleased. "But this guy. You don't insult us—"

"Really." He put a hand on Renaldo's shoulder. "It's not worth a fight."

Renaldo didn't move. The vein in his neck still twitched. But she could see that the others were actually relieved. They began backing off, dispersing across the field. Renaldo was the last, still glaring at the lacrosse boy who had insulted him, before spinning the soccer ball on his fingertips and then following his friends.

Maria found herself lingering to stare at the Frisbee boy. He had brown hair hanging in messy waves that he kept tucking behind his ears. The gesture should have looked girlish, but on him it looked sexy and confident. His skin was amber, almost like a light-skinned Argentinian. Maybe he was? No, he wore a worn-out T-shirt that said FAIR TRADE PRODUCTS ONLY across the chest. He carried himself like a white boy, as if his whole body could part the air, make things happen.

As he bent down to scoop up his Frisbee, Maria found herself blurting out, "You speak Spanish!"

He shrugged. "Some. Last year I was in Costa Rica, digging ditches. I should be better, actually. I'm going to Guatemala next summer and I suck."

Hearing this made her smile. Gringos went all that way to dig dirt for free, while her cousin came here to do the same, for money. "I'm from Mexico," she offered.

"Yeah? My parents have friends who have a house in San Miguel de Allende. But I haven't seen much else. Seems like a cool place."

Maria found herself burning all over, as if he had complimented her, rather than her country. "Thank you," she added.

He stared at her.

"For helping out there. With those guys."

Again he offered a casual shrug. "It's nothing. Just a stupid thing." In Spanish he added, *"Hay lugar para todos."* There's space for everyone.

Again, she couldn't stop grinning.

"Hey, I'm Tash."

"Maria."

For the next hour Maria stayed in the shade of a tree, careful not to sit out in the sun because her skin got too dark, and kept her eyes on Frisbee boy, until Renaldo called to her. *"Vamos!"* he shouted. "We have to go home!"

Maria floated across the grass, aware only of the tall boy with wavy hair. She rolled his name in her mind. *Tash.*

"That was nice of him," Maria said as she buckled herself into Renaldo's beat-up Toyota Corolla. Renaldo's friends were packing up, shoving their water bottles and balls into nylon bags. Some had evening jobs—a few had to start their busboy shifts. Renaldo had night school, and then he had to be up at the crack of dawn for a big stone paving job.

He didn't answer.

"I mean that guy."

"What, you think I'm supposed to be so grateful? I need some high school kid to rescue me?"

"That's not what I meant, Renaldo." She wanted to add, *That's not what* he *meant.* But she didn't dare, especially when her cousin was in one of his moods. Little Bull, her uncle called him sometimes. Always ready to charge.

She knew why Renaldo was sore. Most of those boys were just a few years younger than he was. He'd come over here with his brothers and father a few years before, and all he'd done was work, all the time. He tried to get his GED at nights, but it was hard, with the long hours. Soccer was the only time he could unwind.

He cracked open a can of beer, even though she'd told him how many times that it was illegal in America, and they really meant it here. You couldn't just bribe some cop. But Renaldo always shrugged her off. Baby-school girl, he liked to call her. So innocent. She bit down on her words while he lit a cigarette and turned on the radio, letting the music pulse loud. *Mi primo,* she thought bitterly. My cousin. He flicked his cigarette out the window, the red ember twirling in the wind, scattering on the big green lawns.

The Alvarez family lived on a cul-de-sac in a small Cape Cod—style house, stacked inside like a layer cake: her uncle and his second wife, along with her little cousins and Renaldo, lived in the top part, and she and her mother had the basement apartment. Maria was relieved to be below. Sometimes there was too much arguing, especially among the men, and through the ceiling she heard every word, even the ugly ones. She didn't like either how her *tío* Pedro lorded it over all of them, her mother especially. Maria's mother was Pedro's little sister who'd married a no-good man who was—no surprise—gone a year later, and so Tío Pedro had sponsored Maria's mother to come to the States. Maria, in turn, was supposed to come right home after school to start the beans and rice, and push everyone's soiled clothes into the washing machine, then vacuum and pick up her little cousins' toys.

When Maria first came to Meadowbrook, she was astonished at how different everything seemed. *What an empty, quiet country,* she thought. The huge supermarkets with their pyramids of oranges, the long streets of houses, the way people stared at you from their doors but didn't always wave or say hello. The hushed pockets of quiet. She once sat on her front stoop and a whole hour passed before she saw someone go by on the sidewalk.

To Maria's frustration, living here was sometimes too much like being back in Puebla. Months would go by before she even spoke to an Americano, other than a teacher. And why should she? Every weekend the whole family would load into their cars and vans and drive to Union City to go shopping. Then they'd come back, and the women would spread out in the kitchen to make dozens of tamales—not much different from in Puebla. Or they'd get in their cars all over again and visit some relatives or have a barbecue party at their own place.

This was where she belonged, for now, and besides, Mrs. Alvarez said it could be years before everyone saved enough money to buy the house they hoped for. They couldn't afford anything in this town, anyway, and this is where the good schools were. So they stayed on, the women painting the kitchen avocado green and planting peppers and roses; the men fixing their old cars in the driveway.

As Maria and Renaldo came into the kitchen her *tía* Lucy, Renaldo's stepmother, was leaning against the counter. She hadn't changed out of her gray smock from the warehouse where she packed flowers into boxes, and even with the pretty golden highlights in her hair and her bright lipstick, she looked pale and grim.

"What's the matter?" he asked.

She pointed to a paper. "We had a surprise visit. Some kind of inspector. Said there were complaints. We're violating the rules." And then she began to cry.

A few months ago someone must have complained that they were all living illegally. In fact, the house was zoned as a two-family, and it was perfectly fine for Tío and his family to live on the top part. But they had the feeling many on Ivy Lane just didn't like them being there—especially as the small Cape Cods were torn down and bigger houses were put up instead.

Their whole street was split—half the block was made up of spanking-new houses, with their banks of perfectly planted azaleas and their speckled brick facades. This was one of the little homes to remain, owned by a woman who'd retired to Florida and now rented out the place. The neighbors didn't like how the grass grew a little too tall in the front, or how many cars were parked in the narrow driveway, including Tío Pedro's dented white van, or how Renaldo and his friends liked to sit on the stoop at the end of the day, drinking beer or playing their radios too loud.

"Hey, hey." Renaldo went over and touched her arm. His eyes were bloodshot, from his beers. "It's okay, Mami. It's okay. We haven't done anything."

"I know. But that's the second time—"

"And they found nothing, remember?" He smiled. "Listen, I gotta take a shower and get out of here. But I'll talk about it with my father. We'll take care of it."

"Thank you, *papi*."

Maria's pity swiftly turned to annoyance as she watched her petite aunt rise up on her toes and peck a kiss on Renaldo's cheek. Why did Tía Lucy have to fall apart over everything? Her mother complained that Tía Lucy was always sobbing over something to the men, and was the last one to unload the dishwasher or help out with Sunday cooking. She was the one who gave Maria the most grief for wanting to be with Lola and Jaya instead of the family. "What, we're not good enough for you anymore?" she would say.

Gathering her book bag, Maria started for the door. When

Renaldo saw her, he whispered, "See, *Prima*? We always have to prove ourselves. Or be rescued by your Frisbee boys."

Maria didn't answer, but went down the stairs to the basement apartment that she shared with her mother. She settled into their bed and switched on the TV on mute, to check out the movie listings for later.

This was one of their favorite things to do. Maria and her mother liked to climb into the queen-size bed in their alcove and eat chocolate flan, which they knew they shouldn't, and watch old American movies. Her mother's excuse was that they helped her with her English. Really it was just so delicious to curl up in the covers with Mami and eat sweets and weep and talk about the characters. Especially after listening to Renaldo and his mean mouth. Upstairs she could hear him yelling that he didn't have a clean T-shirt. A few minutes later she heard him stomp across the house and slam the door.

*Stupid Renaldo,* she thought. *Always making trouble.* She didn't care what her cousin said. That Frisbee boy was a real angel. An idealist. Her whole body grew warm again, remembering. *There's room for everyone,* he'd said, tucking his hair behind his ears.

Folding her knees at her side, she flipped through the movie channels. She thought, one day, she would find him, even if he was in high school, teach him all about Spanish and maybe more.

Then Maria noticed that the phone machine, which sat on a little table in the alcove, was blinking. She leaned over, and saw there were four messages. She pressed the button. All from Jaya.

*Chapter 4*

The house fell silent. Walking around the empty rooms, the shadows growing deep on the walls, Jaya was reminded of when she and her mother first came to the States. Mrs. Lal had worked long hours doing elder care, deep in New Jersey, or far away in the Bronx. The closest she got to seeing her mother in those days was the extra light-blue uniform that hung on the shower head in the bathroom, or the rice and pigeon peas in a pot, the smell of her perfume on the pillow. When she heard her mother coming in, she'd hunch down deeper in her bed, pretending to sleep, wishing she'd touch her, just run her hand over her hair, but furious, too, her jaw in a sullen lock.

Then she and her mother came to Meadowbrook, and moved into a sweet apartment in a two-family on the edge of town, where the houses were smaller, with tiny yards and metal fences. The pine floors were slanted and the flame on the ancient Sears stove licked past the edge of the pans, melting their handles. It cost twice as much as what they had in Newark, but Mrs. Lal didn't care. Outside the window Mr. Carlota, their landlord, had planted a grape arbor, the trellis so close, Jaya could reach her hand out her bedroom window and pluck the purple fruits.

"Just like the tamarind tree back home, right, Jaya?" Mrs. Lal liked to say.

But Jaya hated this new place. Mrs. Lal had bought her a weekend pool pass, and Jaya sat miserably on a skinny towel, watching kids cannonball into the water and call out to each other. In town girls sauntered into Starbucks, just back from the pool, dressed in flip-flops and showing their tan lines, talking about the Jersey Shore. Half the time she couldn't even tell the mothers and daughters apart; they had the same little pocketbook hanging from their wrist that can only fit a tiny slim wallet and a cell phone. They sat in the nail parlors, right next to each other, flipping through *Lucky* and *Vogue*.

Most of the girls in Meadowbrook knew each other from way back—wedged under their refrigerator magnets are snapshots of them running through sprinklers when they were in diapers. Back where Jaya came from, they didn't even know what a playdate was. So Jaya learned to fit herself into a place just on the outskirts of everything. When she was sick, she knew not to call her mother at work unless her temperature was really high. Or not to tell her about that sting in her ankle from falling down at volleyball or that the teacher wanted to meet just when it was time to take the Siler twins for their Mommy & Me music class. Jaya knew that her mother could miss work only so often.

———

Evenings, Jaya and her mother walked everywhere, since they couldn't afford a car. They often did this after supper, slowly eating their ice cream cones, watching the first fireflies of the season prick the softening dark, trying to get used to the feel and smell of this place. It was familiar, like Port of Spain. People gathered on porches, talking to their neighbors, but none of the faces called out to them, as they were used to. They could disappear into the shadows and no one would know.

As they walked, Jaya could see something release in her mother, how she was finally left alone to be herself, not Raj Lal's widow, not her own mother's disappointment, the daughter who had dropped out of nursing school.

Jaya wished she felt the same. But as they strolled, she became aware of something growing between them, an angry shadow, thick as vines.

"Jaya, why do you always have such a sour face?" Mrs. Lal would often ask at the end of the day, when they were walking back home.

"Mama, you don't know what it's like here," she complained. "These kids have everything."

"This is one of the best school districts in the country," her mother replied. "I'm doing this for you, Jaya. Don't forget that."

One evening they took a different turn, and Jaya saw the strangest thing up ahead: a huge silver dome, like a blimp landed on the grass. People were walking out, dressed in white, like cricket players in Trinidad.

"Let's go see," her mother said.

When they pushed through the revolving door, they were hit by a sudden rush of wind. "What is this?" Jaya asked, suddenly frightened.

"It's a tennis bubble. There's a machine that blows air and keeps it up."

Jaya didn't like the way sounds bounced everywhere, shrinking her down, making her feel tiny. The whoosh of air in her ears. The huge quilted silver roof felt as if it could any second come crumpling down.

Mrs. Lal seemed to love it, though. She stood there, chin tilted, watching people in their tennis clothes run back and forth under the glare of artificial lights.

That night, as Jaya lay in her new bed in their strange apartment, she couldn't shake that feeling from that tennis bubble. It was like everything that was wrong with moving to Meadowbrook. The two of them on the edges, peering in. Just to buy something simple—a new mop and shelving paper— she and her mother had to take the bus to Bed Bath & Beyond on Route 12. After, they sat at the stop, bulky bags on their laps, a hard wind of passing cars slapping at their faces and hands. They were nothing to those other people, just specks on the curb. They could blow away any minute.

The phone rang. Mrs. Lal was on the other end, sounding very worn and tired. "It's not looking good," she sighed. "They put Mrs. Harmon in intensive care."

Jaya swallowed.

"I need you to go to her desk and look up her nephew's phone number. He's the only one who's allowed to hear the medical reports, and it's making it crazy for me here. He needs to come up from Philadelphia right away."

"Why can't you call?"

Her mother grew brusque and annoyed. "Because you have the cell phone, Jaya. Now, please. I got a lot to watch over here."

"But what about me?" She hated how her voice sounded— so whiny and weak.

"You know what to do. Finish up the dishes and the beds. And there's some soup on the stove at home."

"But—"

"Jaya!"

"Okay." She sighed.

Jaya pushed back the cover on the big rolltop desk that was shoved into a corner of the living room, and began looking for phone numbers. Mrs. Harmon had her own way of organizing. She filed people under the nicknames she gave them—some of them not very nice. Mrs. Lal was listed under *A* for "angel." For the Leonards, who lived on the other side of her hedges, she had them under *N*. They were the Next-Door Nosy Nudges. She was about to give up when she found an index card in a cubbyhole. Across the top, in red marker, was written "Emergency Information!" Then it read: "In case of emergency call Andrew Philip Cramer, my nephew. My lawyer told me to appoint Andrew executor, and Andrew is a lawyer himself.

He's a little dull, but I suppose he's the most responsible person in the family."

Jaya paused, working up her nerve, before she dialed. A man answered. She could hear noise in the background—kids, someone washing dishes. When Jaya explained what had happened, Andrew's voice prickled with suspicion. "And who are you?"

"My mama works for Mrs. Harmon."

"Why didn't your mother call?"

"She's at the hospital now. And she can't call long distance."

He sighed. "This is terrible news. I can't make it up tonight, but I'll try first thing tomorrow morning."

"Wait!" Jaya paused. "Can you call the hospital so that my mother can get the doctor's reports?"

He sounded embarrassed. "Of course. Yes. I was just going to do that."

They hung up, and it was only after Jaya had slid the index card back into the cubbyhole that she realized he hadn't even said thank you.

After putting away the vacuum cleaner and Windex and paper towels, Jaya paused. Long shadows drew across the pine floors. The bare branches outside shivered. Through the window she could still see the bag of mulch slumped by the garden, where she and Mrs. Harmon had been working. And the indent in the sofa where Mrs. Harmon had laid while she was having her stroke.

She reached for her cell phone, flipped it open, and punched in LOLA.

"What's up, girl?" Lola asked.

When Jaya opened her mouth to speak, she couldn't say anything. A rush of hot tears came to her eyes. She kept squeezing back that image of Mrs. Harmon, twitching and spasming on the sofa.

"Lola," she finally whispered. "Come to Mrs. Harmon's. Maria, too. I can't do this. I can't do this without you guys."

*Chapter 5*

The first time Jaya and Lola set eyes on each other was outside James Madison Middle School.

Jaya was turning the corner when she saw a crowd gathered around a girl and boy. A little thrill chill went through her: The girl looked like a movie star, so glamorous and fierce. She wore white capri pants with a slit at the calves, a black T-shirt, tiger-striped mules, and her hair was pulled up in a glittery amber clasp, loose and sloppy, the way models do in magazines.

Most miraculous of all, she was doing a spectacular handstand, her long legs scissoring in the air.

In fact, Lola was responding to Anthony Vitale's boast that he was so good at snowboarding, he might go professional. Anthony was always saying things like that. How he was the best at basketball or Ultimate Frisbee. Or he had the best bike, the best MP3 player. How his dad knew just about everything there was to know about buildings. How dumb school was. His own dad didn't even finish high school, so what was the point? He was going to work for his father's company anyway and make lots of money. School was just one big stupid distraction—that is, until he made the U.S. Olympic snowboarding team.

Lola had no patience for boys like Anthony. He was way worse than her fourteen cousins—he just didn't get it! So she appointed herself as the one to drill into his thick skull that having an idea—a real idea—mattered. That Mr. Cohen was not a dork, and the U.S. Constitution was, yes, *interesting*! Try living in a country where their idea of a constitution is getting shot in the head if you're the wrong religion!

"Maybe your daddy should buy you some lessons, huh?" she called. "Doesn't he have to buy you math and reading lessons so you can learn what a book is?"

"Shut up," he mumbled. "You are so stupid." The tips of his ears were crimson now. It was well known that Anthony Vitale couldn't read properly until he got to third grade, and it was only because Anthony senior had donated the new auditorium that Anthony junior even got placed in the advanced classes.

At this, Lola bent at the waist and landed perfectly, lithe as a gymnast. "No, Anthony. I think we know who is stupid."

By now most of the kids had drifted away, muttering. "She is such a retard!" one girl commented. "That's something my kid sister would do!" another added. They'd enjoyed the Lola-Anthony show, which flared up every now and then, but enough was enough.

Even though Lola heard what they were saying, she couldn't stop herself—she craved these moments of glory, but after, when the kids slipped off, a wave of loneliness crashed through her. She was entertaining, but nobody really cared. She knew the others found her a little too sharp; she always fought a little too hard, and the popular girls, with their tight ribbed tank tops and hip-hugger jeans, were always put off. Lola was just, so, well, too much. Full of brawl, over-the-top, *foreign*. Lola's mother and sister, Nadia, chided her, *Stop with the speeches, Lola*. But that was Lola: always trying to score points.

A few girls had stayed, staring and giggling, Rachel Meisner among them. Lola swung around, fists on her hips. "What are you staring at?"

Rachel gazed at her coolly. "Nothing, Lola."

Meadowbrook girls had this look in their eyes, like they were checking something out, but not quite committing. Even if Lola said the right words—"awesome" and "no way" and "I was pissed"—the effect was never the same.

Everyone walked away except for one girl, who stood with her ankles pressed together, an old-fashioned army satchel strapped across her chest.

Lola noticed different-colored pencils sticking out of the little loops. The girl was pretty, but in a different way. She had skin the color of maple syrup, rich and shiny-looking, and her black hair was oiled and gleaming and tucked into a neat braid.

"You aren't afraid, are you?" Jaya asked.

Lola shrugged as she picked up her knapsack. "Of what?"

"Of talking to him like that. In front of everybody."

"Anthony's a show-off, but he doesn't have anything to show off about. He can't even do his maths by himself."

The girl smiled. "We say 'maths' too, down in the Caribbean."

Lola shrugged again, but in a friendly way. "That's FOB talk."

"What's FOB?"

"Fresh off the boat. Greenhorn. Totally FOB, my sister Nadia tells me when I forget and use a Slovak word. Or dress in some dorky way."

"My name is Jaya," the girl offered.

"Lola."

They stood staring at each other, both suddenly awkward. Lola put her hands on her hips. "Hey," she suddenly asked. "You want to hang out with me? Come eat some food? I have to go help my mother at her job."

"Sure," she replied. "Why not?"

Lola and Jaya began to walk up the block, half with each other, half not. Lola was surprised at how easy it was to be with this girl, like they'd known each other for years. There was something loose and soft about her. She had the most beautiful, thick black lashes, Lola noticed, and she was looking at her in such a slow and thoughtful way.

"These clothes are my sister's," Lola explained. "She gives me her hand-me-downs so I don't totally embarrass her." She laughed. "I'm doing it all the time. I can't keep track."

"I don't have any sisters," Jaya said. "Or brothers."

"It's just you and your parents?"

"My mother," Jaya corrected.

"Yeah, well, it's like my papa's become such a loser since we moved here, he might as well not be here." Lola stopped.

"Whoa! Did I just say that?" She smacked the side of her head. "Sorry. It's just—sometimes, my brain, the words spit out of my head so fast, I can't stop them."

They turned into one of the fancier parts of town, where the new houses had cropped up on freshly carved streets with freshly painted signs. Despite the oversize houses, with their beige brick faces that never seemed to fade and the expensive landscaping with skinny trees, the area felt a bit barren and lonely. Lola stopped at a house, where the mailbox had a hand-lettered sign that said VITALE; in the driveway were two white trucks with VITALE CONSTRUCTION on the sides.

Jaya stopped. "Wait, your mother works here? For Anthony Vitale's family?"

"Yeah." Lola grinned. "She's their housekeeper. How do you think I know so much about him?"

Entering the Vitale house was like being on an HGTV cable program on house renovations. They walked up a perfect lane of rhododendron bushes banked in rust-colored mulch. Two thin birch trees in pots of pale white stones framed the portico, and the door glittered with shiny brass trim, like a general's uniform. Inside, past the two-story foyer, the kitchen was a cathedral to huge stainless steel appliances—a double-door refrigerator that resembled a warehouse freezer; a huge hooded stove, reminding Jaya of some fancy kid's rocket, ready to lift off. The arched windows looked out onto a lawn that might as well be a miniature golf playland—a little gazebo, a pond, and a trampoline.

"Wow," Jaya murmured.

Lola waved a dismissive hand. "Typical American excess. If you can't be famous on *American Idol*, you do it on your block."

In fact, every time Lola looked around the Vitale house, she could see only what it meant for her mother: the sixteen-foot ceiling rafters, which meant Mrs. Svetloski had to stand on a ladder and use a duster with a telescopic handle; what seemed like acres of white Berber wall-to-wall carpet—impossible to clean, especially when someone spilled marinara sauce at Sunday dinner.

Lola grabbed a bag of Cheetos and two sodas and led Jaya down a hall to the basement. Mrs. Svetloski, a stout woman in a gray housedress, gym socks, and rubber sandals, was just heaving up the carpeted stairs. "Lola, no crumbs! I just vacuum."

"I know, I know."

"And while you're down here, fold the laundry!"

Lola rolled her eyes. "You think Anthony can fold his own smelly socks?" She went over to her mother and touched her cheek. "Of course, Mama. I said I would. You rest." Then she frowned. "Mama, did you smoke?"

Her mother gave a weak sigh. "I have a cigarette. My only one for today."

Lola's heart gave a painful twist. She knew her mother was lying—that by now half the pack was emptied, crumpled into her pocket. At least Mrs. Vitale didn't permit smoking in the house. But the doctor kept warning Mrs. Svetloski that it wasn't good, the smoking, not with her blood pressure and diabetes. "You're asking for trouble," Lola warned.

*Trouble finds you no matter what.* Her mother shrugged. *So I invite him in.* Now she smiled at Jaya. "This your friend?"

Lola nodded. "This is Jaya."

Jaya turned to her mother and dipped her head, shyly. "Thank you for having me."

Mrs. Svetloski laughed before heaving up the stairs. "Thank you for putting up with my daughter!"

The downstairs basement held a bar, a plasma TV, a pool table, and then a laundry room that was as big as a bedroom, with a soft yellow armchair.

"Wow," Jaya said.

"Mrs. Vitale's into decorating," Lola explained. "Every other week she comes with some new fabric swatch and wants an opinion." She shrugged. "They're a funny family. Their poor papa keeps buying Anthony tutors to take the fog from his brain." She touched her own chest proudly. "I get straight nineties one year after I come here. I don't need no tutors, no help."

Lola suddenly realized she'd been going on for a while, and turned, a little sheepishly, to Jaya. "So how long have you lived here?"

"About a year." Jaya shrugged. Then she added, shyly, "You know, my mother, she cleans too. She also takes care of children."

"Wait, you're kidding!"

So that was it! The strange sense of connection. Lola fancied herself a rationalist, a revolutionary, and an anarchist all rolled together. She seldom had room for mushy feelings of It-Was-

44

Meant-to-Be. Girlie astrology column nonsense, stuff her sister liked. But this was different. And there was something else she liked about this girl—her quiet formality. How she had thanked her mother, wiped her feet before coming down to the basement. That she said "mother," not "mom," and "children," not "kids." A sadness lurked around her—it was there, in her dark eyes and her careful speech.

Lola jumped up onto the dryer, long legs swinging beneath her. "Maybe that's why——" She searched for the word. Something to describe what she felt. Easy, but more than that. A quiet tether between them, lax and firm at the same time.

"How come you can just come here and act so——" Jaya hesitated. "So comfortable?"

Lola shrugged. "I help my mama a lot. She gets tired."

Suddenly Jaya confided, "You know that girl Rachel? The one you were yelling at?"

"Ugh. Wicked Witch of the West."

"Every Saturday morning."

Lola's eyes widened. "No way!"

Jaya hesitated; she looked like she might cry. Her lashes were spiked wet. "I hate going over to my mother's jobs," she admitted, her voice coiled tight.

"What do you hate most?" Lola asked softly.

It took Jaya a few minutes to get the words out. "I hate . . . I guess that when you first meet them, the people are all friendly and stuff and say, 'Oh, my house is yours.' But then it isn't like that at all. They wish——"

45

Lola found herself suddenly moved. For all her noisy pride, she'd never really said a word about what it was like to have her mother work for the same families of kids she went to school with. She'd stuffed the hard little humiliations into one of her few quiet places. Like the time her mother had actually showed for back-to-school night, and one of the mothers, who remembered hiring her for a party, began gushing to the other parents about what a great cleaner Mrs. Svetloski was. After that, Lola begged her mother not to go to such events. Or she didn't tell her at all.

But there was, in this girl's face, something unguarded, vulnerable. She couldn't hide anything. It was as if Lola could see right into a clear pond, trembles of hurt moving beneath. She could hear the words Jaya really wanted to say out loud: *They wish you didn't exist.*

"They're just phonies," Lola assured her. "You wouldn't want to really know them. Trust me. They don't deserve you."

When Jaya grinned, Lola felt the most delicious sunny sensation pour through her, as if she'd just swallowed a bowl of the sweetest yellow custard, soft and warm. She'd achieved something great, better than getting an A plus, or making Anthony Vitale miserable. She'd made this lovely girl smile.

# Chapter 6

Growing up in Puebla, Maria believed in miracles and angels. She knew the rustling palms spoke to her. Her *abuela* taught her that if the sky turned purple before a rainstorm, that meant a ghost would come to visit her dreams. If an egg yolk broke while making flan, that meant bad luck.

And then came the miracle day when two angels rescued her.

Maria had recently moved to Meadowbrook from Union City, since her *tío* Pedro said there were too many problems there, and now she was being "mainstreamed"—put into the regular class.

But on Maria's first day Mrs. Lansky, her new teacher, nudged her into the front of the room and announced, "Everyone, please give a big hello to Maria, who is from Mexico." She saw a girl lean over and whisper, loud enough for Maria to hear, "Look at those clothes. More like she's from Planet Maria."

"Wetback clothes," the other girl said, and giggled.

Maria flushed. She had, in fact, carefully chosen a flowery print dress for that day. But it was so confusing. Here they didn't wear school uniforms, which made every morning an agony, figuring out what to wear, especially since some girls never wore the same outfit more than once. Maria had only two pairs of jeans, which she diligently washed and pressed with a crease down the center, until she saw that a lot of the boys and girls wore denim that was purposely ripped.

To Maria's dismay, she was assigned to that very same girl's book group. All week they didn't talk to Maria. Every time she tried to pipe up and say something, they were quick enough to ignore or shrug away her words. When it was her group's turn to give a presentation, Mrs. Lansky asked, "And Maria's contribution?"

The girl flicked some hair wisps from her eyes. "She didn't read the book."

Maria said back, "I did read the book. These girls didn't call on me."

Mrs. Lansky turned to Maria and said, "Now, dear, in our school you don't wait for other students to call on you. You just pitch in. You make your voice heard. In America, we have participatory classrooms."

Maria noticed that when Mrs. Lansky spoke to her, she pronounced her words like she had a doughnut in her mouth, exaggerating every syllable.

Grown-ups like Mrs. Lansky seemed to always be disappointed in her in some way—as if they wanted her to be rude. And though they finally released her from ELL, it felt as if she'd been given a guest pass. The other kids screwed up their faces, not able to understand her accent. They were still always testing her. A speech therapist took her out of gym to work on her accent. Maria felt as if she were enduring some lifelong exam, as if she were a project of theirs that was never done.

And she didn't know how to be with the American kids either. Somehow she always felt too babyish, especially when they would talk to grown-ups on the same level. Back in Puebla, if a boy or girl talked back to the teacher, the teachers rapped the students hard on the knuckles. Yet she also felt older than the Americanos, who were so carefree, rushing off to music and ballet lessons every day. She mostly raced home to start supper for everyone, or to help her mother out.

One day after school she was hurrying to get to one of her mother's new cleaning jobs. But she hadn't been feeling so well. All afternoon, through math and social studies, mysterious pains had jabbed at her stomach. Her skin prickled hot, so she kept asking for the bathroom pass, to press wet paper towels against her burning cheeks.

As she began to cross Grove Field, a hard heave rolled through her, spiking and grabbing at her insides. Her knees went soft, and she dropped to her knees, her backpack thunking onto the ground.

*Get up,* she told herself. *Mami is waiting.*

But she couldn't. That pain was followed by another one, even worse than before, reaching up to her throat.

She heard a flurry of footsteps. Two girls—one with dirty blond hair, the other with tawny brown skin and a long black braid—crouched before her.

"You okay?" one asked. She had a strong, bossy voice.

"I'm okay." Maria gingerly touched her own forehead, surprised at how clammy it was.

"You don't look so good," the pretty one with a braid said.

"I lift you up," the blond girl offered. "And we call your parents."

She gasped. "I told you. I'm okay."

"I don't care," the take-charge girl declared. She slipped a cell phone from a hip holster.

But Maria clamped a hand around her wrist. "No. Mami is at work."

They looked surprised. "Okay. We'll take you home, then. Where d'you live?"

Her chin jutted out. "I told you. Leave me alone." Just then a fierce, hot pain clawed at her belly. She let out a loud groan, grabbed her stomach, and spewed out a stream of sour vomit.

To her surprise, the girls were completely unfazed. Calmly the dirty-blond girl fished inside her own backpack, pulled out a gray gym shirt, and gently wiped Maria's face. Then she said to her, "Now, you tell me where you live or I bring you to my mother, who is going to really yell."

She hesitated. "Mami is over on Prospect. Cleaning a big house."

A weird look flew between the two girls, like two electric wires shorting out. Maria had never told anyone outside of her Spanish-speaking friends that her mother cleaned houses. She wasn't ashamed; she just wasn't sure how it would go over.

Americans were funny in that way. They loved to do everything for themselves. Even the men proudly changed ca-ca diapers, right in the playgrounds. But their voices got hushed and small when they asked you to scrub their toilet. So it was hard to figure out what to be proud of and what to be ashamed of, in this country.

"This is a new job. I don't want to bother her—" Another pain snatched at her breath.

"Don't worry. We'll get you there soon."

As each of the girls took an arm and draped it over her shoulders, Maria felt herself sinking into them. She couldn't remember the last time she'd done such a thing, with anyone. They moved as if their bodies were one, a mix of softness and concern, steering her up the hill to Prospect Avenue. This was one of the prettier streets in town, where the houses were Victorian, with wraparound porches and cupolas.

She pointed. "That one," she gasped.

They were in the driveway of a huge house that reminded her of a *quinceañera* dress, decorated in frilly layers of color, blue lapping into green and magenta. They tapped on the rear screen door, and her mother showed up, wearing yellow rubber gloves.

"*Qué pasa?*" she asked. Her face had tightened into fright and worry and annoyance.

Maria let out a whimper. She could see that panicked-bird look in her mother's eyes. Whenever Mrs. Alvarez got scared, she would start dashing around the room, like a pigeon that had accidentally flown into the house. Usually Maria stayed patient,

51

guiding her mother to calmness. But this time she couldn't. Hard fruit pits were digging into her ribs.

"She's sick," one of the girls explained, pointing to her own stomach.

Her mother ran over to the counter, picked up her pocketbook, then put that down, picked up the phone, and settled that back again. "I cannot go hospital," she explained to the girls. "No have money. *Y mi hermano. El es* at job. *El* get angry. Miss work."

"Can we call the hospital?" Lola asked.

"*Sí, pero*——" She pointed to her wallet. "*No tengo*——"

It was amazing. That loudmouth girl, she understood perfectly. Maria's family didn't have that little laminated card that said they had health insurance. Lola pulled out her cell phone and made a call—it sounded like to a family doctor—and talked to someone. After she hung up, she explained, "The nurse says it sounds like food poisoning. We just have to make sure she drinks a lot of water and stays hydrated. If the vomiting doesn't stop in twenty-four hours, then she should go in. For now she should lie down."

"*Dónde?* Where?" A frightened Mrs. Alvarez stood in the middle of the kitchen.

They searched the house, but all the rooms were much too fancy: The beds were high four-posters, with five-hundred-thread-count sheets and fluffy, tufted quilts that Mrs. Alvarez was instructed to air every week. Then the girls discovered a little screened-in porch off the front parlor, with a worn-out sofa.

"Wait, what's your names?" Maria asked as she dropped herself down onto the lumpy cushions.

"Lola," the bossy one said.

"Jaya," the quiet one added, and spread a blanket over her.

Then her mouth again filled with spit and she let go more hot, sour vomit into a rubber bucket the girls held up. Lola and Jaya stayed by Maria's bedside, taking turns giving her sips of water and emptying the bucket. Neither mentioned leaving. It was as if they felt responsible, on duty, somehow.

When Maria stopped heaving, she lay back on the pillow, feeling very small and shaken under the covers, and gazed at Lola and Jaya. They were standing close, smiling with relief. Love seemed to pour from their eyes, their fingertips. She squeezed each of their hands. *"Milagro,"* she whispered.

And Lola and Jaya seemed to feel it too. Jaya told Maria that she looked beautiful, her hair spread around her face in a dark halo, resembling a painting of the Madonna. Surrounding them was a quiet fluttering, like angels' wings rubbing. Something hushed and special settled on each of their shoulders, stretching them beyond themselves.

Something happened on that porch, when Maria whispered *"milagro."* It was a miracle. A sign, that day, they were supposed to find one another. Three daughters of maids and nannies! You couldn't even make a TV show about such a thing, it was so corny. That's how they knew. The three of them were meant to be with each other.

# Chapter 7

It was true. Mrs. Harmon had had a stroke. A really bad one, crippling her speech and paralyzing her whole right side. She could barely lift a fork to push the hospital Jell-O into her mouth. Her eyes were discs of cloudy glass. She wouldn't be going back to the cottage with the low timbered ceilings. She wouldn't be crouching in the garden in her straw hats, or gently shaking dried tea leaves into a bowl.

"This house has to be put up for sale," her nephew Andrew Cramer explained. "As soon as possible."

Mr. Cramer had just driven up from Philadelphia to take care of matters, and he seemed surprised to find not just Mrs. Lal but all three girls at Mrs. Harmon's house. He reminded Lola of Abe Lincoln: tall and reedy, long sideburns down his hollow cheeks. Jaya couldn't help but notice he stared past Mrs. Lal's shoulders when he talked. He seemed embarrassed by how little he knew about his aunt, which made him even more stern and particular.

Mrs. Lal put her fists on her hips. "Mr. Cramer. If I may be so bold. I work with old people all the time, and I can tell you one thing: You take them away from the place they love, and you might as well dig a grave for them. Mrs. Harmon doesn't want to be taken from her house. This place is her heart, Mr. Cramer. She got to be where she belongs, until the day they come to put her in the ground."

"I know this has been very upsetting," he replied. "But my aunt needs twenty-four hour care now."

"I can do that."

"I mean medical help. Professionals." He swept out his hand, as if the state of the house were Mrs. Lal's fault. "And how to pay for everything is a big problem. In case you didn't know, this house is all my aunt has. She's been getting by on Social Security for years."

"At least we can honor her wishes," Mrs. Lal countered. "She told me herself she wanted to stay here until the end."

He shook his head. "It isn't possible." He turned to the woman standing next to him. She was dressed in a slate blue suit and wore a tasteful pearl necklace. "This is Adele Carson. She's a local Realtor, and she's going to help me get the house ready for a sale."

Mrs. Carson smiled. "Though I must warn you, this house is a real challenge. Not a natural sell. Especially in this market. It's really tough these days. That's why we have to do everything possible to make this happen."

*Who's the "we"?* Jaya wondered as they followed Mrs. Carson around the house, her high heels clicking on the plank wood floors. She started with the kitchen, gesturing toward the stained linoleum, several of the tiles peeling off, the blackened brick behind the woodstove, the cubbyhole larder stuffed with plastic bags. "Maybe a fresh coat of paint," she said, and sighed.

Jaya felt suddenly embarrassed, looking at Mrs. Harmon's home through Mrs. Carson's eyes. Everything she liked about the place—its slouchy comfortableness—was exactly what the Realtor didn't like.

"But look at this," Lola said, pointing to the original wavy glass in the windows, the faceted knobs on the doors. "It's so cool and old."

Mrs. Carson sternly shook her head. "All this historic stuff is very nice, but take a look at how these floors creak and sag! And the windows, they're drafty. People these days expect updating. Central air, new stoves, granite counters." They were in the living room now, and she snapped on a switch. "Look at this. Lamps everywhere. Not a single recessed light."

When everyone returned to the foyer, Mrs. Carson explained, "The place must be cleaned, top to bottom, and cleared out, the pine floors refinished and shined to a gleaming varnish, the outside shingles given a fresh coat of paint." Mr. Cramer should hire professionals to manage the estate sale. They would go through the house, putting tags on everything, then come on a weekend and set up a portable cash register on a folding table and put out boxes of Mrs. Harmon's preserving jars, her dented baking trays, her gardening tools.

"I'll need the house cleaned and organized this weekend," Mr. Cramer said to Mrs. Lal. He didn't ask if she was available.

*Chapter 8*

Being the daughter of a maid or nanny, it wasn't like everyone was so bad or mean or stupid. It was just weird. You knew your mother put extra bleach in the underwear of some girl who was walking up the aisle at assembly in her best corduroy jumper dress. Or those shoes you wore were hand-me-downs from the kid in the grade above you, and you just prayed she didn't notice. Or how you hated Monday mornings, when half the class came in sporting sweatshirts with big letters that said I ROCKED AT JONAH'S BAR MITZVAH! Which of course you were never invited to.

That's why it was so amazing that the three girls found each other. It *was* a kind of miracle. After she met Lola and Maria, Jaya's doubts vanished. She forgot about being scared. That terrible feeling of the tennis bubble, cold air rushing in.

The three of them would try to meet on Tuesdays— sometimes other days too—pooling the change they found on their mothers' bureaus for a Starbucks frappé. They found a bench in the park they declared was theirs, sitting in the dappled shade. In the beginning they laughed hard, swapping stories and hurts, amazed that there could be anyone else who understood.

The best part, though, was the bits of advice the three of them would share. Lying about what you were doing for spring break, or making up a story about scoliosis, which is why you couldn't go on the school ski trip, which cost too much.

"What do you do if someone asks what your mother does?" Jaya asked.

"I used to lie," Lola said bluntly. "Then my mother got her job with the Vitales and I put it in his face. Much more fun."

Maria squirmed a little. "I say . . . she freelances. She has a little business."

"Wow, guys, you are good." Jaya laughed.

Maria had other tricks too, about clothes. She had long ago figured out that the kids with the most beat-up nylon packs and worn-out T-shirts were probably the richest. But if you looked closely at these kids, you'd see they had a Gore-Tex rain jacket that cost a lot and that their torn-up sweatshirt was the most expensive one at Abercrombie & Fitch, but they wore it as if it were nothing, just a rag. She'd study what the other kids bought and find the knockoffs in Newark and Union City. She learned not to buy jeans with so many silver studs down the seams or gold lettering across the thighs because that was ghetto, and not in a good way.

Sometimes Maria took them on a bus down Haley Avenue, where, at the 99-cent store, they rummaged in bins and bought stupid cheap things: plastic hoop earrings and imitation leather belts. They'd fantasize about getting the look just right for high school. Maria saw herself walking down the corridors on the arm of an absolutely cool boy. Or Jaya would finally get to use the art facilities there, which had real silk screen presses and huge painting studios.

Maria even persuaded her *mami* to let them come over for the Academy Awards. They gathered on the big bed to eat popcorn and grade all the dresses—Maria's idea, of course. It was then that Maria suggested they all go to the spring dance. "We should go," she said. "We can get dressed up and have so much fun."

"That's for rich kids," Lola declared.

"Who says? It doesn't cost that much."

"All those show-off brats will be there," Lola insisted.

"Why do you care so much what they think? We should just go and have fun." She touched each of them, on their wrists. "Come on. We'll go to the mall and check out the fancy dresses."

The next week they took a bus to the mall—the expensive one, where a lot of girls from school shopped. Even its name— Reese Lake Mall—felt like a country club. The mall had a long curving drive and valet parking, a pale, speckled stone fountain, and a sunken living room area, where men in loafers browsed the newspapers. The three girls rode up the silent escalator, passing mothers and daughters, hair carefully brushed and highlighted. They seemed expert, comfortable, as if shopping were a profession, the calmest of routines. So different from the frantic shopping Jaya did with her mother back in Newark, where a guard ran a magnetic wand over your bag every time you walked through the doors.

In Bergdorf's the clothes were well-folded and tempting, like pastries in a shop. Jaya unfurled a pair of jeans and saw they were two hundred seventy dollars! A wave of queasiness pitched through her. Checking more and more of the tags, she kept feeling like little doors were shutting down inside her. The prices were so crazy, so otherworldly, it left her sad and depressed, as if someone had tricked her. Then she got angry for even caring.

"Let's try something on," Maria whispered. They were in the designer junior dress department, pushing through racks of gorgeous dresses.

A saleswoman in a tight suit was hovering around them like a sharp-winged insect. "You want me to start a dressing room?" Her eyebrows, which had been waxed into skinny arches, rose high.

Jaya shrugged. "Yeah, I guess so."

Again Jaya was surprised. She was so used to stores where she piled the clothes onto her arm until it ached, and then squeezed into a big dressing room where all kinds of women and teenage girls were fighting for the mirror, complaining about their fatty thighs. Here the saleswoman had carefully hung each of their dresses on louvered doors for little rooms that each had a tufted stool. The minute she left, though, they crammed into one room and began wriggling out of their jeans and tops.

Jaya's outfit was a turquoise sheath, with a nice V-cut in the front. She'd never felt anything like it: The silky fabric spilled over her hips like a rush of pure, cold water. The shiny hem flounced perfectly at her calves. She kept turning on her toes in front of the mirror, feeling light as air.

"Wow, Jaya! Forget the dance," Maria said. "This would be perfect for the Academy Awards. Can't you see it? Jaya walking down the red carpet?"

"You are nuts," Lola said as she struggled into a sateen orange number that had too many crisscrossing straps.

There was a firm knock on the door. "How are we doing, ladies? Any luck?"

"Oh my God. We have to get out of here," Maria whispered.

"Fine!" Lola yelled. She gave herself a once-over in the mirror. Her arms hung awkwardly, and her breasts looked stuffed into the bodice. "Ugh," she said.

Jaya glanced at the price tag dangling from the armhole of her dress: seven hundred ninety-five dollars! That glutted sick feeling came over her again, and she quickly tore off the dress.

When they emerged, the saleswoman gave them a sharp, probing look, asking, "How did it go?"

Jaya felt a giggle come up in her. You'd think she was in the doctor's office for something important, like a sprained ankle, and the nurse asking, *Does it hurt when you stand on it?* How seriously everyone took shopping here!

"Didn't fit," Lola coolly told the woman, and they marched out of the department store and back into the mall. By now, as they stepped into an elevator that was like a space-age glass chute, Jaya felt disoriented, groggy from the crazy prices.

"So what do you think?" Maria said, turning to Jaya. "Should we go find some knockoffs for the dance?"

"I'm not sure," Jaya said. She was tempted, for the dance sounded special—how all the kids got to dress up and spin across the polished parquet floor under a ceiling of balloons, the golf course lit up just for them. "I feel kinda funny celebrating since I'm not sure we're going to stay for high school."

Maria and Lola looked at her, surprised. "Whoa, where did that come from?" Lola asked.

Jaya didn't know how to answer. Last week was the end of the month, and Mrs. Lal had stayed up late, sitting at the dinette table with her stack of bills and a calculator. Besides the rent and the heat and the credit card bills, she also sent down two hundred dollars to Jaya's grandmother, who lived with some distant relatives.

"My mama says we can't afford it here. Maybe we'll move in with my father's family. Do high school there."

"You can't do that!" Lola said.

"It's not up to me." Jaya drew away, not liking how their eyes were pressing in on her.

Jaya thought about the time the Lal clan, her father's family, came out to see how they were doing. They found it pretty but boring: no West Indian clubs nearby, no good *roti* places, the supermarket store prices ridiculous. They climbed up the rickety back stairs, crowded into the apartment, and ate on the new plates Mrs. Lal had bought on special at Target. Just before they left, they all walked into town and had ice cream. "That's it?" Jaya's cousin Smita had asked. "That's all that's here?"

Jaya nodded. "There's only one Main Street."

Her cousin made a low whistling sound. "Smita would have a hard time with that."

For some reason, her cousin always addressed herself in the third person, as if anything that was good for her went for everyone else as well. Her queenly air annoyed Jaya, but she couldn't help admiring her cousin too, since people seemed to give her the attention she wanted.

"Whew." Smita rolled her eyes and dug Jaya in the ribs before tottering off on her tiny heels. "Good luck, girl."

Now, Maria reached out and held Jaya's wrist. "Promise me. You'll talk to your mother. We have to go to high school together."

Jaya tried to crack a smile. *Talk to your mother. Convince her.* There was no such thing with Mrs. Lal.

The elevator doors opened and Maria squeezed once more as they stepped into the mall. "Please?" she whispered.

"I'll try," Jaya said.

*There are so many tiny ways you get to know another person,* Jaya thought as the three girls headed to the bus stop. How Maria did her wrist squeeze: She'd circle your wrist with her fingers and hold on, hard. It was the strength of her touch that surprised—soft and firm at the same time. Or how Lola got so agitated when she had some big idea she wanted to tell. Her wispy hair swept across her eyes and she didn't even notice. Two hours could melt away and Jaya would look up and suddenly realize the whole afternoon had passed. That's why their friendship was so right. This hadn't happened to any of them since they'd come to America. They could be outside, together.

In fact, they forgot they were outside at all.

# Chapter 9

First thing Saturday morning Mrs. Lal and Jaya were at Mrs. Harmon's house, where they roughly divided everything up. Ordinary items were put in the living room. Those of questionable value were stacked on the dining room table. The jewelry was sorted into piles—costume or good. And all the valuables, though there weren't many, were put in Mrs. Harmon's bedroom, which could be locked with a key.

Lola showed up at about noon to help out for a few hours. She and Jaya went up to the attic, where they bent under the sloped ceiling and tried to figure out what was what. Lola was amazed at the forest of history. Inside old suitcases with rusted snap locks lay folded lace and drapes, tablecloths embroidered with raised stitching. They found old children's toys: wooden blocks, a broken dollhouse, a chipped croquet set. Jaya's hands pushed through yellowed newspapers and *Life* magazines, the corners curled. Lola knew she had to stop. There were so many other, practical things to do—unhook the garden hose, clear out the shed—but this was too delicious to resist.

"This Mrs. Harmon, she's the real thing," Lola whispered.

Her eyes gleamed. "I bet we could find something really valuable here."

"Jaya!" Mrs. Lal called from downstairs. "Jaya, I need you in the kitchen!"

Jaya crawled over the beams and peered through the square hole. "Yes, Mama. We'll be there right away." She turned to Lola. "Come on. We better do some real work."

Eventually Lola had to go, so Jaya and her mother worked until it was dark, coming home to the apartment to take long, hot showers, not caring whether Mr. Carlota complained about them using too much water. Sunday, Mrs. Lal and Jaya were there until late again. Still there was a lot to be done. So Mrs. Lal asked if she could switch her days for Mrs. Siler, which did not go over very well. At first Jaya wondered why it was that Mrs. Lal was so determined to help, given how she opposed selling the house in the first place. But Jaya had seen her mother do this before. It was just like after her father had died. She poured her grief into work: the harder, the more exhausting, the better. She wrapped her hair in a print cloth, and bent and wiped and sorted. Her face and arms and lashes were silted gray from dust.

On Monday, when Jaya showed up after school, she opened Mrs. Harmon's bedroom door and, to her surprise, found her mother sitting at the vanity.

Next to her was a shoe box they'd designated "valuables"—a jumble of old rings and earrings, Mrs. Harmon's husband's gold cuff links. Mrs. Lal was opening a flap of black velvet tied with satin ribbon, holding up a brooch. It was a filigreed arabesque, shaped like a two-sided harp, studded with sapphires and diamond chips.

Jaya saw something in her mother that made her uncomfortable: a hunger washing up into her glossy black eyes. Mrs. Lal sat in front of the table, head tilted, the brooch pressed to her collar. A small trace of a smile on her lips. Jaya wasn't even sure her mother knew she was in the room, but then Mrs. Lal said softly, "It is beautiful, isn't it?"

"Yes."

"You can always tell real sapphires from glass because they're dark like a midnight sky."

Suddenly she snapped it open and pinned the brooch to her collar, patting the cloth flat. "There now, that's even better." She twisted a little on the stool. "See how that catches the light."

Jaya's stomach cramped. "Ma, please."

"There are earrings, too."

She opened another flap of velvet, and held up a pair of earrings. They winked and sparkled in the sunlight as she fastened them to her ears. These earrings were like nothing Jaya had ever seen. The filigreed tops gently cupped her mother's lobes. Two twisted loops of diamond chips hung down, swinging against her neck.

"Mrs. Harmon told me about these," she explained. "They belonged to her great-grandmother. Her great-grandfather was an ambassador to Turkey. He wasn't supposed to, but he got these as a present. And her great-grandmother wore them to all the important balls."

*Put them back,* Jaya thought. *Please.* Her stomach was twisted tight now. This was just too weird. She wanted to snatch the jewelry from her mother and put them away. And then she noticed tears glistening in her mother's eyes.

The last time Jaya had seen her mother enjoy a bit of dress-up in front of a mirror was when her father was alive. She had accompanied him for his Sunday painting—as she always did—and he'd bought Jaya's mother a present, an abalone comb. It was the kind of thing the tourists liked, but he had lingered near the table, running his thumb along the shell edge, admiring its shimmer from green to black to yellow, like the cloud edges when a storm was blowing in from the ocean. When he gave the comb to Mrs. Lal, she seemed surprised, and immediately went into the bedroom to slide it into her hair, just over her ear.

Then Jaya watched as her father had come up from behind and put his arms around his wife; she rested her cheek on the crook of his arm. Her mother's face became a sweet, blurred oval. For the first time Jaya understood that this was what love could do: It could change your inner shape, make you curve to another.

Now she realized this was what was missing from her mother's life. Someone to soften her away from her own firm self. And as Jaya watched the loops of sapphire and diamonds sparkle and dance against her mother's dusky skin, it was like watching the sea move against hardened oak.

---

Sometime between Thursday and Saturday the sapphire-diamond brooch and earrings disappeared. No one knew exactly how that could have happened. There had been many people who'd come through the house—painters and floor refinishers, the appraiser and the estate sale manager.

At first the estate people, who had been tallying and recording Mrs. Harmon's belongings, considered it a minor detail, a misplaced item that would show up. But when the appraiser called Mr. Cramer and explained that the most valuable pieces were gone from the very small jewelry selection, Mr. Cramer took notice. He made a few phone calls. He asked to meet with Mrs. Lal at the house. And something in the way she answered made him suspicious. What was it? Jaya wondered later. Was it that hidden yearning that flooded into her eyes? Or the way her expression grew distant, her wide shoulders drawn back when she sensed an affront?

Jaya came home to find her mother was sitting at the tiny dinette table, clutching a towel as she talked on the phone. "I really don't understand this, Mr. Cramer," Mrs. Lal said. "You said we were doing such a good job——"

Jaya watched as her mother listened to the voice on the other end. She was squeezing the dish towel, over and over. Then slowly she set down the phone. Her face looked stricken. "I've been fired," she finally said, incredulous.

"Why?"

She shook her head. "Something about . . . irrefutable evidence that links me to the jewelry theft. Can you imagine!"

She gave the towel another squeeze. "He said that it was in everyone's interest if I didn't work there."

Jaya felt as if that tender bubble of air that surrounded them had been punched through. Who were they kidding? Just the two of them, alone. The walls, the floors of their apartment, everything fallen away. And more cold gray air pouring in.

# Chapter 10

"This is an outrage."

Lola sat on top of the washing machine in the Vitales' laundry room, as if holding a legislative session. She had just been reading about Sam Adams and the Boston Tea Party, and had become particularly interested in real rabble-rousers. People whose blood ran hot and quick, whose talk sparked action. "Jaya, we have to do something. Protest."

Jaya's head lifted, her eyes hooded. "To who?"

They went silent. They knew this was the strange part of being a nanny or a housekeeper. There was no company, no supervisor or principal, no human resources department or higher authority. There was just some mother leaving a check propped up by the salt and pepper shakers.

"I don't know, Lola. My mother, she can get another job." Her eyes grew glassy. "And Mr. Cramer. He said he might . . . he might press charges." She could barely get the words out.

"That's unfair! We can't let that happen! Your mother, she worked for Mrs. Harmon, and just because some stupid nephew—what did you say about him?"

"He's her brother's son. They were never close. Mrs. Harmon always said that side of the family was too boring."

"See? Some stupid stranger can just accuse your mother out of the blue!"

Maria sighed. "It's terrible. People can be mean like that. It happened to my mother once. Someone said she took two hundred dollars from their dresser."

"Did she say anything?"

She shrugged. "No. What could she do?"

"But people can't just do that! This was Jaya's mother's main job. And Mrs. Harmon, she—"

"We can't do anything," Jaya interrupted. "It's over."

Lola stared, frustrated, at her friend. *Don't do this,* she thought. She hated self-pity. She hated people who gave up, slumped against life. Just like her father, wrapped in his shawl of surrender. Everything was fate, he said. *What about second chances?* she wanted to shout. *Isn't this why we came here? You haven't even tried!* But Mr. Svetloski was deaf to the noise and hope of her and her sister, Nadia. That's why Lola loved holing up in her bedroom and reading about the American Revolution. She admired those rebels. How they were loud and pushy, how they could make something completely new.

"I say we go see Mrs. Harmon," Lola declared.

The others looked at her in surprise.

"I'm serious. Why not? I bet she can vouch for your mother. She likes her, right?"

Jaya nodded. "A lot. They talked all the time."

"That's what I mean. We can get her to say something. Call her nephew."

"Lola, she had a stroke. A pretty bad one, my mother said. I don't think she can even talk." She shivered, remembering that day, and put on her sweatshirt.

"All right. Then she can write something. What are they called?" She banged her heels against the washing machine. "An affidavit. A statement. We can stop this stupid business right now. Right, Maria?" She was sure Maria would back her up— she was always so sunny and optimistic.

Maria, though, had pinched her face into a doubtful expression. "Can we really do that?"

"Why not?"

"I agree with you, Lola, it's really terrible. But my uncle, he's always telling me, 'Don't get into trouble.' There's so many problems these days. He . . . he just wants me to be good."

"Good!" Lola snorted. She couldn't believe her best friend would utter such a word. Or that she'd have such a frightened rabbit-like look. "Look. We go to the hospital. We can stop this stupid business right now."

"How will we get there?" Maria asked. "It's far away."

"Watch." Lola dug out the cell phone and called her sister. "We need a lift," she told her. She could hear Nadia's irritation, but it was easy enough to guilt Nadia into doing her bidding, since she knew Nadia wasn't doing anything but lounging around in her boyfriend Lon's parents' rec room.

Nadia was like a prettier, older version of Lola, with

striking dark eyes, sharp cheekbones, and a size-two body that just about every girl at Meadowbrook High envied. She did a much better job of blending in than Lola; soon after the family moved to Meadowbrook, she found a crowd of girls who blow-dried their hair into perfect fans that rippled at their backs, and wore tops that showed just a sliver of belly—as much as school code would allow. The only difference was that Nadia didn't go off in the winter to ski in Aspen or come back after spring break with a Cancún tan. Usually she was doing overtime at the A&P in another town, where she worked as a cashier, to save up money for good clothes and her portfolio as a model.

That was Nadia's social trump card: She actually could be a model, and had even gone on a few auditions. Her other big coup was her boyfriend, Lon, who had graduated last year and was going to Rutgers on a football scholarship. He came around enough for girls to admire his curly dark hair and his muscles showing through T-shirts that proved he hadn't gone flabby since his glory days in high school charging the finish line.

A few minutes later, as Lola and the others were coming through the back door, she saw her sister parking in the driveway and stepping out of the car. How did she do it? Lola wondered. The way she moved—perfect. Her white pants and sky blue shirt. The hippie jacket with shag collar that she'd gotten for forty dollars at a thrift store. Her hair piled sloppily in a clip. And the crowning touch on a cold spring day—blue rubber flip-flops. Genius. Light-years ahead of most

Meadowbrook High girls who had clothing budgets the size of their swimming pools.

"So where do you want to go?" Nadia asked.

"The hospital."

"Somebody sick?" Her sister was toying with the key ring, obviously counting the minutes to when she could be done.

"No," Lola said. "Something more important than that. Jaya's mother—"

Lola broke off. She was all ready to make a big speech about the terrible injustice they were fighting, when suddenly she saw her friends through Nadia's cool, appraising gaze. Maria, far too dumpy and babyish with her sweet heart-shaped face. Jaya, a skittish shadow clutching her frayed army satchel across her lap. They looked childish, overeager. Hardly heroic.

Lola pushed her shoulders back, as if defending her friends. "Just take us," she said.

Jaya tried to stay calm. She pressed her ankles together, let her arm rest on the open window, cool air skimming her elbow. They were seeing Mrs. Harmon. They would straighten everything out. Talk to her. Turn this whole thing around.

Inside, though, she was terrified.

Jaya was never good at confrontations. Or sick people. Talking up. Faking it. Daring stunts. She wasn't good at anything except sitting with a sketch pad across her knees, watching and drawing.

"Come on," Maria whispered.

"I'm afraid," Jaya admitted.

"I know. But we'll make everything good again." She brushed Jaya's arm lightly. Jaya softened. She always felt better when Maria touched her. She did her wrist squeeze and looked at you with those big, wet brown eyes of hers. *"Querida,"* she whispered. "Don't let nothing get to you."

But there was something else that kept Jaya ducked into a hole of silence. What if Andrew Cramer was right? What if her mother had stolen the earrings and brooch? Ever since that evening when she'd learned about her mother's firing, doubt had seeped inside her, corrosive as rust. What about all those times when her mother gave herself a few extras, like that scratched coffeepot from the Silers? The way her pupils glittered when she hung up an employer's new silk dress, freshly sheathed in dry-cleaning plastic? Longing and envy poured through her mother's fingertips, her eyes. Jaya saw it all the time. But Jaya could never say this. She could never reveal her torn-up, pained heart.

Inside the lobby Lola strode right up to the information desk, said she was a great-niece, and learned that Mrs. Harmon was on the third floor. Silently she led the other two to the elevators and upstairs. The corridor there was mostly empty, the only sound a *beep-beep* of monitors, the low warble of a TV.

They had reached Mrs. Harmon's room.

Jaya felt as if she were pushing through a wall of hot air. Her palms pricked with sweat as the girls passed a patient, her nest of hair spread on the pillow, two saggy balloons tied to the rail.

And then she saw Mrs. Harmon. In the enormous bed she looked like a tiny yellow doll. Her head kept making a slow jiggling motion on her thin neck.

*Be brave,* Jaya told herself. *Like Mama.* "Hi, Mrs. Harmon," she tried.

One side of Mrs. Harmon's mouth trembled, but she stayed silent. Jaya noticed that her cheek still drooped.

Maria whispered, "Talk about the jewelry."

Several times Mrs. Harmon swallowed and made an odd gargling noise, but no words came out. Somewhere in there was the old Mrs. Harmon, gathering up her thoughts. But the room stayed silent.

"Listen, Mrs. Harmon. I'm sorry to bother you." Jaya bit her lip. "You know your brooch and earrings? The ones your great-grandmother gave you?" She paused. "See, they've been stolen."

Mrs. Harmon fastened her shiny eyes on Jaya. She couldn't seem to get the words out—it was like watching an animal trapped behind glass.

"The thing is, they say it's my mama who stole them. But she—" Jaya broke off. "Please, Mrs. Harmon. You have to help us. You have to tell your nephew. That Mama wouldn't do that—"

A slow lisping sound slipped out of Mrs. Harmon's throat.

Lola dug into her knapsack and pulled out a little paper, on which she had written the question "Do you believe Mrs. Lal stole your jewelry?" Underneath the question she had made two boxes, one for yes, the other for no.

Jaya stared at the paper. A terrible crumbling sensation went through her. She felt as if she could blow away any minute.

"Please, Mrs. Harmon," she begged. "All you have to do is point."

But Mrs. Harmon's hand stayed limp on the page.

And that's when Jaya really began to cry. Everything sifted out of her in this terrible hospital room with sickly green walls—she was no more than ash, a speck, nothing. She remembered how her mother couldn't resist bringing home that pair of shoes with the broken heel from Mrs. Siler. Or how just the other day Jaya had noticed her mother paging through the community college catalog, desire rushing through her eyes.

*Oh, Mama,* she thought as her broken rusted heart fell into pieces all around. *What is the truth?*

*Chapter 11*

They were scared. Singly, doubly, trebly scared. As all three girls squeezed into the back of Lon's car, Meadowbrook looked different. The pretty houses skimming past now hunched against them. Fear coursed in a cold front through them, freezing their thoughts, coating their mouths shut. Nobody could talk.

This business with Mrs. Harmon was harder than they'd thought. It wasn't just about stolen jewelry. It was about old age. And yellow sickly skin and crumbling brain cells and maybe even death. It was about the end of things, about pushing back against something hot and heavy, even as it pulled you down.

Lola found herself remembering a hot summer day, playing dare with her cousins at the swimming hole. Who could jump harder, deeper. A taunting circle, calling up to her. She dove straight down. Someone grabbed her ankles, another her wrists. They surrounded her, grasping her like weeds. Lungs burning, she thrashed, then shot to the surface, air exploding from her mouth. She had never been so terrified. She never forgot the sensation of pushing against water, rope fingers smothering her.

Nadia dropped them off in town, but the three girls didn't feel ready to part just yet. On the corner was the lot where trucks were pulling up and letting out the day laborers who were finished for the day.

A car suddenly surged past, boys laughing. "Get lost!" they shouted at the men who were climbing out of trucks.

Maria flinched. She'd heard the stories: Just the other day, over dinner, Renaldo told his family about a friend from work who'd been cornered by a group of teenage boys wielding beer bottles—he'd gotten away by leaping over a fence. Nobody said a word, though. Everybody was scared about their jobs—even Renaldo, who had a steady gig with a landscaper. They didn't want to make trouble. Not these days.

The dark was coming down swiftly, a cold breeze nipping at their necks and ears. "Come on," she urged her friends.

They found themselves pulled to Mrs. Harmon's place, as if to a magnet. For a few minutes they sat on a brick wall in silence, staring across the street. The windows, bare of coverings, were dark. The front yard was in bad shape: flower beds clogged with wrinkled leaves. The trellis listed to the side. A FOR SALE sign creaked on its post.

"It's kinda sad, isn't it?" Maria remarked.

"Uh-huh."

Jaya noticed a beige-colored car pulling up to the curb. The Realtor, Mrs. Carson, led a young couple through the gate, briskly kicked a bagged flyer off the porch, and then punched a code into the security lock that hung from the doorknob. An instant later the girls could hear voices and heels echoing against the bare floors and walls.

"I can't believe Mrs. Harmon isn't in there and these people are just wandering around inside," Jaya whispered.

"Me too. Remember that time Mrs. Harmon showed us how to make ink out of berries?"

"Oh, yeah."

Jaya had actually forgotten about that day. Most of the time she thought of Mrs. Harmon's as only hers, but a few times she'd brought Lola and Maria along. Mrs. Harmon had been her usual casual and welcoming self, serving slightly stale biscuits and tea, and then teaching them to boil berries in a dented pot and use sharpened feathers to write. Jaya didn't think much of it, but of course Lola had gone crazy, marveling at all the old items that were crammed into Mrs. Harmon's room: a washboard and bucket, a pewter ladle. Funny, Jaya never realized that Mrs. Harmon's house could mean something to Lola. But the place was a part of her, too. Jaya had forgotten that. She was so used to being on her own. By herself.

"Look, guys, I know this was kind of a setback," Lola put in. "But we can't give up. What about getting together tomorrow?"

"I can't," Maria finally said. "I'm meeting . . ." She couldn't help it, but a smile slipped through. "A boy."

"What boy?"

"Tash."

Then Maria explained about the argument with the

81

lacrosse players, how the next time she'd been at the park with her cousin, she and the Frisbee boy had wound up chatting, in Spanish and English. At some point he'd remarked that he wished he could do that more often, because it would make his Spanish so much better. And she'd blurted out, Why didn't they meet and she'd give him lessons? Just like that! She'd never done anything so daring.

Maria had been dying to tell her friends, but with Mrs. Harmon and Jaya's mother's firing, there never was a good time. So she let it build up in her, like the happy silver-confetti feeling before a birthday. But as she explained herself, she could feel Lola's disapproving stare.

"Are you serious?" Lola asked. "That's what you've been thinking about right now? A boy?"

"Why not?"

"How shallow."

Tears stung Maria's eyes and she looked away. She knew Lola could be mean, but she'd never felt her sharpness slice her.

Maria looked to Jaya, hoping she'd defend her. But Jaya seemed to be somewhere else, staring off at the street.

The cold seeped in between them. For the first time they walked with spaces surrounding them, no reassuring bumping of elbows and arms. Without a word the girls parted ways.

As Jaya walked home, she could feel that old bleak feeling leak through her. That there was nothing to protect her. Not even her friends. Up and down her street, cars were pulling into the driveways, doors slamming, kids tumbling out, shouting at their mothers. "Mom, please—just a half hour of Power Rangers!" one boy whined. A few porch lights winked on. It was all so normal, so TV-perfect, but out of her reach.

Mounting the outside stairs, Jaya saw Mr. Carlota through the lace curtains, watching TV. She never knew if he would give her a friendly wave or narrow his eyes and complain that she was making too much noise on the steps.

She returned to an empty apartment, since Mrs. Lal was doing extra babysitting for the Silers. Her mother had left a basket of laundry and a note on the dinette table: "Please finish." She ate her dinner in silence, watching the phone, hoping it would ring any minute. She kept thinking that Mr. Cramer would call up, saying, *It was all a mistake. We found the earrings. We're so sorry.* But the phone never rang, never rescued her from her doubts.

*Chapter 12*

The next day Lola was sitting in the breakfast nook in the Vitales' kitchen, making a diagram. If Jaya was going to be such a depressive and Maria was busy mooning after that boy, she would have to solve this theft on her own. Who would steal a pair of earrings? Well, just about anybody, she figured. They were valuable. They were beautiful. So that left just about the entire town of Meadowbrook.

Not a very good start.

Outside, Mr. Vitale and a few of his men were loading metal heating ducts into the back of one of his white vans. Anthony was tipping up his skateboard with his sneaker. "If you're not going to help," his father yelled, "then get outta the driveway!"

Mrs. Vitale was there too, dressed in a stretchy velour track suit, and getting into her Lexus. "You don't have to yell at him," she scolded her husband. "He can hear you!"

Despite herself, Lola sometimes felt sorry for Anthony. He was a little slow, with a wide, sloping stomach and thick, clumsy hands. He showed no interest in anything except video games and skateboarding. And he couldn't care less about his father's business, even though he boasted all the time that one day he'd be in charge.

It was Mr. Vitale who had turned the family's hole-in-the-wall plumbing supply business in Newark into a local empire. His shiny white trucks were all over town, parked in front of houses. The company's motto, *We Do It All*, was stitched across the right front pocket of his employees' blue coveralls. And they did do everything: heating and central air and gutting kitchens, and now even building brand-new houses. Mrs. Vitale often said she couldn't believe how successful her husband was. Her mother-in-law used to spend all day behind a Formica counter, ordering bolts and screws and yelling at the men with grease under their nails, and now she could join the country club and spend all day in tennis skirts and nobody would think it strange.

Lola wished her father, through osmosis, could pick up on some of that shiny can-do energy. The few times her parents showed up for some end-of-school event—Field Day or Earth Day—her father stood on the side, scowling and bitter. He didn't understand American men, with their casual shorts and athletic calves; their enthusiastic, goofy fathering. "They dress and act like overgrown boys," he grumbled.

Lately things had gotten worse in the family. Mrs. Svetloski had gone to the doctor, who'd given her some tablets and told her she needed to lose about forty pounds, otherwise she'd be straining her heart. Mrs. Svetloski had come home that evening, her face gray, and had lain in bed with her feet up on the pillows. Lola had thought for sure this would be the wake-up bell for her father: Ding-dong! Time to get a job! But no, it had only made him sink further into his own self-pity.

Anthony came into the kitchen and snatched the paper with her diagram. "Hey!" she cried.

"Mrs. Harmon's house," he read out loud. "I know that lady's place. My dad just told me it's condemned."

"Condemned?"

"Yeah. There's all kinds of problems. Like the stove being dangerous. And some beams and stuff. I don't know exactly. He's looking into maybe tearing it down and building condominiums."

"Really?" She nearly shot up out of her chair.

Anthony blinked, pulling back. "Jeez, Lola. What is your problem?"

Lola bit her lip. *Calm down,* she told herself. But her heart was beating so fast, her thoughts were stuttering ahead. "What else can you tell me?" she asked.

"I went with my dad over there. He tried to figure out how much it's going to take to fix that place up. You could blow a lot of money on a house like this, if you wanted to, my dad said, and it might not be worth it. He could get him some guys who can tell him how much scrap wood and the fixtures would be worth. But the location"—and here Anthony's own voice lifted, his eyes gleamed—"he says is really good. Worth a lot of money."

Lola stared at Anthony in dismay. It was as if she were peering into a crystal ball and seeing Anthony Vitale Jr., future real estate mogul. A distant hard drumbeat started up in her head. This wasn't just about the theft. She had to save this place from greedy developers, who were no more than grown-up idiot boys who got Cs in history, and who covered the land in a plague of cheap-wood fake colonial condominiums.

"What did Mrs. Carson say to that?"

"She sounded pretty interested. Like, a year ago my dad might have done it in a second. Only business isn't too good. So he isn't sure."

Just the other day Lola had heard Mr. Vitale tell Mrs. Vitale that he was cutting back on his operation and would have to lay off some guys. "The real estate bubble's popped, babe," he added, kissing the top of her head. "Go light on the Saks card."

Anthony peered at Lola's notes. "Why do you want to know about that house?"

Lola hesitated.

"Come on."

Lola felt a warm flush come over her. How could she tell Anthony, of all people? Maria and Jaya would kill her. Or would they? she reflected, remembering with a sore pang their trip to the hospital and the tensions between them.

So she started to tell him just a little—how Mrs. Harmon had had a stroke and been taken away—but before she knew it, voice shaking with anger, she had let him know about Jaya's mother being falsely accused of stealing the earrings and brooch. To her surprise she was a little upset, even scared. Tears stung the backs of her eyes. Embarrassed, she wiped them away.

"You should just go in there, then," Anthony said. "Maybe you'll find proof or something that could help you."

"Are you crazy?"

He shrugged. "I walk into my dad's jobs all the time. They leave the doors open 'cause there's so much stuff going on."

Lola gazed at Anthony. It was as if the crystal ball had spun around, blurring the other image and giving her a new one: rebel. She even detected a glint of shrewdness in his eyes. Who would have guessed? Anthony Vitale, a subversive in the making.

"Just go in there," he repeated.

It was a dare, hanging in the air between them, like a knife.

"Maybe I will."

Anthony was still lingering. "If you want, I can find out more," he offered.

"That would be great."

Before they knew it, they were grinning at each other. Lola felt a hot flush, all over, as a new insight came to her: It was as weird for Anthony to have Lola in his house as it was for her.

Truth be told, the Vitales were generous people. They had big refrigerators and big hearts. They knew all about her no-good father. Mrs. Vitale sometimes even sent over sympathy lasagna. And health insurance! Her mother had the luckiest, best gig around. She should be grateful. Instead she and Anthony tore at each other's throats, like dogs who couldn't share the same territory.

"Hey, I was going to make a sandwich. You want one too?"

"Yeah, sure."

But they kept staring at each other, as if too embarrassed to look away.

Then Lola's mother called from upstairs. "Lola! You can help me move this bed?"

Lola felt as if she'd just been dropped from the lofty rafters of the Continental Congress onto hard, bitter ground. Oh, yes. She wasn't a grand schemer, a leader of causes. She was the housekeeper's daughter, and there were beds to be made, especially when your mother had a bad back.

As Lola left the kitchen, it all became clear. Helping Jaya and the Founders' Project were one and the same. How could she not have seen it before? The house was a symbol of everything that was wrong with this stupid materialistic town, drowning in a froth of greed. And Jaya's mom was its victim. Lola was going to expose it all to everyone. She'd show them a Founders' Project like they'd never seen. As she mounted the grand staircase, Lola was busy writing in her head. For she knew exactly what she had to say.

# Chapter 13

Maria tried not to stare at the door of Starbucks while she waited at a corner table. For a while she sipped at her frappé, but her stomach was scraped raw from nerves; the milk tasted bitter, like metal. Maybe she could go to the bathroom and douse her perspiring face in water, brush her hair for the seventeenth time, but then what if he thought she'd stood him up?

It was rare she ever stepped inside a Starbucks without Lola and Jaya. Three dollars for a cup of coffee? She could hear Renaldo laugh scornfully. *I'll get you some* café con leche *from a truck.* But this was the place Frisbee Boy had suggested.

And then there he was, pushing through the door like a sun-god, shaking his hair from his eyes, dressed only in a T-shirt and light cargo pants, his fleece jacket tied loosely around his slender waist. Dust specks floated off his bare arms, like a coating of gold powder.

"Hey," he said. When he raised his hand to wave to her, she could see the twined muscle of his bicep under his sleeve. The crushed ice in her frappé ached against the roof of her mouth.

"Hey."

He dropped down opposite her. "Sorry I'm late. I have this ACLU high school chapter stuff I promised to do. I'm president this year." He grimaced. "My dad's idea. For college stuff."

Maria didn't even know what "ACLU" meant, but she said, *"No problemo,"* and told him to get a drink.

He grinned. "Cool."

As Tash (a nickname, she learned, for Theodore Sherman, which he hated) returned to the table with his iced latte, he said, "You sure you want to do this? 'Cause it's not like I can pay you——"

"No, it's not about that." A sharp heat rose from her cheeks to the roots of her hair. How she hated this! "It helps me, too. I'm not in ELL anymore, but the teachers said that sometimes teaching others about your own language helps you improve." They had said no such thing, but she had to come up with something quick.

"That's awesome. My mom'll be thrilled. She's the one who got me going with this volunteer stuff. Some old buddy of hers from the peace corps runs this Costa Rican nonprofit."

Maria nodded. This sounded promising—something that would keep him meeting with her every Thursday afternoon at the Starbucks.

Maria and Tash began to talk—mostly in Spanish, though occasionally lapsing into English since it soon became pretty clear that Tash was a natural and easy conversationalist but his actual Spanish was thin. He seemed to know this too, apologizing for how he tended to "fake" sentences, and this made him even more adorable than ever. She'd never met a boy who so readily admitted his mistakes.

The best part, Maria realized, was that she could learn all about Tash, under the guise of it being part of the lesson. She found out that his mom had been in the peace corps in Guatemala, and then had taught school there for a couple of years. These days she was head of some big foundation in the city and he got to go to pretty cool events. His dad was a tax lawyer, and also worked in the city. He was an only child too, and he lived in a house his parents had built that looked over a ravine on the hilly edge of town. Every morning, he said, he woke up to the sound of rushing water on rocks. Maria had been over to that part of Meadowbrook only once, when Renaldo had taken her in his car and they'd gone bombing down the winding roads, just for fun.

"My dad is a major pain," he explained. "He wants me to go to Yale, his alma mater. But my mom hates when he talks like that. 'Live your life first!' she tells me. 'And besides, you can break your ass to get in, and then you wind up not getting in and feeling bad about yourself. Let it happen!'

"What a hippie," he added, laughing. "She still saves plastic bags and has an organic garden, spending gobs of money on the right fertilizer, even though she doesn't have any time to take care of it."

Maria also noticed he talked about his parents as if they were his friends, analyzing their flaws and their good points, joking about them in this casual, knowing way. If someone were to ask her to name five traits of her mother, she couldn't even find the words. Nice. Good. Hardworking. But friend? No. Just mother.

"*Y tu padre?*"

"He's Mr. Character-Building. He just started this new thing: When we go on vacation, like on our ski trips, I have to use all my own money. No wraparound sunglasses for me."

Maria had never heard about that: having so much money that you pretend you have less money.

*A rich blanquito,* she could hear Renaldo saying. *They do weird stuff.*

There was something different about talking to Tash— different even from spending time with her friends. It reminded her of one of those TV shows where you toured inside people's houses, checking out their carpeted closets and marble baths and brushed-nickel taps, only this was more like knowing other things, the conversations they had over breakfast, the thoughts inside those people with healthful burnished skin.

Maria felt as if she were lying in a summer field, listening to the whiz of a Frisbee. Everything was easy. Tash-easy. American easy.

"*Mi Dios!*" Maria suddenly realized the time. Tío Pedro would really give it to her, since Tía Lucy had asked her to babysit. She jumped up from her seat.

"You all right?"

She hooked her pocketbook over her shoulder, steadied herself. "I just forgot. I have to be somewhere—"

Tash stood too, and suddenly she realized how much taller he was, bending toward her like a lean tree. She, on the other hand, resembled a stout bush, and silently cursed her short, plump body. Next time she'd be sure to wear her wedges.

"Okay." He had on his fleece jacket and lifted his canvas bag over his shoulder, the strap slanted sideways across his chest, a baseball cap cocked backward, so he looked like a bike messenger boy in the city. "See you next Thursday?" he asked.

"*Jueves,*" she corrected.

# Chapter 14

After school Jaya hurried over to the Silers' house. As she opened the back door, she was grateful for the warm kitchen. For a moment she watched her mother at the stove as she slowly stirred boiling water with a wooden spoon. She knew that look so well: the tall, firm back, the broad sloping shoulders. It reminded her of before, when it was just the two of them, back home. When her mother was just hers, and she didn't have to watch her push softened pears into some other kid's mouth.

Sometimes Jaya would look for signs of the other kids. She would find her mother napping with the TV on, and she'd curl up next to her, trying to see their thumbprints on her cheeks, the smear of jelly on her collar, the smell of baby talc and soap on her neck. She would rest her head on her mother's chest, listening to her even breathing, wondering if she could hear the sounds of her day. Did she call out to them, scold them, or praise them, as she did Jaya? she wondered. Did she give their little bottoms a pat when they wandered off the wrong way?

"Mama?" The words were a glittering chain in her mouth, hard as metal. *What really happened to the jewelry?*

"Yes?" Her mother swiveled around, spoon in hand, and

Jaya felt the words slip down into a dark space.

Panicked, she blurted out, "The other day me and Maria and Lola went to Mrs. Harmon's—"

"You did what?"

"I just thought . . ." Jaya's face flushed hot. "I missed her. And if you talked to her, she would listen. She doesn't even know you were fired—"

Her mother was shaking now. "You will not bother that poor woman! And I forbid you to ever do that again, do you understand?"

"Is something wrong?"

Jaya turned around to see Mrs. Siler standing in the kitchen. Though Mrs. Siler was an attorney for some big firm, she still looked like a college girl, her brown hair tied into a sloppy ponytail, a spray of freckles around her cheeks. Everything rattled her—if Mrs. Lal bought regular eggs, not cage-free. Or if she served the children chicken and rice instead of the frozen macaroni pouches with dancing rabbits.

"Nothing," Mrs. Lal replied. "Jaya's just here to help out. And to get going on her homework."

Mrs. Siler turned to Jaya. "Would you mind doing your work elsewhere?" She gave an apologetic smile. "Forgive me, but I'm just one of those sticklers who thinks a kitchen is for food."

"Yeah, sure." Jaya gathered her belongings.

Mrs. Lal always said Mrs. Siler was "a little on the high-strung side." But she wasn't quite sure where she could go, exactly. Everything in the house was set up for either very little people or grown-ups with expensive taste. The playroom held miniature tables and two painted chests of toys, a small kitchen for Isabel, and a fire truck for Jordan. There was matching everything, including laundry bags with their names stitched across. Before Jaya had come to America, she didn't know there could be such a thing—a whole room just for children, color-coordinated and full of their belongings. It was like the kids here had their own miniature world, with special frozen food boxes and plastic bowls.

"Why don't you use the mudroom? There's a table in there."

Jaya opened the door to the mudroom and set up at the tiny table in the corner. Not a very good idea, she soon realized, since the room wasn't insulated and she kept having to blow on her knuckles and jiggle her knees every few minutes. She made it through her social studies homework before giving up. Picking up her things, she headed for the living room.

Suddenly there was a shriek from the other side of the house. Jaya hurried into the playroom, where she found Jordan trying to snatch the stuffed Barney from Isabel. Jaya sat Jordan down with a truck, then she lifted the sobbing Isabel onto her lap. The little girl smelled good, of milk and soap. This was the part of her mother's job she did like. It made her feel like she was inside the glowing circle of other people's kids. She lingered a moment, stroking Isabel's hair, as if soaking in the warm rays of belonging.

Jaya picked up some stray LEGO pieces that had drifted from the playroom and put them into the toy box. No matter how much her mother told her they'd come to this country for her future, her education, she had the feeling that it wasn't true. She'd always be here, attached to her mother, picking up stray socks, serving chicken nuggets, and mopping floors while other kids could go out into the world and be themselves. She'd be stuck in a dark room, gazing out, belonging to no one else.

She found a comfortable chair in a corner. She knew she should get going on her math homework, but she felt like sketching for a little while. She pulled out a stick of charcoal and her pad, and for a few minutes there was just the soothing scratch of charcoal on her paper. She was soon so absorbed in her drawing that she didn't even hear someone come into the room.

"Oh!" Mrs. Siler was standing there, the pale skin around her eyes pinched.

Jaya looked down. She hadn't noticed before, but she had left a gray handprint that had smudged the pink-and-white-striped upholstery. Quickly she took out a cloth she kept tucked in the box and tried to blot the stain.

"Don't use that!"

The handprint had spread into a blotch. "I'm sorry," she mumbled. She wished, right then, she could let out a wail, just like the twins, so her mother would pull her into her arms.

A few minutes later, she walked into the kitchen and found Mrs. Siler talking in a low, intent whisper to Mrs. Lal. They'd apparently been talking for a while.

"I'm really sorry, Simone. It's a little too much. Jaya coming here and doing her homework. Maybe it's just my hormones, now that I'm not nursing. It's just been so hard."

Jaya noticed that Mrs. Siler had this way of talking about how she felt, her hormones, sounding so helpless, and yet somehow commanding you to listen.

Mrs. Lal nodded. "That's okay. Jaya's a big girl. She can take care of herself."

Jaya felt a slow, horrible burning in her chest. Why had her mother said that? She hurried into the living room and began stuffing her things into her backpack. She needed to get out of there, fast. As she wrenched open the front door, cold air blasted her face.

"Jaya?" her mother called.

But she kept going, outside and down the porch steps. Out of the corner of her eye Jaya saw her mother's surprised face, a dish towel in her hands. She wasn't sure if she was fleeing or her mother was hurling her out of that warm circle. All she knew was that it was time to run, as hard as she could, away from there.

*Chapter 15*

It was garden season again in Meadowbrook. The leaf blowers were starting to come out—men with motorized packs on their backs, tubes coiled around their waists, wresting damp leaves from skunky flower beds. All day long, up and down, under the newly budding trees, landscaper trucks drove past, rakes and machinery rattling in the flatbeds, the men spreading out on the lawns, attacking weeds, grooming the grass to a velvet trim.

But this year something was different in Meadowbrook, a feeling, an unease, an edge of chill eating away at the sweet, good spring days. Especially with so much going bad. FOR SALE signs were springing up like mushrooms after a rain. In the park all the nannies were talking about the layoffs and who'd just gotten fired or had their hours cut back. The "other side" of Haley Avenue was creeping up, salsa blaring from some shop where they sold international calling cards. Women in veils walking right past the old barber shop, now an African hair-braiding shop.

And then the sorest point: the day laborers, who waited every morning in the parking lot on Jessup Lane. Nobody liked how they looked—caps pulled low over their eyes, hands pushed into their spattered dirty jeans, crushed Styrofoam cups and cigarette butts left on the asphalt. One woman claimed that the men ate lunch on her deck and left yellow rice and chicken bones scattered on her grass, where the crows were having a field day. A neighbor four doors down expressly told her guys to use the basement bathroom, and they'd tracked through the house to use the one in the kitchen. Then another, six blocks down, said she'd looked out the kitchen window and seen a guy urinating in a bed of geraniums. Gross!

But the pizza parlor—where Jaya, Maria, and Lola decided to meet—was filled with the usual late-afternoon roar. Mothers with little kids were filling up the tables. Jaya saw a couple of boys and girls from her grade dressed in their baseball uniforms, their caps resting on the tables. She and Maria and Lola never did stuff like that. Even if they did go out for teams, their mothers weren't the kind to sit in the bleachers and take them out for pizza after. They only showed up for school activities if they had to, and they always stood shyly in the back.

"Come on, guys. We can't just sit around staring at our slices." Lola sighed. "We have to do something."

"I have an idea," Maria said. "You know that boy, Tash Adler? His dad is a lawyer. Maybe he can help."

"Oh, yeah, how'd your little lesson go?" It was hard not to notice the sour tinge in Lola's voice.

Maria blushed. "Pretty good. We're meeting again. Next week." She actually didn't want to talk any more about Tash.

She knew that Lola didn't believe he liked her at all, that he was just some too-cool high school cruiser.

"Forget about his dad," Lola said. "We have to figure this out on our own. Like, who would steal that jewelry? Then we can show how it wasn't your mother and she can get her job back."

"But there is no job," Jaya insisted. "Mrs. Harmon isn't coming back." She was hunched over in her chair, a blue hoodie drawn over her hair. Ever since the afternoon at the Silers', when she'd run out on her mother, she felt cold all the time.

"Still," Lola said. "It isn't fair. You have to clear her name. You can't have something hanging over you like that." She paused, and then declared, "I say we go right over to Mrs. Harmon's house."

"Are you crazy?" Maria asked. "We're not allowed there!"

"I'm serious. I even got a little info on the place. From Anthony Vitale. His father's thinking of buying it. Maybe even tearing it down to build some gross condos. He says we can just walk in——"

Jaya shook her head. Hot tears squeezed out of her eyes. Her throat felt raw, as if she'd been crying for days. "No. I can't ever go there again."

"But what's your mom going to do?"

Jaya reached around for her satchel, hanging on the back of her chair, and brought out a sheaf of papers. They were flyers, with the words RESPONSIBLE HOUSEKEEPER. AVAILABLE IMMEDIATELY. "Listen, I promised my mother I'd put these up."

"Oh, God." Lola sighed. "I used to hate when my mother made me do that. One time we walked into every hairdresser and nail salon and I had to translate for her. So embarrassing. There was my mother begging to soak people's corns, and there I was speaking for her! I wanted to die. Thank God she got that job at the Vitales'. Even if they drive her crazy."

"But we have to help," Maria said. She stood and pushed her chair into the table. For an instant she looked like a stern school teacher. "Let's go." She added, with a mischievous smile, "And then maybe we can go shopping."

It was just like when they'd first met, the way they just knew how to fit together. They worked as a team, seeking out all the possible places for posting flyers: the supermarket, the light poles along Main Street, at the dry cleaner's, the ice cream shop, the train station, the library, and community bulletin boards.

When they finished, Maria pointed to Vamps and Vixens, and suggested they browse inside.

"Oh, no," Lola groaned.

"Why not? Jaya needs to be cheered up. And you know that shopping always makes me feel better." She added, "Besides, I want to find something nice."

"What for?"

Maria hesitated. "For my next lesson. With Tash."

Lola looked at Maria as if her friend had suddenly emerged from the ocean, a freaky plastic girl with fake button eyes. Jaya's mother was fired for no good reason, Jaya might have to move away from Meadowbrook, and Maria was thinking about dressing up for a boy?

"Come on," Maria urged. "It'll be fun."

Lola didn't exactly agree. She had no patience for shops, especially the kind that Maria liked, with frilly little skirts and crocheted purses that cost fifty dollars and held no more than a lip gloss tube.

"Please?"

"Okay," Lola grumbled as they crossed the street and made their way to Vamps and Vixens.

There were plenty of shops like this around Meadowbrook. Knickknack places that sold mismatched china dishes and silver goblets and bunny rabbit baskets. Or there were the arty stores, crammed with ceramic napkin holders and key pegs, the kinds of things that somehow wound up in Maria's apartment, as a discarded gift from one of Mrs. Alvarez's employers. "Housewife hobby shops," Lola called them. "They don't have to make money or anything. The wives just get to stay out of their husband's hair."

In fact, Mrs. Meisner's shop was a lot of fun. She actually had a good eye. She knew how to mix vintage stuff—old rayon dresses with kitschy prints, and bags made of uphol- stery fabric—with newer, fashionable clothes. Jaya liked Mrs. Meisner. Her two-tone hair stuck straight up on end, as if she'd just been through a wind tunnel; she liked to wear white smocklike shirts and colorful, mismatched costume jewelry that she sold at the shop.

Maria browsed a table of ribbed tank tops so skinny she was sure they could probably only make it up her arm. She knew this was ridiculous. She couldn't afford the jeans crusted with rhinestones that cost more than two hundred dollars. Her mother was lucky if she made that in a day. But still, there was something delicious about pretending. That's what she always loved about coming to America. Even if you couldn't really have something, it always felt as if it were there for you to touch and smell. When she and Mami first arrived, they used to spend Sundays at the mall. Her mother loved to visit the makeup counters, lifting her chin to be spritzed by the perfume salesgirls. Usually she walked away with a few sample packets in her pocketbook.

Jaya, who was admiring the costume jewelry section— old rhinestone pins and crystal earrings—also loved beautiful things. Mrs. Meisner had pinned a few on the vintage dresses and some felt hats. Jaya moved closer, touching carved bangles on a stand. They were made of different-colored wood, and let out a musical click as she fingered them. Their surfaces reminded her of the curving leaf designs she had once admired in a book the art teacher had showed them about calligraphy and illuminated manuscripts. She was digging into her bag, to get her notebook and one of her father's old colored pencils, when someone shouted from behind.

"Hey!"

She whirled around. Rachel Meisner was standing there, glaring at Jaya. Quickly Jaya shoved her pad back into the bag.

"What's in your bag?"

"Nothing. Just my paper and pencil—"

"This is my mom's store. Are you stealing?"

"No, I was just drawing."

"Then you were stealing her designs! What makes you think you can just waltz into a place and copy it down?"

"Are you crazy?" It was Lola, who had come up from behind. "Jaya is an artist. She draws things. She knows more about design than your mother ever will."

*Oh, no,* Jaya thought, her stomach churning. *Please don't start up.*

"I think you all better leave." She whispered something to her friend Madison. She was Rachel's perennial sidekick, walking through the school corridors as if their elbows were attached. She had come from Hong Kong, and one of the first things her parents had done was change their daughter's name from Ming to Madison, a fact that infuriated Lola.

"What did you say, Rachel?"

She shrugged. "Nothing. It's just stuff."

"Yeah, well you better tell that stuff to my face."

"Your ugly face, you mean?"

Jaya began to tremble. She didn't know what upset her more, being accused, or how Lola picked fights with everyone.

Madison stepped between them. "You really have to go."

Jaya was already heading for the door, Maria fast behind. Lola reluctantly turned on her heel and left. Outside, Jaya pulled the flap over her canvas satchel and suddenly realized something was missing—her flyers. She must have set them aside when she'd pulled out her notebook. She went back inside, where Rachel was standing by the counter, holding the sheaf of papers. Obviously she had read what they said. Jaya took them quickly, cheeks warm. Even though Rachel didn't know anything about the theft at Mrs. Harmon's, she felt she could see Rachel's eyes, through her curtain of hair, mocking her. *Your mother is pathetic. You are too. Copying and scrounging off everyone.* Jaya shoved the rest of the flyers into her bag and hurried out.

It was getting late and a breeze had picked up. Lola dug her fingers into her jacket. The cloudy sky showed cracks of darkness.

"That girl is something else," Lola remarked.

"It was a misunderstanding, Lola. That's all," Maria said.

"What are you talking about? She is completely out of her mind. A real nutcase."

"You didn't have to do that," Maria insisted.

"Do what?"

"Pick a fight with her."

"I was defending Jaya! They can't just kick her out! Maybe you'd realize that if you noticed something other than tank tops!"

"But you're always making everything such a big thing! You think you're such a revolutionary. You're just a . . . drama . . ."

"Queen," Jaya supplied.

"And you don't ever want to believe anything bad about

people!" Lola yelled. "It's not all romantic movies, Maria. Everything working out. Like that Tash guy. Do you really think he wants to give you the time of day?"

Maria's lower lip trembled. "You are mean, Lola. I don't even know why I am friends with you."

Stung, Lola shot back, "Yeah, well, I feel like I don't even know you anymore. Obsessed with all these shallow things!"

"And I feel like I know you too much! Always making trouble and fighting with everyone!"

They glared at each other, breathing hard. How could this happen? How could the best of friends become such enemies?

Lola whirled around to face Jaya. "Jaya, come on! Say something! I was trying to help you!"

Maria also turned. How could Jaya stand there and let Lola bully her?

But Jaya was cringing, as if she found the whole scene distasteful. Her arms were crossed, canvas bag strapped across the front, like a barrier between them. "Don't," she said. "Don't do anything for me. Just leave me alone."

With a sob she turned and walked away, still hugging her satchel to her stomach, as if that were all that mattered.

# Chapter 16

Lola couldn't stop moving, couldn't stop being angry. It was a fire licking through her, singeing her bones. That idiot Rachel. Why did they even go into that stupid shop? It was like walking right into the Wicked Witch's lair. The cold breeze had picked up, and she hunched deeper into her jacket. She walked through town as the store lights blinked on and cars slipped out of the train station parking lot, picking up the fathers and mothers who worked in the city. Everything seemed unjust. That Mrs. Harmon was in the hospital. That Jaya's mother was fired. And that Rachel Meisner dared kick them out of a store!

At home she found her father sitting in the vinyl lounge chair, watching car races on TV.

"Papa?"

He didn't even move his head to say hello to her. What else was new? He probably hadn't moved an inch all afternoon. Nadia was out too, so Lola went over to her side of the room and flipped open the computer they shared.

Quickly she signed on, hoping that maybe Jaya or Maria had e-mailed her, to make up. Instead, to her surprise, she found one from Vitalesurferboy@yahoo.com. Funny, they were practically tripping over each other at the Vitales' house and in school, but this was the first time they'd ever e-mailed each other. A tingling sense of danger surged through her, like what she'd felt the other day. "Did you check out the house?" was all he'd written.

"Not yet," she wrote back. "Soon."

She began to pace in the small room, knees bumping on the bed edges. Fights like the one today used to happen all the time to Lola. She always blurted what came into her head, telling someone exactly what she thought, walking them through each and every one of their deficiencies. To her, a personality was something that could be rearranged and fixed. Like Nadia— Lola once told her sister that she shouldn't spend so much time primping in front of the mirror before Lon arrived, since it made her look desperate. But then her sister's face had crumpled, and Lola's first gush of satisfaction vanished. The old loneliness knocked through her. She was more apart than ever.

But Maria! What had happened to her? Sure, she knew Maria cared about clothes and TV and movies. But wasn't the point that they were different? Not like those girls who would call out to one another during study hall, "Hey, anyone for the tanning salon this weekend?" Who turned shopping for a new pair of shoes into a major research project! Who didn't even know who Benedict Arnold was, but for sure could name everyone on *Survivor*.

Lola sat down again, tried to work on the assignment for

Mr. Cohen. She tried to write something down, but nothing made sense. She kept getting distracted, mixing it up with the fight. "Being American, you're supposed to feel like you have a right," she typed. "But what if you don't feel like you have a right to anything? To walking in a store? Or knowing the truth about adults? What if everybody seems to tell you you're weird and just too much? Even your best friends?" She shifted in her chair. Taped up a few inches away were two of Nadia's modeling photographs, her looking so sure and glamorous. Then Lola saw herself in the mirror, hunched over the blue glow of the computer, her own face strained, pale. Not heroic at all.

# Chapter 17

After leaving Vamps and Vixens, Maria stormed down Ivy Lane toward her house. *Shallow!* That word again! How could a best friend talk like that, be so hurtful and harsh? That's not what friends were for. Scouring her with nasty judgments. No, she told herself. She was better off without Lola. And maybe even Jaya, who didn't say a word!

To her annoyance, Renaldo's beat-up Toyota was parked in the driveway. The last person she wanted to see. Always so down and angry. Usually during the week he wasn't home until seven, eight, now that the weather was getting better. Last night she'd heard him and Tío fighting upstairs. Their voices so loud she could hear every word, even as she lay in bed. *You better watch that temper!* Tío had yelled. *You know how many the company let go? You know how bad it is out there? You want to be one of those guys just waiting in the lot every day?*

Maria walked down the side path to the back, to find him sitting on the patio, drinking a beer, tapping his foot to the radio.

"*Hola, Primo,*" she called.

He tipped his bottle toward her. His cap was jammed low over his eyes.

Maria pushed open the sliders. She didn't want to be lectured by him, especially when she was so sore at her friends. But before she even stepped inside, he called to her. "Your Americano left a message. Said to telephone him."

"A message?" Her throat went dry.

"Yeah. He says he forgot to mention that he wants to do the meeting at his place next time."

Maria's stomach gave a raw lurch. Every time she thought about her family knowing about Tash, it was like experiencing food poisoning all over again. She wasn't allowed to go to a boy's house—certainly not a *blanco*'s—without permission.

Renaldo had followed her upstairs to the kitchen, where she saw dirty dishes piled high in the sink, the juice bottles and cups still on the table. She had meant to come home after school to clean up, but then she'd gotten caught up with Jaya and Lola, and had forgotten all about it.

"What is this?" Renaldo yelled. "I come home starving. You haven't even started dinner! And now you're going to some white guy's house?"

"For lessons—"

"Stay away from those boys."

She turned to him. "Why?"

His mouth twitched. "I'll tell you why. You know Lorenzo? A bunch of them jumped him the other night. Two broken ribs."

Maria took a sharp breath.

"That's what they do for fun, *Prima*. Your sweet high school boys. They're a bunch of thugs."

"But Tash, he's not like that—"

Renaldo moved in closer, right hand lifted. She could smell the sour tang of beer, feel him like a hard wind that pressed her back against the wall. When the slap came, she froze. A shock of pain exploded in her mouth. Her cheek stung, hot. He swung again, only this time she managed to wriggle away, just as his knuckles hit Sheetrock, plaster crumbling. Renaldo paused, a confused sorrow in his eyes.

At that moment she hated Renaldo. Not because he'd hurt her. Because maybe he was right. This country was full of hard stuff and hard people. A place where maids could lose their jobs over stupid earrings. Where high school boys beat up Mexicans. Where you didn't have good friends. And the angels were no more than hollow plaster.

# Chapter 18

Jaya raced up the stairs two steps at a time, tore open the door, and flung herself inside the closet. She didn't know what to believe or do anymore. She couldn't hang out at her mother's job. And after their fight the other day, she definitely didn't want to be with Lola and Maria.

Instead, crouched under the heavy weight of coats and jackets, Jaya decided she would look for Mrs. Harmon's brooch and earrings. Maybe they were here, in a suitcase, folded under a turquoise *choli*, or under her mother's wedding sari. Jaya's fingers snapped open the latches and worried the smooth silk, searching for telltale bumps. Maybe her mother was a thief. They were both thieves, trying to steal a life that wasn't theirs.

The closet was where they kept their belongings from Trinidad that they never unpacked. She often came here, to remember home. She'd plunge her hands inside, feeling the slippery rayons and starched cotton saris from her grandmother Rupa's shop, smelling of sandalwood incense and oil. Packed in newspaper were her little gods. Her favorite was Krishna, with his outlandish blue skin, coddling a white cow to his belly, sitting astride a vivid green cushion decorated in a gold frill. His nose was chipped, but she loved the painted black eyes and black topknot, the full and curving lips. He used to sit on a ledge in a shed, where her grandmother did her *puja*, setting out a banana leaf with sandalwood paste and cut-up papaya.

Here in Meadowbrook it always felt like the colors and sounds she knew had faded. The geraniums hung neatly from wire baskets, the flower beds with matched gravel. No vendor coming down the street with his cart selling coconut milk or mango slices. No laundry hung on the line, Mrs. Persaud's panties blazing a brazen pink in the sun. No men sitting outside in the evening, their rum-fired voices curling up into the night.

When Jaya joined her mother on the playground, she could feel the voices of the other nannies flow in and around her. Her mother didn't like to sit with the other Trini and Guyanese babysitters too much—she thought them a slovenly lot. And they were not too fond of her, since Mrs. Lal kept herself haughty and apart, especially as she actually lived in Meadowbrook. *Dat mother say no to goin' back home in April. Can you imagine! They say April too busy a time, and I got to go when they take their break! What they think, I ha' no other life?* The patois made Jaya smile, she heard it so little these days. Mostly it was stowed away, like all those items in the closet. Pushed down deep, with the memories of her grandmother and father.

Once, she'd heard the other voices in the park, from the mothers. They moved around like shifting air, she an unseen

116

rock, their words crashing on her sides. *The thing is, you know these women from the islands. They're not very educated. And I'm worried about the children. Learning how to speak properly. I mean, they're warm and everything. But I'm not sure we can keep her forever.* The other one, murmuring her assent.

*Is that how they see me too?* Jaya wondered. Her teachers, the other kids? That's why she didn't speak too much in school. She feared her own voice might betray her, open up the colors of her old life.

Jaya's hand touched a rippled piece of metal attached to a hard square object. Her breath caught in her throat. She started to cry, realizing what this was: her father's old paint box.

On Sundays the two of them would pack a thermos and cold *roti* and potatoes from the night before, though her father always promised her a treat after. They'd bike to the beach while her mother was still sleeping. *Leave her be,* her father would say. *Your mother needs to crack her schoolbooks later on.* He'd stuff the paint box, his collapsible easel, and a few canvases into the basket up front, and Jaya would balance on the metal seat behind. They'd ride and ride, turn down the alley where they'd pass his old home, and his sisters would call out from the upstairs balcony, *Raj, why you not come round more often?* He'd laugh, his spectacles glinting in the morning sun, and swerve away and call out, *Got betta things to do!*

*Always,* they shouted back. *Always betta than us!*

Now Jaya snapped open the box, and found his old tubes, curled inside their hollows, like dried-out worms. His brushes, stiff with dried paint, fastened in loops on the inside lid. A set of pastels, worn down to nubs. His oval palate and knife. Her father had been fastidious about his supplies, and it was Jaya's job to rinse the brushes in the seaside after he'd dipped them in linseed oil. Then they'd stop at her father's favorite food stand and eat crab and dumplings, ride back through the Sunday crowds pouring off the pavement, and Jaya would look up to see her mother through the metal grate, looking rested, full up from her hours reading her textbooks. How well she knew her mother then. Now she wasn't sure who this mother was, a stranger who scavenged off other people's belongings, whose hard face she could no longer read.

*She's trying to do what's best for you.* That's what Mrs. Harmon had said, that day they were in the garden. Was that true? She could see Mrs. Harmon, crouched over her flower beds. Or stuffing towels along the cracks of her doors, giving her hot tea brewed from the lavender that grew in huge bunches over her fence, dripping with scent.

Jaya uncurled herself from the cramped space and rose, a little unsteadily. She couldn't remember the last time she had cried so hard. She could hear Mr. Carlota's TV downstairs, almost vibrating under her shoes. Shutting the suitcase, she stuffed her father's paint box inside her satchel. She wasn't sure what was next. She knew only that she needed to see Mrs. Harmon again. And she would do it by herself.

Without her friends.

# Chapter 19

"Hey, come on in."

Tash backed up, shoulders pressed against an oak door as big as a church entrance. "Wait, did you walk all the way here?"

"Yeah." Maria ran her tongue over her swollen lip, praying he didn't notice. She'd put ice on it that first night and went to the bathroom every period in school to put on more lip gloss and makeup. Luckily, last she'd checked there was just a little puffiness in the corner of her mouth.

"You should have told me. I would have asked some buddy with a car to pick you up—"

"No, it's okay. I wanted the exercise."

Not true. Walking up to Tash's house had almost killed her, the blood thudding hard in her ears, her breath fire in her lungs. Tash's house was at the very top of the last ridge before the nature preserve. Even now she could see the tops of the fir trees shivering in the breeze, and she could hear a rushing noise, which she figured was the small river he had mentioned.

It felt funny to have come here without telling Lola or Jaya, as if she were playing hooky from their friendship. And she was, in a way. Her cell phone was switched to silent. After the fight outside the shop, being around them hurt too much. She didn't want to sit with Jaya and Lola in Starbucks or on the playground benches, stewing about everyone in Meadowbrook.

Besides, she couldn't change the day! For all his ease and coolness, Tash had an unbelievably busy schedule, like an executive. High school ACLU. School senate. Ultimate Frisbee. And his parents treated him like a grown-up, letting him attend all kinds of events. Just the other night he'd gone to a special showing of *An Inconvenient Truth* with Al Gore himself, through his mother's work. Tash moved in a magical world. Anything—even meeting a former vice president—was possible. Today the meeting had to be at his house, he had explained, because the alarm company was coming to fix some shorted wires.

Maria stared, astonished, at his house. It was really one large room, the slanted ceiling soaring two stories up, the sunken living room down a few low steps. To the right was a big open kitchen with a huge counter, a dining table beyond. But most amazing was the rear, a flank of floor to ceiling windows looking out on the ravine.

"I was just making myself something to eat," Tash said, shuffling over to the counter, where he'd opened jars of peanut butter and jelly and a bag of bread.

"That's all right."

She noticed, hanging on one wall, large framed black-and-white photographs of a little boy—Tash, she realized. They weren't the usual snapshots or posed pictures her own family took at the photography studio in Union City, all the cousins in frilly dresses and suits, gathered stiffly before a frosted blue backdrop. These were like glamorous Ralph Lauren advertisements. Tash at the beach pushing his toes into the sand; close-up Tash laughing on a swing; moody shirtless teenage Tash reading on a screened-in porch. All together they made a silent film story of Tash, its plotline clear: This boy's life is marvelous and picturesque. It gave Maria a tiny sore pain, realizing how this was another way to be rich. His parents gave him back his own self, strung from these beautiful images, and crafted into a story. It's as if they were saying, *This is who you are to the world. Everything about you matters.*

"I thought we'd work downstairs," he said.

Having slapped together his sandwich, Tash took her down a narrow set of stairs. He pushed through a door, leading, she realized, to his bedroom.

Maria froze. She had never been inside a boy's bedroom, not a boy she wasn't related to.

But Tash had already flopped down on a blue beanbag chair, his long legs stretched before him. Clearly girls did this all the time in his world. It was no big deal.

"A bedroom downstairs?" Maria asked, stalling.

"Yeah." He grinned. "We call this the upside-down house." With one foot he kicked the other beanbag. Still Maria stayed rooted in the doorway, palms prickly with sweat. She wanted nothing more than to sink into that luscious soft vinyl; it would be like falling into his spectacular life. But her feet wouldn't move.

"Can we go out there?" She was pointing to the rear of the room, also made of glass gliders, opening to a lower deck, where she saw a small metal table and chairs.

"Yeah, sure." He shrugged as if he'd forgotten it was there.

Her legs felt weak as she made her way across the room to the deck. It was actually too cold to sit outside, but at least she could semi-relax, perched on the metal chair. And the view was spectacular. The deck jutted out over a steep rocky slope that led right to the rushing water.

"You aren't afraid?" she asked in Spanish.

"When I was little, yeah," he replied. "My parents put me in the guest room then, on the other side. But now I really like it. The sound helps me fall asleep."

How lonely, she thought, a little boy in this big house, the sound of water putting him to sleep. For a brief moment she felt sorry for him. She slept in the same bed as her mother, and sometimes her little cousins came downstairs and crawled into bed with her, falling asleep at her side, their sticky hands wrapped around her stomach.

Over the next half hour they worked on their conversation. Tash was getting better—he'd stopped faking it so much—and actually remembered more vocabulary words. "That's what pisses my father off," he told her. "How I never work at memorizing. My PSATs sucked for that reason. Though I told him to chill. We can go crazy with tutors and Kaplan crap later."

Maria nodded, but she actually felt a twinge of annoyance at Tash. He didn't know how lucky he really was.

Back in Puebla she'd gone to a missionary school, and she knew how much her mother counted on her doing well. If she made the right answers, then Mama would send her reports to Tío Pedro and he would sponsor them. When she came to America and was put in ELL, it seemed the Americanos were always giving her tests and more tests. She knew, again, if she filled out those little bubbles the right way, she would move up the next notch and then finally out of the Spanish-speaking classes. Her mother didn't understand much about scores and grades—she'd only gone through eighth grade—but she always smoothed her daughter's hair and said, *If you are ready, God will help you pass.*

The doorbell rang. It was the alarm company, men in identical red knit polo shirts, who were soon prowling around the house testing the system, so it became too hard to concentrate. Maria and Tash made their way back upstairs to the kitchen, where Maria nibbled on crackers. Then there was a mechanical whirring noise coming from the garage, and a woman burst in through the rear doors, lugging Trader Joe's paper bags.

"Hey, Beanpole," she greeted Tash. "Get your butt in the garage and help me with this stuff." Her eyes opened in surprise. "Oh, you must be Maria." Setting down a bag, she held out a hand. *"Me llamo Margaret."*

Maria swallowed. She still couldn't get used to this business of calling grown-ups by their first name. *"Buenos tardes, señora,"* she murmured.

Tash's mother looked like an ad of an elegant older woman, burnished in subtle grays. She had wavy hair, loose and streaked with silver. Dangling against her sunburned neck was a silver and turquoise pendant, a matching cuff around her wrist.

Maria instantly liked her. She was a thinner version of Tash, and talked easily, like him, her white teeth flashing. While Maria and Tash unloaded groceries—Maria was surprised at all the frozen food boxes—Mrs. Adler went downstairs to change out of her suit and came back in a black stretchy outfit, a shawl thrown over her shoulders. Then she took over the conversation in Spanish, complaining that she'd tried talking to Tash in Spanish since he was a baby, but only now had he shown any real interest. "You're so lucky," she said to Maria. "You'll always be bilingual. It's much harder for us."

*Lucky,* Maria thought. She'd never thought of herself as lucky. Not standing in this huge house with the most spectacular view possible.

Mr. Adler had also arrived. He was friendly enough, but not as easygoing. He spent time going over details with the alarm men and then grilling Tash on his classes that day.

"You must stay for dinner!" Margaret suddenly exclaimed. "Anna made this huge lasagna, and there isn't an inch of room in the freezer now."

"I'd like that," Maria said. Then she glanced at Tash. What did he think? But his face was so still. He seemed to have retreated a little, ever since his father had arrived.

"Go ahead. You can call your parents from my office, down the hall," Mr. Adler offered.

As Maria walked away, she could hear Mrs. Adler say, "She's sweet."

Tash said nothing.

*Chapter 20*

Jaya paused outside Mrs. Harmon's room. She wore a little tag pinned to her shirt that said "Visitor" and her name in marker written underneath, by the receptionist. This place was much nicer than the hospital. Down in the lobby she'd seen a TV room, where a lot of old people sat in comfortable chairs, chatting. She still couldn't make her feet go forward. It just seemed too hard, like walking up a hill in the blazing heat back in Trinidad, thick air pressing at her.

Her mother would kill her for being here. But something in her burned to see Mrs. Harmon. She had to. She touched her bag, feeling the hard bulk of her father's paint box inside. *Remember. This is M*rs. *Harmon.* The most rooted person she'd ever met.

She had so many questions to ask Mrs. Harmon, so much more she wanted to tell. But she wasn't sure of anything anymore. Whether her mother was a thief. Or if she should clear her mother's name. Whether her friends were in fact her best friends. And even deeper, she wanted to know Mrs. Harmon's secret: How do you feel like you belong? Do you have to live in a place for hundreds of years, your pale skin and wispy hair the same as those who came before? Do you need to know that the ground is sure beneath you?

Maybe she wouldn't ask the questions at all. That's the way it was with Mrs. Harmon. They'd work side by side in the garden, lost in a companionable silence—a little like being with her father, when he'd painted. Then Mrs. Harmon would suddenly utter some half-smart, half-distracted remark that made its own kind of sense, and Jaya would feel reassured, solid inside herself.

But she hated hospitals. When her father had grown sick, she'd dreaded her afternoon visits, which her mother had required, every day after school. This was his best time of day, her mother insisted, and so he would wait for her, the pillow propped up behind him, a glass of mango juice and pills on the bedside table. He was always very happy when she walked in the door. But she couldn't help noticing his ashen color, his face collapsed to sharp angles. He wasn't the same. He'd become a polite stranger, made of bones and thin skin, asking about her day and admiring the drawings she had brought to him. She began to believe that her real father had gone away on one of his road projects. More and more she thought up excuses not to visit him in the afternoon. Most of the time she was really sitting in the shade under a tree outside school, mad at herself. The more she stayed away, the more she began to believe that she, too, was made of nothing, only air and sand. She clenched against thinking about her father in that hospital bed. But that terrible, sifting sensation kept on. Any day, she knew, her insides could blow away.

Now a woman came near, carrying a tray of food. The little bowl of wobbling Jell-O made Jaya queasy. "Are you here to see Mrs. Harmon?" she asked.

"Yes."

She smiled. "That's nice. She doesn't get many visitors. Just her nephew. He comes by once a week."

At the mention of Mrs. Harmon's nephew, Jaya froze. What if the nurse told him that she'd been here? Would he call the police? Bar her from the nursing home? Press charges?

"Go on, dear. She'll be happy to have a guest."

When she saw Jaya hesitate, she led her right into the room. "Here, let me show you. She's doing much, much better. She can make out some words."

The nurse picked up a pad of paper that was sitting on a little table on a metal arm that fit over the bed. Jaya noticed that on the top was an advertisement for laxatives. "See here. You say something and she will try to write back. She has use of her right hand."

Jaya was standing a few feet away, at the foot of the bed. Mrs. Harmon appeared to be still sleeping, so she inched up a little closer.

Jaya hated how she looked. Her white hair had been combed smooth and spread about her shoulders. She wore one of those nightgowns with a silly ruffled neck, like a little girl's. Jaya knew that Mrs. Harmon would hate this, too. She much preferred her khaki pants and her cardigans, which she ordered from the L.L. Bean catalog. Jaya looked around the room and saw the narrow wardrobe was open, with only a lavender robe hanging inside. Why wasn't someone bringing her regular clothes? If Mrs. Lal were in charge, they'd make sure she had her favorite things. She'd bring a plug-in teapot, her stash of loose teas, and ginger biscuits, and they'd sit across from each other blowing on the tops of their mugs, talking about how the garden was doing and making jokes about the staff. *Simple,* Mrs. Harmon liked to say, whenever she had to deal with the outside world—nurses, opticians, deliverymen. *They are simple people but necessary.*

Mrs. Harmon's lids fluttered open, and she stared right at Jaya.

"Hi, Mrs. Harmon."

Mrs. Harmon grinned, a little too childishly, which made Jaya want to run from the room. Then the old woman grunted, lifted up the pen, and with a trembling hand wrote in shaky letters: Long time no see!

Jaya smiled. She seemed not to remember the visit with Maria and Lola.

How is your mother?

Jaya bit her lip. "Okay." *Tell her,* she thought. *Tell her she was fired.*

Mrs. Harmon tried to lisp a word. "Andrew." But the sound came out too thick. She wrote again. My nephew is a pest. He says he's selling the house.

"Yes." Jaya felt the tears rush to her eyes.

I don't like it.

Jaya wanted to cry. "Neither do I."

The room went quiet. Jaya dropped down onto the armchair and stared out the large window, which looked out onto a parking lot. There was no way Mrs. Harmon could spend the rest of her days in a room with pale green walls and aluminum rails, her only view a stretch of asphalt.

Then she saw Mrs. Harmon had written again.

It's just a house.

Jaya laughed. "I guess so."

Mrs. Harmon pointed. *What's that?* she managed to mouth.

Jaya looked down. Mrs. Harmon was pointing to the satchel that sat bulkily on Jaya's lap. "My . . . my father's paint box."

You lug that heavy thing?

She nodded.

The old woman paused. For the first time Jaya saw a glint of the old Mrs. Harmon, a bit of devilish spark and amusement. She wrote her longest message yet, her fist shaking across the page. Maybe you can draw something for me. I can hang it up. On these putrid walls. Make it more like home.

Then she put her head against the pillow, her veiny hands covering her scribbles, eyes shut. That last burst of writing seemed to have exhausted her. Soon she was fast asleep, making soft wheezing sounds.

Jaya got up and began wandering around the room. She pushed the movable table away. On it was a little slip of paper where Mrs. Harmon had checked her choices for breakfast, lunch, and dinner. Hamburgers and carrots or fish sticks and carrots. Applesauce for dessert. She thought about the jars of tomatoes and blueberries Mrs. Harmon kept in her larder, each one carefully sealed with wax and labeled by date. Come Christmas she gave them out to her neighbors, most of whom probably threw the jars out, Mrs. Harmon would say.

In the corner sat a stack of cardboard boxes. Jaya recognized those from when she and Mrs. Lal had been carefully sorting out Mrs. Harmon's belongings, since of course Andrew Cramer had had no idea what his aunt would want to keep. Now Jaya flipped open one of the cartons and saw it held some clothes. She began digging inside and found what she was looking for: a few of the cardigans, the wrists worn and saggy, and her pants, with faint green streaky circles at the knees. She hung those up in the wardrobe.

In the next box she found a few items from the living room. Two embroidered pillows, an old ashtray from Atlantic City that Mrs. Harmon usually used for spare coins, and a book of crossword puzzles, half done. She set the books and ashtray on the night table. She also dug out Jack and Jill china salt and pepper shakers, a sprig of dried lavender tied with a fading ribbon, and a photograph of Mr. Harmon in a silver frame. All of these she arranged on the windowsill, so Mrs. Harmon could see her things instead of the parking lot. She spread a crocheted afghan at the foot of the bed, and set the two pillows on the chair.

Wiping her hands on her jeans, she thought, *I'm just like Mama, finishing up one of her jobs, giving one last prideful look before picking up the check and locking the door.* And then she felt a rush of darkening sadness, remembering that her mother no longer worked for Mrs. Harmon.

"How nice, dear. You've really made it much more homey." It was the nurse, returned with a tiny paper cup filled with pills.

Jaya didn't reply; she knew that should have made her feel good, but instead she felt the same sadness sweeping over her, like the twilight that greeted her as she made her way out of the nursing home. She hurried down the circular drive. Luckily, the bus was just pulling up as she reached the corner.

As the bus groaned to a stop at Haley Avenue, she noticed a big bright store, a place she'd never seen. Its window was a rainbow display of paints. Across the front was a huge sign: SALE! EVERYTHING 20% OFF! ONLY THE BEST AT MANDY'S ART SUPPLY HOUSE!

# Chapter 21

It was amazing. Dinner wasn't exactly a dinner. It felt more like a class, a discussion after all the students had read a book, everyone offering an opinion. Only there was no teacher calling on anyone. And the Adlers had opinions about everything— about Tash's history teacher, who was a hack loser. "Just get through. I'll give you some better books to read," Mr. Adler said. About the situation in Darfur. "We could have stopped this," Mrs. Adler said, and sighed.

They ate at the big dining room table, with candles lit and wine served, salad and lasagna and glazed baby carrots, a glorious rush of water whispering through the screen. Almost too perfect. Margaret talked about her job: She was working on a huge project that involved tutoring centers in the inner city, and some big benefit where famous people would get shown around, including Bill Gates, if he would only commit to the day.

"Just tell him the awesome captain of Meadowbrook's Ultimate Frisbee team will hawk his software," Tash joked.

Margaret reached over and rumpled her son's hair. "Thank you, darling. Bill Gates doesn't need any promoting."

When they turned to Maria and asked her about herself, she felt that terrible, itchy sweating sensation all over her skin. She ran her tongue over her swollen lip. Her voice seemed to have evaporated.

"What does your father do?" Mr. Adler asked.

"I live with my uncle and cousins. They do landscaping."

"Oh! That reminds me!" Margaret exclaimed. "At the grocery store some hysterical mother was going on about the day laborers. Says they're always ogling her."

"I heard something about trouble," Mr. Adler remarked, helping himself to a last serving of lasagna.

"Hypocrites." Mrs. Adler banged a container of sorbet down, with spoons. "They want their hedges done and then for everyone to just disappear."

Maria could hardly breathe. "My cousin Renaldo has a friend," she whispered.

Everyone stopped what they were doing and stared, waiting for her to finish. She wished, for a moment, she hadn't said anything. Finally she added, "Says he got beat up."

Margaret set down her spoon, her gaze probing. Maria hadn't planned on saying anything more, but Tash's mother looked so sympathetic. She seemed like a marble statue of Lady Justice herself, all white-silver and elegant folds. Maria wanted to tell more, about Jaya's mother. But she couldn't. That wasn't right. It was between them. A private problem.

Instead she told the Adlers about her neighbors, how they had twice tried to slap a summons on them for illegal tenants or how they called up whenever her family had a barbecue and their friends and cousins parked up and down the cul-de-sac. Margaret Adler was suitably enraged. Mr. Adler listened closely. Then Maria noticed how Tash hadn't said anything at all, but was pushing his baby carrots around on his plate. A flush of shame spread through her, as if she had just dumped her soiled laundry right in the middle of their table.

Mr. Adler looked at her with soft eyes. "If there are any problems, Maria, you must call—"

"Richard is a lawyer," Margaret explained. "Granted, most of what he does is white-collar crime."

Tash laughed. "My mom, saving the world."

*Save me,* Maria thought. *Adopt me. Let me stay here, perched in your house above the trees, above it all.*

*Chapter 22*

Mandy's Art Supply House was like *Diwali* or Christmas day, all the shiny presents laid out in a spread of gorgeous color. In the center, lit up by spotlights, was an opened paint box, showing tubes of every luscious shade imaginable. Inside, even the smells were tempting. The clean starchy odor of the paper. The sawdust scent in the back, where they stretched canvas on wood.

Jaya wasn't sure where to begin. First there was the aisle of paper. Watercolor paper. Charcoal paper. All different textures: rough, smooth, shiny. How could she choose? Then she turned the corner and found herself in an area devoted to brushes. Flat, thin, for oil-based, or watercolor. She ran her finger along silky bristles, turned over a wooden handle and saw the price: Forty dollars! She jammed the brush back into its slot.

Someone came up behind her. "You want some help?"

Jaya swerved, as if caught. To her surprise she was facing a girl, not much older than herself, with freckles smattered across her nose. She wore cargo pants with a dozen saggy pockets, a clingy black sweater over a tank top. Two silver hoops glinted in an earlobe.

"I want to draw. Maybe some portraits. Places. Stuff like that."

"Color, or black and white?"

Jaya thought for a moment. "Color."

She nodded. "You might do better to start with a set of good pencils. They're like the charcoal sticks but they don't crumble as much, and you can get a little more control with them. You can also sharpen them all you want." She reached for a metal box and handed it to her. "Here, this is a set with a decent selection. Three different kinds of black, for sketching. It's cheaper that way."

"Thanks." What a luxury, to have so many shades!

"What kind of paper you want?"

"I don't know."

"Follow me."

Jaya followed the girl down one aisle, then another, mesmerized by her slouchy, comfortable walk, the way she was so at home among all these supplies—lightly touching the tops of brushes, little palate knives, running her hands over the bound spirals. She yanked out a good-size pad with a yellow cover. Then she reached for a metal spray can. "Do you have fixative?"

Jaya shook her head.

"Totally stinky and environmentally gross, but you need it, even with pencil work. Otherwise the drawing smudges like crazy."

Jaya swallowed, her throat dry. "How . . . how much is it?"

The girl tapped the pencil package and paper and fixative.

"Let's see. Ten for the pad, eighteen for the pencil set, four bucks for the fixative. That comes to about thirty-two dollars. Plus tax."

"Wow. That's a lot." She could hear her mother add, *Just for drawing!*

The girl laughed. "I know. It sucks. I spend my whole paycheck here. I don't even know why they bother paying me. They should just dump the money back into their account. Send me a bill."

Jaya smiled. She had actually never talked to an American girl about how expensive something was. "How long have you worked here?" she asked.

"Since a year and a half ago. Basically I was taking all these classes and coming in here all the time, until finally the owner said to me, 'Why don't you just come work here?' So I did. I haven't saved a penny, but it's helping me with my portfolio. I'm applying to art school. Ever hear of RISD?"

Jaya shook her head. "No." Mrs. Lal had already planned out where Jaya was going—The College of New Jersey, where they had a very good nursing program.

"So do you want them?"

Jaya dug into her satchel, pulled out her wallet. Inside were two twenties: her lunch and after-school snack money and another twenty that her mother had given her for some groceries. She'd have to come up with some kind of lie. She handed the bills to the girl. A few minutes later, light-headed and giddy, she walked out with her package.

*Chapter 23*

"Where were you?" Mrs. Alvarez greeted Maria, clutching her shoulders with both hands.

After dessert Tash's father had driven Maria down the hill to her house. She had almost refused, embarrassed to have him see her cul-de-sac and saggy little Cape Cod rental, with four dented cars and vans parked in the driveway.

As she moved up the walkway, she saw that all the lights from inside the house were ablaze, spilling their yellow glow onto the front lawn. Shapes were moving around in the window. As usual, the TV and radio were on and everyone was talking all at once. It drove the neighbors crazy. *Is everything a party with you folks?* Suddenly she felt a hard ache come up in her chest. She missed Lola and Jaya. Only they would have understood her mixed-up feelings from the night.

"I told you, Mami. I was at Tash Adler's house. They invited me for supper."

"But so late!"

It wasn't late, she knew that. Most of the time no one in her house sat down for supper until at least nine o'clock, just like in Mexico. It was only ten minutes after nine now. But it was unusual for Maria to stay out at all, even with Lola and Jaya, who kept their time together to the afternoons.

And it irritated her to feel her mother's hands pushing into her shoulder bones, the way her mother had pulled her face in tight to hers. "I need you," her mother said. "I have a job interview."

"When?"

"Next week."

A few weeks before, Maria had come home to find her mother sitting sadly at the kitchen table, staring at a bottle of perfume and a Macy's gift certificate. One of her favorite employers, Nancy Gilbert, had told her she had a new job in California and would be leaving soon.

"Oh, Mami," Maria had sighed. "You take it too personally."

"I know." She'd pressed a wadded tissue to her eyes. Mrs. Alvarez's biggest problem was that she got too attached to the people she worked for. She took over their houses as if they were her own, neatening the tilted-over books on the shelves, lovingly dusting the silver-framed family photos. Sometimes, when Mrs. Alvarez was finished, the sweaters spread out carefully on towels in the laundry room, the children's socks sorted, she would have a cup of coffee with the mother of the house. They would talk about their children, or where to buy disposable cloths for lint, or what they liked to make for supper. The mothers gave her their woolen coats they didn't need, or an extra set of crystal salt and pepper shakers, the gift card still inside the box. Mrs. Alvarez loved all this. It was as if

140

when she stepped inside their door and pulled on her rubber gloves, the house became hers. And when someone's husband got laid off, or they moved away, she cried bitterly into her pillow at night.

"Okay, so why tell me about the interview now?"

Her mother looked at her, hurt. "I made food." She pointed to a tray of enchiladas, *verde* sauce congealed on the folded tortillas.

"I told you. I already ate at Tash's."

Then she pushed her mother's hands off and went downstairs to their basement apartment. What was wrong with her? Normally she was such a cheerful person. She loved showing little kindnesses to her mother. And she knew her mother actually looked forward to these interviews, in her own way. Mrs. Alvarez liked putting on her best dress, running a rouge brush over her cheeks and proudly showing the potential employers a list of cleaners and polishes they would need to stock. But for the first time her mother's fussing didn't move her. It seemed naïve, childlike.

And tonight something worse was coming over her. Everything looked so . . . small. How could it be? How could she look so poorly on the sweet little place she and her mother had fixed up? She was so used to moving around American houses with her mother's eye toward cleaning—how much Pledge the oak table needed. Did the lady want the molding dusted too? Would the vacuum reach up the carpeted stairs? For the first time she realized these weren't just rooms to get through. They were houses where people lived. And thought and argued and ate.

*Thou shall not covet,* she could hear the Sunday priest tell her. Father Enriquez had said that to her the first time they'd gone to services in Jersey City, before slipping the wafer into her mouth. She remembered his gray eyes and his crimson and gold vestments, how comforted she'd been that the services were almost identical to those in Puebla. But why had he picked *that* commandment?

Maria went into the bathroom, washed, and changed into her cotton nightgown. In the bedside table she found her mother's carefully thumbed Bible. She began to page through the tissue-thin pages, her fingers moving past her mother's childish markings, the passages Mrs. Alvarez would repeat to herself when on a bus or a long train ride.

Without turning on the lights, Maria lay down in the dark on the alcove bed. She stayed there for a long while, her whole body rigid, listening to the tread of footsteps overhead, everyone sitting down to eat without her.

She was still there when her mother came downstairs and slid into bed beside her, smelling of the Jergens lotion she spread on her hands and neck each night. The dark pulsed with her mother's hurt.

"Maria," she heard. "You come to the new place, no?"

She didn't answer. Why did her mother have to plead?

"Maria, I'm talking to you."

"Yes, Mami. I'm sorry."

"Next week?"

"Yes."

Then she realized her mother was crying. *"Mi amor,"* her mother whispered. "Don't be a stranger to me. I live in a land of strangers. Please."

*Chapter 24*

For Lola it was bad enough that her friends had left her. But now Mr. Svetloski was disappearing.

That should be a good sign. After all, he was finally rousing himself from the vinyl TV lounge, leaving the miserable two hundred square feet of their courtyard, but nobody could figure out where he would go, without a car. Across Route 12, to drink coffee at Panera?

It all began the day Mr. Svetloski had a twelve o'clock interview at the mall to sell men's shirts at Macy's. Mrs. Svetloski drove him there, and then he told her he'd take the bus back. He didn't walk in until seven that evening, his suit jacket limp and wrinkled, his face gray, refusing to say a word about the interview, muttering only that he had a few "other opportunities" he would look into. For the next few days he left, wearing that same suit, shrugging off all offers of ironing or dry-cleaning, sometimes not getting home until late.

Even Nadia, Miss On My Way Somewhere Else, seemed concerned. She'd just interviewed for a new job herself, as weekend assistant manager at a trendy boutique in the mall, and it looked like she was going to get it. "I don't usually hire someone still in high school," the manager had told her, "but you seem so mature. So European sophisticated. Our customers will love you."

When Nadia related this conversation to her family over supper, her father offered a wan smile, the first real reaction they'd seen in weeks, and said in Slovak, "You know what they say about firstborns?"

"No, what?" Nadia looked coy, her cheeks flushed, as she readied herself for fatherly praise.

"They run so fast, they crush their parents' heads into cobblestones."

Nadia's smile faded. For once, as Lola watched Nadia's empty chair bang against the table, she felt terrible for her sister. And what was worse, her father had not lost his cruel grin.

Lola went to bed that night shaken, puzzled by this strange man with the mean mouth and foggy eyes.

That's why more and more Lola found herself hanging out at the Vitales', half to help her mother, who was finding it harder to drag the vacuum upstairs, and half because she didn't have anywhere else to go. Lola and Anthony even began to hang out at the Vitale office, since Mr. Vitale thought it would be good for Anthony to "wrap his head around something other than his Game Boy," and besides, his secretary was laid up from a hernia operation.

Mr. Vitale's office was a little gray warehouse on a cul-de-sac, past the ShopRite and car wash. There wasn't much of an office, just a desk workstation for his secretary and a fax and Xerox machine. Fluffy coils of insulation sat bound like haystacks by the door, and in the back were metal shelves brimming with building materials, mysterious and potent in their uses: pipes and flats of Sheetrock, strips of unpainted molding, even an old stove that Mr. Vitale was trying to refit. Lola was amazed at Mr. Vitale's competence, his easy mastery of just about anything that passed through the company's corrugated steel doors. And it wasn't just the mechanics of a boiler or roof tacking. He'd learned just enough Spanish so he could stand at the head of the driveway and give fourteen workers from El Salvador their orders for the day.

Strange as it was, the only person she told about her troubles was none other than Anthony Vitale. She and Anthony began to work side by side; they filed papers and checked off when plumbing and building supplies came in. They mailed out bills. They went with Mr. Vitale as he drove around town monitoring his different jobs. "You're finally getting serious, Anthony junior!" Mr. Vitale said one day as he was heading off for a new bid, leaving Anthony and Lola to add up the last receipts and close the shop.

Anthony lowered his eyes. "I guess so, sir."

"It's about time."

It was so confusing. She was supposed to hate Mr. Vitale, prime enemy of history. But it was actually hard to hate such an upstanding good guy. He helped run the Kiwanis club. He sponsored a Little League team, twenty ten-year-olds with gold stitched VITALE & SONS across their nylon backs. He paid for a middle school auditorium.

And he and his wife wrote letters on behalf of their pain-in-the-neck slacker son. This Lola discovered one afternoon when she and Anthony were crouched over the computer, helping input some receipts, and her wrist strayed and she clicked on a folder called "Anthony." In it were all kinds of letters to teachers, asking them to make sure he received extra attention for his "learning deficiencies." "He's a bright boy. He just needs a little help now and then." "Don't give up on him."

"Hey!" Anthony's face flushed, and he quickly clicked the document away.

She stayed his hand. "But it's cool. The way your mom and dad fight for you."

Anthony shrugged. The tips of his ears were crimson.

Inside herself everything was getting muddled. Anthony was different. So were the Vitales. No one was behaving the way she'd expected. Here she had come, right into the belly of the enemy, and nothing was as it had seemed.

They turned back to their work. Lola wrote down in a ledger a bill for a sink faucet—eight hundred dollars. "God, this costs so much," she remarked. "Just for a faucet! All it does is turn water on and off!"

"That's because my dad uses the best," Anthony explained.

"The best!" Lola threw down her pen. "Why do you always use that word? Everything isn't the best. It can't all be the best. Then it's not the best."

His face fell. "It's just an expression, Lola. A way of saying things."

"Yeah, well, it's a dumb way."

He looked away, hurt. "You don't have to say that."

"What?"

"That. It's like you . . . go too far, Lola. It makes people . . ." He paused. "Not like you."

Lola felt as if he'd taken one of Mr. Vitale's pipes and thrust it into her chest. Her whole chest burned. She knew what he said was right. Her sister complained about it all the time. *You can argue your way out of a paper bag, Lola, but you'll never get a boyfriend!* Lola couldn't help herself. Words just came tripping off her tongue, mean and slicing. She knew, somewhere deep down, that sometimes, even when she was right, she was also deeply wrong.

"And you know, Lola, you kind of put it in everyone's faces. Not everyone is as smart as you at school. You shouldn't be so . . ."

"Boastful?" she supplied.

"Yeah."

"Sorry," she said to Anthony, but he had already left the room.

*Chapter 25*

Jaya dropped down onto the playground bench and ripped open her package. All day she'd survived her classes, language arts and social studies, and that god-awful chemistry quiz, by reaching beneath her desk, touching the spiral pad tucked into her satchel.

This is how her father used to sketch—thirty-second drawings—before he'd settle into his painting. He'd draw a group of children running past, or a mother and baby wading into the waves. One, two, three, and magically a person danced onto the page. He filled a whole sheet with these spindly little figures, and another, his hand moving in swift, sure strokes. Later he'd redraw some of the images, giving them volume, adding details: the straps of a little girl's bathing suit, how a mother's face was shaded by her straw hat.

*First get the gist, Jaya,* he'd tell her. *Then you can fill in the rest.*

Her plan was to draw pictures of Meadowbrook and hang them up all over Mrs. Harmon's walls. That way she could be reminded of her old life, all the places she couldn't visit anymore. But when Jaya tried to sketch a boy going down a slide, all she managed was just a few squiggly lines. She tried a girl clambering onto a jungle gym, but it came out like a clump of knotted yarn.

A shadow fell across her page. She looked up, to see Maria.

"Hey."

"Hey."

Maria looked different; she smelled different, some kind of shampooey perfume scent radiating off her glossy curls. A tie-dyed T-shirt, jeans, and boots. Jaya felt a pinch of irritation, sure it was the influence of that Frisbee boy, Tash.

"Where were you? It's Tuesday. I left a message."

"Oh, yeah. Sorry."

Without saying so the girls had called off their regular meeting. Jaya just couldn't handle seeing either of them right now, especially Lola. She was less afraid that she'd get mad at Lola and more afraid that she'd find herself swept into Lola's crazy ideas once more. Lola could do that to her, simply mesmerize her with her bigmouth daring. After, it was like having a sudden ice cream headache, chilly and disorienting.

Besides, the whole business with Rachel Meisner made her nervous. Rachel had these X-ray eyes that flashed right through you, fierce with judgment; she was the talented poetess whose searing haikus adorned the pages of the school magazine. One time Jaya accompanied her mother on the job to help out, and when she opened the door, to her embarrassment, there was Rachel in her messy room, sprawled on her bed, writing in a book with gold-rimmed pages. Rachel shook back her black bangs, looked straight at Jaya, and complained,

"Ma, why does the cleaning lady have to come on Saturday?"

Jaya was pretty sure Rachel didn't ever recognize her in the school halls after that. She found that happened most of the time. The other kids just didn't put it together. But with Lola picking fights, she was making it worse. As if calling attention to the three of them, taunting the world. What if Rachel were to do something mean and vengeful?

No, she thought, reaching for a dark blue pencil. She preferred to duck out of sight. Even if it meant avoiding her friends.

"How's your mom?"

"Not so good." She nodded. "She's doing some extra baby-sitting for the Silers. Trying to get the word on some new jobs."

"It will work out, *mi amor*," Maria assured Jaya, squeezing her hand. "I know it will."

Jaya said nothing. Usually Maria's words comforted her. Now she found them too simple, too sweet. She noticed Maria's notebooks stacked on the bench, covered in stickers of pink hearts and sparkly stars. That had never bothered her before, but now, for some reason, it did. She realized too that her friend always talked about "bad" or "good." What if things weren't either? What if a mother could be both? Could she ever explain to Maria that she'd scoured her own apartment: the closet, the pockets of her mother's coats, all the bureau drawers? That she wasn't sure what to believe about the theft? Besides, Maria, for all her sympathy, seemed distracted.

"Did I tell you? I went to Tash's house."

"Yeah? What's it like?" She actually didn't want to hear.

"So beautiful, you wouldn't believe. Like in a magazine. And his family! They are so nice. They had me for dinner and they talked and talked—"

"Uh-huh." She flipped to another page. Two kids on bicycles were coming into view and she wanted to try them. She could sense Maria twitching on the bench, growing frustrated beside her.

"So you want to go for a walk? Get a frappé?"

Jaya shrugged, tapping her pencil on her pad. "I was drawing."

"It's nice."

She didn't answer.

"Your mother is crazy, not letting you be an artist. You're so good!"

"I'm supposed to be a nurse," Jaya said quietly. She didn't add anything more.

"Okay." Maria sighed and rose from the bench. "I've got stuff to do too."

"See you."

Jaya watched her friend walk away. She could see the hurt in her shoulders. But she couldn't help herself. Too much had changed. Maybe for all of them. Even good, nice Maria had changed into a boy-crazy alien that she didn't want to know.

Just across the way, her mother was sitting on the playground benches with Marleen, while watching the Siler twins clambering on the jungle gym.

Jaya didn't usually like to join her mother at the park; she hated how the women would sit on the benches, clucking and talking to their little charges as if they were their own, with all their endearing and maddening little habits. How Jordan likes his food served on orange plates, and Jessica, she only eats white food—pasta, potatoes, cheese. It gave Jaya a little ache to hear her mother talk in the same way, as if these children were hers.

She was always embarrassed by the gossip: the nanny who was paid off the books and got a welfare check on the side, or the other one who dumped the kids with a friend and then went to the mall. This other nanny slipped a twenty from her boss's lingerie drawer every Friday. Jaya's mother was always hissing through her teeth about people like that.

Jaya also knew her mother didn't like Marleen very much. She always sat with her arms crossed on her plump chest, round face creased with a skeptical scowl, complaining about her employers, while dishing out the latest gossip. But Mrs. Lal had told Jaya she'd have to put up with Marleen if she was ever going to get the word on some new work.

"That's no good," Marleen kept saying, shaking her head, when she heard the whole story about Mrs. Lal getting fired from Mrs. Harmon's.

Mrs. Lal sat up stiffly on the bench, keeping a sharp eye on Jordan. He had a bad habit of shoving wood chips into his mouth. "Well, we'll find something."

"Don't know about that," Marleen remarked. "Word gets

around this place. Especially about some thief thing. It's not so easy."

Irritated, Mrs. Lal gathered up the diaper bag and Tupperware container with Cheerios and cheddar goldfish.

"Jaya," she called, "I'm going to be late this evening. Going to check out the listings at the library."

Then she called to Jordan and Isabel, hoisted them into the stroller, and trundled away. Jaya felt that old brush of sadness, watching her move so slow, nothing like the mother she remembered from Port of Spain.

It was coming easier now. Jaya's wrist relaxed. Her fingers got used to the tips. Her page sprang up, full as an unkempt garden, wild with figures. She drew a mother nursing a baby, a group of kids clustered around the ice cream truck. She could hear her father's voice, coaxing her. *That's it! You got it now, darlin'! Gonna be magnificent!*

It was just like his painting, how he'd use a thin brush to outline the view—the waves cresting on the beach were just some scraggly, faint strokes. And then a few minutes later she'd look over and see that her father had switched brushes, and now was dabbing fitfully into the blobs of color on his palate board. The waves had foamy frills of thick white; the whole view was filling in. How did he do that? How did those ghost lines turn solid?

The sound of her parents was close now. *What a dreamer you are, Raj Lal,* her mother used to tease. He was always making big plans. Finishing his degree. Opening an art gallery. A seafood restaurant. *You and your grand ideas! How you going to pay for everything?* And he'd toss back: *Darlin,' don't you worry about that!* They didn't own a car, but sometimes he'd rent a taxi and take them around Port of Spain, showing her all the roads he was helping build with his company. *See that? Who's dreaming, little lady?* That's what she missed about her father, how he could fill whole rooms, the very air. His paintings propped up every-where, against the walls, drying against the balcony grates. His voice a great billowing sail, surrounding them in color and hope.

When Jaya arrived at Wrightchester Gardens, Mrs. Harmon was sleeping. Jaya pulled out her pad, tore off her drawings, and taped them to the walls. There was one of the library, another of Main Street and the movie theater, a few of the children playing in the park. Not bad, she thought.

"Why, hello there!" The nurse came in, carrying a tray with cheese and crackers and a paper cup of pills. "Here you go, hon. Time to wake up."

Mrs. Harmon's lids fluttered open, and she offered a lopsided grin. "How . . . is your mother?" The words came out in wobbly gasps.

The nurse smiled. "Do you see how well she is doing with her speech?"

Jaya noticed how the nurse's voice had gone up several notches, and her tone had changed, as if she were talking to the air—the way Jaya heard teachers sometimes talk to a room full of kids.

"My mother's really busy," Jaya explained. "She has a lot of jobs."

This, of course, was a big lie. Mrs. Lal was pretty nervous, what with losing the job with Mrs. Harmon. She needed to find some others, but everyone was talking about how bad it was, all around town.

Mrs. Harmon pointed to the walls. "Let . . . me see."

Jaya watched as the nurse slid her hands behind Mrs. Harmon's back and gently raised her up from the pillows, helping her lean into the rubber-covered bars of the walker. Then they moved around the room, making strange little thumps, Mrs. Harmon leaning heavily to one side, her foot dragging sideways. It was a terrible sight. But then she began letting out little noises of delight, seeing the sketches of Meadowbrook—Main Street, kids spilling down a slide. Finally she stopped before Jaya's drawings. Her eyes were watery, and no sound came from her twitching mouth, but Jaya could tell she was pleased.

"You're so good at this, dear," the nurse remarked. "The way you've arranged everything. And now these pictures. I can just imagine her house."

Startled, Jaya looked around at the room, which did look better, more colorful. How stupid of her, she thought. She knew exactly what she had to draw next.

*Chapter 26*

Tash was a little restless today. They'd been over the subjunctive and future tenses. They'd covered some new vocabulary. And only half an hour had passed. Maria watched Tash sit at the Starbucks table, crossing and uncrossing his long legs as he twisted in his chair.

*"Hay una problema?"* she asked.

He rubbed his thighs. "Sorry. I just screwed up. Said I'd meet my friends at the park and I forgot. They're waiting for me."

"Oh."

Maria tried to hide her disappointment. Ever since the fight with Lola and her meet-up with Jaya, Maria had concentrated even more on Tash, reliving every moment of dinner at his house a week before—how she'd taken the salad bowl from his mother, how Mr. Adler had looked at her with his soft brown eyes and offered help. Maybe Tash could be her boyfriend. His family would adopt her as one of their own. After all, his mother had been talking to him in Spanish since he was a baby. Besides, she would be the perfect girlfriend-in-law—polite, bilingual, working side by side with the silver-haired Mrs. Adler in the kitchen.

She'd actually dressed for the occasion—a new pair of jeans she'd bought on Saturday in Union City that fit snugly around her hips, a mauve-colored top, and her wedges. And now Tash was ready to call it quits.

"We could finish up there," she offered now.

He looked puzzled.

"I'll walk with you and we'll practice."

He brightened. "Hey, that's cool." He reached over for her empty cup. "Thanks, Maria. I'm always messing up my schedule. Complete ADD."

As they walked together toward the park, Maria was aware of how much shorter she was than Tash, even with her wedges. She'd have to think about a pair of platform sandals, which would give her another inch. She'd seen them in the window of a shop, and she might be able to persuade her mother to buy them. That is, if she got another job. Which reminded her—she had to meet her mother in an hour at the train station, to go with her on the new job interview.

A group of high schoolers were gathered under a tree. She recognized a few of the boys from the Ultimate Frisbee team. They were lying on the scruffy patch of grass, leaning back on their elbows, gazing coolly over their gangly knees.

"Yo, Mr. Adler," a boy with blond dreadlocks and faded Bob Marley T-shirt called out. "Española lesson done?"

Tash flushed, then pointed to her. "This is Maria."

A few of the guys nodded. Then she realized that one of the guys was actually a girl. She wore her hair cropped short and spiky, a strand of leather with a blue stone around her neck, a worn-out T-shirt that stretched nicely across her breasts, so you could almost see her nipples. And that was who Tash dropped next to, his long legs knocking into hers. She pushed him back, smiling. "How's it going, Tash-boy?"

"I am, like, so wasted from staying up all night finishing my history research paper," he said.

"You? I had that Am Lit exam."

"Oh, yeah. The one last period?"

Maria realized with a pang that they were so familiar he even knew her schedule. "Did she do Mark Twain in multiple choice?"

The girl nodded. "What a bimbo. Is Huck Finn a hero? I mean, does she seriously think that you can answer such a question with an A or B answer? Is this some technique they gave her in teacher school?" She tossed off that last phrase— "teacher school"—with contempt. Maria found herself embarrassed, especially as she'd always figured she'd become a teacher, probably for elementary school, a dozen angelic children surrounding her in an adoring circle.

Even though Maria was sitting right next to Tash, she had a hard time getting his attention. She could feel the warmth of his skin near hers, his stomach shaking every time he laughed. But his body was tautly turned toward the group.

Maria could see Tash and his friends were the "smart" kids, judging from what he'd told her, AP classes stacked up for the semesters ahead, their summer internships. But she was surprised at how loose and easy they were; almost lazy, if she didn't know better. She always thought smart kids stayed in the library all night, like the altar boys and girls at her church who showed up early on Sunday mornings to prepare the wafers and wine. But this group didn't seem to have an anxious thought in their heads. Even the dreadlocks boy, who had a tightly strung, wiry intensity, seemed most focused on getting himself a vanilla glazed doughnut. Maybe, she reflected, when you were high-level—what she sweated so hard to achieve with her number-2 pencil bubble-tests—you could just lie around on the grass and bask in your inborn greatness.

"Come on, man, I'm starving," dreadlocks boy said as he lifted himself off the grass.

Maria stood, brushed off her jeans, and looked expectantly at Tash. He gave an embarrassed shrug.

It was different, being with Tash's friends, as they made their way into town, aiming for the doughnut shop. Time pooled and spilled, so different from the short, tense bursts she would steal with Lola and Jaya, before one of them had to break away to help out at home. And Maria just wanted to keep on this way, trying to soak up some of their ease, until she spotted her own reflection in the bagel store window. She shuddered. The strained expression and bright eyes, the way she was nodding too fast, trying to keep up. She looked like someone. Then she realized who it was: her own mother.

"You hear what happened to Brandon?" dreadlocks boy

suddenly asked. The doughnut shop appeared to be abandoned. Now they were sauntering over to some benches under the clock tower.

"Which Brandon? You mean Mr. I'm So Cool Lacrosse?"

"Yeah, they had another fight with those soccer players."

Maria stiffened.

"Hey, Maria," Tash said. "That's your cousin who plays soccer, right?"

She nodded, swallowing hard. "Um, yeah."

"Well, there's some weird rumors. Thefts. Like we got a gang problem or something."

"I heard the opposite," the short-haired girl shot back. "You ever hear about this stupid game called Jumping Mexicans? Guys get drunk and beat up Latinos?"

"Totally creepy," Tash agreed.

The short-haired girl looked at Maria and asked, "Have you heard anything about that?"

At first Maria flushed. The girl's gaze was too sharp, like a harsh clinical lamp suddenly switched on, showing up her little corners of privacy. She wished she could just crawl under a bush and disappear. She knew about gangs, for real. Back in Union City there was a gang called Sistah Devils that prowled the schoolyard; she always knew which street to duck into to avoid them. A girl across the hall was jumped, and a few weeks later she was sporting gang colors and boasting about being a runner for her boyfriend.

That's the whole reason the Alvarezes moved to

Meadowbrook. But then she thought about Renaldo's friend getting beat up, the occasional jab or nasty name she'd heard in the halls at school. It was confusing. They'd come here to be safe, but now it seemed people looked at them and felt they were the ones who were making the town not safe.

She paused, sucking in her breath. Why was this so hard? Because she was afraid of these boys and girls staring at her? Or because she feared something bad might happen? "*Mi primo* . . . my cousin. At his job he has to pick the guys up every day to work. But some people, they are mad at this. He knows some guy who got chased once." She added, "I guess people aren't so trusting. Like my friend's mother, she got fired for stealing——"

Everyone was very silent, staring uncomfortably at their sneakers. Only the girl kept a sharp gaze on her.

Maria suddenly noticed the time on the town clock across the street. She was late—very late. She tapped Tash on the arm. "I have to go."

Tash smiled. "Oh, sure. But *Jueves, sí?*"

"*Sí.*" Her smile felt false, as dull and tinny as a mouthful of nickels. Besides, the group had veered off—now aiming for cheeseburgers at the diner.

*Chapter 27*

Late afternoon at Starbucks: a melody of satisfactions. The slushy tinkle of scooped ice, the hiss of the espresso machine, frappés with perfect spirals of whipped cream.

Lola, having snagged a perfect table by the window, was bent over her assignment for Mr. Cohen. She'd spread out a stiff roll of oak tag and was creating a large flowchart that began with important principles of the revolution—freedom, individualism, justice. Then she began to diagram recent events and trends that showed how their ideals had been corrupted. Her teachers often told Lola she had good ideas—maybe too many—and she just needed to organize them better.

She tried to hunch against the waves of chatter, but it was hard. No, she wasn't going to let anything bother her. Not the girls just returned from dance class in their stretchy leotards, poking their straws into their cups, ballerina-dainty. Or the boys who leaned their two-hundred-dollar skateboards up against the wall before hitching up their jeans and slouching inside.

Lola had always prided herself on decoding the social constellations of Meadowbrook. There were the girls who moved in packs, and wore the exact same UGG boots and plucked their eyebrows into identical arches. There were the superachievers, whose parents drove either expensive cars with DVD screens flashing over the rearview mirror or beat-up VW Passats plastered with stickers from some fancy college. The occasional Indian or Korean kid whose parents were doctors or Bell Labs scientists, astronauts attached by a special tether to the universe of success.

And finally, the we-don't-give-a-damn alternative sadists such as Rachel Meisner, who blazed cruelly in the middle school firmament and made Lola's life miserable.

"Oh, how cute. You're making a show-and-tell?"

Rachel stood over her table, skirt swaying gently over her calves, holding two iced coffees. Her hair was dyed a shiny black, her bangs a fringe of russet-gold. She'd done her eyes in owlish circles, which seemed to emphasize her Sylvia Plath–diva-poetess air. She wore a leather bracelet studded with silver buttons, a granny skirt over black net stockings, and thick lace-up boots. All courtesy of her mother's store, where Rachel had daily pick of the stock.

She nudged Madison. "I did one of those in fourth grade. Remember?"

A crazy, sharp anguish pierced Lola. Sometimes—especially when faced with someone like Rachel—the Slovak words jammed up against the English ones. Flustered, Lola pointed at Rachel's legs. "Hey, did you pay someone to make those holes in your stockings?"

"Ooh, that really hurt, Lola. What a comeback."

Then Rachel pressed through the door, an iced coffee balanced in each hand. Outside, through the plate glass, Lola could see Rachel join a group of girls at a metal table, their shoulders shaking with laughter.

How did Rachel do that? In one stroke she'd demolished Lola's hope. Lola was nothing all over again. Just a pathetic trying-too-hard outsider who didn't know the moves. She ripped up her sheet of oak tag, tossed it into the garbage, and hurried outside.

When Lola first arrived in Meadowbrook—fresh from the playgrounds of the Bronx—she figured she was sassy enough to conquer even someone like Rachel. She also knew, instantly, that Rachel was someone who should be won—if you wanted some status. So at lunch one day, when Rachel called out to her, "Hey, Lola, are you really from the Bronx? Aren't there, like, shootings there?" Lola took the bait. She swaggered over and offered, "Yeah, sure. All the time." She pointed to an old scar by her ankle. "This is where a bullet nicked me. I saw, like, ten, twenty shootings maybe."

Rachel and her friends giggled nervously.

"I even held a gun once."

The girls fell silent. The air seemed to close around Lola's throat. She was drowning, flailing. But she couldn't stop herself. She had to impress them. Especially when she saw Rachel's attention wander as she whispered, "You won't believe, I was over at my cousin's house, and she has the coolest music. Her dad, he works in the music business, and he can get anything she wants. All these cool bands that no one has even heard of yet."

Lola put a fist to her hip and boasted, "Back in Slovakia, we have so much stuff. Bootleg cassettes."

The girls lifted their eyes. "Cassettes?"

Her voice seemed to falter. "Yeah."

"What is this, a seventies yard sale?" one of the girls said, and giggled.

Then they burst into laughter and drifted away, still laughing. Lola wasn't even sure why she'd lied about the cassettes. But it was too late. They had seen her vulnerability, her strain. For all her posturing, Lola wanted in, just like everyone else. And from then on Rachel Meisner had become a social force field, repelling Lola backward.

Lola looked up at the darkening sky. It was getting pretty late. But she wasn't ready to go home yet. She still had so much more work to do on her presentation, especially since she'd torn the whole thing up anyway. Where could she go? Then she saw, up ahead, a low brick building, beckoning to her like an old friend—the library.

It was funny being at the library at this hour. Everything changed, as if a switch had been thrown. Most of Meadowbrook emptied out: the toddlers, strewing their sippy cups on the carpet and beanbag chairs, the strollers parked in the front, gone. The broken crayons and jackknifed picture books stowed away. The teenagers had disappeared too, the ones who did their homework or got in trouble for text messaging and giggling behind the revolving stands of paperbacks. Even the retirees, paging through *Golf Digest* or returning a plastic-covered novel from their reading group, were back at home.

After five o'clock a new group flowed in: people who'd just come off their shift at a hospital or on a bus route, some of them still dressed in their uniforms and sensible shoes. The place became hushed, the only sound the urgent *click-clack* of keyboards. Every time Lola passed someone hunched over a terminal, they were conducting important personal business: an old woman pecking at a Medicare application. Another doing a practice driving test in Spanish.

To her surprise, Lola found Jaya's mother at one of the computer cubicles, a ghostly light bathing her face, giving it a strange, haggard look.

"Hi, Mrs. Lal."

"Oh, hello, Lola." She glanced at Lola's book bag. "Doing work here, dear?"

"Yeah. A history presentation."

She smiled. "You're always so good at school. I keep hoping some of that will rub off on Jaya."

Lola felt a small pang. Obviously Mrs. Lal didn't know that the girls were fighting. That hurt her even more, as if she'd disappeared from Jaya's life. She fiddled with her bag straps. "Hey, sorry about what happened with Mrs. Harmon's place."

Mrs. Lal's face darkened. "Yes, well, that's behind me now."

She tapped the screen with her pencil eraser. "I'm looking for jobs on Craigslist. One has to move on, after all."

"But I was there, Mrs. Lal, remember? And I'm sure it's just some stupid mistake, and I wish we could—" She bit down on her words, seeing the flash of alarm in Mrs. Lal's eyes.

"That's quite all right," Mrs. Lal said. There was no mistaking the chill in her voice.

"I better go," Lola mumbled, then added, "Say hi to Jaya."

Lola felt as if everything about her were on fire: her chest, her lungs, her hair. She left the library and crossed the street, stopping outside the middle school, which had long since emptied out. She remembered again that scene in Starbucks, with Rachel. It was all so unfair! How Mrs. Lal had to hunt and peck for jobs on Craigslist. And she couldn't do anything about it, especially now that she and Jaya and Maria were fighting.

For the first time Lola had to admit she was jealous of Rachel. Because she knew it would all work out for her. Rachel could be mean and cruel, and everyone would think, Well, that's what smart girls do. She'll go to some arty college and write lots of angry poetry, and her teachers will give her prizes.

Yet no matter what Lola did, she was off, fighting for attention in all the wrong ways, so that even the teachers shrank back. Even her own best friends. But she *had* to fight. Something was tilted and unfair about Meadowbrook. This was supposed to be a meritocracy. She should be on top, simply because she worked so hard, and was pretty smart, too. But it didn't work that way. Because there was something Lola didn't have. She wasn't a leader. And—as painful as it was to admit—Rachel was a leader. She could make her friends follow her, do even terrible things. Lola couldn't make anyone do anything. She shouted too much. She tried too hard. It reminded her of that display case in the middle school corridor, with its shiny trophies. She would just shatter the case, rather than ever getting inside for some great win. She wasn't one of them, after all.

*Chapter 28*

As Maria turned the corner, she saw her mother—ankles pressed tightly together, her round hips and thick, curly hair, and she said to herself, *When I grow up, I do not want to be her.*

More and more, nasty thoughts were starting to plague her: how her mother hadn't learned much English, even though Maria had given her a really simple dictionary and phrase book. That she carried around a frayed market bag, instead of getting herself something nice. That every time they did one of these housecleaning job inteviews, Maria could see her mother scanning the lips of the prospective employer, nodding frantically.

Now a fresh wave of remorse swept through her as a worried Mrs. Alvarez rose from bench. "Where were you?"

"I'm sorry. I had some work after school."

"But we're late!"

"I'm sorry, Mami."

Today her mother had done a shift at a friend's diner in Jersey City and had probably stopped off at the market, for Maria could see the tops of green plantains poking out over the handles of her mother's bag. As they walked the few blocks—fortunately, the house wasn't too far—Maria felt terrible, especially when she saw how nervous her mother was.

"Mami, please," Maria whispered as they pressed the doorbell. "It will be all right."

The woman, Mrs. Broder, was still in her work suit, and Maria could see just a flicker of annoyance in her eyes. "I'm sorry," Maria said as they stepped inside. "My mother was ready, but I was late from school. And she likes me to be here in case there's something she doesn't understand."

This was the part she always hated—the beginning, her mother eagerly trailing behind, her head bobbing, the prospective employer sizing them up.

"The woman who used to clean, one day she just disappeared," Mrs. Broder explained.

That's what they always said, Maria knew. Sometimes it was true; sometimes it was made up.

"My only fetish"—Mrs. Broder paused, to check that Maria understood the word—"is that the moldings have to be dusted and wiped with a damp cloth every week. I just hate when they are left."

A good sign, Maria thought. The more they told you up front, the less chance of misunderstandings later. How many jobs did Mrs. Alvarez cry about losing? *Why couldn't she just talk to me?* she would ask, over and over.

Because they didn't want to, Maria would try to explain. A lot of people actually didn't like hiring people for their houses and gardens and children. They felt too weirded out, guilty, and they wanted you to make it easier for them. Or it didn't occur to them to be forthright. But poor Mrs. Alvarez couldn't see it that way. She took these people into her heart. She might not be the best or the fastest or even the cheapest, but couldn't they see that? Didn't her heart count for something?

*No,* Renaldo often said, with a sour mouth. *Everything is money in this country.*

They continued walking through the house, up and down the carpeted halls, through the arched doorways to the kids' rooms with bookcases and movie posters. They were obviously older children—another good sign, since it meant no sticky jam prints on the kitchen chairs, or toys to scoop into shelves and boxes.

When they returned to the kitchen, her mother whispered to her, *"Noventa dólares."* Ninety dollars.

Maria repeated the sum, in English.

"I paid the other woman seventy."

Maria could feel her mother's nervous breaths behind her. Tío Pedro was very strict about everybody pitching in their share of the rent and utilities. And she could see how Mrs. Broder was weighing out whether to argue. This wasn't about money, she realized. It was about the worth of things, about this woman feeling that her check wasn't just disappearing into a stranger's hands.

"Seventy dollars gets you one thing," Maria said. "But I can see your other woman, she didn't do this—" She reached between a cabinet and refrigerator and pulled out the plastic wastebasket, its lip caked in grease. She opened a cabinet and showed how the spice jar tops were coated in dust. "My mother is very thorough."

The woman smiled. "I like that."

Before she knew it, she was rattling through more of her mother's amazing qualities: how she made a point of wiping the glasses before she put them back in the cupboard; how her favorite thing to do was organize linen closets, folding the towels and sheets, just so. "My mother, she's a neat freak." Maria smiled. The other woman flushed with pleasure. She had gotten to her, Maria could see. And it wasn't that anything she said wasn't true. It's just these were private little traits, what you didn't boast about to strangers. You didn't push yourself forward like that. It was unseemly. But the more Maria talked, the more the woman grew brighter and more alert in Maria's vision, while her own mother faded, and it seemed as if it were just the two of them talking in the room.

"That's great. Can she come on Thursdays? My son has soccer practice the day before and so I can get the uniform washed."

"Sure. Just make sure there's enough bleach by the washers."

"Of course."

She added, "I think you'll be really pleased."

Maria had never done that before. She felt as if the English words she spoke landed securely on the other side. It was like watching a Frisbee loft across the air, falling firmly into someone else's hand. As she watched the woman write down Mrs. Alvarez's schedule, Maria sensed the lessons with Tash, even the time with his friends today, was an exchange that went the other way too. Sure, they spoke in Spanish and covered vocabulary and grammar. But she was learning how to carry herself in English, to be an American in words.

Outside, her mother kissed her on the forehead. *"Mi hija,"* she whispered. In her hand was a slip of paper with the date and time of her first day of work.

Maria knew she should be happy. But she had this funny tearing sensation inside. She was reminded of the first time in class when she'd listened for a whole hour to English and realized she'd stopped translating from Spanish. Now she was so completely inside their English, their way of talking, her mother seemed to have shrunk to someone shadowy, tentative, while that woman, a complete stranger in a gray suit and lavender shirt, had grown solid and real.

As they began the long walk home, Maria suddenly said, "Mama, I can't do this anymore."

*"Qué?"*

"I can't come in there. I can't always go on interviews with you."

Her mother's eyes were bright with alarm. "What are you saying, *mi hija?*"

"You're never going to learn English if I do this all the time." She added, "It isn't right."

Mrs. Alvarez said nothing. Maria almost wished her mother

had yelled at her, as surely Tío Pedro would. But her mother just plodded ahead, shoulders slumped, the market bag rubbing against her legs, as if she deserved no better. The sky lowered. The angels vanished for good. In their place was just a piercing aloneness.

# Chapter 29

"Okay, it's revolution time!"

At James Madison Middle School, excitement bristled from Mr. Cohen's classroom. Giggles floated out the windows, which now had to be cranked open since the weather was turning warm. People rushed out of the bathroom in funny costumes, while hall monitors tried to peek inside the classroom, wondering what was happening.

Dressed in blue pants, a crisp white shirt, and a bow tie sprinkled with stars, Mr. Cohen stood in front of the blackboard and brandished a marker. Corny as can be, but Lola appreciated the kitsch. Only he could make history a cross between a party and a poetry slam. Much more interesting than the usual teacher drones who paged through overhead projections and sent everyone into a drowsing stupor.

Even the slackers had come prepared. Mary Jameson wore a pinafore top and gave a sweet, boring talk on women of the revolution. Noah Feldstein got special permission to bring in a rusty musket and explained about artillery on both sides. And Anthony Vitale—Mr. School Is a Waste—nervously offered a report on colonial architecture, handing out special pictures, courtesy of his father's superfast laser printer and laminating machine.

The double period went by fast. All the ums and ahs of Meadowbrook lingo had been combed into proper sentences. Mr. Cohen furrowed his brow and wrote notes on his pad. Of course everyone would have a place in the revolution, wasn't that the point? But there was no getting around the quest for superstar status: George Washington, Thomas Jefferson. The big heroes.

Lola twisted, impatient, at her desk, gazing now and then at her pages, a lecture on how the America of today had betrayed the ideals of the revolution. Jaya's mother assumed guilty before innocent. Historic houses torn down for cheap condos. Day laborers jumped. Everything this country was supposed to be against. And none of these kids even knew such an injustice was happening in their own sweet Meadowbrook. How could they? They were too busy getting glazed-eyed over their Nintendo games or picking a bikini for their vacation in Saint Barth's.

When it was her turn, Lola took to the front of the classroom like a prosecuting attorney. She snapped open her manila folder and charged on. She'd written her presentation in a heat.

"I am not going to point any fingers," she began. "But I'm here to talk about something you may not even know about. How we are tearing down a historic house, here in Meadowbrook, New Jersey. And in tearing down that house, we are tearing down the foundation of our democracy."

Soon she was weaving bits of the Declaration of Independence and Thomas Jefferson's letters in with today's morally lackluster world. She was all over the place, condemning SUVs and fashion and *American Idol* alike. "No wonder we have prisoners in Guantánamo Bay! No wonder we condemn people without fair hearings! No wonder Americans are hated everywhere! We've grown as hollow as the walls in our imitation houses! Fed on fake profits! We've lost our purpose! Our focus on justice and equality! Jefferson famously declaimed that every government should be torn down every twenty years and a new one planted in the blood of liberty! Those who lived through a revolution knew that no matter how strong the principles we built, man corrupts them. Maybe it's time to tear down and plant again."

Lola was sure Mr. Cohen would love her somersaulting connections, applaud her for her relevance. But something peculiar began to happen. The sentences started to grate, like rusted gears. She could sense a restiveness in the room, even a few puzzled looks. And her own voice, once so cocksure, sounded shrill. She pushed on, but it only grew worse. When she put down her paper, a soft embarrassed silence fell around her.

Mr. Cohen tugged on his bow tie. Usually he said a thing or two about the presentation before calling on the next person.

Lola put her fist to her hip, waiting.

"The thing is, Lola, this is supposed to be about history."

"This is history! Living history!"

"Yes, but—" He seemed baffled. "The important thing was

for you to discover something. To not know your answer when you started. That's what a research question is. You embark on a quest to find your answer. This was—"

"A screed!" someone shouted from the back of the room.

Mr. Cohen didn't say anything. Lola's cheeks were aflame.

"It was a good start, Lola. A lot of energy."

Shamefaced, she wilted into her seat. Her defeat was all the worse because she had such a big mouth in class. Who cared if Rose Chu did a bad, boring job on her report on revolutionary boats—she never said a word anyway. But Lola, she had to do things boldly and loudly, so that when she fell, the humiliating crash could be heard all through the halls of James Madison Middle School. Not about history! How could Mr. Cohen say such a thing? History was her thing! Her special talent!

Lola was so busy roiling, she didn't even notice Rachel slip up to the front of the room. As usual, Rachel was clad all in black, her nails daubed in inky polish, a felt black beret tilted over her hair, and pinned with a tiny rhinestone American flag, courtesy of Vamps and Vixens, of course.

Her presentation was simple. No PowerPoint, no laminated cardboard, no marker scrawls on the easel. Just two single-spaced typed sheets of paper, from which she read.

"This is an imaginary diary," she explained. "I wanted to discover what it might be like to be George Washington during some of his darkest moments. When he had his gravest doubts about his cause."

Lola was surprised by how firm and quiet her voice was.

She'd never seen this before in Rachel. Something in her quieted down too, as if Rachel's seriousness commanded them all.

And Rachel began to read. Softly at first, until her voice rose in short, ragged bursts, especially during some of the tougher moments. She plumbed. She dove. She wove in bits of real information. Winter, Mount Vernon, the Hudson River, steering their boats past ice chunks in the dark of night. "I have reached a nadir. My men wait, outside this tent, and neither do I have hay for their horses, nor hope for the days ahead." Whole swaths of history sprang alive in everyone's eyes. "How can I not see my men's blistered, frost-blackened feet? Or that boy of fourteen, weeping for his mother on the surgeon's slab? Will God, will I, remember his sacrifice? How many more losses must each of these soldiers endure?" It was unsparing. Brilliant. Moving. When Rachel finished, the whole room was hushed. She could see Mr. Cohen was so stunned that he didn't know what to say.

And then slowly everyone began to clap. The room erupted into praise.

Lola had never been so shaken. So absolutely unsure of herself. Rachel Meisner, mistress of suburban idiocy, a genius history writer? Must this brat get this, too? It wasn't fair. History! Rachel Meisner wasn't just an enemy. She was an encroaching empire, gobbling up her territory, blithely annexing Lola's private passions, taking up all the resources, even Mr. Cohen's admiration.

In the locker room Lola wrenched off her shirt and jeans, stuffing them into her locker, and pulled out her shorts. Nadia's, actually, since she'd forgotten to put her gym clothes into the wash. She was so upset that after Mr. Cohen's class she'd actually shot off to the wrong side of the school before the bell rang, then realized she was supposed to be in gym class. Most everyone had already changed and was inside, dribbling around the court.

When Lola slammed her locker, she noticed another locker's door open. Inside, a heap of clothing and papers on the bottom—somebody who couldn't be bothered with things like hooks or shelves. Peering closer, she recognized the closely typed pages, and the title: *GeneralWashington's Diary*. She stuffed her hands into her pockets and touched something funny. She pulled it out. A matchbook. Of course—Nadia's occasional smokes, taken on a summer afternoon. Lola fingered the matchbook, heat licking her insides. She imagined lighting a match, touching it to the page. A corner twisting, shooting into flames. A strange satisfaction reaching through her as the fire spread, destroyed all of Rachel Meisner's work. Across the empty locker room, in the dusty mirror, her own wild anarchist face. Rockets, sparks, explosions, in her mind.

"Lola?"

Mrs. Sanderson, the gym teacher, was in the doorway, whistle and plastic ID dangling from a striped ribbon around her neck. "Lola, what the heck are you doing?"

Panicked, Lola looked at the matchbook in her hand and tried to shove it into her pocket.

But Mrs. Sanderson, an agile point guard, swiftly nabbed it out of her palm. "I'll take that," she declared.

Nightfall. Lola couldn't eat, couldn't sleep or stay still. She just had to walk. She had slipped out of the apartment, unnoticed, and found herself wandering the dark and empty streets of Meadowbrook. Her mother was already in bed; her father, who knows where; and Nadia working a late shift at the A&P. Already the school had called about her little "incident" in the locker room, requesting a meeting with her parents at the guidance counselor's office. Could anything be worse?

She kept moving, hands jammed into her pockets, staring sullenly into the house windows lit like bright fireflies. Inside, she thought, everyone was happy, normal. Children's homework zipped into backpacks, *Jimmy Neutron* turned off, toddlers immersed in bubble baths.

She found herself standing in front of Mrs. Harmon's house. She thought again of Anthony Vitale, his scythe grin encouraging her. Mr. Cohen urging her to discover something.

Pushing through the metal gate, she followed the narrow path to the back, then hesitated. But the kitchen door was wedged open, just a little, with a wooden block. Probably to air the paint and varnish fumes.

*Just a look,* she told herself.

She made her way down the empty corridor, sawdust grinding beneath her shoes. Mostly she saw cardboard boxes sprouting junk. Her blood was pounding so loud, it was like a jackhammer at the back of her skull. She'd find some clue and save Jaya's mother. Show them all. Maybe even find something important. A valuable letter. A secret missive from George Washington himself. Why not? This house had been here for forever.

*Discover something,* Mr. Cohen had said.

And there was the square attic door, beckoning to her like a pulsing Siren. She knew she shouldn't, but she just wanted to breathe that close, sour mildewed air and mothball stench, feel history one more time. She scraped up the stairs, fingers quickly coated in dust, and tugged on the light chain. A lone bulb clicked on.

It was like gazing at the carnage on a battlefield: raw, exposed beams, the innards of foil-packed insulation. They'd done it. They'd disemboweled this house, gouged out its life, its past. A hot ball came up in her throat. Her legs shook. She wasn't even sure she could make her way back down again.

She crawled across to the spot where she and Jaya had been working that day when Mrs. Lal had called them away. And there it was, the old black chest with the broken brass hinge. She pushed open the lid. A dust cloud billowed into her face. Sheaves of yellowed newspaper crumbled in her fingertips. *St. Louis Post-Dispatch*, December 12, 1921, she made out on one scrap.

Her hands brushed against a familiar object, the buckled cardboard cover and the thick serrated pages. Then she remembered—the scrapbook, greeting her, almost like an old friend. Eagerly she spread the volume flat across her knees.

Paging through, she began to calm. It was like a conversation she had forgotten about. She lost track of the time. She was back in the past, imagining this girl who was pasting together a scrapbook of a family that reached back to a time of buggies and gas lamps and the Civil War, and to even earlier, when farmland and pastures rolled thickly beneath the New Jersey sky.

And then a voice broke roughly into her thoughts. "Who's up there?"

Lola blinked, squinting in the dim dusty light. As she lurched up from the floor, she banged her head on a joist, and the scrapbook sprang from her grip, the trunk lid slamming shut. Confused, Lola twisted around, only to jab at a brass lamp that crashed down.

She could hear scuffling down below. Then a rusty hinge as the attic door was flung open. The round head of a flashlight bobbed into view. A face and shoulders thrust up. For an instant she thought it was Anthony Vitale. He had the same wavy brown hair and slightly puzzled look.

"What's going on here?" he asked. Then she realized: It wasn't Anthony, but a young policeman.

*Chapter 30*

A fine Meadowbrook sports day. Grove Field's newly cut grass sparkled. The sky was a cloudless blue. An ice cream truck chimed at the playground curb. And here came the lacrosse team, their little orange pennant bobbing in the breeze, like a navy flag parting territorial waters.

Maria watched the coach lead, pulling a cart piled high with lacrosse sticks and balls. Even the water jugs bore the official crest of Meadowbrook High. Soon he and his assistant coach fanned out over the lawn, pushing a dozen more flags into the softened earth, staking out their territory, while the players pulled on knee pads and sneakers.

When they reached the area where Renaldo and his friends were playing a fierce game of soccer, Coach Bob stood right by the makeshift goal line chalked in the stubby grass, next to an overturned garbage can. He didn't say a word at first. He just pushed up his nylon jogging suit sleeves and gave his well-groomed smile.

"Hello! Hello?" He was a handsome man, silver hair still thick and swept back behind his ears, a regular, even tan.

Renaldo and a few of the players stopped. The others came straggling from behind. Sitting cross-legged on the grass, Maria stiffened.

"Can I help you?" Renaldo was still catching his breath.

"Fellas, I'm sorry. I'm going to have to ask you to clear the area." He spread an arm out, revealing the orange flags, which now made a serious formation around the field.

"You have some kind of appointment?"

The coach laughed. "Of course not. This is practice. For the Meadowbrook High team."

"I thought you have the high school fields for that. This is a public park."

A vein tightened in the coach's neck. "I understand there's been a prior misunderstanding. It's standard knowledge that our fields are overbooked while the Astroturf is being installed. So the teams come here for practice."

"I'm sorry, Mr.—" Renaldo scanned the lettering over his chest. "Mr. Matthews. I don't know anything about that. My guys, we came here early this morning and we're finishing a game."

Coach Matthews sucked in his gut. Maria rose, a queasy sensation rolling through her, and came to the edge of the group.

"That's fine. But we're in a league. And we have a game on Monday."

"Sure. After we're done." Renaldo turned on his heel. *"Vamos,"* he called to his guys.

"Hey!" The shout boomed, furious as a cannonball.

Pausing, Renaldo turned back. By now the high school players were gathered behind the coach. They made a kind of ready-made champion photo op: regulation shorts, clean tube socks and letter shirts, shoulders wide, brisk, confident, orthodontia-straight smiles. Renaldo's friends clumped behind him, each in a wary crouch, skittish eyes low, hands stuck in their jeans, sneakers pushing at the ground. A few were muttering in Spanish. *Let's go. No trouble.*

"I don't know how to say it any other way. You've got to clear the field."

"And I don't know how to say it back to you, mister. You gotta wait."

The vein in the coach's neck pulsed wildly now. He touched his cell phone, clipped to his waistband, as Renaldo moved closer, eyes flared.

"Renaldo," Maria pleaded.

*"Silencio!"*

The team stirred behind the coach. Maria wished she could stop Renaldo. Stop everything. But her whole body had gone numb.

One of the boys shouted, "You don't even live here!"

"Yeah!"

The coach turned angrily to the team players. "Brandon, Trevor, I'm taking care of this."

Renaldo cursed under his breath, in Spanish, "Idiots, think they can push us around."

"Why don't you learn English, buddy?" someone said, and laughed. "Gotta know English even for McDonald's."

Brandon pushed forward, put his hands on his hips. "Seriously, Coach. Just get rid of them."

Then he spun on his heel and walked away. Renaldo made a low bristling noise in his throat. His hands went into fists.

*Don't,* Maria thought.

But Renaldo was headed straight for Brandon. Just as the other guy turned, he took a solid swing and hit him right on the bridge of his nose. Brandon staggered backward, blood spurting from his nostrils, a little cross-eyed with surprise. Renaldo swung again, but this time Brandon was ready, and grabbed him around the neck, tackling him to the ground.

A roar let up among the boys. It was hard to tell who attacked whom next. Two players jumped in, showing a flash of green-and-white uniforms. The boy behind Brandon toppled Renaldo's friend, Carlos, and was pummeling him, hard. The assistant coach flung himself on top of them, but the melee had erupted, everyone throwing punches, the sound of bone on bone, bodies hitting dirt.

Maria saw the coach unsnap his phone from his hip holster. "I got a problem at Grove Field," he yelled. "Get over here. Now!"

A few minutes later she heard the high whine of a siren, radio squawking as a police car swerved to the curb.

Two policemen shouldered their way through the crowd to the scruffy grass, where Brandon and Renaldo lay felled and bleeding.

And a few minutes later, the worst sight of all: Renaldo being led away in handcuffs.

*Chapter 31*

When Jaya woke on Sunday, she felt as if her bed had spun around. Where was she? She lay there for a few minutes, staring up at the ceiling and the furry bar of sunlight that fell through the curtains. The bloated drift of voices rose up from below. Mr. Carlota almost always had the TV on.

Jaya usually loved Sundays. Her mother let her sleep in, so she'd wake up to the smell of chicken curry simmering in a pot on the stove. Still in her robe, Mrs. Lal would greet her with a mug of warm milk mixed with just a little coffee, and then she'd pull out the international card and they'd call her grandmother. *Oh, yes, they're treating me quite well,* Mrs. Lal would say. *The people are excellent. They pay me more than enough. Soon we'll save for a down payment on a little place not far from here.* Jaya's stomach always hurt when she said this, but her mother would give Jaya a wink. It was their little secret, these lies to her grandmother.

If the weather was good, Jaya and her mother usually set out for the yard sales. Her mother dressed differently, in jeans and one of her father's old shirts, hanging loose over her hips, her hair tied back. This made her look younger, like a college girl, or how she looked in the old days, back in Port of Spain. They'd stop at the driveways and rummage through the plastic bins, buying spatulas and sugar containers, wooden hangers still in their plastic wrap. After, her mother would hum as she'd spread contact paper down on the shelves and set the six glasses she'd gotten for a dollar. *Jaya, you know the school system here? It's one of the best. A brand-new biology lab. So much better than what your cousins have in Queens. There's possibilities here, darlin'.*

One morning they had stopped off at a sale where Mrs. Lal was especially interested in a cute Pottery Barn desk for Jaya. The mother remarked, "My daughter Tiffany loved that desk, but we recently did the room over, so she didn't need it." Jaya realized, with a hot flush, that this was a girl in her class. Before she could pull her mother away, Tiffany was coming down the driveway in a pair of white cutoff shorts and purple flip-flops. "Hey, Jaya," she called, giving her a shy little wave.

The mother smiled with surprise. "Oh, you're Mrs. Lal. I remember now. You have an apartment address."

"Yes." Her mother's back went straight. She stopped fiddling with the drawer handle.

"I wasn't sure if you were getting our e-mails about volunteering, and which committee you wanted to be on."

Jaya felt a pain, watching her mother's face go still, its quiet dignity. In Trinidad they didn't have things like PTA car wash fund-raisers, parents showing up to help pin up the art show. She also knew what her mother couldn't say, that they didn't

190

have a computer at home for checking e-mail. Her mother would sneak in some computer time at the Silers', when the kids were napping, though she had to be careful, as this was one of Mrs. Siler's pet peeves. Or she'd stop off at the library after work, when they had evening hours.

Mrs. Lal didn't get the desk that day. And, fortunately enough, there weren't too many embarrassing moments like those. Jaya actually liked going to the yard sales, helping her mother find little bargains to fix the place up—it was like a game and her mother was always cheerful, even silly. At those times she could believe that Mrs. Lal was right, that this was the right move. This was their new home.

This morning when she padded into the kitchen, she saw her mother was already dressed in a pressed oxford shirt and plain slacks, what she usually wore to work. As Jaya took her seat at the dinette table, she noticed there were no chicken parts on the chopping board, no onions and garlic crackling in the pot.

"Sorry," her mother said. "I'm doing some extra babysitting for a new family. You're on your own today." But she sounded wistful. "Do you have plans?"

"I have a lot of homework." In fact, she had planned on drawing Mrs. Harmon's house.

They sat opposite each other at the kitchen table, her mother sipping her coffee and staring out the window. Jaya noticed the gray showing at her mother's roots. The last few weeks had been hard on her. After work she was often in the library, scanning the local message boards, but so far nothing had come of it. "Maybe I was wrong," Mrs. Lal said softly. "I should just pack it up and move in with your cousins."

For the first time ever Jaya felt sorry for her mother. This wasn't the mother she was used to, the one who could just up and move to a town, or stand up to Mrs. Siler when she thought she was too soft on the children.

"What do you think?" Mrs. Lal's voice was uncertain.

Jaya wanted to say, *No! I can't leave Lola and Maria!* But she wasn't sure. Not these days.

"My goodness, look at the time!" Her mother suddenly rose, poured out the rest of her coffee, and rinsed the mug, setting it upside down in the drying rack. "Jaya, what ever happened to your picking up those groceries the other day? I didn't see them in the fridge."

Jaya panicked. "I forgot to tell you. I had these lab fees, so I used the money for that."

Her mother's brow wrinkled. "All right. I'll pick them up on my way home today."

Shrugging on her coat, she paused for a moment, putting her hand on Jaya's hair. "Be good," she said.

Walking up the hill, Jaya noticed the line of cars parked on Mrs. Harmon's block. A few people were climbing the front stairs and, without knocking on the screen door, going right in. Her heart started to lift. Maybe something had happened. A miracle! Mrs. Harmon was completely better! She could talk and walk, and her nephew was throwing her a big welcome home party. Jaya began to hurry up the hill.

As she drew closer, she noticed people walking out the door with bulging shopping bags. Jaya realized, with a cramp in her stomach, what was going on: the estate sale. She stood for a few minutes, stunned, her heavy satchel pressed to her hip.

Then she walked inside, where Mrs. Harmon's whole life was spread out on folding tables or hung from portable rods— old coats, fedoras dimpled with age, a rotary phone. People were shifting around in her rooms as if in a museum where they were allowed to touch the displays. They tested the cushions on her sofa and wing chair; they knocked on end tables.

In the kitchen, on the big pine table where Jaya used to do her homework, was a litter of kitchen junk: old canning jars, a whole box offered for five dollars; juice glasses; a scattering of flatware. Someone was plugging in the blender, making its steel blades whir. "Wow," the lady said. "It's still in its original box! With the warranty!" Others were rummaging around in the pots and dented baking pans.

When Jaya tried to go upstairs, a woman at the cash register pointed to the yellow tape strung across the first step. "Sorry, honey. The second floor is off limits. That's what the estate is keeping."

"She's not dead, you know."

The woman gave her an odd look, and shrugged. "I don't know about that. We were just hired for the sale."

Jaya pushed through the back door and went into the garden.

A mother was near the shed, foraging in a plastic bin of garden implements. Her little boy was torpedoing through the garden, kicking at dead leaves, stamping around in the flower bed, the same one Jaya and Mrs. Harmon had been working on before she'd had her stroke.

Jaya walked over. "Those were just planted," she told them, pointing to the black-eyed Susans, which lay flattened in the churned-up dirt.

The boy gleefully stamped some more.

"Don't do that!"

The mother gave Jaya the same odd look that the woman inside had given her, and pulled her son away.

Jaya looked around. She didn't know why she was so angry. Even though she and her mother had done a good job of sorting through most of the valuables, she couldn't stand the idea of people pawing at Mrs. Harmon's belongings.

She sat down on the wrought-iron bench to calm herself. She knew all the good things—the pewter candlesticks, the painted china with twined roses on the rims, the honeymoon plate from Niagara Falls, the embroidery sampler from her great-great-grandmother—had been packed up, carefully folded into the cartons that now sat in the nursing home. And she could tell that much of the stuff in the attic hadn't even made it down.

Still, her heart ached. She hated the thought that by the end of this day the house would be stripped down. That bits and pieces of Mrs. Harmon would be carried off into minivans and station wagons, all over Meadowbrook, like an old loaf of bread distributed by a colony of ants. Couldn't some things stay put?

After pulling out her pad, she set it on her knees and popped open her new pencil box. The tips, freshly sharpened, gleamed. The garden was quiet now and she had a good view of the house.

Jaya started first with the outline. She felt as if she knew the slumped shape of the cottage by heart, where the roof bulged out just over the attic dormer, and the strange, low slant of the left side, as if the whole house were sliding down the hill. And the stairs, which were not exactly level with the porch, and the crazy pattern of mismatched stones that led from the kitchen door to the shed. She drew and drew, her wrist going softer, looser. She concentrated on getting the shingles just right, the humps of holly bushes in the front.

Soon she forgot about all the belongings inside, letting them sift out the door. It was like seeing the air go out of the house. People kept walking out, carrying full paper bags. One man balanced a twin mattress on his head. It was okay. Jaya just kept drawing, until she was done.

When Jaya opened the door, she was surprised to find the apartment dark. She didn't even notice her mother at first. Then she saw her sitting in a chair by the window, in her bathrobe. Her faced looked swollen; her cheeks were streaked gray from dried tears. Balled-up tissues lay at her feet.

"Mrs. Siler let me go." Mrs. Lal shook her head in disbelief.

"She said . . . it wasn't working out. She didn't need so many hours."

Jaya had rarely seen her mother cry. Even when Jaya's father had died, Mrs. Lal had stood by the funeral pyre, her back very straight, her face still. Now, when she was done crying, she silently took Jaya by the wrist and pulled her onto her knees. Jaya felt awkward and clumsy; she was much too big to sit on her mother's lap. Her shoes dangled to the floor and she kept sliding off.

"And there's something else. About your friend Lola. You know how everyone talks in the park. Yesterday Marleen told me that she'd heard that Lola broke into Mrs. Harmon's house. I could be wrong, but I feel like word has gotten out about me. Maybe Mrs. Siler heard something——"

Jaya flushed hot; she suddenly felt sick to her stomach.

"Mama, Lola went because——" She broke off, not sure what to explain, exactly. Then she let it tumble out of her, that she and her friends wanted to find out who really stole the earrings, how they had gone to Mrs. Harmon to tell her the truth. She tried to capture the lightning-fast arguments of Lola, tossing out words such as "justice" and "power." But when Jaya spoke, it sounded muddled and pathetic.

Her mother went silent for a long while. "It's my fault," she finally sighed. "Having you and Lola come help at Mrs. Harmon's. Mixing you up in my business."

"Mama, me and Lola and Maria, we just wanted to help——"

"Hush." She touched a finger to Jaya's mouth. Her face

looked drawn and sad; she looked, suddenly, years older. "Now listen to me, Jaya Lal. I forbid you to have anything more to do with that girl, do you understand? I have enough trouble as it is."

"But, Mama, she's my friend—"

"I said no."

"But—"

"Jaya."

Jaya struggled to look away. Her mother had pressed forward, cupping her chin tight. Whenever her mother grew mad, her eyes glowed with a fierce light. But tonight Jaya saw something else—a kind of shadow, a fear. Jaya had never seen this in her mother. Even when they came to America and Mrs. Lal didn't know a soul and had to go calling agencies for work, she wasn't afraid. Once they were evicted from an old apartment, and still she kept her cool and found them another.

Right now, though, her neck curved in shame, as if readying herself for a blow that would rain down any minute. The shadow in her was growing, moving between them like a dark river. And Jaya knew neither of them would cross anytime soon.

"You promise?" Mrs. Lal asked.

"Yes, Mama," she whispered. "I promise."

*Chapter 32*

"This is the way it works."

Ruth Dinerstein walked around her desk and came to sit opposite Lola in her expensive leather chair. She was on the short side, with thick ankles. Crinkly black hair and an interesting sweater made of rumpled mauve silk. She had the air of someone who knew she was smart. And the quirky purple glasses and funky strap shoes were flourishes to let you know she was smart in fashion ways too, so don't write her off as a psychology nerd. Lola felt a small lift in her otherwise sodden mood. She liked her, just a little.

"You're going to come here every week. You're going to talk about yourself."

Lola rolled her eyes. She liked her less now.

"You're going to answer my questions and we're going to talk about what's on your mind."

*Oh, please,* Lola thought. Some kind of fake American friendship business. She wished she had been given a regular suspension.

It had been several days since that evening she had been taken back to Green Valley Garden Apartments by the policeman (a nice young rookie, who told her privately that he remembered doing dumb stuff when he was a kid, but please, not to do it again). And then the meeting at the school guidance counselor's office, when her mother burst out, "I have no idea what happens with my daughter! She break the law! She almost make fire!" Her father just sat on the folding chair, baffled and seething. Who were these people interfering in their private life?

It was all Mr. Cohen's fault, actually. He had advocated for her. Said a suspension didn't make sense, not with such a good student. "She needs counseling, I think." Under his breath he whispered to the guidance counselor, "She has issues with anger."

Issues. Issues were *Brown v. Board of Education*. Issues were separation of church and state. Issues were not about some stupid unburdening of her family problems, something that would do better in an anonymous pathetic column in *Seventeen* magazine.

> *Dear Miss Know-It-All:*
> *The other day I almost lit a match in my enemy's locker*
> *(and I felt good about it). I broke into an old lady's house.*
> *I think I'm having trouble with boundaries. I have an*
> *anger problem.What do you think?*
> *Penelope Pyromania*
>
> *Dear Penelope,*
> *Yes, you do. I suggest you talk about it and hold hands in*
> *a circle with every girl you have ever secretly envied. Leave*

*Easter baskets at their doorsteps. Volunteer for the elderly.*
*Read to the blind. You will be surprised at how much of a*
*better person you will be.*

Lola sucked in her breath. No, she would not completely give in. She would do as expected. Come here twice a week after school. Isn't that what Nadia had advised her? *Just do what they tell you,* she said that night, when they lay in their single beds side by side, watching the highway lights press through their blinds. *Give them what they want.* Nadia's credo, Lola thought grimly. Miss Teenage Model Superstar headed to fame, all because she has a moral heart as light and hollow as popcorn.

"Tell me about your father."

Lola looked at the woman, startled. *Ding!* An arrow right in her tender spot. Why did she know to ask that right away?

Ruth Dinerstein regarded the folder on her lap. "I understand he's an engineer?"

"Was."

"And your mother?"

Lola's throat was so dry she couldn't speak right away. "She is . . ." She took another sharp breath. "She used to have black braids." Why did she say that? She meant to say, *My mother is my mother. She has a good job working for an obnoxious rich family that pays her well.* But when Ruth Dinerstein asked her, a photograph of her mother suddenly popped into her mind. She was leaning against a wall, in a funky white shirred peasant shirt tucked into cuffed jeans. Her hair was done into two frizzy braids, and she was laughing. Lola guessed the photo to be when her mother was maybe fifteen, sixteen. But she wasn't sure. The girl in the photo certainly resembled Mrs. Svetloski. She saw the same wide face and gap-toothed smile. Lola could even see a little of herself in her too. But she also looked nothing like the gray-faced woman who came home every night and dropped with a sigh onto the sofa, or the mother who pushed a mop across the kitchen floor at the Vitales', muttering under her breath. "She never goes to her doctor appointments," Lola added.

"And your father?"

Lola shot her a sharp look. Again with her father. "He doesn't pay attention." The air in her lungs came up so short she had to remind herself to breathe.

She could barely remember what transpired for the rest of the session, since she was working so hard to fend off any more of Ruth Dinerstein's unerring arrow questions. She knew she told a little more, about how her father hadn't found a real job since they'd arrived here and about how she'd taken to opening the mail and sorting the bills, so that her mother wasn't too overwhelmed. As she walked out of the office and crossed the street to the bus stop, she felt a strange sense of relief. She'd actually never told anybody about their money worries, not even Jaya or Maria. That seemed shameful, a pathetic reminder of how small Lola's life really was.

The bus ride from Ruth Dinerstein's office calmed her, allowed her to reenter Meadowbrook with a bit of dignity and stealth. At school she had managed to hide in the hordes of kids rushing down the corridors to classes, and then fled right after the last period bell. But it had been days since she'd even walked down Main Street, for fear of running into Rachel Meisner or any of the other James Madison kids, who would surely make her life a torture. Interestingly enough, the only person who actually spoke to her after she was caught was Anthony Vitale. "Getting caught sucks," he wrote in an e-mail. "Power to the people."

As the bus swung past Grove Field, she squinted, wondering if Jaya and Maria were hanging out on their favorite bench. The previous Tuesday she had waited on the bench, like always, but no one had showed up.

And in the past few days Lola had spotted Jaya a few times at school, but they had not even managed a hello. Once, she had gone up to her at lunchtime, and Jaya had turned away, tray balanced in her hands. Lola didn't pursue it then, not in front of all those other kids. Lola tried waiting for her on the steps after school, backpacks swelling and bumping around her, but Jaya had clearly ducked out another entrance and taken a different street home. Her head raged with speeches she would make to Jaya if she could just pick up the phone. *How could you do this to me? Abandon me in my hour of need?* But the words sounded phony, and she never called.

As the bus drew up to Main Street, Lola looked through the window and saw a familiar sight: Jaya's army satchel slung across her shoulder.

Quickly Lola scrambled off the bus, just as the folding doors hissed shut. Jaya was half a block ahead of her, heading toward the supermarket. It gave her a pain, seeing her friend's careful, solitary walk.

Lola raced up to her friend. "Jaya, please," she whispered.

Jaya whirled around. Lola had never seen her like this. Her face was hard, her eyes stones. "Go away."

"But please. Let me explain——"

Jaya put up her hand. "No. It's really bad around here. My mother lost another job. She doesn't even know why. And you go breaking into Mrs. Harmon's house! What were you thinking?"

"I was trying to help——"

"Are you crazy? That's illegal, right?"

"I know, I know. I got a little carried away. But, Jaya, we have to stop them. These fascists——"

"Stop!"

"Stop what?"

Jaya looked at her, frustrated. "Look around you. Haven't you heard what's going on in this town?"

Lola was silent.

"You don't get it. You can't just do what you want, Lola. Say whatever comes to you. We're not the same as all those other people here. We can't even pretend. We can't . . . we can't do anything."

Then she watched Jaya grab a cart and push it inside the supermarket, metal wheels rattling on the rubber mat. The worst of it, Lola realized, wasn't that her best friend had ripped out her insides, which she probably deserved. It was that the other side had won. They had defeated her in the worst way. They had made strangers of those closest to her heart.

# Chapter 33

"Oh, girl, good to see you!" Smita took Jaya by the arm and led her into the house. She was wearing skintight jeans and a navy blue halter top, her bare, bronzed shoulders pushed back. Jaya knew her cousin was doing it just to bother her aunt, who thought her youngest was getting much too slutty-looking since she'd started high school.

Most of the women and girls had gathered on the two big sofas; Smita's mother, Auntie Sharmila, had installed panels of mirrors on one wall, so it felt as if there were twice as many of them in the long room, nodding, murmuring, and laughing. For Jaya, used to the quiet of just her and her mother, it was disorienting to be with so many people.

The men were out back, where they had fired up the barbecue and cracked open some rum and beers; the radio was on, playing the local Caribbean station. *Gon ta be a warm one, folks. All you breakin' open da coolers today, mon? Let's hear it for some smooth soca right now.* On the counter separating the dining room from the kitchen was an array of foil pans. Jaya could smell the chicken curry and *dal*, the chow mein. Even the folded-up triangles of *roti* smelled great. Jaya's stomach rumbled. She hadn't eaten much for weeks, it seemed, ever since her mother had been fired. It was as if she were willing herself to get smaller, to make it easier to disappear from Meadowbrook altogether.

Mrs. Lal was sitting right in the middle of the sofa, several cousins and aunts gathered around her. An uncommon place for Simone, but they had pulled her in and sat her right down, made her tell the whole sorry story of Meadowbrook and her firing from the Silers.

Jaya knew it could have been worse. Mrs. Siler could have fired Mrs. Lal on the spot, no severance pay, nothing. But Mrs. Siler was very calm and efficient, a real human resources pro. Their needs were changing, she explained. She would give Mrs. Lal three weeks pay—certainly very fair. On the question of a referral she was a little vague. "I'm certainly happy to tell them that my children adored you." Somehow her crisp dismissal hurt more than if she'd blown up, accused Jaya's mother of all kinds of terrible crimes. Then, Mrs. Lal had told Jaya, she'd have known where she stood.

"That's no way to treat you!" Helene, one of the older women, said.

They made clucking noises with their tongues. "Got to watch them," Helene advised. "Me buy something, me put the receipt and money right where she can see it."

"Helene, don't you act like no saint! What about that time you just walk out!"

"Oh, that!" She flapped her hand. "That lady crazy!"

It was strange, but today her mother looked more relaxed than Jaya had seen her in a long time. Unusual to see her in the middle of all of her father's relatives. They were the raucous do-nothings, her mother always said. But today her father's relatives seemed like hearty good-spirited people; every few minutes the doorbell rang and somebody came in, bearing another foil tray of food. A bit of the old spark was showing in her mother, especially when she leaned back her head and howled with laughter, hearing about how some cousin thought he'd bought land in Florida and went down there and learned it was a toxic dump. "Robie never very swift!" she said, and laughed. They traded other stories, about relatives and people from back home.

Some were doing better than others. Auntie Sharmila and Uncle Pratash were definitely well settled, judging by the flat-screenTV and sound system, some kind of discount he got from the Best Buy store where he was manager.

Smita perched on a stool and piped in, "It's better you came here, Auntie. I don't know why you want to live all the way out there."

"Don't worry," Auntie Sharmila added. "Me find you something better. They won't ask references, nothin'."

"But where we going to live?" her mother asked.

"You come stay with us awhile. Jaya can stay in Smita's room." Then she added quietly, "My brother would want it." She glanced at the wall where a large photo of Raj hung, showing him at his high school graduation, with his too-big glasses and his crooked teeth. Her aunt's eyes glistened. Jaya felt a hot pressure dammed up behind her lids. She always hated this moment, how her mother's body stiffened, her face became hard. *They trying to guilt me with his death,* she would say. *I need to lead my life. Not a widow's life.*

But this time it was different. Her mother's gaze softened, her lips parted, as if she were looking at the photo for the very first time. And she even allowed Auntie Sharmila to slip her arms around her shoulders.

*Chapter 34*

"These are short-term jobs," Mr. Salerno explained. "We get called in after a house is sold. Or a landlord needs some apartment cleared."

Even though it was a Saturday, Maria and her mother were sitting in a small cubicle on the second floor of an office building on Haley Avenue wedged between an auto body shop and a Laundromat. A few days before, Mrs. Alvarez had answered an ad in the newspaper, which had read: CLEANING PEOPLE NEEDED. FAST. EFFICIENT. PAID IN CASH. Mr. Salerno had called back almost right away, asking if she could come in for an interview.

Maria knew her mother didn't like this kind of work. She'd once had a job cleaning offices on the night shift, and though the money was good, she grew frightened, cleaning out wastebaskets in the corridors of empty offices, the only sound the buzzing fluorescent lights. Every time the security guard jangled his keys, she nearly jumped out of her skin.

Maria had told her mother she didn't want to go on any more interviews, but Mrs. Alvarez had begged Maria to come on this one, and finally she had relented. After all, maybe this was better for her mother. Just a company: No attachments, no tears or straining hard to please. Just one hundred dollars at the end of a long day scrubbing down cabinets and floors.

So Maria had agreed to come. Back at home everyone was afraid, especially with Renaldo's troubles. Maria remembered the night Tío Pedro brought Renaldo home after they'd posted his bail, how Renaldo had come through the door holding an ice pack against his left eye. Mr. Riccardi was furious when Renaldo missed a half day the morning after the fight because he couldn't move out of bed. Since then, Renaldo really tried. Even Maria could see that. He was always the first one up in the house, hair freshly washed and slicked back, pacing the patio in his cuffed jeans, flicking his morning ashes into the hedges. But it was like living with a grenade waiting to go off. The house was awful these days: doors slamming, voices too loud, everyone on edge. "This family gives me nothing but trouble!" Tío Pedro yelled. "And no respect!"

Sitting here, in the small office cubicle, Maria could see that her mother was nervous. She had filled out the application, which she pushed gingerly across the desk, but she asked no questions. "How often do you have work?" Maria asked Mr. Salerno.

"A lot of this work is short notice," he was explaining. "I need to pull together a crew and get them in and out."

"How many for a crew?"

"Depends on the size of the job. If it's a big house, I'd rather have three or four. Goes quicker for everyone and we can get it all done."

They shook hands, and Mr. Salerno squinted at Mrs. Alvarez's application. "Frankly, I've recently lost a few people. If you can deliver me the team, I'll give you a bonus of fifty dollars. Makes it a whole lot easier for me."

Maria turned to her mother. *"Si usted tiene otras mujeres, hay mejor,"* she said to her mother.

*"Yo tengo muchas amigas. Ellas son muy buenas."* Then she added, "Hardworking!"

Mr. Salerno smiled. "Good. I think I'll have something in the next few weeks. I'll call you soon with the details."

When they stepped outside and began walking toward the bus stop, Maria asked her mother, "Who are you going to get for the crew? Do you mean Tía Lucy? She doesn't even do the boys' laundry. She sure isn't going to do some extra cleaning job."

Her mother didn't answer.

"Mami?"

Mrs. Alvarez whirled around, her black eyes flashing. "What is wrong with you! My brother needs help—" Her voice was cracking.

"But—"

"Where have you been all these weeks? We are not good enough for you? You are in a dream! We have trouble. Real trouble with Renaldo! I need . . . I need you to be good, Maria. *Entiendes?*"

Maria was so surprised by her mother's outburst, she couldn't answer. *Good.* She rolled the word in her mind as the bus groaned to a stop, and she stepped inside. But what did that mean anymore?

*Chapter 35*

Jaya and Smita took a walk around the neighborhood after lunch, even though Jaya felt so groggy from the food she could barely move. But Smita seemed eager to get out of the house—to sneak a cigarette, which she kept cupped in her hand for fear that the elderly neighbors might spot her.

"We could have so much fun," Smita said. She prattled on about the high school, where the principal was "a real witch with a military mentality," but her older sister taught her how to get around the rules.

Jaya could see her cousin was showing off. She was taking her on a tour of Richmond Hill, as if Jaya's moving there were all settled. They walked around the block to a house identical to her aunt and uncle's, where a group of girls were clustered on the front stoop, wearing tight tanks and jean skirts. "Hey Smita-girl," they called out. Smita shot them a saucy smile and they chatted for a few minutes, then strolled on, passing yet another house, with some more teenagers gathered around a car, the music booming loud through the open windows.

The neighborhood was clearly her cousin's queenly terrain.

The houses here were tight together, two-family shingle houses with tidy yards in the front. It was all so familiar, just like back home. People called out to one another; cars slowed on the street, soca and reggae and rap pulsing from deep bass speakers. The little shop on the corner sold crates of salt fish and bottles of syrupy *maubey* in the refrigerator case. Smita and her friends sometimes snuck into the clubs on Jamaica and Liberty Avenue, where they danced to music from back home. Here you weren't on the edges of things, since everyone was mostly from Guyana or Trinidad.

And it did sound exciting. Jaya soon lost track of all the names that were strung out before her. *That boy there, he went out with my sister, until she met Damien, and you see that girl? Her brother crashed a car the night before last and he just walked away!* But Jaya also realized she didn't know Smita very well. Smita was the past; she was home in an old way, back from when Jaya played with her cousins in the alley behind her grandmother's shop. Not like with Maria and Lola. They had to get to know each other, bit by bit, on the benches. They'd *found* a way of being together. And then she remembered, with a raw pang, Lola's break-in. No. Lola wasn't a friend. A friend wouldn't do what she'd done.

"You have a boyfriend?"

Jaya flushed. They were leaning against a wire fence, gazing at a group of boys on the basketball courts. Some of the boys had taken off their shirts, showing the waistband of their underwear, their backs gleaming richly brown in the sun. "No."

"Friends?"

"Yeah."

Again she thought about Lola and seeing her at the super-market a few days ago. She'd never done anything like that, been so cold and mean, cut someone off.

"Hey!" Smita called out. "Come say hello to my cousin!"

One of the boys let the basketball go and sauntered over. He was tall, and wore a gold chain that sparkled in the hollow of his throat. He grinned, wiping sweat from his jet-black hair.

"Hello." His voice was soft and low.

"Roy's a deejay. Does all the parties I was tellin' you about."

"You gotta come sometime," he said.

Jaya's tongue suddenly felt foolish and thick in her mouth; she could just muster a nod.

"You'll have lots of friends here," her cousin remarked as they turned away from the courts. "No doubt. Smita will make sure of that."


They left at ten o'clock to catch the last train to Meadowbrook from Penn Station. Uncle Pratash was driving them to Jamaica Station, and Jaya sat in the back with a shopping bag full of food, the *roti* and curry and lo mein soaking warm and greasy against her ankles. Auntie Sharmila, a little tipsy, leaned over the passenger seat, the glow from the overhead light showing her henna highlights. "I don't know why you have to live so far, Simone. We're family."

Her mother brushed cheeks with Auntie Sharmila and whispered, "Thank you."

It was a long trip. First the Long Island Rail Road ride into New York City, then the wait on the uncomfortable seats in Penn Station, and finally their New Jersey Transit train arrived on its track. Jaya settled into her seat, leaned her head against the cool glass, and watched the black tunnel slip past, giving way to bleak stretches of the meadowlands, its dry rushes lit up by white highway lamps, showing oily blotches of water. Her mother and she stayed silent, as if they both knew what lay ahead: giving the landlord notice, packing up their belongings, and hiring a van to drive all the way over to Queens. After today it did seem strange, being so far away from the little bit of family they had in this part of the world. It made her mother's choice to live in Meadowbrook seem perverse, full of capricious pride. And yet. Why wasn't she happy? Why did she feel this sad ache in her bones?

Somewhere in the back of her mind Jaya wondered, Did she do this? Did she let her mother know that she wasn't cooperating in this crazy Meadowbrook idea all those times she'd complained? Especially once she'd started fighting with her friends and she had nothing tethering her to the town? She thought again of them standing in front of that tennis bubble, how excited her mother had been, and she frightened. Her mother often complained, *Why do you have to mope so much? Can't I ever get any enthusiasm from you?* And now that relief lay right before her—her own bed practically made up, right next to

215

Smita's—she should feel better. But she didn't. This was a lousy way to leave.

As Jaya and her mother stepped out of the Meadowbrook station, the damp earth, the quiet, was a shock, hitting them like velvet. Everything was muted, the only lights glimmered from the movie theater arcade, where someone was sweeping the pavement. A lone car glided past. The scent of evergreens and early hyacinths hung in the air.

Mrs. Lal suddenly paused, drew back her shoulders, and lifted up her chin, her eyes searching the ridged tops of the trees. "Smell that, Jaya. You want to give that up?"

The space of understanding lay between them, waiting. Jaya almost reached out to feel the reassuring nub of her mother's elbow. But she couldn't. Not yet.

# Chapter 36

Maria stared at the silver mobile phone folded shut on the Starbucks table. Her stomach hurt. Her palms were damp with sweat. She tried rehearsing what she would say, forcing her voice to go light, casual. The way those high school kids talked. Finally she punched in the numbers.

"What's up?" Tash asked. His voice sounded muffled and sleepy on the other end, as if she'd woken him from a nap.

"Did you ask your father?" Maria blurted out, abandoning all pretense of cool. "About helping my friend? And my cousin?" She paused, her voice hoarse. "It's gotten really bad. At home, too."

She couldn't find the words to explain, not to a stranger, how they had paid the bail and Renaldo had come home yesterday evening. His eyes bloodshot, him smelling of beer. Then he had explained: When Mr. Riccardi had learned Renaldo was involved with the fight at the park, he'd fired him, right on the spot. Now, every morning at the crack of dawn, Renaldo bicycled to the church parking lot. He was one of those other guys, shifting on the hot asphalt, keeping his eyes low and humble, hoping for work.

There was a pause. "Oh, shoot, Maria. I'm sorry. I forgot."

Her heart pounded in her ears.

"I'll ask him tonight. I promise."

"Please do." Her voice was a squeak. "It's important." As she hung up, she realized, *It isn't important to him.*

Just as she was shoving her cell phone back into her bag, to her surprise, who should walk through the door, but the elf-girl she'd met with Tash. Maria tried to scrunch down in her chair. But the girl was making her way right to her.

"Hey."

"Hey."

"You're Maria, right?"

She nodded.

"I'm Genine. Remember, from the other day? Hanging out?"

Without asking she slid into the chair opposite Maria. The girl was a study in black: worn messenger bag stretched across a faded black T-shirt with a silk screen image of Che Guevara; black jeans and high-top sneakers. Her hair, cropped close and sticking up like pine needles from her scalp, was dyed black, and Maria could detect wisps of more ordinary brown strands showing through. And she still wore that same leather rope with the polished stone, glistening against the hollow in her throat.

"So I heard about some stuff going down at the park. What's up with your cousin and the other guys?"

"It's . . . it's not good." Maria paused. "My cousin's got a court date in a few weeks. And . . . he lost his job. He says it's harassment."

"Maybe it is," Genine said flatly.

"Renaldo has a temper."

"So what? That's not against the law." She gave her a sharp look. "And your friend's mother?"

At this, Maria winced. "It's really bad," she whispered. She paused, not wanting to say what came next. "I think Jaya's going to move away. She says she doesn't feel like she belongs here anymore."

The girl pushed her chair closer to the table. She had the tiniest features, almost miniature: delicate nose and mouth, violet-colored eyes. She was an elf: small, intense. "There's a lot of talk in town. People are saying they should ban those guys who stand on the corner. Even crazy stuff. Ticket the soccer players if they don't live here. Put a cap on how many renters there can be in town. Get rid of the ELL classes in the schools."

A nauseous surge rolled through Maria. She hated this. More trouble. It suddenly hit her how she never talked about these problems with anyone, not even with Lola and Jaya. It was different for them. They didn't have neighbors sending the police over to complain. And that wasn't their cousin waiting for work in the church parking lot, ducking when some stupid kid threw a beer bottle out a car window.

"How do you know all this?"

Genine grinned. "I'm curious. I poke around." She paused. "Listen, I was wondering. Can I interview your cousin?"

Maria looked at her, surprised.

"Don't worry. If he doesn't want me to use his name, that's

219

cool. I write for the school paper. And I just think it would make a really important story. Nobody knows about the crap that's going down in this town. They just kinda jump to conclusions about people. You know, guilty before tried."

Maria hesitated. She could hear Lola's voice. *Just watch these politically correct kids. They act so morally superior and they're just beefing up their résumés for college.* But in a way, Maria thought, maybe this girl was the same as her. Hadn't Maria done the same thing with Tash? Pretending to offer Spanish lessons, when really she'd wanted him to like her, however pathetic that was?

And this girl, she had a certain steady, unwavering focus, the kind that made you nervous.

"Yeah, sure, I guess so," she replied.

*Chapter 37*

Lola made a list. Of everything that was wrong with her father. His widening belly. His sallow skin. His accent. His insistence at drinking tea in a glass even though they had four new brightly colored mugs from IKEA. His refusal to print out a résumé, even though Nadia had typed one on the computer. His habit of stopping everywhere and asking directions, no matter where they were. How he showed up at parent-teacher conferences and lectured the social studies teacher that they should have a special course on Prague and middle Europe, the great confluence of East and West. Worst of all, his lack of fatherliness. To think that Mr. Vitale, of all people, would help her see her father's great gaping lack! But it was true. For the first time she saw with utter clarity what was wrong with her life: Her father just didn't measure up.

After she'd given Ruth Dinerstein her carefully detailed items, instead of enveloping her in sympathy, Ruth said, "Lola, you're angry, aren't you?"

"Of course I am! He's not holding up his share!"

"Lola, your father is depressed. He can't do any of these things. He's not able."

"Not able! He has a degree! He's smart!" She leaned forward, elbows at her side, head down, like a charging football player. "Do you know how many people used to work under him?"

"Lola. Do you understand what depression is?"

A flash of anger coursed through her. What she wanted to say is, *Why do I have to understand? Is that my job? Do Rachel Meisner or Anthony Vitale or any of those kids have to worry like this? Do they hide the heating and the gas bills so their mother's blood pressure won't go up?*

"It's an illness. Your father has an illness."

"Oh, please." She hunched down. No way was she going to buy this mental health nonsense. Americans were too soft. They bought every new theory like a trendy diet. She smiled to herself. That's what her father used to say. Before he became such a slug on the couch.

"Lola, can you tell me what you're thinking?"

"No."

"And why is that?"

"Because it won't change anything."

"Why do you feel that way?"

"Feel! Why is everything feeling? Do you ever think that it's time to just do? That people do! They get up every morning and they do! They don't wait, they don't complain, they just do. There's too much feeling around here!"

"Doing, like almost lighting a fire in a locker room? Or breaking into a house?"

Lola narrowed her eyes, wishing she could zap the woman into oblivion. The arrow had found its target, all right. "You're trying to make me feel bad for what I did."

Ruth Dinerstein looked at her hands and said nothing.

"I have a theory," Lola began. "All this stuff that's available. Family services. Food stamps. Tutoring for the stupid kids. And then for the rich kids. Stanley Kaplan-Take-My-Money. Tennis clinics, a hundred dollars. What, your backhand needs a prescription? I have a theory that this country is going down because it makes everything so soft. That's not what they meant."

"Who's 'they'?"

"The founders. Of the revolution. Do you think Sam Adams stopped to have his head checked when he got so mad at the British?"

Ruth Dinerstein leaned back, a smile softening her face. She seemed to be considering Lola's point. Instead, to Lola's surprise, she asked, "Why do you hate Rachel Meisner so much?"

"What's not to hate? She's spoiled. She's—"

"Yes. But she's not your friend. Why do you focus on her?"

"I don't. She picks on me. She and her friends, they put it in our faces. All the time."

"And why do you think that is? Is she aware of how much of an effect she has on you?"

Lola winced. She hated to admit it, but sometimes she lay in bed obsessing about Rachel. Wanting to both topple her and be her at the same time. It never occurred to her that Rachel

223

might enjoy this, stoke Lola's temper for her own satisfaction.

Abruptly, Ruth Dinerstein stood. Today she wore silvery sandals with thin straps. Nadia would definitely approve. "Thank you for coming."

"We're done?" Lola asked, incredulous.

"For today, yes."

"But what about——" She wanted to say, *My whole speech? My theory?* Wasn't Ruth Dinerstein just going to say that nothing was wrong with her, and they should just forget about the stupid sessions and let her go?

Ruth Dinerstein held out an arm, as if to make sure Lola didn't go anywhere but through the door. "Next Tuesday, three thirty?"

Lola turned away, pushing her fists into her jacket. "Yeah. Sure."

Lola decided to walk home, to cool off. She hated what she saw in Ruth Dinerstein's gaze, that she was nothing special. That everything that was happening was some stupid teenage angst therapy. Didn't she see? She was a revolutionary! A thinker! The worst fate would be to be ordinary. A middling nothing.

But as she turned into the park and found herself settling onto a bench, she couldn't stop going over what Ruth Dinerstein had said. Why did she focus so much on Rachel, of all people? The truth was, it was Jaya and Maria she missed. Couldn't she just be satisfied with them? Maria didn't care about Rachel.

Neither did Jaya. Why did she have to turn everything into some kind of friendship team competition?

Even now, as she stretched out her legs, she remembered how the three of them would sit on this bench and talk. They hated to leave, even though someone usually had to rush off to do chores at home. For Lola it was like eating her favorite dessert, caramel custard, over and over, until she was sick with happiness. Sometimes, not even an hour after she'd left them, she'd take the cordless and sneak into her bedroom and call up Maria or Jaya, to share something she had noticed about her father or a funny bit on the news. How quiet the last few weeks had been. How deathly silent.

They just wanted to stay together. And she had blown it.

# Chapter 38

Dynamite.

If Maria could come up with one word for Genine Barra's article, that would be it. A veritable bomb. A tiny, well-aimed explosive, set off in the center of Meadowbrook's conscience. The girl wasn't an elf, Maria realized. She was a little terrorist. Maybe—unlike Lola—a real revolutionary.

And she moved fast. The Sunday after their encounter at Starbucks, Genine interviewed Renaldo. The whole time she held her flat little voice recorder, no bigger than a cigarette pack, tilted toward Renaldo, nodding and listening as he spoke, her small violet eyes watching intently. The more he talked, the more his voice grew small. How he feared for his job. How hard it would be if they got rid of the day laborers. How he just came here to make a living. After Genine left, he called her a "sweet girl." Maria smiled. Not exactly a word she'd use for Genine. She was as sweet as black licorice, sharp and tangy.

Four days later Genine's article appeared in the *Meadowbrook High Gazette* with a huge headline: WHO'S THE REAL GANG? Beneath was a split picture showing shadowy men waiting on the corner and the lacrosse team posed in their classic horseshoe formation. People were furious. Genine was called into the principal's office and given a verbal thrashing by the coach. The article was put up on Meadowbrookonline, and one writer posted, *I pay taxes so some brat can stick it to our team and defend a bunch of illegals?*

By the next morning, after lots of homeroom text messaging, the high school chapter of the ACLU decided to hold a meeting, and Genine invited Maria to come.

As they hurried across the park toward the Gothic spires of the high school, Genine gave a telegraphic rundown on herself, how she always knew she wanted to be a journalist when she grew up. Wished she were old enough to go and report on the war in Iraq. Her parents were divorced—her father already onto some new, younger family that she hated—and she and her always-depressed mother lived in a small colonial on the edge of town.

Once inside, Maria tried not to stare too foolishly at the bulletin boards and trophy case with its weathered footballs, the photographs of the cool theater kids putting on *The Rocky Horror Show*. As it was, Maria barely felt like she belonged at James Madison Middle School, but to be allowed here, in these hallowed corridors of older teenagers, brought right into the inner sanctum of student leaders—she might as well have been given a personal invitation to the White House.

And she was confused. Was she doing this because she really wanted to be a part of their protest, or because Tash Adler was president of the ACLU high school chapter?

It had been more than a week since she'd seen Tash. He'd canceled last week's Spanish lesson, and had never gotten back to her about his father. Now, when she stepped into a classroom where they'd pulled the chairs into a circle, she saw Tash talking to some girl with blond hair, her pink sweatpants rolled low beneath her hips, showing a glimpse of thong. Jealousy scored right through her. Tash gave her a little wave and smile. "Hey, Maria," he said. "Glad you could come."

"*Hola*," she shot back. She couldn't help but notice how he didn't move from talking to the girl, and used his distant, public voice. She took a few steps forward, then squeezed into one of the chairs, feeling suddenly cloddish and fat.

Tash clapped his hands. "Okay. Let's get this show on the road. I called this meeting because, as Genine's article showed, we have a situation in town, where immigrants are having their civil liberties threatened." He went on, carefully laying out his argument. Once again Maria saw the angel emerge, the same boy who'd once said, *There's space for everyone.* The very distance in his voice now made him a leader. He took what to her was a simple, embarrassing problem, and made it abstract, a test of principles.

"You all know about this stuff. Like the rumors. And the situation in the park, with the soccer players." He paused. "We have to do something. An action."

"But what kind?"

"I say we leaflet the town," the boy with dreadlocks said. "Get people to know what's going on. Have you heard what people are saying?"

"Pure crapola," someone else said.

To Maria the whole meeting was turning strange. They were talking about Renaldo and his problems, the soccer games. She had the eerie sensation of watching her own family become a public cause. It was like seeing one of those photographs of a missing boy on a milk carton. Would she and her *tíos* and cousins soon be plastered on leaflets all over town?

"Maybe we should ask Maria," Genine said.

All eyes turned to her. This was growing more surreal by the moment. She and her family were not just a story, but an issue to be studied. "I—I don't know," she stammered.

Her mother would be mortified if she knew she was here. In her family you didn't do this. You didn't stand out, make a fuss about yourself. You did your job and you disappeared. Especially when there was so much trouble.

Maria looked at the group: all strangers. Pimply boys, girls in misshapen sweaters, and that blond flirt with the thong sitting much too close to Tash. She tried to wrestle down her jealousy. Could she really join these *blancos*? These boys and girls carried another kind of privilege that went beyond their Abercrombie & Fitch T-shirts, their expensive suede clogs. It was these words. Big words they used so lightly, as if they owned them.

Could there be another kind of coveting? she wondered, thinking about the priest's admonition to her. What about being jealous not of their clothing labels but of their way of talking?

It had always been Lola who'd let fly these bright, lofty words: liberties, rights, the Constitution. Such ideas puzzled

Maria. She had known English only to get through a day. Another test. A visit to the doctor. But as the talk heated up, it was like learning English all over again, in another way. And the more she had listened, the more she realized she didn't want to remain in the basement, doors slamming overhead, whispering with her mother, trapped in the clammy, confining dark. She wanted to gather all her small slights and fears, bring them up and out into the open air.

"It's okay," she said slowly. "My family would appreciate it. But you have to know—they won't join in. That doesn't mean they don't care. They just . . . they don't want to make trouble."

There was quiet in the room.

"I say we show up at Grove Field," one boy suggested. "With signs that say—What was that cool phrase you used, Tash?"

Tash looked right over at Maria and smiled, as if there were a private line opening up warmly between them. His Spanish lessons. Her political lessons. "*Hay lugar para todos.* There's space for everyone."

"Yeah, that's it!" the boy cheered.

"Totally awesome, man. We'll do T-shirts. We'll march in front of Brandon and his boys with their cute little uniforms—"

Everyone was talking at once, excited, pitching in ideas. "I'm really good at making posters," one girl offered. "I'll bring lemonade," another said. "Oh, Lauren, pretty please, bring your lemonade." A boy punched her in the arm. Maria wasn't even sure what the joke was, what was funny and what was serious. It was so confusing. Was this about Renaldo and his troubles, or showing up the varsity lacrosse players? She wasn't sure. They'd even begun to chant. "*Hay lugar para todos!* Bran-don move over! Make space!"

Then Tash jumped up onto a chair. "Hey, hey, guys! Let's vote. Who says we show up at Grove Field? T-shirts, the whole nine yards—"

Arms shot up, then more. The whole group. A forest of hands.

Maria grew dizzy. Slowly she raised hers, too.

# Chapter 39

"He's gone again." It was Nadia on the phone, sounding both hysterical and annoyed. "I dropped him off at the unemployment office for some kind of job training thing. But when I went to pick him up, apparently, right at the end, he got angry and stormed out. Nobody knows where he went."

Lola's heart skipped a beat. She was standing in the kitchen, trying to keep her voice low, since Anthony was at the kitchen table. Mr. Vitale, who had come in for an apple, paused. She could feel his concerned eyes upon her.

"I just don't have the time to deal with this," Nadia said.

"And I do?"

"Lola," she warned, "I've got to be at work now."

Mr. Vitale's face softened when she explained what had happened. "Don't worry." He tapped Anthony on the arm. "Let's go with Lola and see if we can track him down."

Quiet surrounded the truck cab. Lola could think of nothing more humiliating than sitting next to Anthony and his father, going in search of her own father at the county unemployment offices. But Mr. Vitale kept it light. He joked with the two of them about the pathetic showing of the Yankees and how Anthony needed serious work on his throwing arm if he thought he was going for tryouts next year.

The security guard was locking up the front doors by the time they arrived. He explained that a short while ago Lola's father had demanded to see his case worker, and when told it was too late, he'd stormed off. He pointed vaguely toward the big intersection.

*Oh, great,* Lola thought. Her father had run away. Like a sulking four-year-old who hadn't gotten what he wanted.

Mr. Vitale, who was leaning up against the truck, called out to her. "Lola, any luck?"

"I'm just going over that way. You stay here. In case he comes back."

"Okay, but don't go too far, all right?" It was hard not to notice the worry in his voice.

As she headed out of the parking lot, Lola started to panic. Would her father do something stupid? The ground was darkening with spots. She looked up to see drops scattering from the overcast sky.

Up ahead was a bridge with a slender pedestrian walk, the kind of structure her father used to help build, back in Slovakia. Rain was starting to slant down, hard, soaking her sneakers. As she moved forward, she could feel a thrumming vibration, shaking through the asphalt and cement. Below, bleary head-lights from commuter traffic were pressing toward her, more flowing down a ramp in a river of gleaming danger.

Then she saw the confused silhouette of her father, leaning over the guardrail.

"Papa!" she screamed.

His head jerked up. It was hard to hear over the pounding wind of moving cars, or to see in the dim light if that was a look of recognition. Lola sprinted closer.

He was wearing suit pants and a white shirt, no tie. The wet fabric clung to him, as transparent as skin.

"I've changed my mind," he called out. "I've reversed my resignation."

"What resignation?"

"At Atko. They still need me."

Lola swallowed. That was his old job. The last one, before they'd emigrated.

"Papa?"

She was still a few feet away, and she watched, terrified, as he edged closer to the guardrail and bent at the waist. She was reminded, suddenly, of a gymnast on the horse, the way they thrust their thighs out to the side, swung themselves over.

In a surge of fury Lola raced forward.

"You can't do this!" she shouted. Wind punched her voice hollow.

Her father turned. He seemed surprised by her anger.

"You can't! You have to get a job and sell shirts at Macy's! Work in a shopping mall and sell mobile phones. You have to go to training and not walk out. You can't leave."

234

The strange, dazed expression from before vanished. "You don't understand, Lola—"

"I don't want to understand!"

He stared at her, exasperated, as if she, not he, were the maddening one. "You know what this place was telling me to train for, Lola?"

"What?"

"Television technician. They give me a test. Some twenty-two-year-old community college idiot is telling me that I should want to sit in a little room and put together wires and solder and make a box of junk." He spat on the ground. "You know how many people I am in charge of at Atko?"

She knew, of course. She had heard many times, but she didn't want to set him off even more.

"Three hundred! Three hundred people in my division. Three hundred people I could fire just like that!" He snapped his fingers, and they made a wet rubbing sound. "Guess how many projects I do at one time? Forty! Bridges. Tunnels. Roads. Anything they give me!"

"I know that, Papa." She sighed. "But we're here now."

The rain had matted his gray hair flat against his skull, making his pale face shine, bone white. It was like looking at his death mask. "Lola. I used up all my savings. I gave up everything."

She did not answer.

"I'm fifty years old, Lola. I brought you here. This is the best I can do."

The cars pounded below. They were surrounded by a grainy

dusk, exhaust haze and pollution mingled with the weak rays of a lowering sun. It was just like her family—while everyone else was rushing somewhere, straight ahead, even in the slashing rain, they were stuck in some terrible half twilight, never able to go forward. Her father wasn't crazy. He wasn't going to jump. But he wasn't going to move, either.

Lola began to weep. This was it, the steely truth of her life. What she had been fighting ever since they'd come to America. This was a lonely land of firsts, where no one, not even your parents, could help you cross over. And she had no choice but to do it by herself, and leave her father behind. As she began to walk back toward the Vitales' truck, it came to her. You pushed ahead, in the chilling rain, hoping you didn't die from being first.

*Chapter 40*

When Jaya reached Wrightchester Gardens, she found Mrs. Harmon sitting up in her bed. She looked more herself. She wore one of her pale lavender cardigans and a blue striped oxford shirt, and her hair had been put into a dignified knot. Even the lousy food must have done her some good, because a bit of color had returned to her pasty cheeks.

The room didn't look bad either, now that Jaya had set out a lot of her belongings. The bed was covered in the crocheted afghan. On the floor was a braided rug, and in one corner a TV set. An old tea service was even laid out on a tray, the cups chipped.

"Tea!" she called out to Jaya.

It was just like the old days. Mrs. Harmon twisted around, and with a shaking hand reached for an old tin on her bedside table. "Let me help," Jaya offered, but Mrs. Harmon stubbornly refused, waving her away. "No!"

In the past few weeks Mrs. Harmon had improved. Her words came out, slow and thick, in a voice that was peculiar—a nasal sound that began near the roof of her mouth, slipping sloppily out one side. It reminded Jaya of how deaf people spoke, which made her a little sad, because she would have to get to know a different Mrs. Harmon, an old lady who spoke like this.

Mrs. Harmon was also more irritable than before, but in a funny way, it was as if the stroke had made her stronger. She burned with a hard, focused brightness, even if her mind had a way of taking its own stubborn course, sometimes getting stuck in knotty little corners.

She shifted herself on the bed, so she could use her good side to shake out the dried lavender. She did allow Jaya to switch on the electric kettle and put the hot water into the teapot. A few minutes later, after she'd checked the tint of the tea, she told Jaya to pour.

"How . . . is . . . your mother?"

"She's good." Jaya stared at a trail of steam winding up from her cup.

Mrs. Harmon asked, "Your friends?"

Jaya was surprised. She'd brought Lola and Maria around only a few times. "Busy."

Mrs. Harmon made a grimacing face, as if trying to remember something. "Lily?"

"Lola." Jaya's stomach hurt. What would she think if she knew Lola had broken into her house?

"Spark plug." She blew on her cup and sipped. "She had a temper."

There it was again, that canny way that Mrs. Harmon could be, like a pencil flashlight, so sharp.

"Mrs. Harmon, Lola . . . she—" Jaya paused. "I don't see her much anymore."

"Why?"

Jaya wanted to say, *I don't know how to talk to her. Or to Maria.* "Things changed between us."

They sat for a few minutes, sipping their tea. "What's that?" Mrs. Harmon pointed to a package wrapped in brown paper.

"Oh, I forgot!" Jaya proudly tore open the paper. Inside was her drawing of the house, her most involved yet. She had used most of the pencils, shading carefully to show the shingle siding, the stone path that curved to the garden, the carefully planted flower beds. She'd even had it framed, going back to Mandy's Art Supply House, where she'd found a cheap black one on sale.

"My goodness! You went to all that trouble!"

But Jaya could see she was pleased. Her eyes glistened as she took it from Jaya, gazing at the drawing for a few minutes.

"Hey, Mrs. Harmon, aren't you ever sad? Losing the house? Lola, she says it's a . . . travesty. It was in your family all those years."

Mrs. Harmon shrugged. "I *was* upset. Andrew is a fool. He'll get nothing for the place. He just wants it off his hands."

Then she began to talk in earnest. The veins on her neck bulged. Her eyes strained. But she was determined to get it out. "It's funny. What I really miss are my friends. I keep thinking about the time we took a bus cross-country. Four of us. We had two hundred dollars. We ate . . . pancakes. Pancakes, pancakes, pancakes." She wheezed a strange thick laugh. "That's what I remember. And . . . I've got my things. Thanks to you. And your mother, bless her heart."

This was the lengthiest speech Jaya had heard Mrs. Harmon give since her stroke, and she could see how much effort it had taken, for she sank back against her pillow, catching her breath.

If Mrs. Harmon could do this, Jaya wondered, why couldn't she speak up about her mother and all that had happened? Was it as Lola said, that she was a coward? Always hiding and ducking away?

*Say it,* she told herself. *Tell her.* "Mrs. Harmon?"

"Hmm?"

Jaya bit her lip. "Can I draw you now?" she asked instead.

Mrs. Harmon smiled, and then shut her eyes. She looked exhausted, as if this conversation had knocked the wind out of her. Jaya could see the spidery red veins across her lids, a quick pulsing beneath. She had fallen asleep.

Jaya's hands shook as she reached into her bag for the colored pencils. And she began to draw. While the sun lowered through the curtains, she sketched the sleeping Mrs. Harmon in unsparing detail: the liver-colored spots on her neck; her hands, with their knotty whorls for knuckles. Jaya didn't flinch from drawing, even though a little spittle showed in the corner of her mouth. This was much harder than drawing the house. But she reached deep inside herself, into that fright that had scored into her such a long time ago; the hospital afternoons when she had had to look at the man who had sunk to bones. Now, even as she was nearly blinded with hot tears, she kept at it, drawing the ugly and the sad and everything that hurt.

Once she was done, she ripped out the drawing from the pad and propped it against Mrs. Harmon's lamp. It wasn't her best drawing, she knew. But it was good enough.

"Good-bye, Mrs. Harmon," she whispered. The old woman's lashes fluttered, but she did not stir.

When Jaya turned to leave, she saw Andrew Cramer standing in the doorway.

*Chapter 41*

Lola just had to walk. There was only room for three in the truck, so she let her father go with Mr. Vitale and Anthony, and walked the whole way from the unemployment offices, heading into town. She should have been exhausted, but she wasn't. She was strangely refreshed. The downpour had long since receded, leaving a wet shimmer on the newly mowed grass. The last of the sun had dipped behind a bank of clouds, and the air was cut with a moist chill, strange for almost-summer.

She walked through the town park, beneath drooping tendrils of weeping willows, past the playground, where little kids clambered on a jungle gym with accordion red tubes, while the nannies watched from the benches.

When Lola first arrived in Meadowbrook, she'd found the park to be a comfort, especially after the noise, hot pavements, and congestion of the Bronx. She was reminded of the village fields in Slovakia, especially after the rains, when mist lifted off the grass and her hair was soaked cool. Now she felt strangely refreshed, lighter. She thought about that old story of her father carrying his father on his back, for miles and miles. It was if, on the bridge, her father had given her permission: She didn't have to carry him anymore. Wasn't that something?

As Lola made her way around the edges of the park, she noticed someone familiar. It was Maria, sitting all by herself, a soggy piece of cardboard propped beside her, with the words HAY LUGAR PARA TODOS.

"Maria?"

When her friend looked up, her face crumpled into a hurt little smile. She looked different, as if the sweet roundness of her face had been chiseled sharp. Her eyes shone with a new, sad depth. If Lola hadn't known better, she could have sworn her friend was at least five years older.

"Hi," Maria offered.

And then she gave Lola a hug. Squeezed her tight, held her a long time. It was still the same old Maria. The one who touched and held on. How Lola missed that. And then she realized what she had been living without, what the hollow space inside was. She'd forgotten that she was not completely alone.

"Are you okay?" Maria whispered.

"Now I am," she replied.

"Me too," her friend answered.

## Chapter 42

"Well, hello."

Andrew Cramer stood awkwardly in the doorway, as if waiting for her invitation. In his arms was a huge bouquet of white lilies, wrapped in a cone of lavender paper.

Jaya was so dumbstruck she could only nod. Her heart banged sharply against her ribs.

He took a few more steps into the room and set the lilies down on the windowsill. They looked too big and extravagant next to Mrs. Harmon's worn things. *Don't you know?* Jaya wanted to say. *Your aunt hates lilies. She says they're only for funerals.*

"I was wondering who'd done such a good job with all my aunt's things," he said. "It's very nice, what you've done here."

Jaya shrugged. "I wanted her to feel at home. She'd lived in that place her whole life."

An uncomfortable expression darkened his face. "Look. I'm sorry about your mother—"

"It isn't right!" Jaya blurted out. Then she bit down on her words. Her heart was thumping hard in her chest.

"It may not be," he said gently. "But there was a serious theft."

"How do you even know that she took the jewelry?" Jaya couldn't believe the words that had shot out of her.

"It's true. I didn't for a fact. But I couldn't take a chance. No reasonable person would."

Reasonable. What did that mean? That this nephew who didn't even know his aunt was in charge of everything, and her mother told to go away? She didn't understand anything anymore. But for the first time she felt like it wasn't enough to just crawl away into her quiet hole and ignore how much this hurt. She wanted to do something. To prove him wrong. She wanted to say, *Every one of these things my mother chose and carefully packed in newspaper or folded with mothballs. She's the one who knows your aunt. Not you, who brings her lilies and couldn't even name what kind of tea she likes.* But Jaya didn't say any of that. What could she really say?

Nothing, she realized, as she shoved her pad into her satchel. She had no proof. Nothing.

Opening the front door, Jaya was surprised to find the apartment looking cheerful, the curtains washed, their bright yellow-checked color filling the windows. The linoleum tile clean, showing the gray seams; she could see their sweaters spread out on the drying rack in the bathroom, damp arms bent over the sides, as if in prayer.

Humming under her breath, her mother emerged from the bedroom. She looked better than she had in weeks. Her brow was smooth; her skin had lost its dull, unhealthy look.

Jaya realized something was different in the apartment, too. The walls were stripped of their framed photographs. Two of her father's paintings were propped against the wall.

"What's going on?"

Her mother didn't answer at first. Then she set her hands on Jaya's shoulders. "I've decided, Jaya," she said. "We're moving to Queens."

Jaya looked at her, confused. How could her mother say they were moving when she'd made the place so welcoming? "I thought it best," she added.

Jaya let out a small cry. "Why can't you ever ask me?"

"What do you mean?" Her mother looked surprised. As if such a thought had never occurred to her. "What's the matter? I thought this is what you wanted!"

Maybe it was. For so long, aching in her bones. That underneath she had never believed in this thin sham of a life in Meadowbrook. And now, staring at her mother and remembering Mr. Cramer at the nursing home, she felt she'd been caught in a crime, yearning and scavenging, like her mother. Maybe they were thieves and they should disappear, without a trace.

Why, then, did she run to her room and slam the door, not caring if Mr. Carlota, their landlord, complained? Why did she start tearing around, desperate to find something that reminded her that she did live here? Something to reverse this, turn everything back, like a tape loop, to before, when she was happy in Meadowbrook?

Propped on her bed was a little heart-shaped pillow, stitched with Valentine-red letters: YOU ARE THE BEST! Maria had given it to her, when Jaya had been upset over failing a science test. Corny and girlie, but now Jaya threw herself down onto her mattress and grabbed it like a lifeline. Over her closet mirror was a strip of photos from a Walgreens booth on Haley Avenue, the three of them mugging and sticking out their tongues.

Why, she wondered, squeezing the pillow to her cheek, couldn't she stop crying?

*Chapter 43*

Maria and Lola sat opposite each other in a red booth at the diner, pressing their palms against mugs of hot chocolate. Maria felt stupid and cold, unable to shake off her chill.

She'd sat at Grove Field for hours on the grass with her little sign, damp seeping through her jeans. Just as Renaldo had said, she was a dumb dreamer. Finally only Genine had showed, wearing a boy's muscle shirt, the words MAKE SPACE! penned in ragged letters across her lean chest.

"Where is everyone else?" she'd asked. Maria had shrugged. Genine had pulled out her cell phone, begun punching numbers. "Hey! What is with you guys?" she kept shouting. As Genine snapped her phone shut, Maria could see she was very embarrassed. "They said they were studying for some big exam. I'm sorry, Maria. I really am."

The two of them had sat glumly on the grass until finally Genine had had to go too. Maria had remained, growing chillier and angry. Angry at herself for believing. For being fooled by those Americanos.

And then there was Lola, standing over her, wan and

bleary-eyed. Maybe her real angel. Or at least a real friend.

"So what happened?" Lola asked.

"They didn't come." She took a sip of her chocolate. "Okay, go ahead. Say it. Mr. Cool is a fraud. You told me. Watch out for those bigmouthed political kids."

For the first time Maria realized that to Tash she was an idea, something he could notch into his mental résumé of altruistic experience. *I made friends with a Mexican girl.* It was the kind of thought she never would have had a few months, even a few weeks, ago. A wistful sadness brushed through her, as if she were saying good-bye to something, like leaving the little stone house she'd always lived in, back in Puebla. But in a strange way she felt peaceful, too, having arrived at a colder, more sober place.

"I wasn't going to say that."

"Then what?"

"That . . ." Lola offered a tired smile. "You look different. Pretty. Older."

Maria blushed, tears welling in her eyes. Lola reached a hand across the table, gave hers a squeeze. She'd never done that before, and Maria's hand felt good, warm.

"I'm sorry."

"But why, Maria? Why did you run after him?"

Maria flinched, drew her hand away. "You're just jealous!"

"Maybe—" She stopped. "Maybe I am," Lola added softly.

Lola had to admit she wasn't just jealous about Tash. It was about Maria getting involved with their little protest at the park. Even if it had been a failure. It wasn't fair. She was supposed to make this a big deal. Okay, she'd confused it in her mind, mixed too much together. But it was as if Maria had stolen something from her, her specialness, by hanging out and copying those high school kids. Since when did Maria become such a firebrand? She almost didn't recognize her friend anymore, Little Miss Revolutionary Frida Kahlo, with her fierce black eyes.

Lola tapped the soggy board, which was propped up against the booth seat. "Pretty cool, Maria."

"Well, the whole thing was a flop," Maria admitted.

"Yeah, but——" Lola squeezed her hand again. This was getting to be a habit. "You know, I'm proud of you."

Maria looked astonished, as if she couldn't associate that word—"proud"—with herself. Sweet, maybe. Or good. A little silly. But she never thought of herself as someone who impressed. "I thought I was shallow."

Lola winced. "Sorry."

Maria sucked in her breath and asked, "And what about you?"

"They're making me see a therapist."

"Really?"

"Really."

"How do they pay for it?"

Despite herself, Lola grinned. Only Maria would ask such a question, worrying about money. "It's some kind of referral thing through the school district." She took a sip of her hot chocolate. "I guess they're trying to make me a little nicer."

Maria smiled. "You're nice enough. In your own way." She paused. "So what's therapy like?"

She shrugged. "It hurts." She added, "A lot."

In fact, for the past few days Lola had stopped obsessing about Rachel. Instead, all she could think about was her mother. She lay awake at night imagining her mother suddenly fallen ill and taken away in an ambulance, stranded on a hospital bed, stuck with tubes, her eyes milky gray. "My mom is having a lot of stress tests. They're worried about her heart."

"Oh!" Maria's hand flew to her mouth. *"Qué pasa?"*

"She's okay for now. But I don't know what will happen." She glanced away, wiping her stinging eyes with the back of her hand.

Maria stroked her wrist and told Lola about what had happened to Renaldo, about him getting fired, and all the trouble in town. And then they didn't talk anymore. It seemed they had said enough. They had spoken in a way that they never had before, or that Maria hadn't even know she could do. It was like emptying out an old chest of discarded things—all her disappointments, ugly, tired, embarrassing. They both felt exhausted, but also a little relieved.

"Have you seen Jaya?" Lola finally asked.

"Once or twice." She swallowed. "I tried to talk to her, but she brushed me off."

"We have to call her."

Maria lifted her face to Lola. "You think?"

She nodded. "Definitely."

They both gazed out the plate glass window, searching the dim streets. As if somewhere among the moving shapes, commuters streaming along the pavement, nannies heading home to the train, high schoolers bowed down with backpacks, their friend could be found.

# Chapter 44

"You're going to what?"

Jaya said it again gently, as if reading out loud directions on a cake mix box. "Come August we're going to move. Mama says after the school year is done. That way I can spend one summer month here, and then get ready to start high school in Richmond Hill."

"But you can't!" Lola couldn't believe it. They were meeting in the Vitales' laundry room, and she stared sadly at the plastic bowl of chips and cream cheese dip that she'd laid out on the folding table. This was her little way of turning their reunion into a grand occasion. Now her plan seemed dumb, pathetic. Her friend was disappearing on her, for good. It wasn't fair.

The day before, while sitting in the diner, Lola and Maria had called Jaya. To their surprise, Jaya, her voice husky and low, had sounded glad to hear from them. Maria was even worried she was sick, there so much sniffling on the other end.

But now that they had actually gotten together, it wasn't going that well. Lola and Jaya just stood across from each other, leaned up against the humming machines, in tense silence. Jaya looked strangely beautiful. She must have lost weight in the last few weeks, for her jeans hung loose on her hips, and she had a mysterious gaunt-eyed look.

"You could say you were sorry," Jaya finally blurted out.

"I did. I tried to." Lola added, "You didn't have to treat me like a leper. It was bad enough the entire middle school hates me."

"But, Lola, to break into that house——"

"I know, it was stupid. I thought I was helping."

"Besides," Jaya added. "My mother told me I couldn't see you."

"You don't always listen to your mother. That's not being a friend."

To her surprise, Jaya nodded, solemnly. "You're right. But I'm here now."

Lola struggled to add, "And it was hard, with Rachel Meisner making everything worse——"

"*Mi querida,*" Maria interrupted, holding up a hand. "Sometimes you pick fights too. Besides, Rachel's not the problem. Not those other kids either. The whole point is . . ." She trailed off. "We're all here. Now. I don't want to be with anyone else. I just want to be . . . here. With you guys."

Lola was surprised by the tears that pricked her eyes.

"It'll be okay," Jaya interjected. "We can visit on weekends."

"Can't we do something to help?" Maria asked.

"It's too late," Jaya said.

Maria was furious. She leaped off her perch on the dryer and began to pace. She had a need to get out of this stuffy room, smelling of steam and Clorox, out into the sunny day. That had been happening a lot lately. Ever since she had gone to that meeting and showed up at the park with her little sign, she couldn't bear to stay quiet. Just being in a basement made her antsy and irritated. She didn't want to remain below, silent, in the dark.

"Enough of this," she declared. *"Vamos."*

It was just like the old days, pooling their coins and sharing a frappé. The weather had turned suddenly sultry. Girls strolled past in tank tops, flip-flops snapping at their heels. The ice cream shop overflowed with kids, the pavement crowded with a litter of strollers.

Though it felt good to be together again, it was different, too. For the past few weeks they'd been so separate, figuring out everything on their own. Now it was as if they were stitching the friendship back, but with sadder threads. They talked and suddenly realized there were lots of things they actually didn't know about one another. How really frightened Lola was about her mother. And Maria admitted how bad it was at home, especially with Renaldo. She even told about him slapping her.

"That's awful!" Jaya cried.

"What a bully!" Lola fumed.

"No, wait." Maria put up a palm. "He is, but——" She struggled to say what came next. "Guys, I know we go through a lot of the same things. But it's harder, for me." She took a breath. "For my family." Then she added softly, "Sometimes I'm even scared to go on the street alone."

Lola and Jaya, wide-eyed, fell silent as they walked. When they reached the middle school, they stretched out on the lawn, watching cars pass, children waving, splay-fingered, from their car seats; the high school track team jogged by in a flash of orange-striped nylon shorts. It was growing late. The first commuter train had arrived, disgorging parents who hurried past, talking on their BlackBerries about what to buy for dinner. All three girls had gone quiet and sober. It was time to go home, to help their own mothers. Still they lingered, not yet ready to pull apart.

"Hey!" Maria sat up on her elbow. "We should do that."

"What?"

She was pointing to the sign: SPRING FEVER DANCE.

Jaya smiled sadly. "I don't know. Especially after everything that's happened. It's too much."

"But that's the point! We can't let them do this to us." Then Maria pulled each of them close. Lola and Jaya felt it—her excitement, her fierce strength. It was like an electric current, drawing them tight.

"Who cares about those other kids?" she whispered. "I say we go to the dance. In our most gorgeous, best dresses. And we have the best night of our lives."

---

When Jaya walked into the apartment she went right up to her mother, who was sitting at the dinette table hemming a skirt, and said, "Mama, I want to go to the spring dance." She didn't ask. She just told her.

"But, Jaya, we're leaving——"

"I know. But that's the point. That's why I want to go. To say good-bye." She was surprised at her own firmness.

Mrs. Lal set down her needle and cloth. A gentle smile creased her face. She even showed a bit of excitement, as if remembering her own dressing-up for dances. "I tell you what. There's a Junior League rummage sale happening at the church this Saturday. We can find you something nice there."

Jaya's heart sank. That was the last place she wanted to buy a dress. But her mother was being so nice for a change, she felt she had to agree.

*"Por qué?"* Mrs. Alvarez asked when Maria explained about the spring dance. Why would she want to attend anything outside of the weddings and confirmations and baby showers that filled up their family weekends? When Maria explained that even Ernesto, a boy the family knew, was going, her mother relented. "All right," she agreed, and they found a dress she had worn to a cousin's *quinceañera*. "But you be a good girl. You don't dance with strangers."

That Saturday, Jaya and her mother descended into a church basement that stank of sweat and dust and was jammed with tables of knickknacks, books, old computers and printers, with women like her mother dragging heavy nylon bags along the floor. Her mother headed to a back room, her fingers flying expertly across the shoulders of dresses.

"Take a look at this." Mrs. Lal held up a long shiny brown dress, the top made of a crocheted knit. Not bad, but Jaya wasn't going to let on.

"Go ahead. Try it."

"But there's no dressing room!"

"Put it on over your clothes."

Jaya stripped off her cardigan and pushed her arms through the stretchy fabric. She looked ridiculous, her sneakers and jeans sticking out beneath the silky hem.

"Hi, Simone," someone called out.

Oh, God. Rachel Meisner was moving toward them, wearing a blue volunteer apron. "I thought that was you, Simone."

Jaya always found it odd that her mother was called Simone, but Rachel's mother was Mrs. Meisner.

"How do you do, Rachel." Her mother used her cool, formal voice. "You working here?"

Rachel shrugged. "My mom's idea. The Junior League and all." She said this as if *of course* Mrs. Lal should know—didn't she stay up all night thinking about Mrs. Meisner's schedule and volunteer commitments?

"We're trying to find a dress for Jaya. For the dance."

"Oh, yeah?" Rachel nodded toward the racks. "There's some cute stuff. My mom likes to cruise these things for her store." She went behind the counter and pulled out a hanger with a black dress made of layers of delicate scalloped lace. "I was saving this, but I bet it would fit you."

"Thanks." Jaya swallowed, hard, and numbly took the outfit.

"I know it's a little Goth, but my mom tells me it's actually worth a lot."

Even though Rachel was being nice for a change, Jaya wished, as she tried the dress on, that she could disappear beneath the stuffed bulge of heavy winter coats hanging in a rack beside her. She couldn't help it. She still felt like the maid's daughter, a woman who scrubbed out the lime deposits from the shower tile. She felt placed, stuck in a dusty secondhand groove, never able to budge.

Fortunately, the dress didn't fit.

Two days later, when Jaya woke, it was as if her mother had seen right into her dream. A maroon dress lay spread across the foot of her bed.

She lifted it up. It was made of slinky rayon, spaghetti-thin straps stitched to a band of wispy lace on the bodice. The shiny tags—from Lord & Taylor—were still dangling from the label. *How could she?* Jaya didn't even want to know.

Jaya took off her nightgown and put on the dress. The fabric slipped down around her waist and hips in a lush swoop; its wine color gleamed richly against her skin.

Her mother was sitting at the kitchen table, reading the

paper and blowing on her mug of hot coffee. She smiled as Jaya walked in.

"Perfect," her mother whispered. "Just perfect."

For Lola it was less of a fight. Ruth Dinerstein had told the Svetloskis to encourage anything that "integrates her into the social world of Meadowbrook." "Meddling garbage," Mr. Svetloski grumbled. But Nadia said, "She's going to have no friends if you let her go on like this." And for once Lola was actually grateful for her sister's intercession.

The evening of the dance, Nadia agreed to put on Lola's makeup and get her into a borrowed dress before heading to work.

"This is so stupid," Lola fumed, jabbing pins into her scalp to make a bun. "Why bother?" In a fit of rebellion, her hair was still wet and unbrushed, and the high heels, earrings, and loaner makeup case Nadia had picked out were in a tumble on the bed.

"Stand still," Nadia told her as she began drawing up Lola's hair. Then she gave her mascara and blush, and brushed glittery blue powder across her lids. She sternly swiveled her by the hips to face the mirror.

Lola let out a small, surprised gasp.

Nadia smiled approvingly. Lola's long, pale arms dangled at her sides. At her waist was a perfect bow. Her shoulders were creamy bare and elegant. She was beautiful.

"Ready?" Nadia asked.

"You bet," Lola said, and grinned.

*Chapter 45*

WELCOME, JAMES MADISON EIGHTH GRADERS! A satin banner floated over the Meadowbrook Country Club entrance; balloons clustered from the columns like hanging grapes.

A line of cars—SUVs, station wagons, BMW sedans—came gliding up the circular drive. In twos and threes and fours the eighth graders emerged, girls in satiny dresses, uncertain on their wedge heels, boys slouched into jackets they'd worn before only for confirmations and bar mitzvahs. Nobody looked quite right, but there was a sheen to them all, as if they were rehearsing for a next, bigger step in their lives.

Jaya, Maria, and Lola walked up the stairs and stood nervously on the gold-banded foyer carpet, feeling as if they'd passed through a silver curtain to Oz, the side of Meadowbrook they'd never seen. Before them was a glass atrium, and beyond, the azure oval of a swimming pool garlanded in twinkling white bulbs.

They could just make out the eddying swirl of dancers in the ballroom. The lights were dim, the raking pulse of a strobe making it hard to tell who was who. Comforting in a way. They stayed close to one another as they inched toward the food spread, nibbling miniature quiches, aware of the darkened bodies around them. Mr. Cohen and a few teachers were patrolling the edges of the scene, giving corny theatrical nudges to the boys huddled in a corner. *Go ahead. Give it a try. Dancing won't kill you.*

Anthony Vitale walked up in a suit that pulled at his shoulders, hair gelled into spikes that looked like peaks of black meringue, and he crushed a few ridged chips into his mouth. "You want to dance?" he asked Lola.

Lola froze. She had said she would come to this event. She hadn't actually thought she would have to dance. Right in the middle of the dance floor. In front of everyone.

"Come on," Anthony urged.

Lola looked panicked at Jaya, who took her hand. "We'll all go," Jaya said.

They slipped into the crowd. At least there was the cover of dark. But to go right into the sweaty center of James Madison Middle School? It was so much easier to be on the outside, mouthing off, criticizing. Jaya put a hand at the small of Lola's back, steered her deeper into the room. Anthony circled on the other side. And Maria and the boy Ernesto came near. Somehow Lola made her feet move on the varnished floor, losing herself in a teeming thicket of bodies. Every now and then the strobe light flashed, showing Anthony's grin, or the iridescent shine of Jaya's dress. They danced to two, four, seven songs. They shimmied; they bumped; they cracked up when Anthony suddenly dropped to the floor, kicked his legs out, and tried a break dance. They had never laughed so hard.

And as Jaya spun around, she thought, *If this is the last thing I remember about Meadowbrook, at least I'm leaving on a good note.*

It was break time for the deejay. Most of the girls left the dance floor, limp dresses sweat-lacquered to their thighs, and drank clear cups of sugary punch while the boys stripped off their jackets. A humid wind blew through the French doors, so everyone streamed out onto the patio. Here the glare of outdoor bulbs and round metal tables made it easier to clump into familiar groupings. While Lola went to the bathroom, Maria and Jaya drifted toward the low brick wall, where they could make out the golf course mounding softly in the dark.

Jaya remembered long ago, sitting with her father during their Sunday paint sessions, his easel propped open. Not far away had been a hotel, and she could usually hear the drift of music for the tourists. She could almost smell the jar of turpentine, see his oily dabs appear on his canvas. Would he ever have believed that his daughter would wind up here, so many thousands of miles away from Trinidad, in an expensive, grown-up dress?

Jaya had pulled so still into herself, she didn't even notice who was approaching her.

"Uh-oh," Maria whispered.

It was Rachel. Wearing a midnight blue dress that made her look like a long Grecian column. Around her neck was a choker made of twisted wire and navy beads; a matching bracelet wound up her wrist. She'd pinned her hair into a sloppy bun, strands trailing coyly down her cheeks, showing off long blue stone earrings that sparkled from her ears. Jaya wasn't sure how Rachel did it, but there was something both casual and sophisticated about her.

"Hey," she said. A few of her friends had gathered around her.

"Hello." Jaya's mouth was cottony, puckered-small.

"Funny seeing everyone in their getups. I wouldn't have recognized most people here."

"Uh-huh." Maybe if she just answered in monosyllables, Rachel would go away.

She lightly touched Jaya's strap. "So you *are* a size seven," she murmured. "I told my mom to give it to you. Looks cute."

Jaya felt her skin go raw. *It can't be. It can't.*

The other girls giggled.

"Glad to see it didn't go to waste."

"Idiot."

Jaya looked up to see Lola, who had just returned from the bathroom, standing behind Rachel. Her beautiful, pale arms were shaking.

When Rachel twisted around, her whole demeanor changed, her body now taut and mocking. "You say something, Lola?" Then she added, "I'm surprised you're here. I thought juvenile delinquents weren't allowed. They break you out so you could come?"

Maria put a hand on Lola's arm. Lola knew. She mustn't. If only for Jaya's sake.

Lola clenched herself tight, watching in misery as Rachel

and her friends drifted off into the dark, smiling, leaving the terrace for the golf course. It was the worst kind of magic. The Wicked Witch of the West had won. Again. She disappeared into a puff of contemptuous smoke, darkness popping with her scornful laughter.

Once they were gone, Jaya broke away and fled onto the back lawn. Crouched near the hedges, she wrapped her arms around her stomach, bent over her knees, and wept. Hard, bitter cries, the kind that no one should see. How could her mother do this to her? Take a castoff from Rachel Meisner! Pretend it was new! Hot stupid tears kept flooding out of her. And it was only when she had finally stopped crying and wiped her cheeks that she saw something glittering on the ground. She bent over and scooped it up, cool and teasing, into her palm. Then it came to her. A piece of memory, a tiny knot of an image. Sapphire and diamond loops, dangling from Rachel's earlobes.

Rachel Meisner was wearing Mrs. Harmon's earrings.

*Chapter 46*

"Unbelievable."

The girls sat together on a bench outside the country club, admiring the chip-encrusted earring, curled tight, like a sparkling snail, in Jaya's hand. Music and strobe lights still pulsed through the French doors and windows. But the girls had forgotten about the dance. This seemed too good to be true. The real thief, right under their noses!

"We should bring it back to Mrs. Harmon. Or call her nephew," Jaya said.

"No, we have to find out the whole story," Maria insisted. "Figure out how she got them in the first place."

"She?" Lola asked.

"Rachel." Jaya said this firmly. "She was the one wearing them. For sure."

"I don't know," Lola said.

"Why? Are you scared?" Maria asked.

Lola felt a hot flush. Then she nodded. "I guess. A little."

She thought about how a few minutes before, Rachel had gallivanted off onto the golf green without a care in the world. Losing the earring along the way. How fitting. And then Lola realized how much she let Rachel frighten her. That in some way, she agreed with how Rachel saw her. Some part of Lola, deep down, was ashamed. All that show-offy stuff she did was to hide that, yes, she was a housekeeper's daughter. And, yes, she did fold towels and sometimes mop the floor, and she didn't have a lot of money, and she didn't know too much about which braided belt was the one to buy that year. And that was the frightful power Rachel had over her.

The three looked at one another, nervous.

"Come, *mi querida*." Maria stood, tossed her hair back from her shoulders, which suddenly looked broad and strong. "She's just a girl."

They stood, brushed off their dresses, grabbed their tiny purses, and tiredly made their way through the crowded rooms of the country club and out the front entrance. Cars were starting to glide up in the drive, to pick up the chatty, exhausted eighth graders. They began to walk, down the block, tottering slightly on their heels, straps digging into their swollen feet. Maria shivered. She wished that she had brought a shawl to cover her bare calves and arms, as her mother had urged. As they began heading up the hill, a car shot past, honking, older boys shouting out the window. The girls huddled tighter. "Ooh, baby!" the boys called.

Maria's face crumpled; she looked stricken, terrified.

This time, though, it was Lola who reached out and gave the wrist squeeze. "It's okay," she told her.

*Chapter 47*

Monday afternoon Rachel was sitting on a stool behind the counter at Vamps and Vixens, her friends gathered around her. Maria was the bravest. She walked right up to the register and opened her palm. "Did you lose this?" she asked.

Rachel went pale. Her friends giggled.

"Maybe now your mother will lift your curfew and you can get out of this jail!" Madison joked.

"Shut up." Rachel warily turned to Maria, Jaya, and Lola. "Where'd you find it?" She reached out to grab the earring, but Maria pulled back her hand. She was thinking about how Genine asked questions—cool, calm, methodical. Not just taking the rosy surface, but pushing harder, deeper into things.

"Where did you get it?" Maria persisted.

Rachel shrugged. "It's from the store. My mom let me borrow them. She always does." But even as she said this, they could tell how embarrassed she was.

"Yeah, if you bring them back, Miss Can't Keep Track of Things," Madison said, laughing.

Rachel whirled around. "Will you please stop!" She gazed

at Jaya. "Listen, you can have the pair if you want. It's not a big deal. Like, we give you stuff all the time."

Jaya felt her skin prickle with shame. And then, for the first time, she saw how much Rachel needed to make others smaller. She remembered Rachel's room, her clothes, books, iPod, shoes, flung everywhere. A room of too much, as if she didn't know what do with it all. Her insides all jagged and dark and messy. No wonder she could be so mean. It was as if she were shooting those sharp pieces of herself at others, seeing if they hurt.

"Actually, we need to talk to your mother," Jaya said.

"Why?" She glanced nervously over her shoulder.

"We just do."

"You should come back another time. She's not here."

There was a clicking sound as a curtain of beads parted and Mrs. Meisner appeared. "Rachel, what's going on?"

"Oh, hello there," Mrs. Meisner said. She seemed to be searching for a name.

"Jaya."

"Yes, Jaya. Of course. What can I do for you, dear?"

Jaya pushed the earring across the counter. Mrs. Meisner looked sharply at her daughter, and snapped, "I thought you told me you lost it."

"It got found," Rachel whispered.

"I was just wondering," Jaya said. "They're so nice. Where did you get them?"

Mrs. Meisner thought for a moment, one finger balanced

on her chin. "Some old lady. I pick stuff up from estate sales." She smiled as she picked it up. "Yes, it is lovely. Those sapphires almost look real. I'd actually put them aside in my desk, when Rachel decided to borrow them for the dance." She glared at her daughter.

Maria pressed in. "Did you by any chance find a brooch that goes with the earrings?"

Mrs. Meisner looked puzzled. Then she reached down and pulled out a velvet tray covered with a jumble of costume jewelry on the tray. "Hmm. No, I don't remember that. I guess not. Why do you ask?"

Jaya swallowed. This time she would have to find the words and say out loud exactly what she meant. She couldn't duck away into her own head. She couldn't disappear into a sad memory. "Mrs. Meisner, you know how my mother works for you and all." Jaya paused. "She . . . she lost a job. Some people said she stole those earrings. And a brooch."

"Oh, dear." The room went quiet. She could see the upset in Mrs. Meisner's eyes. "I'm so sorry, Jaya."

Jaya couldn't speak. Her cheeks were flaming hot. But she had done it. She had said the worst, right in front of Rachel. She hadn't disappeared.

Lola stepped forward. "Do you think maybe you could hold them for us? And write some kind of note saying how you bought them?" Lola was thinking so fast, she wasn't actually sure of her plan.

"Of course. Whatever I can do. I'd be happy to." She shook

her head. "Would you like me to write something quick, right now?"

"Yes, please."

Mrs. Meisner gave her daughter a caustic look. "Hear that, missy? She said 'please.' A rare word in our house."

Jaya could hardly breathe as Mrs. Meisner pulled out a pad of paper and swiftly wrote a note. "Some people," she muttered. "Making snap judgments." Clearly she was putting all her anger into her words. Then she slipped it into an envelope and handed it to Jaya. "I hope this helps. And, please, have your mother call me."

"Thank you." It was all Jaya could do not to cry right there. It was so surprising, this sudden kindness from adults.

As they left, they could hear Mrs. Meisner yelling at her daughter, "I don't know what the deal is, Rachel, but I've had it! My inventory isn't some kind of candy store for you. Or your friends, either. They work here and make themselves useful, or they get their butts out."

As they walked down the street, for once it was Jaya who knew what to do. She knew they had only half the story. The brooch could be anywhere, sold off to another buyer from the sale. Still, she had a hunch. It was like one of her father's unfinished paintings. The outside strokes were done. But there were still details that needed to be filled in, on the inside. The picture of what had happened at Mrs. Harmon's house wasn't whole yet. And it wasn't just the brooch that was missing. Something more was left. A piece of doubt. A last detail. A thread of dark yearning that had spun loose that day she'd spied her mother at the vanity table trying on the jewelry.

"We have to go to Mrs. Harmon's house," Jaya said firmly.

"Oh, no," Lola said. "With all the trouble I've been in, I can't go within a thousand feet of there."

But Jaya knew. The answer still lay in that house.

Then Maria put a hand on each of her friends' arms and smiled. "I have an idea."

*Chapter 48*

It isn't hard, if you're a daughter of a maid or nanny, to become one.

You know how to draw your hair back neat and fix your face into a serious but gentle expression. You show them with your eyes that you're responsible. You wear your most sturdy shoes and bring a stash of rubber gloves. If you buy some detergent, you remember to leave the change and receipt on the kitchen counter.

You make your hands useful. You plump the pillows and chase the dust bunnies out of corners, even if they don't ask you to. You remind them about a new container of Ajax and straighten their underwear drawer, just for extra. You arrange the children's stuffed animals in a pretty circle. You coax your voice to please. You show that you can be in charge but be quiet and take orders too. You slip inside their lives, hand in glove, as invisible as a breeze through a window, so they know you're there—and not there.

Mrs. Alvarez led the girls up the path to the porch, where Mr. Salerno was standing. Another man was carrying in huge flats of cardboard boxes. "Get ready for a long day," he told them.

"*Cómo?*" Mrs. Alvarez asked.

"The way it works is this: The estate people left everything. It's our job to do the final cleanup." He pointed to the big green Dumpster in the driveway. "Broken stuff, leftover furniture, goes there. All the personal effects in the boxes, set on the porch for pickup by the Salvation Army."

"We will take care," Mrs. Alvarez said.

"That's good," Mr. Salerno replied. "'Cause this place has to be ready by tomorrow morning for the walk-through."

"Why?" Maria asked.

"They're closing on the place."

"What's a closing?"

"The official sale, when one owner buys it from the other. The bank signs off and so forth. But the new owner does a walk-through right before. That's why everything's got to be clean and cleared out. You don't want some last-minute haggling at the lawyer's office." He looked at his watch. "Listen, I've got a couple of other jobs to see about. You girls keep me posted."

The minute his truck backed out of the driveway, they hurried inside. And stopped, as if pressed back by an invisible hand. The place was eerily empty. There was only one piece of furniture, a couch set back against the bare wall, with a sign, PICKUP 4 P.M. In the middle of the room were a few boxes— probably what hadn't gotten sold at the estate sale—filled with items like dusty canning jars and frayed pot holders.

*It's just a house,* Jaya told herself.

Maria nudged Jaya from behind. "Come on," she whispered.

The girls streamed through the strangely bereft rooms, their voices echoing off the walls. Mrs. Alvarez began dumping garbage into thick plastic bags, and they made their way upstairs to the bedrooms. There they found a forlorn mattress leaned up against a wall and a few more boxes, showing the nubs of old shoes.

While Maria helped her mother and Lola went up into the attic to check for any last items, Jaya headed for Mrs. Harmon's bedroom. Almost everything was cleared out. The last time she'd been in the bedroom was when she'd been helping her mother and she had watched her sit at the vanity table and pin the brooch to her collar and put the earrings on. The earrings were safely wrapped in tissue paper and at Vamps and Vixens. Clearly her mother hadn't stolen them. Now they needed the rest of the proof, an incontrovertible brick in their wall of defense. But standing here, Jaya wavered. There was some gap here. Even if they did find the brooch, Jaya was still shadowed by the guilty thought that her mother had done something wrong, though she wasn't sure what.

She noticed that the closet door was yawning open. That was different. It was the only closet with a lock and key, where valuables had been kept. Obviously it had been cleared out. An old vacuum was propped against the jam. And on the shelf was a box wrapped in a rubber band. As Jaya reached up and pulled the box down, it made a jangling noise as she brought it to the floor. Written on the lid, in her mother's handwriting, was the word "Valuables." When she opened it, though, she could see there was nothing valuable inside: buttons, a badge from the garden club, a lot of cheap rhinestone brooches, large bead necklaces, and earrings of colored glass. She put it aside. There was nothing here.

She looked back one more time and noticed a small pile in the corner—a few folded bedsheets, a broken lamp. And another shoe box, similar to the one from the closet. She squatted down. This one said "Costume Pieces" on the lid. Inside she found some wadded-up tissue. And, to her surprise, there was one small gold band, with an inscription inside. A gold locket. Good stuff, she thought, and dug underneath, pulling out a black velvet pouch swelling with something heavy and bumpy. She untied the satin ribbon and pulled out the object. It was the brooch, shaped like two arabesques, diamonds and sapphires winking in the filigreed gold.

Somehow, Jaya realized, the box lids must have gotten switched. The box with the costume jewelry had been shown to the appraiser, who had immediately seen it stripped of good pieces. Much of the real jewelry had been sold as junk at the estate sale, to sharp-eyed customers like Mrs. Meisner. Jaya could just picture it. She'd been to enough rummage sales with her mother to imagine the spread of old-lady jewelry, of twisted gold brooches and fussy earrings jumbled alongside a curling iron. Mrs. Lal always said, *Jaya, you'd be surprised at the things people throw out around here.*

For once, she realized, her mother was right.

Even from far away Jaya could see Mrs. Harmon and her nephew, he struggling to push the wheelchair on the white gravel.

Mrs. Harmon's face brightened when she saw the three girls. "Jaya!"

Andrew Cramer flushed, wheels jouncing on the tiny stones.

"And your friends! I knew you'd make up."

Jaya stepped forward. She took a breath. *Fill it in slowly,* she told herself. So she explained everything that had happened since Mrs. Harmon's stroke, taking her time. She wasn't scared at all. Lola, staying quiet, handed Mrs. Harmon the box with the wrong lid, and the letter from Mrs. Meisner.

Mr. Cramer still looked surprised. "I—I don't understand," he stammered.

"You made a mistake," Maria said. "It's not as if people are always good. But you jumped to conclusions. And you shouldn't have."

The whole time Mrs. Harmon listened quietly. She squeezed the rubber handle of her wheelchair with her good hand. She stared at the box, at the wads of tissue, and finally at Jaya. Then, in her funny nasal voice, she said to her nephew, "You are a ninny."

*Chapter 49*

For their last session Ruth Dinerstein was wearing a blouse that looked like wet newsprint grafted onto silk, and she had the biggest, broadest smile on her face. Positively positive, Lola thought. Now, this was a first. Usually she had a little skeptical furrow in her brow, as if raking over every word, doubting how Lola put things.

"So," she said, still grinning, "that took a lot of guts."

Lola shrugged. "I guess."

"You've certainly made your mark, Lola. You and your friends. Isn't that what you wanted?"

Again Lola shrugged. What was with her therapist today? Did she take some kind of happy drug? Or did she think that Lola's recent bout with success meant she'd be pulling in a better hourly fee? Lola couldn't understand what all the fuss was about.

But life, as far she could tell, remained the same. The doctor said her mother was going to have to stop the heavy lifting at the Vitales'. The job was too much of a strain on her heart. Her father was still a pathetic mess, and chances were the family would be going on public assistance and food stamps. Another great American tradition, Lola thought morosely.

"Look, Lola. That took a lot of initiative. Helping your friend. Going into the house. You must be proud of yourself."

"I wasn't supposed to be there. We were kind of stealing. What's the difference between before and now?"

"I'm talking about something else. The feeling that you've accomplished something. That you had a hunch and you followed it through. Is there some reason why you can't acknowledge this success, even to yourself?"

"I guess." Lola wasn't sure why, but she didn't have anything more to say. Usually she couldn't shut herself up. Words streaked out of her in a hot, fizzy stream. But today she felt tired, a comet that had momentarily flared in the sky. Sure, it was fun to slip the brooch into a Ziploc bag and bring the whole thing to Mrs. Harmon; sure, she fantasized about all of the kids in the lunchroom nudging one another and whispering "ooh" and "ah," but she didn't trust any of it. She would soon go back to her decline toward obscurity and freakishness. Jaya would move away.

"Everyone still hates me," she finally declared.

Ruth Dinerstein smiled. "Is that what bothers you? That you're not popular?"

"Of course not," Lola said. "Haven't you been listening to me all these weeks? They're a bunch of spoiled, lazy idiots. They know nothing. Why should I want to be liked by them?"

Ruth Dinerstein pulled down her stretchy newsprint

blouse and began to speak, softly. "Lola, you spend so much time hating those kids. The kids who have everything. The Americans. But you don't realize. You have something they'll never have. Something they can never buy. A real fire inside you."

And then Ruth Dinerstein did the most remarkable thing. She got up from her leather therapist chair, walked across the tasteful three-foot rug that separated them, and briefly laid her palm on Lola's head.

"You lucky, lucky girl," she whispered.

That lovely word Ruth Dinerstein had given Lola—*lucky*—twirled through her as she got off the bus. A quiet filigreed sound, lifting over the town with its little white church steeple, its clapboard houses nestled against the rising hills. Hers, in a way. Lucky.

Lola knew she needed to get back home, but even from two blocks away she could see the hulking shadow of an excavator, bent over like a yellow dinosaur, near Mrs. Harmon's house. She hurried up the hill and stood right outside the garden gate. The scene reminded her of those colorful books she'd seen in the houses where her mother and all the nannies worked, variations of dump trucks and steamrollers.

The dinosaur throttled to life, unfolding its scoop. The crane lifted up over the lopsided garage, and its metal arm swung out and sank its teeth into the roof. The small building collapsed easily, like a softened cake, shingles spattering onto the grass.

Two more swings of the arm, the frame began to shimmy, and a whole side smashed downward. Dust plumes rose into the air. Half the garage was down now, the trellis crushed under a torrent of falling plaster. The men let out a shout, the crane was turned off, and they carted away the debris to a waiting Dumpster.

Before she could help herself, Lola was running across the street to a pickup truck, where Mr. Vitale leaned over the hood, busy with one of his assistants, poring over a huge set of blueprints. *Stay calm,* she told herself.

"Hey, Mr. Vitale?"

"Yeah?" He looked up, surprised.

"Um, do you have to tear down that house?"

"What house?"

"The old lady's one. Mrs. Harmon's. Can't you, like, donate it to the town?"

Her words began to skid out, lightning-fast, overexcitable. "I know you can do it. Please. I've been in your office. I've mailed your invoices. I've seen what you can pay for. It can't be just auditoriums and baseball teams. You gotta save the important stuff too."

He threw a pencil down. "For Chrissakes, Lola. I was just tearing down the damn garage before it kills someone. We're taking a look at the rest. Especially while they figure out this historic registrar business."

"Oh." She dropped her hands to her sides. She'd done it again. Gone overboard.

Then she noticed Mr. Vitale was shaking. Was he angry? No,

she realized, he was laughing. "You don't have to laugh at me," she mumbled.

"I'm not. It's just, if I could bottle that passion of yours, Lola, I'd be rich."

Straightening up, he walked over and touched her arm gently. She felt him soften as he guided her away from the site, sprinkling bits of sparkling magic father dust. "Jesus, Lola," he whispered. "You are something else."

"I know," she replied, rubbing a sleeve over her stupidly wet eyes.

"And we're here for you. Don't forget that."

This time she couldn't stop the tears that flowed, hard and fast, down her cheeks. "I know that, too," she replied hoarsely.

*Chapter 50*

Maria woke up Sunday morning to find her mother already dressed, sitting at the table, reading her Bible. Mrs. Alvarez had had her hair done the day before, and it was crimped into waves at her nape. Around her neck was a strand of imitation pearls. "You come with me to church," her mother told her.

"But, Mami, I promised I'd meet my friends—"

In fact, she'd also planned to squeeze in finding Tash before she met up with Lola and Jaya. The Frisbee team would be practicing at Grove Field today. It had been more than a week since he'd stood her up over the protest, but she had been obsessing about Tash for days, ever since they'd found the jewelry. She had to see him one more time, before school let out. If Jaya could stand up to Mr. Cramer, she had some standing up to do too.

Mrs. Alvarez didn't look up from her Bible. *"Es necesario."*

Maria pulled on a new pair of pants, ran a brush through her hair, and accompanied her mother to the bus stop. It had been a long time since they'd gone to church together. This was a new one that her mother had joined a few months before, since going back to Union City was becoming too much of an ordeal every Sunday.

The bus was mostly empty, grinding slowly along Haley Avenue for all the local stops. The only people who got on were cleaning women and janitors, men in their navy blue or olive green jackets, an occasional group of women headed for church. She heard mostly Spanish and sometimes Portuguese. Back when they'd lived in Union City, Maria used to accompany her mother on the bus to the jobs in the suburbs, sometimes falling asleep on the jouncing seats during the long ride back. Still, she'd liked it. Her mother would read her Bible, lips moving silently, and allow Maria to eat her supper out of a plastic container, like a lot of the other passengers, the smells sifting up in the warm bus aisle. Sometimes they called across and even compared recipes. It seemed like ages since she and her mother had sat like this, side by side, friends almost, and she felt sad for letting it go.

As they stepped off the bus, Mrs. Alvarez turned to her daughter. She had worn her church suit and the only pair of high heels she owned. Her Bible was zipped carefully into its worn silk case. Maria touched her mother's shoulder, felt the little cotton padding beneath.

"I got more jobs," Mrs. Alvarez told her. "Through that man's company."

"That's great!"

Her mother still seemed to have more to say. "You do not do that," Mrs. Alvarez said.

on you. It may not be a big deal for you. But it is for us." Then she added, "For me."

Tash's face seemed to be covered in a red mottled rash, making him look, for the first time, a little ugly. She noticed how small his ears were. "Sorry," he mumbled. He sounded about four years old.

As Maria watched him cross the park and get into the Adlers' silver car, which soon went gliding down the street, a terrible sadness crashed through her. She thought of her mother walking away from her after church. And this flawed angel, slipping away. Just a boy with baby skin. Not a man, like Renaldo, with a hard mouth and hard eyes. That's what was so tough about this country. It was hard and soft. You smashed your heart on its hardness, and you knew, to survive, you'd break some hearts too.

# Chapter 51

Jaya sat down at the dinette table. It was as if everything inside her had gone still. She thought about how good she'd gotten in her drawings these few weeks. Steadier. A slow filling in. She felt sure and solid. She set the little bag down on the table, the brooch and earrings inside, along with a note from Mrs. Harmon.

Her mother, working at the stove, hadn't noticed. Mrs. Lal had already started pulling things down from the walls in the kitchen. The Peg-Board was stripped of the soup ladle and spatula, the set of quilted blue pot holders, the pots and pans that they had bought, a dollar apiece at a yard sale.

"Mama," she called.

Mrs. Lal didn't move.

"Mama, I need to talk to you."

Finally she turned around, wiping her hands on her apron. Jaya had always admired her mother's hands. They were broad, the fingers long, like a pianist's. Jaya had seen them do so many things: scrub bathtubs, peel potatoes, snap sheets on beds. She'd seen them fly up into fists when she was angry; touch her father's hair, one last time, before his older brother put the flame to the funeral pyre.

"What is it?"

Without a word Jaya pushed the bag toward her mother, watching steadily as her mother unwrapped the colored tissue paper, and the brooch and earrings dropped into her palm. "Oh, my," she gasped.

For Jaya, too, it was almost a shock, remembering that day when her mother had sat fingering the jewelry at the vanity.

Mrs. Lal opened the note and read:

Andrew says I am crazy to entrust
these valuables to a fourteen-year-old
girl. But he has made a mess of things
as it is.
Dearest, I had no idea. Look and see
they are found. Come bring them back
and make me your licorice tea.

Yours, Abigail

Mrs. Lal raised her eyes. "How on earth . . . ?"

At first Jaya didn't say anything. She listened for the careful rhythm inside. Then she began the story: how she and Lola and Maria had wanted to figure out what had happened. How they'd seen the earrings on Rachel Meisner, traced them to the estate sale, and gone back once more, to find the brooch. And how Mrs. Harmon had let her bring the jewelry, so her mother could see them for herself. She took her time explaining. She didn't leave anything out. Except the doubts, gnawing deep inside. *Don't be afraid,* she told herself.

Her mother turned the brooch and earrings over in her palm. "I can't believe it," she whispered.

"That's not all," Jaya said finally.

Her mother stared at her, waiting.

"I thought you did it. I thought you stole them."

Nothing happened. The ceiling didn't blow down, wind scouring them both. Instead, just a simple quiet.

Finally her mother smiled, eyes glistening. "I thought about it. For a while."

"Really?" She waited for her mother to speak.

"You have no idea. How beautiful I felt, putting on these things. For a little while I just let myself go. Pretended that was me, wearing those expensive earrings, having enough money."

"What happened?"

"Honestly, after that, I forgot all about them. I put them aside. I think that's how it got all mixed up. I realized that after. But it was too late. They got labeled the wrong way."

"As costume jewelry."

She nodded. "It was just a moment. I couldn't help it." The wetness in her eyes began to spill over. "It's not fair. I didn't know I'd feel this way, coming here. Scrubbing the toilet of some woman younger than me. They treat me like . . . like I'm never going to be anything else. Most of the time, I don't care. I can take it. But sometimes . . ."

Her mother was pressing the heels of her hands into her eyes. "What a stupid, stupid mistake. Now you see where that leaves us."

Jaya's own hands felt clumsy as she reached across the table and tried to comfort her mother. But this was so uncommon, so strange between them, that she could only offer a few stiff pats. And she realized, even in comforting her mother, she wasn't done with all she had to say.

"Ma, there's something else." She paused. "I don't want to go. I don't want to leave Meadowbrook."

Her mother tiredly lifted up her head. "But, Jaya. Sometimes you seem so unhappy."

Jaya was surprised to hear her mother had even noticed. "Maybe I was. But it's different now. I have friends."

Mrs. Lal wiped her eyes with the edge of her sleeve. "It's no good anymore. You see what's happened. I have no work. It's gotten tough around here. I don't know how I'm going to make it up again."

"Mama, Daddy wouldn't want it. He wouldn't want you to give up. To run away from this place. I know it."

Then she let her voice go down low as she imitated her father, the patois rolling out softly. "Come on, darlin'! What's life worth unless you keep up some dream, huh?"

Her mother was weeping now, but she made no sound. Jaya didn't say anything more. The shadow between them seemed to stretch even bigger. They seemed to be on opposite sides of the room now, separated by a watchful quiet. Then her mother stood, came to her, and rested her hand softly on her head. It was the most natural gesture ever. "I miss your father," she whispered.

Jaya grew very still. "I know," she replied. "I do too."

# Chapter 52

It seemed like summer had arrived in Meadowbrook, as sudden and loud as a last-period bell. How had Jaya not noticed it before? The day lilies burned bright orange and yellow. The trees flushed green. Main Street was festive with pink T-shirts and shiny nylon shorts.

Friday afternoon, almost the end of the school year, and the middle schoolers shot down the steps with rocket-fire energy, tackling one another on the pavement, sprawling on the metal chairs outside the pizza place. The only thing pinning them to the earth was their superheavy packs bulging on their backs. High school seniors moved down the street looking slightly dazed and pleased with themselves, not quite believing it was nearly over. It was as if they were about to graduate not just from high school but from the whole town.

As Jaya walked up the hill, the air was filled with weekend chores: the steady insect *hum-hum* of lawn mowers, fathers home early, putting up the window screens, mothers shaking out cushions on the deck chairs. The whole town was unfurling, greeting the warm days ahead. Later there would be ice cream trucks and the chlorine-rich days at the swimming pool.

Crossing the street, Jaya spied a father tossing a ball to his son on a front lawn, giving him tips on his throwing arm. The old feeling returned: bleak air, pushing through her skin. Who was she kidding? She could disappear any minute. Not like these people. They were solid; they knew they belonged here.

Then she spotted Lola shifting impatiently in front of Starbucks, holding their shared frappé, Maria worriedly scanning the passersby.

"Hey!" Lola was waving.

"We thought you weren't going to come!"

"Of course I'm here."

It felt good to walk together, just the three of them, elbows bumping, sipping their cold drink, their talk spooling into the lowering dusk. They walked and chatted, their talk looser, stretching themselves further than before.

"So, you know what I did?" Lola asked as they began to climb the hill.

"Uh-oh."

"I told Mr. Vitale not to tear down Mrs. Harmon's house."

"Lola!"

"Are you crazy?"

Maria said sternly, "Lola, you can't just do *loco* things like that. You have to be patient. Just slow your brain and body."

"Okay." Lola grinned. "From now on, I promise, I'll listen more."

"Yeah, right." Jaya laughed.

"No, really. I'm getting better at all that stuff. Like the Vitales. They're not so terrible. They're . . . good."

"Even Anthony junior?" Maria asked.

"Even him," Lola said, smiling.

They'd arrived at a little semicircular park, its bench emblazoned with carved hearts and spray-painted names. Make-Out Point, it was called by all the high school kids. Maria, Lola, and Jaya had rarely come here before. It seemed off-limits, somehow.

Suddenly Lola seized both their arms. "Oh my God, guys. In all this craziness I forgot to tell you what happened with my sister."

"Nadia?"

"Yeah, well, Miss Better Than Us All got called back on an audition. And she actually got a part in some TV commercial! Selling a hybrid car or something." She turned to Maria, genuinely excited. "You wait, Maria. One day she'll be a famous actress and you'll go to the Academy Awards with me, and you'll need a dress!"

Maria flushed, a little angry. "Stop it. It's not just about dresses and all that. Next year, when we go to high school, I want to do stuff. Like maybe join something. A club."

"Come on, just a tight little silk number?"

Maria cracked a small mischievous smile. "Well, maybe, if we go to the awards, I can be like Angelina Jolie. Giving to all those causes."

All three burst into laughter. They jumped onto the grass and pretended to walk down the red carpet, standing in front of the cameras and boasting about how they always knew Lola's sister would be famous.

"No, wait, check this out," Maria insisted and climbed onto the bench, arms out. "I want to thank all of my fans and supporters for electing me president of the student council—"

"And beating Tash Adler!"

Maria blushed. "Yes, and I also want to acknowledge my supertalented friend, Jaya Lal, who has won every single art prize—"

"Bravo!" Lola clapped.

They laughed and laughed until their ribs ached and they finally dropped down onto the bench, exhausted, amazed that they could be so easy in this little corner of Meadowbrook, where the bench slats were carved with stories and secrets, a place they never imagined could be theirs, too.

"Seriously," Lola said, turning to Jaya. "What did your mother say? Are you going to move?"

They wiped their eyes, grew quiet.

"She said she'll give it through the summer." Jaya tapped her bag, showing a sheaf of bright pink flyers. "She even gave me these."

"I guess that's better than nothing."

"And I was thinking maybe I'll try and get a Saturday job. I saw this place . . . this art store. I thought I'd fill out an application."

They sat for a few minutes, listening to a truck rattle down the hill.

"And Renaldo?" Lola asked.

Maria stared at her hands. "It's not so good. Tío says nobody's going to hire him if he has a record. Even for something small."

Staying here wasn't going to be easy, Jaya thought as she settled back against the bench. Not for any of them. They'd be patching it together, week to week, no guarantees. She'd still hear that panic in her mother's voice every month when it came time to pay the bills. But Jaya knew she wanted to try.

Meadowbrook spread before them, with its steeples and parks. It was as if she were seeing the way her father wanted her to, dusk making the colors even more vivid. The hydrangeas bloomed a deep violet, the lights of Main Street a warm, glimmering strand. She thought of all three of them, coming on airplanes, from three different parts of the world. Living in apartments with slanted floors. Making the most of things. She saw their mothers rising when the windows were still dark and foggy, pulling on their stretchy rubber gloves, pushing mops, folding towels. While they learned to put the rice pot on the stove, phone the electric company, feel these walls, these streets, as their own. To call this place home.

# Acknowledgments

Thanks to my hardworking readers: Marc Aronson, Christina Baker Kline, and Gail Hochman. Namrata Tripathi swept in and gave the manuscript a fresh wind of enthusiasm and generous feedback. My hardworking au pairs kept Sasha and Rafi content while the manuscript was being written: Edith Acuna Enriquez, Dijana Andrijasevic, Luana Ribeiro dos Santos, and Juliana Narcizo; Anna Lopez kept my home, and thus my mind, tidy. Purva Bedi's lovely performance gave me new insight into the material, as did the nannies, who shared their stories and inspired me. When I was a newcomer to the suburbs, my students fine-tuned my ears and eyes. Finally, I am grateful to the New Jersey State Council on the Arts for a fellowship, and to William Paterson University for much-needed time to complete this book.

Turn the page
for another compelling story from the
*other side*
of the American dream:

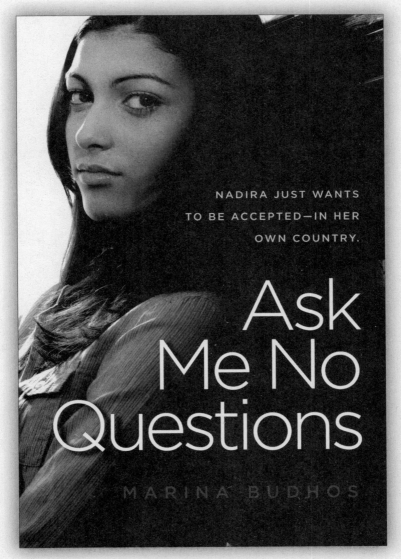

NADIRA JUST WANTS
TO BE ACCEPTED—IN HER
OWN COUNTRY.

Ask
Me No
Questions

MARINA BUDHOS

Available now from
ATHENEUM BOOKS FOR YOUNG READERS

# ONE

WE DRIVE AS IF IN A DREAM.

Up I-95, past the Triborough Bridge, chunks of black ice floating in the East River. Me and Aisha hunched in the back, a green airline bag wedged between us filled with Ma's *luchis* and spiced potatoes. Abba in the front, clutching the steering wheel, Ma hunched against the rattling door.

We keep driving even as snowflakes clump on the wipers, and poor Abba can barely see. *Coconut flakes,* Ma jokes. *We'll go outside and scoop them up, and I'll make you some* polao. But the jokes lie still in our throats.

Up the East Coast, past all these places I've seen only in maps: Greenwich, New Haven, Providence, Rhode Island. Hour after hour, snow slanting down. And in my head, words keep drumming: *Special Registration. Deportation. Green card. Residency. Asylum.* We live our lives by these words, but I don't understand them. All I know is we're driving straight through to that squiggle of a line on the map, the Canadian border, to apply for asylum.

Unspoken questions also thud in our minds. *What happens if we get stopped and they see Abba's expired license? Should Ma wear slacks and a sweater so she doesn't stand out so much? Should Aisha drive, even though it's supposed to be a secret that she knows how?* We ask some of these questions out loud, and others we signal through our eyes.

When we reach Boston, Aisha wakes up and starts to cry. That's where she hoped she'd live one day. Aisha always knew that she wanted to be a doctor going to Harvard Medical School. Even back in Dhaka she could ace her science and math exams, and when Abba was in Saudi Arabia working as a driver, he used to tape her reports to his windshield and boast about his daughter back home who could outdo all the boys. In those days Abba wasn't afraid, not of anything, not even the men who clucked and said Aisha would be too educated to find a husband, or the friends who worried that he'd be stuck with me, his fat and dreamy second daughter. Sometimes I hate being the one who always has to trail after Aisha. But sometimes it feels safe. I'm nestled in the back, not seen.

Ma pats Aisha on the hand. "Don't worry," she whispers. "All this, it's just for a while. We'll get you in to a university in Canada."

"McGill!" Abba booms from the front seat. "A top-rate school!"

"It's too cold!" I complain.

Aisha kicks me. "Shut up," she hisses, then speaks softly to my father's back. "Whatever you say, Abba."

Aisha and I, we never hit it off, really. She's the quick one, the one with a flashing temper whom Abba treats like a firstborn son, while I'm the slow-wit second-born who just follows along. Sometimes I think Abba is a little afraid of Aisha. It's like she always knew what she wanted, and he was put on this earth to answer her commands. Back in Dhaka when Abba wasn't sure about going to America, she cut out an article and put it in his lap: a story about a Bangladeshi girl who'd graduated top of her class in economics and now worked for the World Bank.

"We may be one of the poorest countries in the world," she told Abba. "But we're the richest in brains."

Abba laughed then. Where did an eight-year-old learn to say such things?

That's the way it always was. Oh, did you hear what the teacher said about Aisha today? "Your sister!" The other girls would whisper to me. "She's different." But what kills me is that Aisha always says the *right* thing. She asks Ma if she's low on mustard oil for cooking, or Abba if he asked the doctor about the better ointment for his joints.

It's hard to have a sister who is perfect.

In Portland, Maine, Abba pulls into a gas station. He

looks terrible: Dark circles bag around his eyes. He's wearing one of his favorite sweater vests, but after ten hours on the road it looks lumpy and pulled. Ma scrambles out of the car to use the bathroom. As she pushes across the station, I notice the pale bottom of her *shalwar kameez* flutter up around her jacket. She presses it down, embarrassed. The attendant is staring at her, the gas pump still in his hand. He's Sikh, with soft, almond shaped eyes, and he smiles at her sweetly, as if he understands, and Ma gets up her nerve and pushes inside the metal door.

After, she takes one look at the two of us and says softly, "We need to stop for some food. These poor girls, they look faint."

When we go inside the small diner, Ma looks funny sitting in the booth, drawing her cardigan across her chest, touching her palms to the ends of her hair. Even though Aisha and I hang out at Dunkin' Donuts and McDonald's all the time, my family rarely goes out to restaurants. Ma's always afraid that they'll ask her something and the English words won't come out right. Now she glances around nervously, as if she expects someone to tap us on the shoulders and tell us to leave. "What if they say no at the border?" she whispers. "What if Canada turns us down?"

Abba sighs, wearily rubbing his eyes. "It could happen. No one guarantees asylum."

We've been over this again and again. We know the risks. If Canada turns us down for asylum, we have to go back across the American border, and Abba will probably be arrested because our visas to America have long since run out. And then we don't know what could happen. Maybe one day we will get U.S. residency. Or maybe we'll just be sent back to Bangladesh. But maybe—just maybe—Canada will let us in.

Abba continues, "Look, Aisha has to begin university in the fall. This is for the best." But he doesn't sound so sure.

Aisha leans her head on Ma's shoulder, her frizzy hair falling in a tumble over her cheeks. "Don't worry, Ma. It'll be okay. We'll get to Toronto and you'll open your restaurant, right?"

A little burn of envy sears right through me. I don't know how Aisha does it, but she always cheers up my parents. Ma and Aisha look a lot alike: They're both fair skinned and thin, and they're these incredible mimics. Ma's always picking things up from TV, where she's learned most of her English.

"Abba, why don't you tell us a story?" Aisha asks.

Abba sits back, his fingers resting lightly on the Formica tabletop, his face relaxed.

I should have asked that. After all, it's usually me who sits around with the elders listening to their stories. Nights when Aisha's in her room studying, I'll sit curled next to Abba and Ma, my head against their legs, and they'll tell me about Bangladesh and our family. Even though we left when I was seven, sometimes if I close my eyes, it's as if I were right there. I remember the *boroi* tree outside our house, the stone wall where Ma slapped the wash dry, the metal cabinet where Abba kept his schoolbooks. Abba carries his stories carefully inside him, like precious glass he cradles next to his heart.

"I'll tell you about the stationery."

We all grin. We've heard this story before, but it's comforting—like sinking into the dense print of one of the old books Abba brought with him from Bangladesh.

"Your great-grandfather used to work as a printer. When he was old and ready to return to our village, the man he worked for gave him a box of the best stationery with his own name printed across the top. Grandfather used to keep that stationery in a special box with a lock. Even when he was old and blind, sometimes he brought it out, and we children would run our fingers over the raised print. Grandfather never wrote anyone with those pages. Who was he going to write to on that fine stationery with the curvy English print?

"After I saw your mother, I wanted to impress her. So I sneaked into my grandfather's room, and I stole a sheet of paper, used my best inkwell and pen, and copied out a beautiful poem. When Grandfather found out, he was furious!"

"Were you punished?" I ask.

Abba nods. "I was, and rightly so. Not only did I deceive my grandfather, but I was not off to a very good start with your mother! She thought I was a rich man who could write poetry. But I was only a poor student who could copy from books." He glances over at Ma. "And I'm still a poor man!"

"Hush," Ma scolds. But I can see she is pleased. She looks gratefully at Aisha, and my stomach twists with jealousy.

"Are you done with those?" I ask, pointing to the last of my sister's fries.

Her nose wrinkles. "No, greedy girl." And she pops the rest into her mouth.

I remember when we first arrived at the airport in New York, how tight my mother's hand felt in mine. How her mouth became stiff when the uniformed man split open the packing tape around our suitcase and plunged his hands into her underwear and saris, making us feel dirty inside. Abba's leg was jiggling a little, which is what it does when he's nervous. Even then we were afraid because we knew we were going to stay past the date on the little blue stamp of the tourist visa in our passports. Everyone does it. You buy a fake social security number for a few hundred dollars and then you can work. A lot of the Bangladeshis here are illegal, they say. Some get lucky and win the Diversity Lottery so they can stay.

Once we got here, Abba worked all kinds of jobs. He sold candied nuts from a cart on the streets of Manhattan. He worked on a construction crew until he smashed his kneecap. He swabbed down lunch counters, mopped a factory floor, bussed dishes in restaurants, delivered hot pizzas in thick silver nylon bags. Then Abba began working as a waiter in a restaurant on

East Sixth Street in Manhattan. Sixth Street is lined with Indian restaurants, each a narrow basement room painted in bright colors and strung with lights with some guy playing sitar in the window. They're run by Bangladeshis, but they serve all the same Indian food, chicken tandoori and *biryani*, what the Americans like. Every night Abba brought home wads of dollars that Ma collected in a silk bag she bought in Chinatown.

The thing is, we've always lived this way—floating, not sure where we belong. In the beginning we lived so that we could pack up any day, fold up all our belongings into the same nylon suitcases. Then, over time, Abba relaxed. We bought things. A fold-out sofa where Ma and Abba could sleep. A TV and a VCR. A table and a rice cooker. Yellow ruffle curtains and clay pots for the chili peppers. A pine bookcase for Aisha's math and chemistry books. Soon it was like we were living in a dream of a home. Year after year we went on, not thinking about Abba's expired passport in the dresser drawer, or how the heat and the phone bills were in a second cousin's name. You forget. You forget you don't really exist here, that this really isn't your home. One day, we said, we'd get the paperwork right. In the meantime we kept going. It happens. All the time.

Even after September 11, we carried on. We heard about how bad it had gotten. Friends of my parents had lost their jobs or couldn't make money, and they were thinking of going back, though, like my father, they'd sold their houses in Bangladesh and had nothing to go back to. We heard about a man who had one side of his face bashed in, and another who was run off the road in his taxi and called bad names. Still people kept coming for *pooris* and *alu gobi* on Sixth Street; still Abba emptied his pockets every night into Ma's silk bag. Abba used to say, "In a bad economy, people want cheap food. Especially cheap food with chili peppers that warms their bellies."

But things got worse. We began to feel as if the air had frozen around us, trapping us between two jagged ice floes. Each bit of news was like a piece of hail flung at us, stinging our skins. *Homeland Security. Patriot Act. Code Orange. Special Registration.* Names, so many names of Muslims called up on the rosters. Abba had a friend who disappeared to a prison cell in New Jersey. We heard of hundreds of deported Iranians from California and others from Brooklyn, Texas, upstate New York. We watched the news of the war and saw ourselves as others saw us: dark, flitting shadows, grenades blooming in our fists. Dangerous.

Then one day my cousin Taslima's American boyfriend came over and explained the new special registration law: Every man over eighteen from certain Muslim countries had to register. Saudi Arabia, Morocco, Pakistan, Bangladesh. Some did, and were thrown in jail or kicked out of the country. More and more we heard about the people fleeing to Canada and applying for asylum there, instead of going into detainment. Abba's friends came over in twos and threes. Ma served them sweets and *doodh-cha*—milky tea—and they'd talk. About starting again in the cold country up north. A new life. The Canadians are friendly, they liked to say.

"There comes a time," Abba said grimly, "when the writing is right there on the wall. Why should we wait for them to kick us out?" He added, "I want to live in a place where I can hold my head up."

One evening Abba came into our bedroom, a quiet, sad look on his face. "Take that down," he said to Aisha. He was pointing to her Britney Spears poster, the only one she was allowed. Ma opened the closets and folded all her saris and *shalwar kameezes* into the nylon suitcases we used when we came here. We could tell no one—not even our best friends at school—what we were doing.

Abba asked me to bring out my map of the northeast. After I laid the map open on the dining table, Abba showed us the thick arteries of highways, the spidery blue line of the border. "There," he said. "We have to go there and apply for asylum."

I swallowed, my throat very dry. What happens if they don't let us in? I kept thinking.

The next morning we woke to a scraping and coughing noise and saw the blue Honda by the curb.

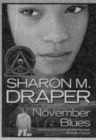

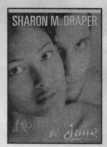

# PRAISE FOR JON M. SWEENEY'S BOOKS...

"Sweeney achieves a fine balance between excellent scholarship and sweet accessibility for every average reader. To learn the life of Francis, to learn to love that life, and at the same time to experience the time in which he lived, this is the book to read."

—Walter Wangerin, Jr.,
author of *St. Julian* and *The Book of God* (for *The Road to Assisi*)

"An informational yet personal account of the transformative power of the Catholic and Orthodox churches' special role models. Sweeney, in very accessible concepts and language, presents a marvelously contemporary and inclusive theology of sanctity and saints . . . both a miniature encyclopedia on saints and a book of spiritual reflection."

—Catholic Library World (for *The Lure of Saints*)

"A rich resource of information, insights and beauty. . . . Both critical and reverential, Sweeney offers tribute to a young woman of courage who became Mother of the Lord and then herself an icon for unending prayers of intercession, consolation and thanksgiving."

—Bishop Frederick Borsch,
Professor of New Testament and Chair of Anglican Studies,
Lutheran Theological Seminary (for *Strange Heaven*)

"This attractively presented little book is truly pocket-sized and portable, but full of rich content."

—The Living Church (for *The St. Francis Prayer Book*)

"Sweeney examines his story and its meaning with unusual humility. He doesn't claim superiority to the people he came from, only an inability to accept all that they taught him. . . . His tone is thankful and affirming, meant to shore up bridges rather than burn them down."
—Betty Smartt Carter,
Books & Culture (for *Born Again & Again*)

"[Sweeney's] book walks non-Catholics through the notion of seeing saints as prayer partners and understanding how saints are canonized. . . . In the end, he believes Catholics allow for the kind of spiritual mystery that, at times, better matches life experiences."
—The Dallas Morning News (for *The Lure of Saints*)

"Jon Sweeney is a fine, informative writer. He has a way of discussing a variety of religious matters in clear, common sense terms. . . . Highly recommended."
—Church and Synagogue Library Association

"Sweeney presents a lively mix of material on saints from all ages who have 'fertilized everything with God.'. . . Best of all, these profiles of holy men and women might inspire you to take more seriously your own calling and aspiration to live as a saint today."
—Spirituality and Health magazine (for *The Lure of Saints*)

"One imagines Popes John XXIII and John Paul II, both deeply devoted to Mary and to Christian unity, reading Strange Heaven with glad smiles and prayers of thanksgiving."
—*Crisis* Magazine

# LIGHT
## IN THE
# DARK
# AGES

*The Holy Conversation of Saints Francis and Clare*

# LIGHT
## IN THE
# DARK
# AGES

*The Friendship
of Francis and Clare of Assisi*

Jon M. Sweeney

PARACLETE PRESS
BREWSTER, MASSACHUSETTS

*Light in the Dark Ages: The Friendship of Francis and Clare of Assisi*

2007 First Printing

Copyright © 2007 by Jon M. Sweeney

ISBN: 978-1-55725-476-4

**Library of Congress Cataloging-in-Publication Data**
Sweeney, Jon M., 1967–
   Light in the dark ages : the friendship of Francis and Clare of Assisi / by Jon M. Sweeney.
      p. cm.
   Includes bibliographical references and index.
   ISBN 978-1-55725-476-4
   1. Francis, of Assisi, Saint, 1182-1226. 2. Clare, of Assisi, Saint, 1194–1253.
   3. Christian saints--Italy--Assisi--Biography. I. Title.
   BX4700.F6S93 2007
   271'.302--dc22
   [B]                                                                      2007007060

10 9 8 7 6 5 4 3 2 1

Published by Paraclete Press
Brewster, Massachusetts
www.paracletepress.com

Printed in the United States of America

FOR CHRISTINA

*with respect and affection*

# LIST OF ILLUSTRATIONS

"The Holy Conversation of Saints Francis and Clare,"
contemporary icon by Marek Czarnecki, reproduced in black and white
... frontispiece

*All of the other illustrations are reproductions of Giotto,*
*or School of Giotto, frescoes from Assisi, Padua, and Florence.*

# CONTENTS

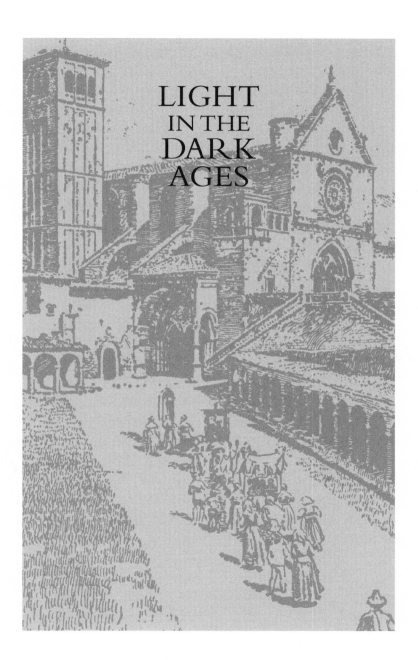

# LIGHT
## IN THE
## DARK
## AGES

CHAPTER

I

# BEGINNINGS

Wrapped in the colorful silks imported and sold by Peter Bernardone, most of the highborn girls in Assisi paid close attention to matters of courtship, honor, and family. Seasonal events in the cathedral church and the governor's estate occupied their minds, and their hearts were wooed by the songs of young would-be troubadours carousing in the streets below their bedroom windows after dark. Francis Bernardone was once one of those young men. But by all accounts, Clare Favorone was never one of those girls.

Francis and Clare were both children of Assisi, Italy, where being baptized into the Church was once the equivalent of citizenship. They came from what we would call upper-middle-class families. Clare was a young teenager when Francis began his slow process of conversion. She was about fifteen and he was twenty-seven when she first heard him preach about poverty and joy at the San Rufinus cathedral. Her family home bordered the great church, and she was accustomed to regularly attending services there. Hearing Francis preach probably stirred the beginnings of conversion. Feeling God's presence wouldn't have frightened her, for she was never easily frightened. Only two years later, Clare began her own rejection of vanity, self-interest, and wealth. She quietly renounced worldly affairs

3

in March 1212 and became the first woman to join Francis and his friars. These were simple gestures, but they were nevertheless recognized by Clare's contemporaries as the first marks of an independent woman.

The life of Francis is well-known, but Clare's less so. Her first biographer tells us that she secretly wore hair shirts—rough garments of asceticism and penance—from an early age, and while we may not take such a description as absolute fact, the point is that Clare was different.[1] She didn't pine for the latest fabrics and dyes that Peter Bernardone brought back with him from his trips to France. She wasn't looking anxiously for her future husband or counting the days until her wedding. From an early age, she seemed to others to be out of step with the expectations of a fortunate girl from a promising family.

Within four and one-half years of Clare's conversion, we have evidence from a letter written by Jacques of Vitry, who was elected the bishop of Acre in 1216 and traveled to Perugia upon the death of Pope Innocent III, that there were many vibrant communities of friars and sisters throughout Italy. Disappointed with the heresy and worldliness that he discovered during his travels in Italy, the Frenchman described the early Franciscans this way, as he discovered them for the first time:

> Many well-to-do secular people of both sexes, having left all things for Christ, had fled the world. They were called "Lesser Brothers" and "Lesser Sisters". . . . They are in no way occupied with temporal things, but with fervent desire and ardent zeal they labor each day to draw from the vanities of the world souls that are perishing, and draw them to their way of life. Thanks be to God, they have already reaped great fruit and have converted many. Those who have heard them, say: "Come," so that one group brings another. . . . During the day

they go into the cities and villages giving themselves over to the active life in order to gain others; at night, however, they return to their hermitage or solitary places to devote themselves to contemplation.[2]

And so it was. The Franciscan movement began in simple ways, with bold but modest intentions, and grew rapidly. The Franciscans presumed to live like Jesus. Francis, Clare, and their early followers were part of a select group of Christians through the ages who have been passionately spiritual and ardently practical at the same time. In the long history of faith, spiritual vitality has flowed best when humans have rediscovered Jesus and tried to replicate his life in their own. Moral and practical decisions have been infused with spiritual vitality in those eras when the words of Jesus were followed most closely.

The Franciscans' worldview praised beauty and ethics both. They were of one spirit with the first Christian churches in Rome and Asia Minor, the Desert Fathers and Mothers of late antiquity, the first followers of St. Benedict at medieval Subiaco, reform-minded Carmelites under St. Teresa of Avila and St. John of the Cross, and others who have imitated the life and emulated the teachings of Jesus. Through their partnership, Francis and Clare brought light into the darkness of the late Middle Ages.

In the words of Dante, Francis was the "Morning Star" or Sun that rises from the East to shine new light upon the dawn. His life was full of poetry—both lived and spoken. His greatest biographer, Paul Sabatier, goes so far as to describe the impact of Francis on his era this way: "[His life] closed the reign of Byzantine art and of the thought of which it was the image. It is the end of dogmatism and authority. Uncertainty became permissible in some small measure. It marks a date in the history of the human conscience."[3]

This book is a chronicle of the spirit that animated Francis and Clare. Through their joy-filled and sometimes foolish lives of poverty and charity, both Europe and the Christian faith changed. The darkness of the medieval worldview was enlightened in ways that would lead to reformations of religious thought, poetry, and song, a renaissance of realism in art, Scriptures in local languages, ways of practicing faith outside of church, and new understandings of God and the world. For at least a generation, Francis and Clare and the first Franciscans changed the heart of faith. And since their time, they have inspired millions of us who desire to capture something of their spirit.

At the same time, there is an undeniable sadness attached to this story. The movement that Francis began in 1209 and that Clare continued after his death and until her own passing in 1253 was fraught with conflict and dissention. The original ideals that inspired so many early followers began to fade away within two decades. We will explore all of these themes in the chapters below.

Each chapter begins by telling one of the key stories of the early Franciscan experience and then explores issues and themes from their spirituality. The chapters are organized in roughly chronological order. For example, chapter 3 describes the stages of Francis's conversion and also introduces the concept of living in voluntary poverty. Chapter 4 opens with the story of how Francis first heard the voice of God and discusses the corruption of the thirteenth-century Church. Chapter 5 tells of the beginning of the Franciscan movement while exploring foolishness and joy—two key aspects of the personality of Franciscan spirituality—and the stormy relationship between Francis and Clare and their parents. Chapter 6 describes Clare's conversion and discusses what it means to imitate Christ. And so on. Each of the sixteen chapters raises questions that explore the spirituality of Francis and Clare, the origins of their movement, and how beliefs and practices from eight hundred years ago relate to what we do today.

It will become obvious throughout *Light in the Dark Ages* that I admire the saints from Assisi and that I believe we should model ourselves after them. However, this book is not without criticism of their ideals and practices, particularly in chapters 5, 6, and 8. Whether you are reading this while sitting at home, on retreat, on pilgrimage, or as part of a group study, each chapter will point you in new directions. The stories and issues traced throughout the book form a basic outline of the early movement and in the process show their relevance, as well as their incongruities, with our lives today. That is, after all, the point of my writing and your reading these pages: we seek to not only understand who Francis and Clare were, but also how to live in the spirit of their ideals today.

In 1986, Pope John Paul II coined the term "the spirit of Assisi," expressing what millions of people have felt since the deaths of Francis and Clare. Assisi certainly holds memories and stories of a time not to be forgotten, but more important, there is a vitality to the early Franciscan way of life that still draws people in our time. This doesn't mean that we necessarily aim to become professed religious, joining one modern Franciscan order or another. But for millions of people today, those little flowers of faith are not saccharine monikers, but rather instances of what can happen to sweeten up any human life, as well as the community of those around it.

## THE SOURCES FOR OUR STORY

I should say a few words about the sources used for understanding the lives of Francis and Clare. Controversy surrounds the ways in which their lives are interpreted, and these controversies wind all the way back to the first days after Francis's death. There were many early attempts to tell the story of his life, and sometimes the interpretations clash.

Most important among all of the early biographies are those written by Thomas of Celano and Bonaventure. Thomas was a contemporary of Francis who joined the Order in 1215, while Bonaventure was a second-generation Franciscan who never knew the founder. Thomas of Celano wrote the first two lives of Francis and the first biography of Clare. For that reason, Thomas is enormously important for understanding the relationship between them. In the case of both Francis and Clare, Thomas's biographies are the closest we have to understanding their lives and experiences.[4] Throughout the present work, I will refer to Thomas's two biographies of Francis as *First Life* and *Second Life*, for clarity and simplicity's sake.

It was about twenty-five years after Thomas's *First Life* was published that Bonaventure—who was then the minister-general of the Franciscan Order—authored his revision. Most of Bonaventure's book came straight from the stories of Thomas of Celano, but he reinterpreted them for a new generation. Three years after writing, Bonaventure declared his to be the only *authorized* biography, and copies of Thomas's two earlier books were ordered destroyed. This is an early sign of how the Franciscans, not even one generation removed from their founder, sought to control the interpretation of his life. We will discuss this more in detail below.

Uncovering the real Francis beneath layers of legend has been the vocation of many great scholars of the last 120 years. Chief among them is Paul Sabatier, who wrote the first modern biography of Francis in 1894.[5] At the time of Sabatier's writing, the *Fioretti*, or "Little Flowers," was well known. *The Little Flowers of St. Francis* is a collection of tales that were told and retold by the generation of friars who lived after Francis's death. These tales were the spiritual treasure of those men and women who valued the original ideals of Francis most of all. They believed that Thomas of Celano's two biographies of Francis were more faithful to the true intent of their founder than was Bonaventure's. *The Little Flowers* contained fifty-three tales in its original, vernacular, Tuscan compilation—the language that Dante and Boccaccio would soon use for their own epic stories.

Two other important texts had not yet been discovered by the end of the nineteenth century: *The Legend of Perugia* (written around 1312; first published in 1922) and *The Mirror of Perfection* (written around 1318; first published in 1898). These collections of tales have intrigued historians, offering further evidence that the official interpretations of Francis's life are not always the most accurate ones. The picture painted of Francis in these collections is different from the common portrait of him, emphasizing his earthiness, combativeness, foolishness, insistence, and occasionally his quixotic way of communicating with others.

*The Mirror of Perfection* was so named because it was said by its authors to be "the Mirror of Perfection of a brother Minor; to wit, of the Blessed Francis, wherein we may most sufficiently behold as in a glass the perfection of his calling and profession."[6] Sabatier himself first published *The Mirror* in 1898, controversially claiming in the book's subtitle that it was a firsthand documentation of the life of St. Francis written in 1228 by Francis's close friend and confidante, Brother Leo.[7] If it had indeed been written so early, it would predate even Thomas of Celano's accounts. But in the twenty or so years after Sabatier made this claim, evidence surfaced that suggested a date of composition about ninety years later than Sabatier had hoped. This later evidence ultimately became irrefutable. As often happened throughout the Middle Ages, it was a copyist's error that led to Sabatier's mistake about the priority of *The Mirror*. Before the age of printing, texts were copied by hand, allowing mistakes of content to enter in. In this case, the mistake was in the dating of it. The copyist miscopied one of the Roman numerals, changing it from MCCCXVIII (1318) to MCCXXVIII (1228).

To this day, no one doubts that the essence of this great collection of stories comes from the friars who were closest to Francis: Angelo, Rufinus, and Leo. There is something undeniably fresh, immediate, unpolished, and argumentative about the tales in *The Mirror of Perfection*. Most of the stories are repeated from Thomas of Celano's *Second Life*, but the original wording (of Leo?) is sometimes altered. Together, *Second Life* and *The Mirror* represent the companions of Francis who believed that the leaders of the Order had turned their backs on the true Franciscan ideals. Absolute poverty and humility were being replaced by property and learning. Leo and his companions were called the Spirituals, or friars of the strict observance. As the scholar John Moorman says, "Sabatier was wrong in dating [*The Mirror*] so early; he was right in recognizing it as a source of the greatest importance since it emanated from the reminiscences of Brother Leo and his companions, and those who had known the saint most intimately."[8] We will return again and again to these texts throughout this book.

Meanwhile, much of what we know of Clare, outside of Thomas of Celano's biography, we have from oral traditions handed down since the friars left her deathbed to continue their work. Some of these stories and legends were recently compiled by the Italian historian Piero Bargellini into his compassionate work *The Little Flowers of Saint Clare*. Bargellini was first and foremost a great

Florentine, serving as Councillor for Arts and Gardens, and was in the 1960s the mayor of Florence. But long before that, he was an artist and a writer who wrote influential books on St. Bernadino of Siena, various other aspects of Franciscan spirituality, and Dante.

Along the way to discovering what happened in those early years of the movement, we also will have assistance from various other experts and biographers, including the great nineteenth-century enthusiast for Francis and Clare, Frederick Ozanam. Ozanam (d. 1853) was beatified in 1997 by Pope John Paul II at the Cathedral of Notre Dame in Paris. But long before that day, Ozanam wrote a beautiful book called *The Franciscan Poets of the Thirteenth Century*, first published in English translation in 1914. Portions of that work are interspersed throughout the chapters below.[9] Ozanam showed how Francis and Clare breathed new life into the spirit of thirteenth-century Italy, and by extension of their followers, the rest of Europe. G. K. Chesterton once said, "St. Francis was very vivid in his poems and rather vague in his documents." Ozanam explains the background and substance of that vividness.

More books have been written about Francis of Assisi than about any other figure in history except Jesus himself. But rarely in those books do readers have an opportunity to assess what Francis actually did that was so extraordinary. The present work will help you to do that. Walk with me through those early years of the movement begun by Brother Francis. See how Sister Clare became his partner, the rudder to his sail, yin to his yang, the other half of the foundation to a spiritual renaissance that transformed Western faith, society, and religion in ways that were threatened, even lost, within their own lifetimes. Explore with me the sometimes simple, sometimes larger, ways that we can live in that original Franciscan spirit today.

*The Resurrection*

We need Francis and Clare today, as much as we ever have. "Our generation already is overpast / Yet love of Christ will win man's love at last." Robert Bridges wrote that simple couplet in memory of his friend Gerard Manley Hopkins nearly a century ago. He was writing about the mistakes of their generation, one that knew the First World War and its accompanying misery and pessimism that was unlike anything their parents had faced. Francis and Clare also lived in a time that felt lost in its myriad conflicts among countries, religions, and classes. Our own day, dawning a new century and millennium, feels similarly overpast.

We need Francis and Clare today. Our souls and bodies need their wisdom and their sensuous approach to life and spirituality, and we need them to remind us of what it means to take steps toward living like Jesus.

Through our desire to see and touch the risen Christ once again, we are privileged to encounter certain individuals among us who are farther along in their paths toward wholeness, in whom we see much, much more clearly the image of God in Christ. . . . So our penchant for telling stories of those people in whom Christ was born, lived, and died again, this perennial hagiographic impulse of Christianity, so to speak, is inevitably part and parcel of our faith in a risen, incarnate God.[10]

The spirit of the earliest Franciscans is contagious; may we all become infected!

# ABOUT THEIR RELATIONSHIP

Tere are more famous couples from the Middle Ages, but none who had a more profound effect on their time and place than Francis and Clare of Assisi.

In the century before our saints were born, all of Europe knew who Abelard and Heloise were. Heloise was Abelard's student, and Abelard was the most famous theologian of his day. He also liked to claim that he was the only undefeated philosopher in the world. He never lost a debate, and his charisma was undeniable. Abelard and Heloise became lovers, creating a scandal throughout Paris. Heloise gave birth secretly to a son, but soon, the two lovers were forcibly separated by her family. Abelard was violently castrated and exiled, while Heloise entered a convent. But the love letters they exchanged rank among the most poignant in all of literature. Together, they confused the spiritual and secular, a mix of genuine love and serious lust, and the sort of secrecy that marks challenges to power for the wrong reasons.

There are also legends of an earlier famous couple, Benedict of Nursia, the father of Western monasticism and author of his influential *Rule*, and his sister Scholastica. According to Pope Gregory the Great's famous biography of Benedict, Scholastica represented the female version of all that Benedict strove to be. The most popular story told about the pair is one that seems to recur in the first biographies of Francis and Clare: it is the story of a meal they shared.

According to the legend, Benedict and Scholastica, monk and nun, visited with each other only once a year—and even then they were not alone. Benedict's disciples would accompany them. They would share a meal in a picnic area not far from the monastery gate. But as happens in the stories of saints, Gregory the Great's text explains that spiritual matters took precedent over bodily needs: "They spent the whole day praising God in holy conversation. Night was already falling when they finally took their meal together."[11] This is a recurring theme in the lives of holy men and women: food becomes an afterthought. And, of course, Jesus himself taught that spiritual teachings are more important than daily bread. Gregory continues:

> The evening grew later and later as they sat at the table in holy conversation. Scholastica then made a request: "I beg you, Benedict, not to leave me tonight so that we may talk until morning about the joys of heavenly life." Benedict responded, "What are you talking about? Under no circumstances can I stay outside my cell."

> The heavens were calm and not a single cloud appeared in the sky. When this holy woman heard her brother's refusal, she folded her hands and rested them on the table. She leaned down, put her head on her hands, and prayed to God. When she raised her head, such powerful lightning erupted, and thunder and a flood of rain, that the venerable Benedict and the brothers with him could not set foot outside the door of

where they were sitting. The holy woman had poured out a flood of tears, drawing rain to skies that had been calm.

When Benedict saw that he could not get back to the monastery because of the storm, he was irritated and complained, "God have mercy. Sister, why have you done this?" And she replied to the holy man: "I asked you, and you would not listen. So I asked my Lord, and he has listened."[12]

And so they discussed heaven for the rest of the evening. Scholastica died just three days later.

The medieval imagination was full of these stories by the time that Francis and Clare came along. But unlike Abelard and Heloise, Francis and Clare did not have a physical or sexual relationship. And unlike Benedict and Scholastica, they were not brother and sister. The friendship of Francis and Clare falls somewhere in between. Their story is, in fact, quite complicated.

He was twelve years her elder, and she would have known very little of him before his conversion. As an adolescent, Clare observed Francis's unusual behavior, as he publicly rebelled against his father and the expectations that were placed upon him at home. Then, as a teenager, Clare began to admire him. She heard him preach, and watched as he began his public ministry. She, too, began to doubt the future her family was planning, and she felt the proddings of the Spirit within her. In the bold tradition of women saints who spurned the domestic life,[13] Clare took the radical step of deciding to join Francis and his merry band of men who were transforming the Umbrian hill-towns with their singing and dancing, marriage to *poverty*, and an alternative spiritual path to cloister and hearth. She fled her home one night and joined the Franciscans down in the valley at their modest compound of huts circling the ancient chapel of St. Mary of the Angels.

Francis and Clare then became an unusual couple. The sources all indicate that they had a natural affection for one another. They were not married and they never had an affair, but their love for each other was felt palpably by those around them. G. K. Chesterton calls it a "pure and spiritual romance," an apt description, although they spent very little time together. Clare was an important confidant to Francis, and a link between his childhood, with all of its extravagant worldliness, and the mature, life-changing decisions that began to mark his early twenties. Their affection for and trust of each other fueled the early Franciscan movement and gave birth to a joy, beauty, and spirit that had long been absent from faith.

However, it has always seemed to make for a better story to have Francis and Clare *in love* with each other. Some of the early sources give hints that support such a view. Thomas of Celano, the first biographer of each of them, called theirs a "divine attraction"—these two saints wanting to be together. And when Thomas describes Clare's childhood reputation as a spiritual giant, he also implies that Francis was intent on meeting her. Thomas compares Clare's holiness to plunder, and Francis to a conquering knight. He writes that Francis "was dedicated to snatching his plunder away from the world."

In the canonization proceedings for Clare that happened just after her death, one of Clare's sisters testified that it was Francis who made the first visit to see Clare, while she was still a teenager living in her father's house. Given Francis's apostolic life at that time, and the way in which marriages were usually prearranged by parents, this seems highly unlikely. The events were more than forty years in the past when Clare's sister was remembering them. Could it be that she remembered things in this way because the values of the day stated that a woman could not make such contact with a man outside her family? There may have been some intent to preserve the family reputation.

According to *The Acts of the Process of Canonization of St. Clare*, written by Thomas of Celano in 1253, Francis and Clare did indeed meet several times before her conversion, and on one occasion the text reads that Clare snuck away clandestinely to hear him preach. But there is no hint of dating or flirting in these passages. Francis was twelve years older than Clare. When he was going through his first dramatic moments of conversion she was barely twelve. She was fourteen when Francis renounced his father and all his wealth in the public square before the bishop and all of Assisi. And when Clare later came to join Francis's movement in the dead of night, her heart and stomach would have been full of terror—not the excitement one feels before a first kiss! They were friends, and they shared a kinship that was more important than romance.

Fifty years ago, Nikos Kazantzakis, the Greek novelist, made popular the notion that Francis and Clare shared a relationship that was sexually charged. In *Saint Francis*,[14] Kazantzakis had the book's narrator, Brother Leo, say to his spiritual father:

> I am the only one . . . who knows about your carnal love for Count Favorini Scifi's daughter Clara. All the others, because they are afraid of their own shadows, think you loved only her soul. But it was her body that you loved earliest of all; it was from there that you set out, got your start. Then, after struggle, struggle against the devil's snares, you were able with God's help to reach her soul. You loved that soul, but without ever denying her body, and without ever touching it either.[15]

According to Kazantzakis, Clare was one of the girls whom Francis had wooed like a troubadour before his conversion, singing at her windows from the street below. When Clare later came to the Portiuncula in the middle of the night in order to become the first woman Franciscan, she urged Francis to believe that she wanted to love only God. "Last night I heard you calling me by name. It was you, Father Francis. You were standing beneath my window once more and calling me. 'Come! Come! Come!' you said. So, I came."[16] Francis then tried to flee. He was scared of his own latent lust, despite the fact that, by this time in the novel, Francis had almost completely lost his eyesight. But the other friars compelled Francis to stay and listen to the pleading of Clare. And so he did, and he began to interrogate her. Can you really go about town barefoot? Can you, a woman from a wealthy home, stomach feeling hungry? Will you, the daughter of a count, be willing to beg for your bread? And Clare answered affirmatively to every question. "I can, I can," she said, but Francis retorted, "You cannot!"

Kazantzakis had Francis participating in the ancient subjugation of women, believing women to be less than men in intellect, spirit, and honesty. He had Francis say, "I don't trust you women. Eve's serpent has been licking your ears and lips for too many centuries. Do not lead me into temptation. Other ladies will gather around you, and you'll all climb up to the convent roof to ogle the brothers. . . . No, get up and return home. We don't want women!"[17]

What a shame! We could psychoanalyze this novelist and come up with explanations for why he made his saints so confused (remember the schizophrenic Jesus of *The Last Temptation of Christ*?), but suffice it to say that it probably did not happen that way.[18] It is true that saints often disappoint us, but it is also true that we disappoint the saints, particularly when we assume sexual relationships for them where there were none. Why do we seem to want our holy men and women to have sexual experiences? Perhaps sex becomes the simplest path to understanding them as like ourselves. Nowhere is this more evident than in the current, but also medieval, fascination surrounding Jesus and Mary Magdalene. More than a millennium and a half before Dan Brown ever conceived *The Da Vinci Code*, Origen's theological opponent, Celsus, suggested that the Magdalene and Christ were lovers. There are even debates as to whether or not Martin Luther may have said something similar. A decade ago, a liberal American Episcopal bishop, John Shelby Spong, wrote that Mary Magdalene may have been married to Jesus and subsequently bore his children. But just as there is only a fraction of evidence to suggest such things—compared to the evidence to support the more conventional views—so, too, there is little reason to believe that Francis and Clare shared any romance other than one that was jointly with God.

After Kazantzakis, Italian director Franco Zeffirelli created his film *Brother Sun, Sister Moon* (1972), in which Francis and Clare are portrayed as young romantics who turn an interest in each other into a mutual interest in the spiritual life. In the first scene of the film, featuring Alec Guinness as Pope Innocent III, the twenty-year-old Francis playfully chases the young teenager Clare as she makes her way to a lonely grotto bringing food to some outcast lepers. Francis is horrified when he sees the lepers and he runs off. The next time they are together on screen, they gaze at each other as Francis marches off to war. Their third scene is in a field of poppies on a sunny afternoon; they have a sweet conversation as Francis's parents eavesdrop and discuss a possible marriage. Later in the film, when Clare comes in the middle of the night to join Francis's movement, *Brother Sun, Sister Moon* shows a scene almost bubbling over with erotic energy that is being turned to spiritual ends.[19]

The myths of Kazantzakis and Zeffirelli have warped the imagination of a generation of those who would be interested in learning about Francis and Clare. How are historians to compete with a best-selling novel and a hit movie? There is something compelling about unrequited love, especially erotic love that seems somehow forbidden. Some modern biographers have even led readers down this path, driven either by the desire to tell a compelling story, or simply to connect the story with the prevalent myth. Gloria Hutchinson writes that the beginning of the Poor Clares was the same as that "romantic scene idealized by Franco Zeffirelli in *Brother Sun, Sister Moon*."[20] One of the best recent biographies of Francis declares, "Clare may have fallen in love with Francis at first, as many believe she did."[21] And another of the most important communicators of the spirituality of Francis and Clare has suggested that it was romantic love that drew them together:

> She had known almost at once that she would follow him. . . . She soon learned, however, that they could never be together, for then they would not be free, they would not be who they really were, two pilgrims in love with the Lord, two souls who were closer apart than they could ever be together. Together they might end up loving each other more than the treasure they had found in one another's heart.[22]

They were two strong, magnetic personalities who could communicate with each other easily by glance, note, or shared prayer, whether they were in the same place at the same time or not. They were likely together on fewer than a dozen occasions over the space of twenty years, most of them only for a matter of hours. But they understood each other, supported each other, and complemented each other's strengths and weaknesses.

The great Spanish mystic and philosopher Miguel de Unamuno once wrote: "Even in the purest realm of the spirit, without the shadow of any vice, man seeks support in woman, as Francis of Assisi did in Clare."[23] This is very similar to Genesis 2, when God says, "It is not good that the man should be alone; I will make him a helper as his partner." They were friends who felt a kinship in passion for turning away from the world and following Christ. They shared a feeling that their parents could not understand how they felt about the future and what it meant to be successful. There were likely no romantic yearnings and surely no sexual relationship between Francis and Clare. They did not have a relationship *past* that need interest us. When Francis cut Clare's hair (as a sign of her tonsure, or promise to live for Christ) on that fascinating first evening—after she had run away from home to join him and the friars—there was no scent of perfume in the air. Clare was immediately a *brother*.

# TO KISS A LEPER

I f history teaches us anything, it is how similar human weaknesses have been throughout the ages. Human foibles, faults, and wickedness wind a pattern throughout the history of civilization. Human beings are as similar to one another in weakness as are great religious figures in strength and wisdom. Across the religious traditions, we see how the exemplars of all faiths have had to overcome basic tendencies toward greed, self-preservation, lust, laziness, and many another sins recounted in stories and scriptures. Saints are taught, not born.

The best teacher of Francis Bernardone was the Holy Spirit at work in his own conscience. In the beginning, in his early twenties, Francis began to spend time alone for the first time. He drew away from the childhood friends who had previously engaged his lusts for fame and friendship, and he wandered to deserted places in the Umbrian hillsides. Francis was particularly drawn to abandoned churches—and there were many of them in thirteenth-century Italy. We can see in him the medieval feeling of devotion simply upon entering a church. These quiet spaces made possible other divine action within him.

If Francis had not finally felt the need to be by himself after years of teenage waste and solipsism, what happened in him next would have been impossible. On the path to conversion it is necessary to have the space, quiet, and freedom to see ourselves more clearly for what we really are. Francis began to see who he was and then, with God's help, to see what was possible in a human being, instead. This is one of the common features of all saints: they have private relationships with God. Their closet expressions—quiet, uncomplicated, and alone with God—become the foundation for the sanctity that they later show.

Francis began to give of himself to others. Thomas of Celano[24] tells us that he followed the example of St. Martin of Tours and gave his clothes to a destitute knight who had lost his own garments and armor in a recent battle. But, where St. Martin had cut his cloak in two, giving half of it to a beggar, Francis radicalized the commitment of a follower of Jesus and stripped completely, removing those "fine, tailored clothes" of his father's for one of the last times. Jesus said: "[I]f someone wishes to go to law with you to get your tunic, let him have your cloak as well. And if anyone requires you to go one mile, go two miles with him."[25] This sort of self-sacrifice became a pattern with Francis, and the occasions for it usually began in simple times of solitude.

Other steps followed on the path toward Francis's becoming, again in the words of Thomas, "a different person." The changes within him were the same sort of qualitative difference that happened in the New Testament story of Saul becoming Paul, or that can be seen in any saint since the biblical era who has been transformed from world-centered to Christ-centered. Francis's decisions were being transformed by a desire to do the right thing, or God's will, which he determined by reading the Gospels. He became self-critical and was able to see his former, unconverted life as dissipate. He found various means of repentance and penance. Saints help others toward conversion with their easy understanding of sin, as well as their awareness of what it means to be released from sin.

Francis's conversion next found expression in his recognizing the inequality that existed between the advantaged and the disadvantaged, the healthy and the ailing, and the loved and the loveless. The love of God began to build in his heart, and God's love gradually replaced the loves that Francis had previously held with ardor for things of the world. To his rollicking friends he soon seemed distant and less enjoyable to be around. As he became more solitary, he began to exhibit moments of divine inspiration. The notion of what might happen in future events, and an awareness of human motives, all became more accessible. This is another aspect of sanctity that appears miraculous to those of us on the outside looking in, but is, in reality, more common than we think. Saints have developed heightened sensitivities to and perceptions of the thoughts, desires, and needs of those around them. This ability may be more common than is typically imagined.

At about this time, he walked to Rome—no small feat for a man in Umbria. But a pilgrimage during the Middle Ages was meant to be slowly traveled, usually on foot, or perhaps riding a horse or a donkey. All indications are that Francis walked with a few companions, but in spirit he was very alone with God during those early days.

While in Rome, they visited the Church of St. Peter. These were the days before the great basilica that was built during the Renaissance, adorned with the work of Michelangelo. The site was the anciently meaningful one where St. Peter had been martyred in Nero's Circus some thirty years after Christ's crucifixion. A small church—a shrine, really, erected in the third century—was called Prince of the Apostles. But by the fourth century, the first St. Peter's

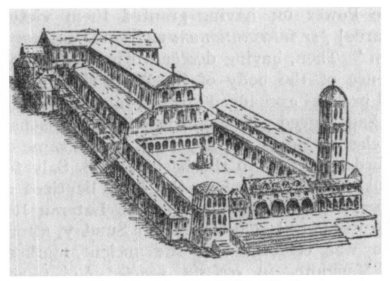

*The medieval St. Peter's Basilica in Rome*

Basilica was built by the Emperor Constantine. It was there that Charlemagne was crowned Holy Roman Emperor on Christmas Day, AD 800, by Pope Leo III. Lothair, Louis II, and Frederick III were similarly crowned by popes in that space. It was this St. Peter's—not the renovated and expanded one that caused Martin Luther to begin his attack on Pope Leo X in the early 1500s—that Francis was visiting. Again, Francis stripped off his fine clothes, but this time, he exchanged his garments with the sundry ones of a beggar who sat in front of the great church.

Francis still possessed a great deal of money at this time. We know this because he gladly made a large offering of coins while visiting the usual pilgrimage sites in Rome. He had always been the boy who was fun to have around because of the money in his pockets, but on this occasion, the money began to spill in the direction of the needy.

All of these conversion experiences culminated one day when Francis, back in Assisi, approached a leper while riding his horse. The leper of the thirteenth century was a vagrant, cast out from society as well as from church. Leprosy was incurable at this time, and those who were afflicted were anathema. Lepers were the same incurable, contagious outcasts as they had been in Jesus' time. First-century Palestine and thirteenth-century Italy were both pre-science. The common response to the disease was inherited from ancient days going back to Leviticus 13:45–46: "The person who has the leprous disease shall wear torn clothes and let the hair of his head be disheveled; and he shall cover his upper lip and cry out, 'Unclean, unclean.' He shall remain unclean as long as he has the disease; he is unclean. He shall live alone; his dwellings shall be outside the camp."

During the Middle Ages, local priests performed a ceremony in which the priest would recite: "I forbid you to enter church, monastery, fair, mill, marketplace or tavern. . . . I forbid you ever to leave your house without your leper's costume . . . to live with any woman other than your own . . . to touch a well, or well cord, without your gloves . . . to touch children, or to give them anything . . . to eat or drink, except with lepers."[26] Lazarus was the patron saint of lepers in the Middle Ages because, although the Gospels do not diagnose him as a leper, the symptoms appear to be unmistakable when he is described in Luke's Gospel: "There was a rich man who used to dress in purple and fine linen. . . . And at his gate there used to lie a poor man called Lazarus, covered with sores, who longed to fill himself with what fell from the rich man's table. Even dogs came and licked his sores."[27]

Leprosy is actually still with us, although not in Palestine or Umbria. Somewhere between one and three million cases of leprosy are to be found in Brazil, India, Madagascar, Mozambique, Myanmar (formerly Burma), and Nepal. We know today that the disease is treatable and only mildly contagious. The kind of physical contact that the first Franciscans boldly had with lepers will rarely if ever result in transferring the disease. But Francis did not know that.

Francis knew that Jesus had cared for lepers. Ten lepers, according to Luke's Gospel, "approached him. Keeping their distance, they called out, saying, 'Jesus, Master, have mercy on us!'" In healing them, Jesus showed his willingness to look at, speak to, and befriend those that the rest of humankind had deemed unclean and sinful.

Lepers became the final test of Francis's conversion. We are told that there was nothing that frightened young Bernardone more than a leper. When he approached the leper while riding his horse near Assisi, his first instinct was to avoid him; he rode past the man feeling a sickening revulsion in his stomach. But then he brought his beast to an abrupt stop. He dismounted and ran back to the leper, grabbed the man by the shoulders—and kissed him! Legend tells us that Francis then remounted his horse only to turn back and see that the man had disappeared!

Was the leper a divine messenger, sent to test Francis? Was he only the object of a dream? Francis worried for many days that he had only been dreaming. Perhaps the test was not real and perhaps then Francis's "passing the test," so to speak, was also then not real. Sometimes when you want something so desperately your imagination runs faster than your life's actions themselves. With all of his heart, Francis wanted to be holy, to purge himself of sinfulness and to replace it with goodness.

The *Second Life* of Thomas of Celano tells us that Francis then set out to find more lepers. He rode and walked to their caves and huts, tucked away in places not intended for visiting, and gave them coins and kisses. Sometimes he would take along a companion, we are told in *The Legend of the Three Companions*, another early text, and after caring for the lepers Francis would leave his companion to go inside a cave and pray alone. "Inspired by a new, special spirit, he prayed to his Father in secret, wanting to keep secret what he knew was happening inside of him."[28] It was the contact with lepers that culminated in his conversion, according to Thomas of Celano: *mutatus perfecte iam corde* in the original Latin, or "a perfect change of heart."

Francis's care for lepers may remind us also of what Jesus did after his death and before his resurrection. The Apostle's Creed says simply, "He descended into hell." Some theologians (such as the reformer John Calvin) have explained that Christ's descent into hell was largely metaphoric, symbolizing the spiritual and physical torment that he underwent on our behalf. But more compelling is the interpretation that Christ actually descended into a physical place called Hell in order to demonstrate that releasing people from sin includes releasing them from pain. Psalm 107 foreshadows this sort of Messiah: "He brought them out of darkness and gloom / and broke their bonds asunder. / Let them thank the LORD for his steadfast love, / for his wonderful works to humankind. / For he shatters the doors of bronze / and cuts in two the bars of iron."

## POVERTY BOTH ROMANTIC AND LITERAL

Above all else, Francis wanted to be poor. Embracing those with leprosy was his first step into a multifaceted *marriage* to poverty.

Francis and Clare combined romance and idealism in their lives together with a stark literalism. The most obvious example of Francis's romantic side is seen just after his conversion, when he wed himself to what he called "Lady Poverty." As Clare would later do, Francis said that he took a different spouse than was

*29*

expected of him. Expressed throughout his writings, his love for
Lady Poverty shows the heart of a romantic and the spirit of a
troubadour. Umberto Eco describes this spirit: "The formation
of symbols was artistic. To decipher them was to experience them
aesthetically. It was a type of aesthetic expression in which the
Medievals took great pleasure in deciphering puzzles, in spotting
the daring analogy, in feeling that they were involved in adventure
and discovery."[29] Lady Poverty was Francis's primary symbol, puzzle, analogy, and adventure. His love for the feelings of human
love was transformed into a love for the love of God.

*The Marriage of St. Francis and Poverty*

Francis was not actually the first troubadour-turned-religious.
Folquet of Marseille composed many troubadour songs in the 1180s
and 1190s, only to quit his amorous ways and become a Cistercian
monk, and later a bishop. There were also stories in the reverse.
Most of the love poets known as the Goliards were, in fact, professed
religious in rebellion. They wrote verses ridiculing the institutions

of the Church and mocking the sometimes poor relationship between piety and reality in the lives of the religious.

But just as Francis enjoyed the drama of being *married* to Lady Poverty, he was also literal in his pursuit of *voluntary* poverty—both as a personal commitment and as a community guideline for his brothers and Clare and the sisters. He resisted every effort of his brothers to own even the most reasonable things: spiritual books, worship manuals, buildings for sleeping, churches. His vision was to be completely like Christ, who told the first disciples to go about preaching without anything for the journey. All would be provided, Christ said, including daily food and future clothing. Francis severely punished friars who even touched coins; they became unclean in his model for faith just as lepers became washed in God's love; and he forbade anyone from preparing food that was intended to be eaten tomorrow.

Francis enjoyed the expressions of faith that would cause others to take notice, but he also desired to make himself despised, an anti-hero, on many occasions. He once insisted that his good friend Brother Bernard step on his face, as punishment. He later singed his flesh when tempted toward lust, and rolled naked in the snow to get rid of temptation. He smiled while being ridiculed by the young boys of Assisi in the early days of his conversion. There is very little that is sweet about this

As all true knights were devoted to the service of some lady, Francis had to choose his. Indeed, a few days before his conversion, when his friends found him wrapped in thought and asked him if he were thinking of taking a wife, Francis replied: "It is true I am contemplating taking the noblest, richest, and most beautiful lady that ever lived." This was the description he gave of his ideal, the type of all moral beauty, Lady Poverty.

He loved to personify this virtue according to the symbolic genius of his time. He imagined her as a heavenly damsel, then the lady of his thoughts, his betrothed, his spouse. He gave to her all the power which the troubadours attributed to the noble ladies celebrated in their poems—the power of wresting from the souls captivated by her all worldly thoughts and inclinations, of elevating such souls to the society of angels. But to the troubadours these platonic loves were merely witticisms, while the invisible beauty that had ravished St. Francis wrung from him the most impassioned cries. Open any of the medieval poets and you will find no song more bold, no words more impassioned, than this prayer of the penitent of Assisi: "O my most sweet Lord Jesus Christ, have pity on me and on my Lady Poverty, for I burn with love for her, and without her I cannot rest. O my Lord, who did cause me to love her, you know that she is sitting in sadness, rejected by all."

—*Frederick Ozanam*

side of Francis. He could be as literally minded as some of the more radical reformers who came after him.

His commitment to being reviled reminds me of the teachings of the Danish philosopher Søren Kierkegaard. What are the qualities of those whom God chooses for a special life, such as that of a saint? The answer is more ordinary than we might think: We don't earn God's favor, and we are not predisposed toward sanctity. Kierkegaard explains that if you are considered righteous by others, if you are regularly invited to be in a position of leadership in your church, if everyone admires and respects you—it isn't Jesus Christ that you are tracking. In contrast to centuries of teaching as to what the "personality" of sainthood might be, Kierkegaard says instead: "It appears that to be a Christian, to belong truly to Christ . . . in truth should mean in the world, in the eyes of men, to be abased, that it should mean all possible hardships, every possible sort of derision and insult, and mean at last to be punished as a criminal!"[30]

Francis felt emotions deeply, and identified with people intimately, in ways that resulted in the sort of active love that is called *charity* in the epistles of St. Paul. Like one of the Japanese priests in Shusaku Endo's famous novel *Silence*, Francis knew the difference between empathy and this deeper sort of love: "His pity for them had been overwhelming; but pity was not action. It was not love. Pity, like passion, was no more than a kind of instinct."[31] Early Franciscan poverty was the ground that caused charity to grow. Francis understood how money and ownership breed competition and jealousy, and how owning nothing makes it possible to give unreservedly because one has nothing to lose.

These were the practical bases for early Franciscan poverty. A friar who owns land feels obliged to use it properly by building a suitable house. A house will include the tools of worship, statuary, crafted windows, candlesticks, books, and resources for instructing others in the faith. These things need defending from possible intruders. And so, even a modest religious house becomes one with a degree of wealth that makes men prepared to hurt those who would attempt to take it from them.

Francis and Clare did not believe, as did some heretics during the Middle Ages, that the world was essentially bad, or evil, or alien. Heretical groups such as the Cathars preached that poverty was essential in order to separate oneself from the earth and the things of creation. A Cathar would no more own land than he would enjoy a good meal or admire a flower. Francis and Clare were optimists and idealists in combination with their literalism, and they found joy in voluntary poverty. Their voluntary poverty had everything to do with freedom and nothing to do with separation. As one eloquent Franciscan puts it today, "While the world is filled with God's overflowing goodness, it is poverty that allows one to experience this goodness by becoming radically dependent on God."[32]

Poverty was also, quite simply, the way to be like Jesus. God's becoming a human being was an act of profound, voluntary poverty. But then, on the level of detail, both Francis and Clare believed that it was not an accident of history that there was no room in the inn. The swaddling clothes and manger (an animal's feeding trough) were no accident either, for this different sort of king. The public ministry of Jesus was unsuccessful by worldly standards; he had twelve men and two or three women with him before his passion; at the Cross, he had only his mother and John. None of these facts were accidents. They were all evidences of the voluntary poverty of Jesus. Every fact about the life of Christ was intended to teach an aspect of Francis and Clare's new way of life.

With Francis and Clare, the Christian became mendicant, homeless, and homely. That's what being married to poverty was all about. In all these things they imitated Christ. Francis became the poor Christ in the actions of his life, while Clare—due to the accident of thirteenth-century European history that said women could not live apostolic lives beside men—became the poor Christ in contemplation. So, as Francis teaches us what to *do*, Clare shows us how to *be*. Both of them made Jesus visible, audible, and recognizable through their lives.

# REBUILDING THE CHURCH

S till wearing his father's fine clothing but questioning almost everything, Francis Bernardone left Assisi by the city gate known as Porta Nuova and wandered aimlessly into the hot sun that bathes the hillside as it winds down away from town. Fresh from his experience of kissing the leper, Francis was full of excitement. Thomas of Celano claims with a hagiographer's bravado that "his heart was already completely changed."[33] That is doubtful. Francis still had thoughts of his former friends, who were nipping at his heels most days and nights in hopes of returning him to a life of frivolity. Most of them would soon fade into the distance completely, and none would ever join Francis in his new life.

Bonaventure says that the sensitive young man "sought lonely places, dear only to mourners," which is to put too dour a spin on it. The romantic sought out rocky paths, dilapidated buildings, ancient castles, and ruins, all of which stoked his imagination in ways that books or conversation may enflame the thoughts of others less sensuous.

He visited the fallen church of San Damiano again and again during those early days, probably both before his brief sojourn as a knight gone off to war against Perugia, and then afterwards, when he had come back home in disgrace. He walked there on many days when his father did not require his help in the shop. He walked there on many days when his mother believed, or perhaps hoped, that he was instead off to see some girl. He did not yet have an idea of what his vocation was to be.

San Damiano was probably tended by a priest, but a poor or absent-minded one. It was a church without much of a congregation and without the sort of appointments that made other churches in Assisi great. The building was in the beginning stages of ruin, but that is exactly why Francis felt drawn to it. Certain places imprint themselves on us and make us feel completely present in something larger, as if our lives are a jigsaw puzzle and the discovered place holds one of our missing pieces.

It is intriguing that we don't have accounts of Francis talking with the priest of San Damiano, asking for advice regarding his life's direction. Instead, it is the altar that drew him, and the icon that hung above it. That icon of Christ on the cross was one of the most striking in all of Umbria. Francis looked into the eyes of Christ there, feeling absolutely sure that they were the eyes of God, looking back at him. He looked at icons as medieval people did; he was wandering down to San Damiano so often because he wanted to *be seen* by Christ.

Even Martin Luther, a medieval man in many ways, later understood what it meant to look deeply at, and be transformed by, an image of Christ: "Through mercy and grace, Christ on the cross removes thy sins from thee, carries them, and strangles them; keep this always in mind and doubt it not—this means, look at this holy image and make it thy own."[34] It was in these moments—which turned into hours—that Francis began to yearn to be like the One who was looking back at him. Francis knew very little of the life of Jesus at this point in his life, but he began to learn the stories and the teachings, perhaps sometimes from the lonely priest of San Damiano.

On one special occasion, Francis was alone in the chapel: Bonaventure says that he was lying prostrate on the floor; other texts written by Francis's closest friends simply record that Francis had gone into the church to pray. No one was with Francis to observe what happened next. Bonaventure wrote that what happened caused Francis to lose consciousness for a time, in a mystical ecstasy; but again, other texts make it sound less miraculous, more important. He heard a voice speak to him from the icon (which now hangs in the side chapel of the Basilica of St. Clare of Assisi) and believed it to be the voice of Christ.

When Francis returned from the abandoned church, having just heard the voice of God, he had no one to whom he could tell his story. He was almost completely alone. Bonaventure says, "The servant of the Most High had no one to instruct him except Christ." Later, he would tell his first companions that Christ simply said to him: "Francis, go and repair my house, which, as you can see, is falling down."

*The Legend of the Three Companions*—written by friars Angelo, Leo, and Rufinus almost twenty years before Bonaventure's official *Life*—tells us that it was this moment before the cross of San Damiano that initiated Francis's identification with Christ and, in particular, with his passion. Could it be that Francis was seeking a connection to the institutional Church when he prayed before icons in churches? Perhaps he wanted God to tell him what to do, how to be a Christian of true commitment, and he expected a different answer. Francis sought a *connection*, to be sure, but was it spiritual only, or ecclesiastical as well? When he received his word from God, he did not run off and join a monastic order. That's an important piece of information.

Joining the Benedictines or the Cistercians would have been the most logical thing for a young man to do in circumstances like Francis's, fresh from a private communication from God. But Francis knew, as did everyone at the time, of the massive corruption in the Church. He began his work, instead, in a mendicant, reform tradition (epitomized by Peter Waldo and Joachim of Fiore a few decades earlier), only tangentially related at first to the Catholic Church. Francis left San Damiano with his mission in mind, and he plunged his hands in both pockets and gave every coin to the attendant priest, who happened to be nearby. He was on his first mission: to literally repair the fallen chapel.

## THE THIRTEENTH-CENTURY CHURCH

The century before Francis was born was one of the most corrupt in the history of the Christian Church. The pursuit of or hold on power and influence, as well as the desire for economic gain or security, were often the factors that led to decisions being made. Power brokering was more important than spiritual matters or doctrinal teaching. It was so bad in those days that it was often said that the majority of parish priests and bishops were practicing either simony (extorting money), keeping prostitutes, or both. They were not just corruptible and prone to adultery, but they were extortionists and worse.

One of the reasons for which the first Franciscans were important to their era is that their reforms of poverty and simplicity were so necessary for reforming the Church. One trustworthy early friar, Salimbene of Parma, explained in very frank language:

I have found some priests lending out their money to usury and enriching themselves merely for the sake of their bastards: again, I have found others keeping taverns . . . and spending their nights in sin, and celebrating Mass next day. And when the people communicate, [the priests] thrust the consecrated hosts which remain over into clefts of the wall: though these are the very body of our Lord. And many other foul things they do and horrible to be told, which I pass over for brevity's sake.[35]

Salimbene's life bridged the time between the end of Francis's life (he was born five years before the saint's death) and the quarter century of Clare's life that followed. Salimbene came to know many of the first religious friends of Francis, including Bernard of Quintavalle, the first disciple. Salimbene writes often of Bernard, "with whom I dwelt for a whole winter in the Convent of Siena. He was my familiar friend. To me and other young men he would recount many marvels concerning the blessed Francis. Much good have I heard and learned from him."[36] His recording of the Church's corruption was damning. Salimbene offers many colorful, descriptive portraits of those who were using the Church for personal ends. Most memorable is the corruption of one of the bishops of Parma, a self-professed nonbeliever who even refused deathbed rites, saying that he had been bishop only for the money.[37] Abbot Guibert of Nogent wrote in France at about the same time: "What can I say? Not even monks, let alone the secular clergy, abstain from raising funds under suspicious circumstances, or shrink from speaking heresies on matters of faith in my presence in order to do the same."

The situation in France and Italy was such that it could not even be covered up. There was widespread opinion among the good elements of Church leadership that the pope must deal severely with the rotten characters, but there was also fear that sanctions would be so widespread as to induce the faithful into the heresy known as Donatism, a rejection of the Church because of the bad elements in it. This was the late Middle Ages: the Church stood at the center of public life; religion—which in these communities was only Christianity—was not a private affair, but a series of public pieties and obligations, all of which ran through local priests and bishops for their authority. Nevertheless, in encyclicals published between 1074 and 1109, Pope Gregory VII told all Christians that they must reject the sacraments given from the hands of corrupt priests. These letters, sent out into the parishes and read aloud in public squares, caused riots.

Six different popes ruled this troubled Church, spread across two continents, from the time of Francis's birth to the time of his conversion twenty-four years later. These were difficult times, which led to consolidations of power. During Francis's and Clare's lifetimes, the bishop of Rome became more and more influential in the lives of Western Christians. At almost precisely the time that Francis began his conversion, the bishop of Rome took on the spiritual power and responsibility that has marked popes ever since. He became the sole person who officially denotes sainthood, speaks with final doctrinal authority, and blesses new movements. Innocent III (1198–1216), the pope who first gave permission to Francis's movement, is the one who claimed these real powers for all future popes by saying: "We are the successor of the prince of the Apostles [Peter], but we are not his vicar, not the vicar of any man or Apostle, but the vicar of Jesus Christ himself."[38]

Despite all of these troubles in the churches, bishops and popes rarely garner mention in texts such as *The Little Flowers* or *The Mirror of Perfection*. Instead, we hear of friars, farmers, lepers, revelers, rambunctious children, merchants, and other common folk.

*The Pope's Dream (when Innocent III dreamed
that Francis would hold up a falling church)*

It is clear where Francis's priorities and those of the friars who
followed most closely in his footsteps lay. From the earliest days
of his conversion, Francis spent relatively little time worrying
about what Rome thought of his actions. His relationship to the
Church was always one of an obedient son who nevertheless tried
to keep himself removed from its centers and people of power.
He could see the ways in which papal authority could change the
ideals of a religious movement. When Francis's contemporary St.
Dominic was frequently heading to Rome for talks with cardinals
and popes, Francis was usually avoiding the trip. Rarely do we see
Francis running to his local bishop, or to Rome, for permission to
do something. His attention lay elsewhere, but also, he knew
better than to always be asking.

But soon after the saint's death, his Order entered the arena of
religious politics and power struggles, competing with Benedictines,

Dominicans, and Cistercians. When a Franciscan entered into a dispute with a university colleague, landowner, or civil authority, or was accused by the Inquisition of doctrinal or moral error, the resolution of the dispute rested largely on who had the more powerful support in Rome. Whom you knew became the test of who was right. This was not true in Francis's day. Francis was wary of any friar's pursuing power or influence of any kind. In fact, he would not have liked that a Franciscan, Nicholas IV, became pope within a generation of his death (1288), or that another, John Peckam, became the archbishop of Canterbury (1279–1292).

When Francis turned to do as Christ told him at San Damiano— "go and repair my house, which, as you can see, is falling down"— he did not have in mind ways of fixing these big problems within the Church. That would have been impossible for him. Instead, he understood himself as one simple man who could easily do as God told him to do: repair churches, one by one, with his hands. He did not begin a funding campaign. He did not begin a recruitment effort, seeking helpers. He began gathering stones, which was difficult work for such a small man. As *The Legend of the Three Companions* relates, "he had been very refined while living in his father's house."[39] Francis began the task of rebuilding churches, starting with San Damiano itself. G. K. Chesterton writes:

> He went about by himself collecting stones. He begged all the people he met to give him stones. In fact he became a new sort of beggar, reversing the parable; a beggar who asks not for bread but a stone. Probably, as happened to him again and again throughout his extraordinary existence, the very queerness of the request gave it a sort of popularity; and all sorts of idle and luxurious people fell in with the benevolent project, as they would have done with a bet.[40]

He, in fact, never left behind the task of maintaining churches. Even in his later years, Francis would always carry a broom when he went off to preach in a church. He would preach and then sweep the floor clean.[41]

# CHAPTER 5

# *WHO IS MY FATHER?*

There is a startling tradition in history of young men and women spurning their fathers (and sometimes their mothers) for service to God alone. Francis stole from his father in order to give to the poor, and then, when confronted about his wrongdoing in the public square before the bishop of Assisi, refused to repent. Isn't repenting what a saint would have been expected to do? Apparently not, according to the early texts. Neither Thomas of Celano nor Bonaventure nor any of the early companions question Francis's motives, although it is mentioned that the priest of San Damiano, to whom Francis wanted to give the money, would not accept it.

Francis's actions in the piazza were a surprise to all who witnessed them, and this is why the story comes down to us with such drama and intensity. Francis turned his back completely on his family, stripping naked and leaving even the clothes off his back as payment of his earthly debt to his father. He shocked his contemporaries not only by his extravagant commitment to God, expressed profoundly for the first time in that public confrontation, but through the plain rejection of his father. Francis said before everyone in town: "Until this moment, I have called you my father, but from this point forward I will confidently say, 'Our Father,

44

Who art in heaven.' It is with God my Father that I have laid up my treasure and with whom I have fastened my entire hope and trust.'"[42] The son disowned the father.

There is no question that all of this would have brought tremendous shame on Peter Bernardone, as well as suspicion on the son. But there are no apologies from the early biographers. Before the encounter between father and son, in fact, *The Legend of the Three Companions* emphasizes that Francis spent time fasting and weeping, both symbols of a saint's asking for God's guidance, "casting his hope completely on the Lord, who in turn, filled him with inexpressible joy and shone before him as a marvelous light."[43]

After the public demonstration against the father, we also never again hear of Francis's mother. In the life of a saint as sensitive as Francis, it seems unusual that we would know almost nothing about his mother. Surely, a converted man would still have room in his life to love his mother, a woman who, it seems, protected him more than once from the wrath of her husband. After his son had stolen those garments from his shop and sold them to give the money to the poor, Peter Bernardone beat him and locked him in the cellar of the family home, according to tradition. Tourists to Assisi can still see the place where Francis's childhood home once stood, and outside it there is a statue depicting his father and mother; his mother appears holding broken chains that symbolize how she freed him while her husband was away. Bonaventure tells it this way: "After a little time, after the father's departing, his mother—who disliked her husband's ways of dealing with their son—freed Francis from his bonds, and let him go from the house." There is no mention then that Francis thanked his mother, embraced her, or even spoke with her. Instead, "Francis gave thanks to the Lord Almighty, and returned to the place where he had been before."[44]

Thomas of Celano recorded years later how Francis picked his spiritual brother, Elias, as "the one he chose to be as a mother to himself."[45] The son disowned his mother, as well.

This may be the most dramatic case in history of a son's sinning against his father, completely dismissing both father and mother, and yet going on to become a tremendous saint. And yet, the ambiguities go unmentioned by Francis's early biographers.

Throughout the late Middle Ages, the primary model for a troubled relationship between father and son was the parable of the prodigal son as told in Luke 15. Abundant visual images and narrative retellings of this parable at the time of Francis's conversion demonstrate that the story dominated the imagination of people. The lesson of the parable would have included the idea that penitence and reconciliation were the prescriptions for wayward sons—not the sort of grandstanding that Francis did.

Some of the first Gothic cathedrals featured stained-glass windows that told the parable of the prodigal son. These were erected during the difficult years of Francis's conversion. The parable had become— just at the time of Francis's coming up—one of the most popular iconographic representations of what it means to sin and then find redemption. The benevolent father of the tale told by Jesus was likened to God the Father, who, no matter what a young sinner may do, is ready and waiting and willing to receive. Francis likely never saw the stained-glass windows installed at the Chartres (1200), Sens (1207), Bourges (1210), or Poitiers (1210) cathedrals—featuring tellings of the popular parable—but he was deliberately acting contrary to what had become a popular expression of the relationship between fathers and sons.[46] Why wouldn't the Assisi bishop, the priest of San Damiano, or later, Pope Innocent III, have asked Francis to reconcile with his father? In the parable, the prodigal son, after squandering his inheritance, is reduced to caring for pigs and even to eating what they eat, for he has nothing left. Finally, he decides to travel back home and ask his father's forgiveness.

According to the pedagogy of Jesus' parable, Francis could have squandered away his father's wealth (by selling the stolen cloth) but then returned home to ask forgiveness. If things had gone that way, it would have also meant re-imagining the time that Francis spent in between the selling of the cloth and facing his father before the bishop. Some of the texts say that that period of time was as long as a month, as Francis hid from his father, fasting and weeping and so on, before gaining the confidence to face him. What was seen as wallowing with pigs became something saintly, for Francis. The father of the biblical parable says to his servants after embracing his son who has returned from sin, "Bring the calf we have been fattening, and kill it; we will celebrate by having a feast." Francis did nothing of the kind. Instead, he would have his heavenly Father say this to him, rather than his earthly one. Other teachings of Jesus tell us that the heavenly host rejoices when even one sinner repents (Luke 15:7). It would seem, though, that Francis had no need to repent. But why?

By the time his father confronted him before the bishop, Francis knew his Gospels well enough to know that he was rebelling against his parents in a way that was similar to what Jesus himself had done. In Luke's Gospel we find the scene of Jesus as a twelve-year-old boy in the temple in Jerusalem, when he stayed behind to talk with the scholars and priests against the wishes of his parents. After searching for him for three days in a strange city, Mary found Jesus there. "They were overcome when they saw him, and his mother said to him, 'My child, why have you done this to us?'" Isn't that how any mother would feel? She added, "See how worried your father and I have been, looking for you." And young Jesus replied, "Why were you looking for me? Did you not know that I must be in my Father's house?" Luke concludes, "But they did not understand what he meant."[47]

In the tradition of a holy man or woman who despises the things of the world and *hates* his own life, Francis turned away from his family as he turned toward God. He was following the words of Jesus in John's Gospel, chapter twelve: "Anyone who loves his life loses it, and anyone who hates his life in this world will keep it for eternal life."

## REDEFINING FAMILY RELATIONSHIPS

For eight hundred years now, people have been drawn with curiosity toward the lives of Francis and Clare. We look on the personalities and intentions of the first Franciscans as one of those moments in the history of the Church when religion was fresh and vibrant. But both Francis's and Clare's religious lives were based upon a rejection of their families. What does all of this mean? Why would it be necessary to abandon one's earthly family for a spiritual one?

We must consider the monastic understanding of *conversion*. In the sixth century, St. Benedict of Nursia wrote in his *Rule* of the importance of undergoing what is called *a conversion of life*, a total renunciation of what is past in order to focus solely on what is godly. "Admission to the religious life should not be made easy," Benedict wrote, saying that only a man who keeps knocking at the front door, asking for entrance to the monastery (and to the life), should be admitted. Most men will go away after a short while of being ignored or rejected, and Benedict advises making one wait for several days! Then, once a man enters into the life, it is intended to be harsh and difficult, "won" (not earned) by great effort and determination. This includes turning away from everyone who had previously comforted or cared for the candidate. And then, "If he owns anything, he must either give it to the poor beforehand, or deed it to the monastery, keeping nothing for himself, for he owns nothing, not even his own body. When this is done he is to change his clothes for those of the community."[48] His old self is now dead and his converted self has begun.

By converting, Francis was turning away from the bondage of the world, which he believed to include his father and mother. The freedom of childhood had become for him (literally, at one point, at least) shackles and obstacles to true freedom in Christ. Francis had shown, up until that final, absolute break, how a repentant man can sometimes still be in chains. But he also showed that confession and contrition are sometimes not what is called for, but instead, complete and total conversion.

Sometimes, however, the language of monastic conversions can be overblown. Thomas of Celano describes the world that Clare left behind as "the filth of Babylon," a description that would be somewhat absurd if applied to her comfortable home and seemingly loving family. Clare's actions were similarly dramatic and bold, if somewhat less ostentatious. When she fled her family in the middle of the night and stealthily made her way to meet Francis and his group of friars at Portiuncula, Thomas of Celano alludes to a phrase from Hebrews 13; she moved "outside the camp," he said, describing Clare's leaving the safe and familiar for the unknown. Throughout the conversion narratives of both Francis and Clare, as well as in classic monastic texts such as Benedict's *Rule*, when saints leave their families behind, it is as if a soldier has gone off to fight.

When the men of Clare's family came for her, she refused to listen to their arguments and she would not allow herself to be removed. Imagine if your teenaged sister or daughter had run away from your family home and had gone to live with a group of men considered by most people to be lunatics. What would you have done? Would you have looked on your runaway sister or daughter as being well on her way to sainthood? Turning one's back on one's earthly parents was seen as necessary if it meant that one's identity could be fully realized in God. When Clare arrived at Portiuncula on that first night, in the words of one biographer, she "gave to the world her letter of divorce" as she took on the hair, clothes, and vows of a woman married to Christ.[49]

Clare advised others to make the same sort of distinctions in their lives when they were called to a religious life. Conversion was total. In one of her letters to Agnes of Prague, Clare calls her disciple Agnes the "daughter of the King of Kings" in contrast to her earthly state as daughter of the King of Bohemia, Ottokar I (d. 1230). Clare also rejoiced when Princess Agnes chose virginity over marriage. Why? Is there something wrong with marriage? No, but to Francis and Clare, a conversion that involved choosing virginity, like choosing poverty, was complete and permanent. Or, at least, it was more complete and permanent than are, for instance, decisions to sin less or to do good more often.

The ultimate beauty of a Franciscan life in the early days came through its proximity to replicating the life of Christ. Christ was poor—he owned nothing; and Christ was chaste—he never married. The physical hardships of poverty and virginity were exactly the point, for Francis and then Clare, of a converted life; they were twin aspects of true Gospel living.

They both intended to do nothing less than turn the world upside down. *Light in the Dark Ages* is a very broad claim for the title of this book, but it is true. Not that the medieval period was so dark, as the old textbooks used to claim; it was actually a tremendous time of faith and piety that we should admire in many ways. The label "Middle Ages" originated at the very beginning of the Renaissance in the late fifteenth century. Its purpose was to distinguish between the classical era of Greek and Roman civilizations, and the rediscovery of those classical forms in the emerging Renaissance. The creativity of Francis's and Clare's lives and movement was one of the most important markers in the time leading up to the color of the fourteenth and fifteenth centuries.

The wars, corruption, and disease that Francis and Clare faced were dark indeed. We most often imagine them with birds, and flowers, and rabbits, and calming wolves to rest by their sides, but we might just as well listen to them as prophets who sought an entirely different way of living.

They believed that any negative effects of conversion, such as leaving behind parents, are easily surpassed by the true freedom that comes from a total lack of attachments. Clare spoke at least for women when she declared in her first letter to Agnes that to be faithful and converted is to become "the bride, mother and sister of Jesus Christ." In Matthew 12, Jesus said, "Anyone who does the will of my Father in heaven is my brother and sister and mother." Clare added "bride" to the mix. Francis said that we are indeed all three of these at once, when we are fully converted. In what is referred to as the second version of "The Letter to the Faithful," Francis said that the Spirit of the Lord will dwell with those men and women who have persevered in faithfulness. Then, he described the various functions of those who take on new roles in the redefined family relationships that come with conversion:

> They are spouses, brothers, and mothers of our Lord Jesus Christ. *Spouses* when the faithful soul is united to Christ by

the Holy Spirit. *Brothers* when we do the will of the Father. And *mothers* when we carry Christ in our hearts and bodies through love and a pure spirit, giving birth to Jesus through all holy activity, showing ourselves as an example to the world.

Clare and Francis wanted to live as they believed Jesus intended for people to live, with lives transformed by a reordering of what it means to be family—bride, mother, father, sister, and brother. Imagine a group of people who truly follow these teachings of Jesus and you will see how the first Franciscans lived with each other. The old claims of biological families—for marriages, children, inheritances, work, and commerce—no longer apply. One's father and mother may be not biologically but spiritually chosen. One's brothers and sisters are every person whom we meet.

Jesus turned the law of Moses on its head when he declared that our neighbors are those to whom we owe the most. The prophet Isaiah had foretold of that servant of Israel who would come and bring forth justice to the nations in this way. In chapter 42, Isaiah even extends our neighborly commitments to people whom most of us would never expect to care for. Similar to Francis and Clare and their care for lepers, imagine if we actually imitated Jesus to the point of doing what Isaiah said was to be done: "I have given you as a covenant to the people, a light to the nations, to open the eyes that are blind, to bring out the prisoners from the dungeon, from the prison those who sit in darkness." What would happen if Christians were to lead the way in opening the doors of prisons, inviting "those who sit in darkness" to come and sit among us; to advocate for early release programs for those who do not pose a threat to the community; to forgive them, reconcile with them, and embrace them as our brothers and sisters? What if more Christians were to do the same with lepers, and those modern-day lepers who suffer from diseases that are still vague, unknown, and dangerous? That is what Francis and Clare were doing, and it was turning the world upside down.

There was a time when Francis was staying at the Franciscan friary in Monte Casale, which was situated in a wilderness known for harboring thieves and dangerous men. One evening, three men who had become infamous in the area knocked on the door of the friary looking destitute and asking for food. The young friar who answered the door was known as Angel. Rather than invite the men in and feed them, Angel said to them, "You are not worthy to even walk on the earth, for you do not show reverence to humans or to God, who created you. Get out of here!" Francis rebuked Angel and forced him to run after the men with alms, while Francis prayed to God to soften the men's hearts. The hospitality shown that night led the three thieves to eventually become friars themselves.[50]

Our saints intended to redefine—as Jesus had before them—what it means to be a child, sister, brother, mother, and father. Jesus said to his parents in the temple at age twelve, "Why were you looking for me? Did you not know that I must be in my Father's house?" Later, in the Sermon on the Mount, Jesus' message included redefining who we are and to whom we are related. When the disciples were arguing before the Passion about which one of them was the greatest, Jesus said that children were the greatest. This was shocking to them! Our over-sentimentalizing of children and childhood today blurs our ability to see the scene clearly: in antiquity, children were of very little value to adults and viewed as incomplete human beings.

Just as the Apostle Paul later defined love in his first letter to the Corinthians, Jesus defined family and neighbor in ways that had never before been understood. Jesus said: You have heard that the Law says not to murder? I say: Do not be angry with your brother. Do not even insult your sister. Your sacrifices are ineffective if you have unresolved conflict with another person. You have heard that the Law says not to commit adultery? I say: Even the thoughts of your minds and the wishes of your imaginations betray you. You have heard that the Law says an eye for an eye and a tooth for a tooth? I say: Do not even resist someone who wants to do you harm. If someone wants to steal your coat, give him also your cloak. You have heard that the Law says you should love your neighbor and hate your enemy? I say: Love your enemies and pray for them, too. All people are your neighbors. All men are your brothers. All women are your sisters. Obey your Father in heaven. What Jesus was doing was very new, unusual, and full of reformation of what it means to be in relationship.

Francis and Clare restored nobility to the human being. This was one of their greatest gifts to their age. G. K. Chesterton wrote:

> Workhouses and lunatic asylums are thronged with men who believe in themselves. Of Francis it is far truer to say that the secret of his success was his profound belief in other people. . . . Francis always assumed that everyone must be just as anxious . . . as he was. He planned a visit to the Emperor to draw his attention to the needs of "his little sisters the larks." He used to talk to any thieves and robbers he met about their misfortune in being unable to give rein to their desire for holiness. It was an innocent habit, and doubtless the robbers often "got round him," as the phrase goes. Quite as often, however, they discovered that he had "got round" them, and discovered the other side, the side of secret nobility.[51]

We call Francis the saint of peace, but often forget that his caring was both personal and political. It was common for Francis to step into the middle of some political dispute between the wealthy and the unfortunate in Assisi in order to see that the poor's interests were represented properly. Francis believed that the sign of a person who has been transformed or is becoming transformed by the Spirit of God is peacefulness and carefulness in dealing with other people.

It can be difficult to relate to this aspect of Franciscan spirituality today. We have built up tremendous boundaries for ourselves, and between ourselves and others, don't-touch-me-or-invade-my-space boundaries. Francis did, too. He was wealthy and privileged—his father taught him to carry himself in such a way that that would be evident to all. That is why he deliberately made himself less sure, less confident in his appearance, or in the way in which he carried himself. In order to understand this spirit today, we would have to attend our next business meeting, church service, or society event by removing our shoes or untucking our shirts, or walking around touching strangers on the shoulder, or messing up our hair, doing something outside our normal, safe, physical boundaries. We would do these little, *foolish* things to ourselves and then pretend as if nothing was different.

According to Francis and Clare, our identities are not summarized by biology, ancestry, or socialization. We are like Nicodemus, who couldn't understand how this realignment of human relationships could possibly work. When Jesus told him that all things change when we are born of the Spirit, Nicodemus asked Jesus two questions that have forever pigeonholed him as some sort of a dunce: "How can anyone who is already old be born? Is it possible to go back into the womb again and be born?"

But Nicodemus wasn't a dunce. We are still asking these questions today when we continue to follow traditional ways of understanding family. Francis and Clare taught that we don't really know who Jesus is. He is in the hungry, the poor, the oppressed, and the dispossessed. What Jesus is today he may not be exactly tomorrow. The first Franciscans formed their life in this tradition—wanting to be Jesus in the changing, ever-challenging world.

# NO FROWNING
# SAINTS

F rancis was being watched while his conversion was underway. Unlike most of us, who undergo conversions that are private and mostly internal, Francis's was played out in the piazzas of Assisi. His neighbors watched as he began to leave his father's table and beg for his daily bread, work not in his father's shop but with his hands to rebuild fallen church buildings, learn to pray the liturgical hours without help from monk or monastery, leave the piazzas and their crowds behind and head off into the valleys of the surrounding countryside, and preach repentance to others, even as he was himself learning what that meant. They saw Francis transform from a high-spirited teenager to a melancholy soldier to a cheerful man with nothing.

An almost flamboyant sense of drama marks the earliest efforts of Francis to distinguish himself from worldly concerns, family constraints, and even spiritual norms. The scenes are familiar to those who have read any of the biographies of the saint. He returns from a local, warring conflict against Perugia in disgrace and shame, probably having deserted; he begins to hear the voice of God speaking to him from a crucifix in an abandoned church; he steals from his father in order to give to the needy; he faces his father's wrath and accusations in the public square in front of the bishop's home and not only returns the money to his father but also strips naked, offering *everything* to him that is rightly his; and he wanders off alone into the wilderness around Assisi, known only to lepers and robbers.

*St. Francis Renounces His Worldly Goods*

Denial of self was paramount to Francis in those early days. At first, he felt that he had so much to give up before he could honestly call himself a follower of Christ. Working with his hands, doing diffi-cult work, was not only his obedience but also his penance.

A rich man of Assisi by the name of Bernard of Quintavalle was one of those observing Francis. He was intrigued by the younger man and respected his work around the city, saving abandoned churches and seeking to better the lives of others. But Bernard, being very successful, felt that he knew the qualities that would make a genuine leader rather than a charlatan. Bernard wanted to see the unkempt Francis up close and over a period of time. He invited him one night to his house.

Bernard asked Francis to have supper with him. Francis readily accepted, anxious to have a dedicated audience. One of the great historians of the Franciscan movement writes: "What took place within the walls of that house during that night has deeply affected the history of the Christian Church, for it was during those hours that the Order of Friars Minor was born."[52] While they ate together in Bernard's lovely home, we see none of the behavior that would later distinguish Francis from his wealthy hosts in similar situations. In later years when Francis was invited to eat with cardinals or lords, he would do things like beg for bread outside in the street while a sumptuous meal was being prepared for him and the others by servants inside, and he would return to the table with his meager scraps, insisting on eating only those. But that came later, in Francis's mature religious life, when he possessed a confidence that was absent from his early years.

Bernard asked Francis many questions about religion and Christian discipleship during their time together. They were there for a long time—so long, in fact, that Bernard eventually asked Francis to stay the night. Bernard knew that Francis's roof was often only the stars, and he had probably begun to take a real liking to the young man. *The Little Flowers* says that it was Bernard's "secret wish" from the beginning to test Francis's faith to the point of inviting him to spend the night, but that may be a later editor's interpretation. It turned out that the two men had many things in common.

So Bernard had a bed prepared for Francis in the same space in which he himself usually slept. Francis prepared himself for bed and got in, pretending to fall soundly asleep. Within a short while, Bernard too began to snore and, at that sound, Francis rose to pray. It turns out, however, that Bernard was the cleverer of the two, since he was also pretending to sleep, wanting to observe something of Francis's private life. As he continued his pretend snoring, what Bernard saw convinced him of his guest's unfeigned spirit. There was young Francis rocking slightly to and fro, praying over and over again as if he were searching deep inside himself for something. *Deus meus et omnia:* "My God and my all."

Soon after that evening, Bernard of Quintavalle became the first of Francis's disciples. Bernard and another man who was very successful in both law and Church, Peter of Catani, came to find Francis, probably while he was carrying rocks from Assisi down to San Damiano, asking how to join him in the work. This wasn't simply a case of two men wanting to carry some rocks or help out for a day. There was something about Francis's commitment and spirit that communicated a complete change of life. His was a life of thorough *conversion.* There was deep meaning in Francis's otherwise rudimentary work that struck others as profound and important.

At first, Francis was full of hesitancy, not really knowing how to take on followers. His first instincts were to be sure to do everything correctly. He knew that there were groups of mendicants and ascetics frequently wandering in Italy and France and elsewhere who were outside the boundaries of orthodox faith. Francis wanted to live the life correctly. Even in his later years, he would never become overconfident in his own instincts; he was always questioning himself.

Francis suggested that he, Bernard, and Peter go to the bishop's house in Assisi and open the Scriptures together for guidance. Once they arrived, the tradition tells us that Francis opened the Gospels randomly, searching for wisdom in that haphazard way that people do when they are at a loss for what comes next.

Tradition says that they read three passages. First, Francis opened the book at random and probably asked one of the other men to read what his eyes first set upon. Bernard read Matthew 19:20–21.

> The young man said to [Jesus], "I have kept all [of the commandments]. What more do I need to do [to have eternal life]?" Jesus said, "If you wish to be perfect, go and sell your possessions and give the money to the poor, and you will have treasure in heaven; then come, follow me."

Francis picked up the book again, and leafing forward, searched quickly for another relevant passage. This time, he probably asked Peter to read what his eyes first landed on. It was from Luke 9:1–3:

> [Jesus] called the Twelve together and gave them power and authority over all devils and to cure diseases, and he sent them out to proclaim the kingdom of God and to heal. He said to them, "Take nothing for the journey: neither staff, nor haversack, nor bread, nor money; and do not have a spare tunic."

Finally, Francis may have read the last passage himself, turning back toward the beginning of the ornate book of Gospels that they had borrowed from the luxurious home of the bishop. He returned to Matthew's Gospel, which would later become the one that he quoted more often than any other, and read from chapter 16, verses 24 and 25:

> Then Jesus said to his disciples, "If anyone wants to be a follower of mine, let him renounce himself and take up his cross and follow me. Anyone who wants to save his life will lose it; but anyone who loses his life for my sake will find it."

That was all that Francis, Bernard, and Peter required in order to create their first rule of life. The three quickly returned to their homes to help Bernard sell all that he owned. Both Bernard and Peter were highborn, but Bernard was rich. They carried money out to give to the people of Assisi, its hospitals, pilgrims, and various places of need. There are many stories of Francis, Bernard, and Peter standing in the piazza distributing Bernard's money to the poor. We can imagine the commotion that this must have caused in town, as people buzzed around, grabbing for goods and coins but also wondering how it all could have happened. When Bernard's valuables were brought forth, the people surely filled his hallways like bees entering and leaving a hive. This further commotion would have cemented the notion of Francis's insanity in the minds of some, while intriguing others.

When Francis had begun begging for his bread two years earlier, his father was horrified at the sight of it and disowned him publicly before the entire town. Not only did Francis beg alms in the piazzas, but Thomas of Celano tells us that at some point he also began "begging for leftovers door to door,"[53] something that would have surely embarrassed his family. Francis also began declaring that his bride was Lady Poverty, no doubt another subtle jab at his father's expectations for him. Every Umbrian father wanted a woman of high character, good family, and decent dowry for his son to marry; Francis had Lady Poverty instead. Finally, when Francis began leading Bernard and Peter into this new life, it was the greatest disgrace for Peter Bernardone. Now, Francis was leading other noble people to do the same. The very public nature of what was happening must have made his son's conversion all the harder to stomach for Peter Bernardone. But what brought shame to his father brought glory to Christ, Francis thought. The ways of God confound the wise, the reasonable, and the predictable.

Isn't it amazing that men were willing to follow a ragtag Francis on a mission when they had so much to lose? They wouldn't have done it if Francis was only one in a long line of dour and disapproving saints. People have always been attracted to Saints Francis and Clare because they seem to have come so close to that enigmatic command of Jesus to the first disciples: "Be perfect." However, neither of them became a saint through their writings, or by athletic acrobatics of self-denial. It was Teresa of Avila, a later saint, who once poked playfully at the *frowning saints* of Christian tradition, saying that she never wanted to become one. "O Lord, deliver us from sour-faced saints!" she used to say. Francis and Clare would have agreed. Early self-denial transformed in them into the sort of joy and freedom that characterizes those who have given up everything for good.

## Joy Turns to Foolishness

Francis and his new brothers often took their message to the lively outdoor places that still characterize Umbrian towns. As one old travel guide explains: "Italian life has always had a gregarious, outdoor character; hence the importance of loggias and piazzas. No one here has patience to sit still indoors for long. Italian chairs of all periods are notoriously uncomfortable. There are more bars serving standing customers in a hurry to get outside again than *caffes* with tables and chairs. Almost the only thing Italians have patience for is a good talker. To this they are ready to listen for hours."[54] The work of rebuilding the Church happened in the piazzas and cafes of Assisi and surrounding towns as Francis and

Clare drew others to join in the good work. There are many tales of the first Franciscans spreading the word of their new life in the open air. And by all accounts, Francis was always a good talker.

The early Franciscans became experts at the unpredictable. Within a few years of the conversion of Bernard and Peter, when they had all become as close as brothers, there was a time when Bernard began to spend many hours each day in quiet contemplation, away from the activities of the other friars. Bernard had, in fact, become seriously adept at meditation, so much so that his reputation for long periods of mystical communion with God had earned him a reputation outside the community of friars. He was known throughout the area as a man who communed with God.

But Francis did not approve of contemplation when it was practiced to the exclusion of all other forms of faithfulness. Francis remembered that first day, years earlier, in the bishop's home when the three of them had read from Luke's Gospel that Jesus called the first twelve disciples to do two things: "to proclaim the kingdom of God and to heal." What was good for Jesus and his disciples would also be good for Francis and his. So, Francis searched out Bernard one morning as Bernard was deep in his meditation and commanded him to leave his quietude and go to the nearest Assisi church and preach from his heart to the people. Bernard resisted. I am not a preacher, he said. For his disobedience, Francis commanded poor Bernard to go immediately and preach in the first church he could find—and in his underwear.

A short time elapsed after Bernard's faithful leaving to do as he was told before Francis said to himself, *Who am I, to send my faithful brother Bernard, one of the first people to believe in my mission and one of the most respected men of Assisi, to go and preach in his underwear!* Francis reproached himself and prepared himself to go and join Bernard, and the two men preached together—in their underwear! From that pulpit, Francis spoke eloquently of the vanity of fancy garments and their contrast with an eternity of God's love. It is said that many people were converted to following Christ on that day.

## STRENGTHS AND WEAKNESSES

Saints are people who live and act with great certainty. They have discovered a freedom that eludes most of us during our lifetimes. By *giving away* possessions, status, and ego, Francis boiled the meaning of life down to what is most essential. This is what he intended when he described freedom in simplicity. It does a Christian no good, Francis understood, to *take back* or *hold onto* things; our false self reemerges and we lose a portion of God's freedom and happiness.

There were occasions in the life of Francis, however, when we see his false self reappearing. We should never make the mistake of thinking that he was perfect. For example, he seems to have always had trouble living in his father's

It is difficult for us to imagine today how important the Christian basilica was during barbaric times. There was often no other civilization other than what was within its walls. After the fall of Rome, the light of science and art was threatened with extinction, and the basilica had to supply an education for the people. Within its walls was the power to illuminate the mind and inspire the imagination.

It was deemed important that people should go forth from the basilica instructed and well satisfied, and that they should return there with joy—as to a place where they found truth and beauty. In order to satisfy this ideal, a church had to contain a complete theology and a complete sacred poem. This was the aim of those artists who covered the churches throughout Italy with mosaics, and not only the apse of their buildings, but also often the naves, the vestibule, and the frontal with the history of both Testaments amplified by the legends of the saints and crowned by the visions of the Apocalypse. Nothing can equal the effect of that noble figure of Christ which stands out prominently on a background of gold, standing in the midst of an encircling heaven, having on His left and right saints who offer up their crowns to Him. Below may be seen the Lamb resting on the mountain from which issue the four streams, symbolic of the Four Evangelists. Twelve sheep emerge from the two towns of Jerusalem and Bethlehem, signifying the Christian host recruiting in the synagogue and among the Gentiles.

Finally, amid the details that ornament these works of art appear stags and doves, lilies and palms, all the symbols of Christian antiquity that have been preserved and interpreted by an uninterrupted tradition. And, to show in a striking manner that it was not intended to

shadow. There were times when Francis rebuked his brothers with such ferocity that we almost see the elder Bernardone, rather than the son. This happened most of all when friars wanted to own things that Francis felt were unnecessary. He would combat these desires in others with a spirit that was unlike him, as if he were once again arguing against his father. He could also be fierce in denying their wishes, and occasionally mean. Even *The Mirror of Perfection*, that loving collection of tales written by his closest companions, recounts that Francis could be ornery when discussing with a friar the idea of owning more than one tunic. "He used to bitterly accuse those who wanted good fabric for their tunic, finding fault with those who believed contrary to him, and would then sew rougher material into his own."[55]

The same sort of old or false self seems to have reappeared in the arduous process of taking control, and then losing control, of his own Order later in life. "[Francis] wanted to obey, not to command,"[56] explains one scholar. But we see Francis frustrated at those times when he was caught between the desire to hold power and authority in order to do good things with it, and the shame and disappointment he must have felt when the same was taken away from him. Again from *The Mirror of Perfection*, we at first see that Francis resigned the office of minister-general of the Order, appointing Peter Catani in his place: "Francis remained forever, from that time forward, a subject, bearing himself humbly in all things until his death, even more than all of the others." But two short chapters later, *The Mirror* recounts a conversation in which Francis tells one of his brothers the real reason why he resigned his office: he didn't feel that the friars were following his leadership. On his deathbed, he rose and cried out, "Who are those who would steal my Order and my brothers from my hands! When I come to General Chapter, I will show them who they are!"[57]

Francis and Clare lived with certainty when they were far away from power and authority. People who do great things usually act with little doubt, and both of our saints had confidence in their mature years, listening to the Spirit of God in their consciences.

> be a source of secret instruction reserved for the initiated, but to give to all the key of these illuminating pictures, they were accompanied by inscriptions. Verses could be read beneath each mosaic which explained its meaning, pointed a lesson, sought to move the spectator, and draw from him a tear or a prayer. These grand and austere walls, these Roman churches became like so many pages in which were celebrated the miracles of the saints, the princely founders of the basilica, and the famous dead sleeping beneath its roof.
>
> —*Frederick Ozanam*

Mahatma Gandhi wrote in his autobiography: "I am far from claiming any finality or infallibility about my conclusions. One claim I do indeed make and it is this. For me they appear to be absolutely correct, and seem for the time being to be final. For if they were not, I should base no action on them." In his *Testament*, Francis said, "No one showed me what I had to do, but the Most High himself revealed to me that I should live according to the pattern of the holy gospel." Clare pursued holiness so doggedly that she would, at times, challenge her superiors on matters of faith and practice. Most famously, Clare provided the first example of a hunger strike undertaken as a means of changing the status quo. After Francis's death, Pope Gregory worried about the Poor Clares being too much exposed to the influence of men—the friars—going in and out of the  convent. The men would bring food and other goods to the women's monastery, and they would also come to preach and teach. Clare valued her brothers so much that she could not tolerate their being taken from her.  So, she told the sisters to stop taking food and other things from the hands of the friars if they would not also be allowed by the minister-general to come into the enclosure and teach. The sisters would not eat if they could not also spend time with their brothers. When the minister-general reported the situation to Pope Gregory, he immediately reversed his decision.

She was undoubtedly tough. On another occasion, Clare challenged political and military powers in ways that were uncommon for a cloistered woman. One of the most famous episodes in Clare's life— reproduced in iconography of all kinds over the centuries—took place more than a decade after the death of Francis. It happened in September 1240 at San Damiano. Emperor Frederick II (who, ironically, had been betrothed as a younger man to Clare's disciple Agnes of Prague) was warring with the pope and hired Saracen mercenaries as part of his invading armies. They would hit and run, destroying their various targets, many of them religious foundations throughout the Italian city-states that were dear to the pope and also relatively unprotected. When these foreign fighters surrounded the monastery at San Damiano, while the other women very understandably hid somewhere inside undoubtedly praying fervently for their safety, Clare led a procession of one outside into the yard holding the Eucharist (or, Christ himself) before her, "striking" at the men with its power. In the paintings of this scene, Clare is usually depicted as holding high a monstrance that contained the Eucharistic host. Scholars know that the monstrance was not actually created until sometime after the Council of Trent in the sixteenth century, but nevertheless, the message is clear: Clare used Christ as her instrument in battle. In this instance, Clare also shows herself to have been powerful in a way that Francis was not.

But just as Francis and Clare were both charismatic leaders, they were not organizers. They also were not good administrators. They were too busy to worry about the future, and they felt too free to spend much time brooding over ideas, something that would have tied them down to libraries, desks, and books. Their leadership was high on charisma and low on follow-through. To take even a small detail, for example, the only gardening that we know of Francis and Clare doing was flowers, to show the beauty of creation. They saw no point to sowing seeds that would one day in the future feed them. Miguel de Unamuno echoed Francis and Clare a century ago when he wrote, "There is no future; there never is any future. What is known as the future is one of the greatest of lies."[58] Today is always what mattered, what was real.

Francis and Clare's convictions were so ideal as to confound worldly realities. They refused to even handle money, or to take possession of any single thing. They felt free to borrow shelter or space or things, but never to have things as their own. They wanted to follow Christ, whom they saw as a stranger and a homeless man. So, for instance, if Francis had been given a large sum of money in order to fund a chain of leper hospitals across Europe, he probably would have turned it down.

In 2005, a collection of fine art was donated to the Province of St. Mary of the Capuchin Order in New York State and New England. The Capuchin friars did not refuse it, as Francis likely would have, but put the collection up for sale through Christie's auction house. One of the paintings alone (a landscape by J. M. W. Turner) fetched nearly $36 million. The painting was sold to Stephen A. Wynn, the owner of the Bellagio Casino in Las Vegas, and the funds were invested. The income has been set aside to be used to fund the Order's efforts in Latin America, Guam, and other poor centers throughout the world. Nevertheless, all evidence suggests that Francis and Clare would not have approved. They would have refused the gift as a temptation to vice.

Francis's and Clare's personalities were such that they were most free when they were following a simple path of living by a *Rule* and listening to the Spirit. Does this mean that they failed to leave the world with meaningful change and permanent reform? Perhaps in some sense, it does. They did not build hospitals, orphanages, or schools; they did not create foundations or fund philanthropies that would outlive them. Their work was of a much more personal nature. The influence of the dynamic is more difficult to characterize than is the influence of those who organize and administer.

The lives of Francis, Clare, and the first Franciscans were marked by charity and compassion that does not compare with the sort of work that is done by large organizations. They did not want their movement to be yet another career path for social advancement and power in the Church. They wanted only simple and joyful men and women. They always believed themselves called to a life of following Christ, and they cut away anything that stood in the way. They were not as interested in changing institutions as they were in impacting individual lives. They cared for people immediately, rather than caring for their needs longer term. But the sheer numbers of Franciscans in the first decades had an enormous impact on the world, and after the passing of Francis and Clare, those friars and sisters began to do some of those things that the founders had avoided. Francis, Bernard, and Peter began the movement in 1209, and by 1250, there were about thirty thousand men and women. Hundreds of Franciscan friaries existed within a decade of Francis's death, and a thousand by 1275.

Their legacy is full of extraordinary strengths and also basic weaknesses. Within a few years of receiving his first followers, Francis became known throughout Assisi for his simple greeting: "Peace and all good"—or, in Italian, "*Pace e Bene!*" During his lifetime, that was the purpose of his daily life, nothing more and nothing less. Clay plaques all over Assisi proclaim the same today.

# TRYING TO BE LIKE JESUS

The procession through town each Palm Sunday morning in Assisi involved nearly every citizen. Small chapels and businesses were closed on that important day so that all could be present for the march into the city center, the hearing of the complete Passion sung from the Gospel of Matthew, and most of all, the general communion.[59] The populace gathered outside the city walls with branches and flowers in hand, waiting for the procession to begin. The walls of medieval cities in Italy and elsewhere made it possible to reenact the first procession of Jesus into Jerusalem with a certain degree of accuracy. The people of Assisi were reminded, both by the words of their bishop and also by the symbolism of the march through the city gates, that this was as Jesus had entered the city of Jerusalem for the last time.

There was a heightened drama given to the reading of the Passion. A melodious Italian baritone would recite the words of Christ, while a deliberately harsh male voice would call out the chants from the crowd and the words of the disciple who betrayed him. It was this sort of dramatic rendering of the Passion that allowed the uneducated to understand what was happening, despite the use of a Latin text.

All of highborn Assisi was there on Palm Sunday morning, March 18, 1212. The day stood symbolically between the activities of the Lenten season and the business of Holy Week. The Saturday before Palm Sunday was the occasion for the last preparations of the boy and girl catechumens. The catechumens were all young children, much younger than Clare was in 1212. The rituals of preparation included breathing on the children, chanting Gospel verses above their heads, and anointing each child as set apart from the world, for Christ. One week later, on Holy Saturday, the neophytes would all be baptized formally into the Church.

At the conclusion of Mass on Palm Sunday, it was customary for each girl of marriage age to personally greet the bishop, presenting herself to him in a manner befitting a lady. For most of the girls in town, this event represented a high point in the year and was worried over, and prepared for, for weeks. It was a prelude of their marriage ceremonies to come, when all eyes were on the bride processing glamorously and joyfully down the aisle, back then just as now.

As we have already seen, Clare distinguished herself from all of the other girls by refusing to show herself as an eligible woman on that day. As all of refined Assisi watched, Clare refused to stand to greet the bishop, something that all of the young women did in order to receive his blessing and to show themselves to the rest of the town. Thomas of Celano tells us that it was Francis who instructed Clare in how to play along with the drama of the Palm Sunday routine. He even told her to dress in her finest clothes and to go forward with the other girls to receive her palm frond from the bishop, according to Thomas. It seems possible, however, that it was Clare herself who decided not to participate. If Francis had declared his marriage to Lady Poverty, Clare could also find another spouse. Her religious life began on that day.

## THE ART OF SPIRITUAL IMITATION

Faithful to the principles of hagiography, Clare's spiritual life was said to have actually begun before she was born. It seemed to the medieval imagination that, if Clare did the great things that she did in life, she must also have been remarkable before birth and after death. That is how saints were once *made* in the pages of hagiography.

The very first story told of Clare's spiritual life is, in fact, modeled on the Gospel accounts of the Annunciation to the Virgin Mary. Like the Virgin Mother, Clare's mother was said to have experienced a divine intervention with regard to a pregnancy. While already pregnant with Clare, her mother Ortolana was praying in the church of San Rufinus begging for mercy and comfort in child-birth when a voice from God said, "Woman, do not be afraid, for you will give safe birth to a child whose light will illuminate the world." This is why Ortolana named her Clare, which literally means *light*.

This sort of imitation of saints from the past was common practice in the composing of a new saint's legends. Christians inherited this sort of imitation from Judaism, where important figures such as Moses, Isaiah, and Jonah became types of people who would come later. The Gospels tell many stories, such as the feeding of the five thousand, in a way that show Jesus as the *new Moses*. The first recorded Christian martyr, St. Stephen, summarized this understanding in the eloquent sermon he preached before the high priest, recorded in Acts 7. Stephen compared Jesus to Moses in that both were powerful in words and deeds, sent by God to rescue his people, rejected by those same people, but then returned to free them from bondage.

As Jesus was the new Moses, so, too, did Jesus tell his followers to *follow* him. St. Paul later said the same, "Be imitators of me, as I am of Christ."[60] And so on it goes, as Christians have ever since sought to model themselves on those who have gone before. The hagiographer who models a saint's life by interpreting it through this sort of lens is doing something perfectly legitimate. Francis and Clare modeled their lives after Jesus and the Virgin Mary, and so did the first Franciscans model their lives after Francis and Clare. Being *Franciscan* was, after all, the whole purpose of becoming a friar or a sister—to become like Francis and Clare.

Unlike some other saints, however, Francis and Clare became renowned for their exact attention to detail in following Christ. They were imitators to a remarkable degree, seeking to eat as Jesus ate, sleep as he slept, travel as he traveled, and to do and not do what the Gospels tell us that Jesus did and didn't do. After Francis's death, Clare praised him in her *Testament* by saying that he was an imitator of Christ to the point of following in Christ's very footprints. Today, we read something like this with a spiritualizing eye, but it was not originally intended that way. The distance of twelve hundred years meant nothing to Francis and Clare; they modeled their apostolic lives as if Jesus was their contemporary.

*The Mirror of Perfection* provides some interesting detail of these measures taken by Francis. Here are some of the occasions in his life when he consciously did as his master had done down to the smallest, seemingly insignificant, details.

| Chapter of Mirror[61] | Example of imitating Christ | References to the words of Christ |
|---|---|---|
| 3 | Refusing to own even spiritual books, as an expression of complete poverty. | "Take nothing for the journey: neither staff, nor haversack, nor bread, nor money; and do not have a spare tunic." (Luke 9:3) |
| 4 | Teaching the dangers of arrogance in learning to a novice who wanted to pursue studies. | "To you is granted to understand the secrets of the kingdom of God; for the rest it remains in parables." (Luke 8:10) |

| Chapter of Mirror | Example of imitating Christ | References to the words of Christ |
|---|---|---|
| 9 | Refusing to stay in a cell if it was said to be his. | "Foxes have holes and the birds of the air have nests, but the Son of Man has nowhere to lay his head." (Matthew 8:20) |
| 19 | Instructing cooks in the communities not to prepare food the night before it was to be eaten. | "So do not worry about tomorrow." (Matthew 6:34) |

A French writer has called this attention to mimicking the life of Jesus "naïve, almost manic imitation."[62] Another, more positive spin explains that Francis was both unaware of more complex ways of reading the Scriptures and uninterested in discovering them: "The son of a prosperous merchant who had passed his youth in irresponsible and extravagant gaiety, he was ignorant of the theological commentaries on the words that might have slurred over their challenge, and he accepted, impulsively and with joy, their literal, practical application."[63] There are many additional examples from Francis's life and writings as well. For instance, in his *Later Rule*, Francis instructed all of his brothers to not only preach in language that is well chosen and chaste, but to always preach with brevity: "because our Lord kept his words brief while on earth." Bringing healing comfort to lepers was an imitation of Jesus, who healed ten lepers in Luke 17.

Francis's rebuilding of San Damiano was his first act of spiritual literalism. He was always one to do precisely what was asked, spending relatively little time trying to discern more subtle meanings to what he felt God had said directly to him. "Go and rebuild my church" was what the figure on the crucifix said as he knelt before it seeking meaning for his life. And so, literally, Francis rebuilt the Church by first rebuilding churches. Francis would not have gained the followers that he did if he had not been literal in his commitments. It was precisely his idealism that drew people to join him. There is simple beauty and attraction in doing what needs to be done regardless of other consequences.

There is an art to spiritual imitation, and it isn't only done through the physical details of life. Søren Kierkegaard taught that faith is impossible without a personal, passionate inwardness that takes hold of one's life. Each person's passion will be individual, but never unique, if it is truly formed around the God to whom we focus all of our attention. Trying to be like the great saints that have come before us is part of Christian discipleship. Imitation of Jesus is more important than praying to him—more important, even, than holding certain beliefs about him. As Simone Weil once argued in a letter to a priest, "Christ does not save all those who say to Him: 'Lord, Lord.' But he saves all those who out of a pure heart give a piece of bread to a starving man, without thinking about Him the least little bit."[64]

A simple joy attached itself to the early Franciscans, as friars and then sisters attempted to follow Christ's commands to the letter, asking very few questions that might fill a modern mind with doubts. Their love for obeying gave birth to a special sort of knowledge. As Jesus praised children for their simple faith, it is this same sort of deliberate simplicity that filled Francis and Clare with a knowledge of God in the soul that is quite different from any book knowledge. For whatever reasons, they could not have made a personal synthesis of the two—firsthand faith and book knowledge—as Thomas Aquinas or Bonaventure later did. Francis and Clare's commitments were Gospel-literal. In many ways, one might say that they followed Christ in every detail, except for when Christ went into the temple where discussions of ideas take place.

## THE TROUBLE WITH LEARNING

Their movement assumed that Scripture study and theology were of little value to a friar or sister. A true man of God would not want or need such things, Francis believed, for the Gospels would be sufficient. Due to the absence of formal theological study and teaching, we may assume that the early friars held and tolerated a wide variety of opinion on such matters. Silence breeds imagination. But Francis had no time for speculation of any kind. He was a man of action and believed that academic study could make it so that a person no longer sees the rest of the world clearly—as the librarians in Jorge Luis Borges's story "The Secret Miracle," who went blind looking for God among 400,000 volumes. It was as if Francis said to his followers: "Follow me, following Christ. Do as I do. Work, preach, practice charity; don't own, worry, or look to the future; and believe as you will."

Francis believed that, particularly among those men who are drawn to full-time religious life, learning can often substitute for, rather than support, spiritual practice. He probably knew the famous sermons of Bernard of Clairvaux on the Song of Songs that included Bernard's opening statement about the passionate, firsthand experience necessary to understand the mysteries of God: "Only the touch of the Spirit can inspire a song like this, and only personal experience can unfold its meaning. Those who are versed in the mystery may revel in it. All others should burn with desire to attain to this experience rather than settle for merely learning about it."[65]

When talking with a young friar who wanted to own books for himself, Francis once used an analogy that explained his position most clearly: There are great soldiers who have fought in heroic battles, and they are usually followed by other men who desire only to tell the stories of the soldiers' valor, rather than duplicate the heroic deeds in their own lives. Similarly, Francis explained, there are those who live in spiritual practice and deepening faith, and then there are those who desire only to read about such possibilities.

On another occasion, Francis accepted some students of canon law who wanted to become friars, but in their cases, part of forsaking the world according to the *Rule* was to leave behind their studies. This happened in Bologna, and the men's names were Pellegrino and Rinieri. Francis instructed Pellegrino "to follow the way of humility in the Order" by not using his learning or even becoming a priest. He asked the young student to be a humble lay brother. Rinieri, meanwhile, became the minister to the friars of the region known as the Marches of Ancona, a place that will feature prominently later on in our story.[66]

On still another occasion, Francis taught his brothers that even if an eminent cleric were to join the movement, Francis would want him to renounce his learning at least to some degree, as learning itself is a form of riches. Revealingly, the man who came to be known as the Poverello, or *little poor man*, explains: "Learning makes a man difficult to teach. One needs to be able to take something rigid, such as the expectations of Christ, and bend it into oneself through humble disciplines."[67] This sounds a lot like the camel going through the eye of a needle, but not quite so difficult as that.

In place of book learning, a life of simplicity was supposed to involve a keen connection to the earth, creatures, and humans, in ways that were unlike those of saints before them. In a very real sense,

"All knowledge," said the holy doctor, Bonaventure, "is contained in two books. The one, inspired from within, embodies all the divine ideas—the prototypes of all the substances to which they have given birth. The other book, inspired from without, is the world in which the thoughts of God are imprinted in imperfect and perishable characters. The angel reads from the first, the beast from the second. Creation was imperfect while it lacked a being who could read in both books at once, and who could interpret the one by the other. That is our destiny, and philosophy has no other use than that of leading us to God by all branches of creation."

No one spoke the language of symbolism more boldly than St. Bonaventure in his all too little-known pamphlets. The very titles of these would be appropriate for hymns and dithyrambs: *The Six Wings of the Seraphim, The Seven Roads of Eternity, The Journey of the Soul to God.* The good doctor knew that it was not mere intelligence that would

the generation led by Francis and Clare was the one that brought heaven and earth much closer than they had been since the days that Jesus was walking around in Palestine. Before Francis, it was unheard of for a saint to speak of specific species rather than a more abstract creation, or to turn to creatures for understanding, rather than to God alone. Francis and Clare brought the earthly and the spiritual much closer together. They saw the world simply and differently from most of the other people around them. The earth was full of God in ways that books could not be. "There lives the dearest freshness deep down things . . . / Because the Holy Ghost over the bent / World broods with warm breast and with ah! / bright wings" (Gerard Manley Hopkins, from "God's Grandeur").

Nevertheless, the Franciscan movement began at "a significant juncture in the evolution of medieval theology: at a moment of intellectual, ecclesial, and spiritual ferment."[68] It was ironically Francis's charisma that attracted some of the brightest minds of the day to his way of life, and after the deaths of Francis and Clare, the life of the mind would become more important within the movement.

Had he lived to see it, it is tempting to imagine that Francis might have appreciated the way that Bonaventure was able to synthesize book learning with a firsthand experience of God. At the time of Clare's death in 1253, Bonaventure was already the most important theologian among the earliest Franciscans, and four years later he became their minister-general. Bonaventure was anxious to quiet the founders' anti-intellectual impulses. He himself came to be known by the glorious title "Seraphic Doctor," referring to his angelic character mixed with a rigorous mind. Like his Dominican contemporary Thomas Aquinas, Bonaventure was comfortable following Jesus into the temple. At the beginning of his *Life of St. Francis*, he calls

help us to recognize the eternal beauty that hides itself behind the veil of nature. In order to elude what despoils it, in order to pursue it—we must also have love. Love is the foundation of that wisdom that trusts less to syllogism than to prayer.

Love is also the culmination of wisdom, for do not imagine that Bonaventure would have been satisfied with the barren knowledge of the Creator and His attributes. Having arrived at the point where reason fails, he burned with a desire to penetrate further. He wished, he says, to lay aside the powers of reason for a time and to direct all his understanding and being towards God until his will might be merged in God's. But, when asked by what means that would be possible, Bonaventure urged the necessity of grace and not knowledge, desire and not thought, prayer and lamentations and not the study of books, the spouse and not the master, God and not humanity.

"Let us die then to ourselves," he continued. "Let us enter into the mysteries of the darkness. Let us impose silence on solicitude, on desire, on the phantoms of the senses, and, in the train of the Christ crucified, let us pass from this world to our Father."

—*Frederick Ozanam*

Francis a "professor of evangelical perfection"—an accurate phrasing that nevertheless shows Bonaventure's love of learning as well as the saint's seriousness for the imitation of Christ.

# JUGGLERS FOR GOD

S cholars have debated for centuries whether or not Francis or the bishop knew beforehand that Clare was coming to Portiuncula. Although there are traditions that say certain friars hurried her through the narrow streets of Assisi, and that the friars stood in the plain near Portiuncula with torches in their hands to beckon her coming, it is just as likely that she was completely alone that first night.

The structure of Portiuncula—which was known at that time by its religious name, *Santa Maria degli Angeli* (St. Mary of the Angels)— was built in the early Middle Ages, and there is a legend that it was originally intended to surround relics of the Virgin brought to Umbria from the Holy Land. The chapel was owned by the Benedictine monks of Monte Subasio. In 1211, the abbot gave Francis permanent use of it, and Francis gathered the friars together in small and temporary dwellings around it.[69] Their lives centered around the small altar inside the chapel throughout the day when they were not out working and preaching.

Many scholars have supposed that Portiuncula was the chapel that Francis repaired when he had finished at San Damiano. No place was more special to St. Francis; *Portiuncula* means "little portion of earth," a name that Francis gave to the place, and he would later die within its walls. It still stands today as a lovely medieval jewel surrounded by a much-less-attractive modern church known as the Basilica of St. Mary of the Angels. This is usually the first stop for pilgrims arriving in Assisi, as the basilica is within one hundred paces of the train station. Just outside the basilica, beside the first souvenir stalls, the buses stop to carry people for the short journey up into Assisi itself.

To walk briskly from Clare's family home to Portiuncula would take at least thirty minutes. That was a long time to have to worry, or to look over her shoulder for pursuers. Surely she knew that her actions would not only infuriate her family, but could put Francis at personal risk. Italian law called for financial and other penalties against men who married women without their family's consent. Any romantic such as Francis would have known this and would also have seen how Clare's coming to Portiuncula could be wrongly perceived. By all indications, though, Clare was not preoccupied but rather determined in her flight that night.

She surely had family running after her as soon as she was found missing. Perhaps that is why Francis cut Clare's hair that first night. Her golden curls can still be seen as one of the relics at the Basilica of Santa Clara in Assisi today. Francis made her a *sister* without any semblance of deliberation whatsoever. Afterwards, still within hours of her coming, she was bundled away to the Church of San Paolo at Bastia, part of a Benedictine monastery a few miles from Assisi. It is there that her family first accosted her, trying to convince her to return home, and then, a few days later, attempting to remove her forcibly.

A few days after arriving at San Paolo, Francis arranged to move Clare to the Benedictine convent of San Angelo, on the slopes of Assisi's Mount Subasio, where she was promised more protection and quiet. Sixteen days after her initial flight, Clare's sister Catherine, soon to be called Sister Agnes, joined her there. The two of them would have been viewed as runaways by many Assisans, and religious fanatics by most of the rest. Their parents and family members became determined again to convince the young women to return. This time, though, they focused on Catherine, physically dragging her away down the hillside until she was almost unconscious. It appears that Clare finally begged them to leave, appealing to what affection they might still feel for their daughter and sister, who was dying at their hands, determined to enter the religious life. It is uncertain exactly how long Clare and Catherine then stayed at San Angelo. They were joined by at least one other woman during that time, namely, their aunt, Pacifica, who was about twice their age. Together, the three of them formed a unique sort of family and were eventually moved into San Damiano after Francis begged the Benedictines and the bishop of Assisi (the same man who gave Francis his cloak when Francis disrobed before his father) for permission to use the church.

Is it only by accident that Francis arranged for Clare to live at San Damiano, where he had first heard so clearly the word of God? I don't think so. He must have hoped and expected that Clare would listen for that guiding voice just as he had.[70] A community quickly grew up around Clare to match the friars surrounding Francis. The sixteenth-century Franciscan historian Luke Wadding offers in his *Annales* the names of fifty women who comprised the convent at San Damiano by 1238. After Clare, Catherine, and Pacifica, the next sisters (later to be called *Poor Clares*) included Benvenuta, Cecilia, Amata (Clare's niece), Christina (a childhood friend of Clare's), and Philippa—all names that figure prominently in Clare's religious life and in the growth of the Second Order. Clare's own mother, Ortolana, joined her daughter at San Damiano within a few years. Legend has it that she waited until after the death of her husband but then sold all of her possessions and distributed the money to the poor—just as Francis instructed and Brother Bernard had done. Ortolana arranged for her brother-in-law to care for Clare's younger sister, Beatrice, and was invested by Francis himself. Beatrice later joined the Poor Clares herself upon reaching the age of eighteen.

## PRECEDENTS FOR THE POOR CLARES

It was the rare mother or father of the thirteenth century who desired their daughter to enter religious life rather than marry. As one medievalist has summarized, "Marriage was not only a sacramental act, it was a civic act. . . . Its rituals laid the foundation of the civic order."[71] In fact, given the corruption in the Church in Clare's day, it would be safe to say that in 1212, no one was encouraging young women to consider the religious life—especially intelligent and attractive young women. And to join Francis was not even as promising as joining a convent. To join Francis was the sort of action that would rightly terrify any parent.

The tradition of religious women was well established long before Francis and Clare. St. Paul instructs Timothy to honor widows, an ancient Jewish practice, but he also speaks of "the real widow, left alone, [who] has set her hope on God and continues in supplications and prayers night and day."[72] In the same letter, plus in his first letter to the church in Corinth, Paul praises women who are virgins, urging them to practice devotion to God's work in lieu of passion to a husband.

Less than three hundred years after Paul's ministry, St. Pachomius (d. 346), one of the founders of monasticism, built a convent for religious women. St. Jerome (d. 420), too, urged both men and women to consider religious life as an antidote to the lax practices and corruption that he already detected in the secular, or non-monastic, clergy. Jerome would found a convent in Bethlehem with St. Paula (d. 404), the patron saint of widows, one of several prominent widows whom he mentored. Jerome spent most of the last three decades of his life working in that abbey, translating the Scriptures and writing his famous biblical commentaries.

Reform movements were necessary also in the centuries leading up to Francis and Clare. The first Cistercian monastery for women was established in what is now Dijon, France, in 1125. St. Dominic founded a convent of nuns only five and a half years before Clare fled to join Francis at Portiuncula. Having seen a vision of the Virgin Mary on the feast of St. Mary Magdalene in July 1206, Dominic understood from her that he was to establish a convent at Prouille, France, where he was busy trying to convert a heretical group known as the Albigensians. Before the end of December that year, the first Dominican convent had opened and was named for St. Mary Magdalene, who still at that time was identified with the penitent prostitute from the Gospels—in other words, a repentant, changed, and committed woman.

And so, when Clare fled to join Francis and his band of friars late that night, her actions were not exactly unprecedented, but they *were* unusual. There was no women's house for her to join. Where would she sleep? What sort of religious work would she do? Would Clare join the men during the day, working with them side by side? Some scholars suggest that this is indeed what happened in the first weeks of Clare's and Catherine's joining the movement. The earliest biographers tell a different story. Regardless, there was a recklessness in both Clare and Francis on that first night. They were fools, just as Christ had been a fool on the Cross. What G. K. Chesterton explains about Francis was also true of Clare:

> The conversion of St. Francis . . . involved his being in some sense flung suddenly from a horse. . . . [T]here was not a rag of him left that was not ridiculous. Everybody knew that at the best he had made a fool of himself. . . . [T]he word fool itself began to shine and change.[73]

Faith became playful in the expression of early Franciscanism. When the Church was beset by corruption and irrelevance, and kingdoms and local governments were more concerned with military conquest than with caring for citizens, the best spiritual response often included playfulness. Sometimes we need a remedy for malaise and trouble that resembles foolishness.

Francis called himself and his brothers *Jongleurs de Dieu* in French, or "God's Jugglers," because they were often the jovial men who would sing and dance with the people. They didn't always have to preach. In her intriguing book *What the Body Wants*, Cynthia Winton-Henry says, "Play is honest. You can't play unless you are yourself." After his conversion, Francis came to understand who he really was, and then he was able to be playful.

Francis was a poet and singer of songs, singing of the joy and cheerfulness in Gospel living and poverty. Three hundred years after his death, a Florentine historian made reference to "praise songs in Italian to the Sisters of Santa Clara" written by St. Francis that sadly are no longer extant, a fact that has depressed Franciscan scholars ever since.[74] The only Italian song of Francis that is still known to us today is the remarkable *Canticle of the Creatures*, which we will look at in detail in a later chapter. In their cheery approach to faith, Francis and Clare believed that they were provided another antidote to the gloom of their era, but also, they were imitating the joy of the first Christian communities.

In various collections of Italian verse, Francis of Assisi's *Canticle* is presented as the very first vernacular Italian poem. Francis's ministry took place at the beginning of the vernacular movement in Europe, both in the church and in literature. The Lateran Council of 1215 (almost ten years before the *Canticle* was written) said that all Christians had to recite certain core prayers such as the Our Father and Ave Maria in their own language, rather than in Latin, by confirmation age.[75] Francis's creativity was a part of the ferment of his age in preaching and speaking in the vernacular. What really set him apart was his composing new work in Italian.

## STRATEGIC FOOLISHNESS

The early Franciscans reached into new communities, as well, by playing the fool. The texts

The spiritual genius of Italian poetry developed in the atmosphere of the catacombs. We must descend there in order to discover the source of what was destined to come later. There, in those early days, lived a people in the modern sense of the word, comprising women and children, the weak and the small, such as ancient historians despise and hold of no account—a new people, a medley of strangers, slaves, free, barbarians, all animated by a spirit alien to the rest of antiquity and suggestive of a new order of things.

This society had an ideal that it was eager to express, but the ideal was too comprehensive, too impassioned, too new, to find adequate expression in words. It required the service of all of the arts. In that early stage of its development, poetry was unclear and imprecise, but it animated all of the arts including architecture, painting, sculpture, and engraving. All of these are symbolic and characterized by figurative expression and the attempt to make the image reflect the idea, to reveal the ideal in the real.

Imagine the catacombs: A network of long, underground corridors, stretching in all directions beneath the suburbs and outskirts of Rome. Do not confuse them with the spacious quarries dug out for the purpose of building the pagan city. The Christians themselves excavated the narrow corridors which were to hide the mysteries of their faith and to be the resting-places for their tombs. These labyrinths are sometimes as much as three or four stories high and they penetrate to a depth of eighty to one hundred feet below ground, but in many parts they are so narrow and low that it is difficult to make one's way through even with lowered head. To the right and left are several rows of broad, deep trenches scooped out of the wall, in which bodies of men, women, and children were once placed side by side. As if to confuse the pagan searchers, the underground passage makes a thousand detours, and to this day these very detours speak of the horrors

tell us that Francis and Clare "desired to bear shame and insult for the love of Christ" and that "they traveled the world as strangers and pilgrims."[76] They were also smart enough to realize that this sort of life and approach would attract more people to their cause and movement.

Francis seems to have known that others would be drawn to a life of joy and simplicity. He once sent Brother Bernard to the nearby town of Bologna to begin the Franciscan movement there, preaching the good news of their way of rediscovering the life of Christ. Bernard's strategy was one of simple humility and foolishness. He walked into the city in his ragged robes (the Franciscans were known for the ugliest of monastic garments), and he sat in the city center reading the recently written *Rule* of St. Francis quietly to himself. Bernard stood out among the crowd of people in the square. He was poorly dressed, smiling at passersby, and was reading to himself in public—something that people rarely ever did in those days. Children began to mock him, thinking that he was a local idiot. In the Middle Ages, children could be even crueler than they are today, and they threw stones and mud at Bernard, calling him names. But Bernard only smiled, and greeted them with the love of Christ.

Some adults joined in mocking the friar while others curiously watched. Day after day Bernard came and went to the public square of Bologna doing these things until finally someone approached him, a lawyer who was impressed by his spirit and humility, and asked him what he was reading. Within days there were followers of Francis in Bologna. It is said that Francis "gave thanks to the Lord and then began to scatter his poor disciples of the Cross more widely . . . and many communities were established in many places."[77]

True joy will have subtle effects on one's environment.

of those early days of persecution when the cruel hunter chased his prey through these winding labyrinths.

No building raised by human hands teaches nobler lessons than the catacombs. In those murky passages the visible world and all trace of light is denied to all who penetrate those depths. The cemetery encloses all the hidden treasures of darkness, and the oratories, built at various points for the celebration of the holy mysteries, are like daylight breaking in upon immortality to comfort the souls for the night below.

These oratories are covered with pictures that are often crudely executed and that are clearly the work of unskilled hands. Yet often when the light of a torch is thrown upon the sacred walls, images are revealed whose design, form, and movement recall the best traditions of ancient art. Also, behind this simple art lurks a principle that was destined to animate and transform it: The true faith of the martyrs is depicted in the expression of these beings represented by those early artists with eyes raised to heaven and hands outstretched in prayer. We discover, in these desolate places, a very different spirit.

At the entrance to a vault appears the Good Shepherd bearing on his shoulders a lamb and a goat, indicating that he saves both the innocent and the repentant. In four panels decorated with garlands of flowers and fruits, we see stories drawn from the Old and New Testaments, arranged in couples, as if to suggest allegory and reality, prophecy and history. We see Noah and the Ark, Moses striking the rock, Job on the dunghill, the Miracle of Cana, the feeding of the five thousand, Lazarus leaving the tomb, and most prominent—Daniel in the lions' den, Jonah cast out by the whale, the three Children in the furnace. We see no traces of contemporary persecutions, no representations of the butchering of the Christians, nothing bloodthirsty, nothing that could rouse hatred or vengeance, nothing but pictures of pardon, hope, and love.

The effects of song, jocularity, human touch, and sharing goods among members of a community not only lower blood pressures and increase life expectancies, but they blow fresh air and optimism all around. We cannot overestimate the power that joy played in fueling the growth of the Franciscan movement. It is these intangibles that best explain why thousands upon thousands joined the two founders, and then why things also floundered, years later, in their absences.

There are deeper aspects to early Franciscan foolishness, as well. They not only played the fool, something that is already difficult enough to understand in our modern idiom, but they humiliated themselves. Francis would often ask his friars to step on his face, for instance, or to verbally remind him of his lowliness, as measures against pride. He sought to imitate Christ crucified, who allowed himself to be debased, mocked, and utterly without hope in the minds of others.

Francis and Clare each also desired to be martyred like Christ, desires that would always go unrequited.

Just like juggling for God in the piazzas, all manners of foolishness were aimed at teaching spiritual lessons. For example, one should never be too reliant upon financial and material resources. Francis believed that all Christians should follow the teaching of Jesus not to worry about tomorrow, sharing with others who are in need. For this reason, when Francis went out to beg alms before sitting down to dine at the bishop of Ostia's house, he wasn't just being eccentric—he was challenging the structure of wealth and want. When he asked his brothers not to own personal prayer books, he wasn't just being literal in his pursuit of poverty—he was setting himself apart from the joint and institutional wealth of the monasteries of his day. All of these were aspects of conversion, according to Francis and Clare. They taught that there are many things, tendencies, and sins that

Christian sculpture also had its beginnings here, and figures may be found that are roughly hewn, without proportion, without grace, with no other worth than the ideal that they represent. A leaf expresses the instability of life; a sailing boat, the fleeting of our days; the dove bearing the branch proclaims the dawn of a better world; the fish recalls baptism, and, at the same time, the Greek word which translates it unites in a mysterious anagram the majestic titles of the Son of God, the Savior. On one nameless tomb there is a fish and the five miraculous loaves of bread, suggesting that here rests a man who believed in Christ, who was regenerated by baptism, and who partook of the eucharistic feast.

As paganism gradually declined, the chisel of the Christian became bold and more productive. Instead of those indefinite emblems that he outlined on brick, he boldly cut the marble and produced the bas-reliefs of his sarcophagi that decorate the museums of Rome and the churches of Ravenna today. In them, we meet again the biblical subjects from the catacombs, but other scenes are added. This richer and more definite symbolism announces that the time of the persecutions was over, and that the holy mysteries no longer needed to be celebrated in secret.

The designers, no longer wanting to express their thoughts in drawing or sculpture alone, turned to speech, as well. The first inscriptions are of a brevity that has its own eloquence. "This is the place of Philemon." Some of them are amplified by means of tender and comforting expressions such as "Florentius, happy little lamb of God." Or, "You have fallen too soon, Constantia, miracle of beauty and wisdom." This was the beginning of a poetry. The spiritual muse no longer could be silent.

—*Frederick Ozanam*

we all must turn away from, in order to see and experience God. In this view of the world, salvation equals a reconciliation that is more thorough than just between God and the individual person.

In many ways, their conversions included a turning away from formalism and professionalism. They encouraged people to leave career paths and secure futures, as if there really was, or is, such a thing. They embraced what I would call *vocational downward mobility*. Success was measured by heavenly means. Francis and Clare embodied spiritual practices that brought these teachings home in their lives. Francis once compared the obedient life of faith to a dead body that does not complain, is immovable, and completely unimpressed by appearances. Brothers Leo and Angelo and others, sounding like James and John at the Last Supper, once said to Francis, "Tell us the highest form of obedience," and Francis said, "He is most obedient who does not judge why he is moved, does not think about where he is placed, does not ask to be moved, and when he is moved to a higher office, keeps his complete humility by accusing himself all the more while he is being honored."[78]

The Second Order (the Poor Clares) spread almost as rapidly as the First Order had done, and often with the same sort of unpredictability. Just as Francis had done, Clare often sent sisters to other regions and countries without any advance warning to bishops or cardinals ruling those areas. The Poor Clares spread within two decades into France, Spain, Belgium, and Bohemia in these ways. To Spain, for instance, Clare sent sisters Agnes (her niece) and Clare (Agnes's niece) by rudderless boat. Like the Irish saints who wandered the seas without sail in order to be led properly by the Holy Spirit, Agnes and Clare shocked the people of Barcelona when they landed on shore and emerged from such a vessel. The women only had to mention who they were and that they were sent from Assisi before they were accepted, and soon the first Poor Clares house was established in Spain.

They were poor, just as Christ was born and died poor. In her *Rule*, Clare wrote: "For the love of the most holy and beloved Child who was wrapped in the poorest swaddling clothes and laid in a manger, and of his most holy Mother, I admonish, beg, and encourage my sisters to always wear only the poorest of garments."[79] She was picking up on something that Francis had instituted for the friars.

Poverty was signaled when Francis chose the cloth for the first Franciscan tunics. The Benedictines wore black, symbolizing humility, and the Cistercians white, for purity. Both choices rested on solid motives, but they also represented the dyeing of cloth into black or white. Francis would have known colors better than anyone in Assisi except for his father, the cloth merchant, whose business it was to search the trade routes for the most alluring dyes and fabrics of the day. Francis would have known that some dyes were made from snails and other animals. But also, Francis saw colors as a form of haughtiness. He is said to have chosen the dirtiest cloth he could find—a sort of dirty brown—for the friars' tunics, but the truth is that he chose a cloth that was a natural color without any preparation necessary.

Cloth without dye may seem trivial, but it had profound symbolism in that day. Many medieval ascetics believed that color itself was a sign of transience and impermanence, and that it may not have existed before the Fall. In the story of Creation, nothing is described in terms of color. Could it be, they wondered, that the devil created the illusion of the first color when he tempted Eve with the forbidden fruit?

When it came to their clothing, Francis and Clare were concerned with poverty in both its appearance (how does it appear to others?) and in its reality (actual money spent). The undyed tunic and cord around the waist presented the first friars with the coarsest, least desirable materials. It was intended to be functional, extremely inexpensive or free, and to appear as a statement of intentional poverty, as well. Such actions only made the first friars appear madder, and less relevant, to those on the outside.

Still, our saints' personalities are never easily grasped, and they were not easygoing people. Just as they rejected color that stood for power or vain beauty, they loved natural color and the species of creation. If some of their contemporaries believed that the devil created the illusion of color in the Garden of Eden, others noticed that God's first act in Creation was light, and without light—as we have known since Isaac Newton—there is no color. So, perhaps all of the colors were created on day one. Francis insisted that the brothers plant flowers so that they might bloom and spin and glorify their Creator, and he reveled in their appearance beside the simple huts at Portiuncula. Clare did the same, and her flower gardens became a special place for Francis to visit.

We can imagine both of them praising the loveliness of *Sister Flowers* along the road or in the garden on one day, marveling at a sunset, appreciating a good song sung well, and complimenting the talented juggler or painter, and then the next day depriving their bodies nearly to starvation, leaving ailments and bodily pain untended to the point of permanent damage. They were probably a constant puzzle to most of their companions and closest friends.

CHAPTER

9

# RENEWING THE
# BONDS OF CREATION

I n the first fifteen centuries of Christian faith, mystics and reformers were always at pains to see the universe as something more than simply rotten. Experiencing God up close led mystics to see a radical separation of the spiritual from the material. And the reformers, frustrated at their inability to change the course and corruption of human events and mistakes, felt helpless in the face of evil. Francis and Clare were both mystics and reformers, and they struggled in both of these directions. Some of their predecessors, such as the leaders of the Cathar and Albigensian movements, were overcome by them.

The earth was viewed by other mystics as inherently evil, and all of its creatures, including human beings, hopelessly fallen. The soul was all that could be saved. For this reason, the medieval mind saw physical deformities and diseases such as leprosy as the result of some sort of previous sin. The human body was seen to be rotting rapidly; saints meditated on skulls and other symbols of mortality, hoping to focus their minds on what was heavenly instead.

What sets Francis and Clare apart from the other prophets of their age—and what, in fact, turns any prophet into a saint—is their ability to know God intimately as mystics, and to fight for justice as reformers, yet still to view the created universe as good rather than rotten. If it is created, redeemed, and sustained by God the Father, Son, and Holy Spirit, then it is good. Their love for the Creator was one with their love for the creation.

Love was, for them, something more palpable, earthly, and rooted in life than it was for most of their mystic contemporaries. Beatrice of Nazareth (d. 1268), for instance, is typical in speaking of divine love over and against human love. In her treatise *There Are Seven Manners of Loving*, the ultimate rung is a mystic union that removes one completely from earthly existence. There would be altogether different metaphors for this sort of cocoon today, but Beatrice's are unmistakably removed from the creation:

> So the soul has climbed in spirit above time into eternity, it is exalted above all that love can give into the eternity which is love itself, which is beyond time, which is set above all human modes of love, the soul has transcended its own nature in its longing for the life which is there. . . . And now this earth is for the soul a cruel exile and a dire prison and a heavy torment: it despises the world, the earth revolts it, and here is nothing earthly which can console or satisfy it, and it is for the soul a great punishment that it must live in this estrangement and appear so alien.[80]

Francis and Clare were a different sort of mystic. They were more like Buddhism's bodhisattvas who simply will not permit themselves the opportunity to soar into these reaches of enlightenment, but rather set themselves to the task of helping others along their way. We see this again and again in the details of their lives. They exhibited a sensitivity to the living and organic things around them that sets them apart. Francis, for instance, even cared

for the inanimate objects of creation with a sensitivity that is sim-
ilar to Buddhist teachings about kindness toward all sentient beings.
In one of his most beautiful paragraphs in *The Golden Legend*,
Jacobus of Voragine explains the following about St. Francis:

> The saint would not handle lanterns and candles because he
> did not want to dim their brightness with his hands. He walked
> reverently on stones out of respect for him who was called Peter,
> which means stone. He lifted worms from the road for fear they
> might be trampled underfoot by passersby. Bees might perish in
> the cold of winter, so he had honey and fine wines set out for
> them. He called all animals brothers and sisters. When he looked
> at the sun, the moon, and the stars, he was filled with inexpress-
> ible joy by his love of the Creator and invited them all to love
> their Creator.[81]

The earthiness of early Franciscan love was rooted in the earth
itself. Francis and Clare shared a pre-Copernican view of the universe (Nicolaus Copernicus, d. 1543). The pre-Copernican view
imagined earth at the center of the universe and humankind at the
center of everything. This perspective permeates much of Christian
tradition, including the Psalms and the translators of the King James
Bible. But you wouldn't know that Francis and Clare looked at the
created world with this lens by reading their writings or the stories
of their lives. They brought new life to the psalms that were loved
and prayed by Jesus himself, such as this passage from Psalm 8:
"When I consider thy heavens, the work of thy fingers / the moon
and the stars, which thou hast ordained; / What is man, that thou
art mindful of him? / and the son of man, that thou visitest him?"
(KJV). But they also showed how it is possible to look up at the skies
and all around at the creatures of creation, praising and blessing God

as a Creator who nevertheless does not value only humans.[82] The human being shares the universe with other created beings in the early Franciscan worldview.

We rarely see either Francis or Clare doing typical religious things in traditional religious places. Valleys and hilltops became Francis's field of faith. He found God in the woods and in creatures as often as he did in churches. Sacred and profane were designations of geography and location before their lives and teachings brought them much closer together.

By the official teachings of the day, an altar was supposed to be present in order for prayer and sacraments to take place. The late Middle Ages was the era of only religion, not spirituality. Local bishops would sanction a new religious space by blessing the altar inside a church or chapel. The laity—other than the very rich—did not own personal prayer books. Even private devotions were said in church, usually before or after Mass or Matins. For many people, singing or saying the Latin liturgical hours or Paternosters ("Our Fathers") was possible only when led by the clergy or a monastic community. A sacred place in and of itself, a church was the primary space for experiencing God. Many medieval chronicles detail how pilgrims would sometimes travel to a church only to find its doors closed. Rather than go elsewhere, they would pray while kneeling outside or while touching the outside wall with a hand or head.

Early Franciscanism brought changes to all of this. By preaching to the people in piazzas and other public places, Francis signaled that God's Word was active outside of church. There was a sense in which the words of prayer, piety, and preaching were seen to partake sacramentally of the Word Itself, and creativity entered into one's experience of God. In song and poetry sung in the vernacular, they made spirituality seem possible to those who were untrained in formal religion. Spirituality at home began to be possible. The distinctions between a theologically literate clergy class and an obedient, pious laity class began to break down. Franciscans led the way, through the creation of what was called the "Third Order" of Franciscans (in 1221), in finding ways for laypeople to live vowed lives of spiritual significance, but without leaving behind the world of family, jobs, or other responsibilities. It was also at this time that letter writing became an important vehicle for spiritual encouragement, personal Bible reading and study grew, and discussions of theological issues in the workplace originated.

In the decades and centuries immediately after Francis and Clare, home altars became common in Italy. These were places set aside in the home, still common in some Catholic homes today, where a person would replicate the setting of a church for purposes of personal prayer, adding images, icons, rosary beads, and mementos of various kinds. Before Francis and Clare, we have little evidence of these. Similarly, vernacular spiritual writing was almost nonexistent before Francis and Clare. But in the century after their deaths, the lives of Francis penned by Thomas of Celano were among the most popular choices for daily reading, and the vernacular Italian works of spirituality became almost too many to count.[83]

## CARING FOR CREATURES

The connection between Francis of Assisi and animals is the single fact about him that most people know. We have tales of his encounters with animals, fish, invertebrates, and plants. In all of these ways, Franciscans emphasized that creation includes more than humankind. Just as they redefined what it means to be family, they further widened the fraternity to link humans and creatures in the same relationship with God.

On one warm afternoon, Francis wandered outside of Assisi, questioning his motives for ministry, asking God if perhaps everything he had done up until that point had been for the wrong reasons. He wondered if he should have simply gotten married and raised a family as his father wanted him to do. Francis was always the most critical of himself, but it was on just such an afternoon that Francis first met the birds and spoke to them as if to equals. That day marks the beginning of the environmental movement, the beginning of the era when we began to understand ourselves as intrinsically connected to all of creation.

Many other legends arose surrounding Francis's love for animals, and chief among them were stories about the Wolf of Gubbio—whom Francis tamed of his savagery in exchange for a commitment from the townspeople of Gubbio to feed him for the rest of his life. In the early twentieth century, a book called *The Chronicles of Brother Wolf* brought the wolf to life again as a full-fledged disciple of Francis. These newer legends were written in the spirit of those friars who regretted the institutional turn taken by the Order after Francis's death.

In "Brother Wolf Joins the Poor Clares," the anonymous author tells of how the friars in charge disdained the wolf after Francis's death, and how the wolf eventually went to live with the sisters instead. "Now among some of the Brothers was a certain dislike of Brother Wolf, which after our master's death showed itself in various words and murmurings, scorning and spurning and pushing aside. No food was put out for him, and no water, which was worse, and Tertius [the friar-narrator of these tales] fared little better, so that there was nothing to share with Brother Wolf."

After this rude treatment of Francis's brother Wolf, the creature is driven away with a stick by one of the friars. He wanders briefly, imagining that he might return to Gubbio, but instead finds his way to San Damiano, where he waits outside for a short time with an injured foot.

> When they opened the door wide [Brother Wolf] crept inside, looking upon them with eyes that were full of tears and pain. And they too, when they saw the evil case that he was in, and that foot, fell to mourning as women will, and very quickly they summoned the Sisters, though it was past Compline, when none may speak, but they with warm water and soft oils washed and dressed it and bound it up.... After that he lived with [the Poor Clares] and left them no more.[84]

This may indicate that dedication to caring for creatures as equals with humans fell off after the deaths of Francis and Clare.

The stories of Francis are also full of birds of a variety of species, including falcons, doves, pheasants, crows, and others. On one occasion, a small waterbird landed on the side of the boat he was traveling in on his way to Greccio. The bird nested in Francis's hands, like a cat might do in one's lap, and Francis blessed it. Later, when Francis arrived at the Greccio hermitage, a falcon "covenanted with him" and undertook to make noise each evening at the hour when Francis would rise to say the liturgy of the hours. The falcon would do the same in the early morning as well, except on those occasions when Francis was ill, when he would remain silent. On another occasion, we hear of a rich man in Siena who sent a pheasant to Francis when the saint was known to be ill. The pheasant was supposed to be killed in order to provide much-needed meat that would strengthen the constitution of all who ate it. Meat was often prescribed in those days as a remedy for curing illness. But Francis, of course, did not slaughter the bird but rejoiced over it and spoke with it. The pheasant lived for a time with the friars and took to hiding under their tunics in their cells when the friars attempted to remove the bird to the outdoors.[85]

## CRICKETS, FISH, LAMBS, AND BEES

Just as he had encouraged the birds to sing, Francis did the same with a cricket at Portiuncula. "Sing, Sister Cricket," he instructed the creature, which was sitting in the bushes beside his cell. He held out his hand and the cricket sat upon it and sang. This happened again and again for eight days. The same thing happened when a fisherman on the lake in Rieti caught a fish and presented it to Francis. Rather than keep the fish for food, Francis set it back into the water. The fish followed the boat for some time afterwards and would depart only when Francis blessed it.

We have numerous stories of Francis with lambs. Lambs have, since the days of the ancient Israelites, been associated with God's redemption. The cousin of Christ, John the Baptist, mysteriously announced to his audience as Jesus approached, "Look, there is the Lamb of God who takes away the sin of the world." And St. Paul later cleared this up, by referring to Jesus as "the Passover lamb," a gloss on the Jewish Scriptures that forever linked Christ with the freedom of slaves that happened long before in Egypt. Jesus himself told the parable of the lost sheep, and that lost animal was a lamb in the eyes of Francis:

> So he told them this parable: "Which one of you with a hun-
> dred sheep, if he lost one, would fail to leave the ninety-nine in
> the desert and go after the missing one till he found it? And

when he found it, would he not joyfully take it on his shoulders and then, when he got home, call together his friends and neighbours, saying to them, 'Rejoice with me, I have found my sheep that was lost.' In the same way, I tell you, there will be more rejoicing in heaven over one sinner repenting than over ninety-nine upright people who have no need of repentance."[86]

Bonaventure's *Life* of Francis explains that the saint loved lambs because "he had a special tenderness for the creatures that by their likeness and nature demonstrate the gentleness of Christ, and because they are a type for Him who was already known in the Old Testament."[87]

Just as he did with turtledoves and other creatures, Francis would barter or raise money to buy back lambs, saving them from slaughter. Symbolism meant nothing to him; he would care for lambs as Jesus had done, because he looked on these gentle creatures as if they were Christ himself. He once mourned the death of a lamb, "in the presence of all," according to Bonaventure, that had been killed by another animal. Lambs became Francis's most earnest animal audiences. For anyone who has tried speaking to animals of various kinds, it is much easier to imagine a congregation of lambs listening to Francis speak, anxious but steady eyes fixed on his every movement, than it is to imagine birds paying attention. The tales of Francis and lambs are almost too many to count. The creatures showed various acts of piety, such as bowing a knee at the altar to the Virgin in Portiuncula, and are often spoken of as the pupils of the Poverello.

Francis always called creatures his brothers and sisters, but most often, he called them sisters. There is a strong sense of the mother in Francis's metaphors and in his spiritual guidance. At one point, Francis compares himself to a hen caring for her chicks. He also encourages the brothers to be mothers to one another. He clung to the feminine side of God, cherishing those metaphors that not only broaden our understanding of who God is, but also temper the over-emphasis that has always existed on the masculine in God. Francis adored God as Mother and he and Clare both sought to imitate Christ, but also the Virgin Mary, the mother of God. It is only by discovering the mothering, loving, caring nature of God in Christ that the world will be healed of its pain and sorrow, Francis believed. As one scholar has put it, "The authoritarian father of Francis wasn't a possible Christian model of a good ruler. Therefore Francis chooses to be a mother."[88]

*Justice*          *Injustice*

We even have stories of creatures that have come to rest and play in places where Francis once was. Bees—which have long been symbols of sanctity for their hardworking ability to create sweetness without taking away from any other creature—took up residence in the ceramic cup that he used for drinking while on Mt. Alverno. Sometime after he had left the mountain, the cup was seen there, full of honeycomb. There is a sense that the presence and touch of Francis improved the expansion of God's creative activity.

In some tales, we may reasonably doubt when the author tells us that fish and crickets left Francis's presence only when the saint gave them permission to do so. Francis was surely not a programmer of animal and insect minds and actions. But there is no need to doubt that Francis had an ability to touch creatures in a way that is unavailable to most of us.[89] He learned a sort of sensitivity to the earth and its creatures that eludes most people.

There are very few similar stories of Clare engaged with creatures. Her life was lived primarily indoors, and her experiences were not so much with animals as they were with people. She was a healer of human sickness and a counselor of troubled souls. One gets the sense that Francis enjoyed caring for creatures himself, but often brought troubled people to Clare. In fact, when we do encounter Clare with a creature in one of the early texts, it almost seems to be portrayed by the editors as a *sanctifying* of the Francis tradition, taking it further away from reality, and so further away from what is believable.

The primary example of this can be found in the story of Clare and a fierce wolf that was plaguing the people of Assisi. This tale is told in *The Versified Legend of the Virgin Clare*, a document compiled immediately after the canonization process had ended.[90] Clearly in the tradition of Francis and the Wolf of Gubbio, we see Clare also facing the terrors of a wolf that is hurting people, even eating them. Francis had brokered peace, emphasizing the ways in which animal and human creation are intertwined, and had respected the beast as well as the people. But in Clare's story with the wolf, she never actually enters the woods, encounters the animal, or discusses a solution with anyone. According to the tale, a mother of twin boys has already lost one of them to the jaws of a wolf when another wolf breaks into her home and steals away the other boy. The wolf drags the child into the forest and the mother cries aloud to Clare (probably in prayer, rather than in person, although the setting is unclear), begging her for help. The neighbors search for the boy, and eventually find him; the wolf has left deep bite marks on the boy's neck and body, but he has ultimately left the child, presumably after the prayer was offered to Clare.

> His mother runs to Clare herself,
> shows her son's scars to everyone,
> and offers her praises to God and to Clare.

The immediacy and earthy relevance of the Franciscan spirit are already being lost in the transmission of the tradition, and in this sanctifying of it. Clare's work is interpreted as of the more divine, wonder-working sort. We see the same sort of change in the stories of St. Anthony of Padua, who was one of the most prominent Franciscans in the years immediately following Francis's death. Like Francis, Anthony preached, but in Anthony's case it was to fish, not birds, and he did not preach to them out of love but in order to demonstrate to a crowd of heretics in Rimini that they should believe without reason (as fish would do). The story in *The Little Flowers* is lengthy, and features the fish coming partially out of the water to nod their heads "in peace and gentleness" as the saint talked. Later, the same fish have listened to Anthony's words and they not only stick their heads out of the water but they "open their mouths . . . to give praise to God."

These experiences of Clare and Anthony lack the earthy understanding that Francis seemed to possess. On the Feast of the Nativity, for instance, he would insist that oxen and donkeys be "spoiled with extra feed and softer hay" because they had kept the Christ child warm on that first day.[91] He practiced a close relationship with creatures that was as uncommon then as it is now. Like no saint before him, Francis desired to touch the earth and also be touched by it.

CHAPTER

10

# BEING CRUCIFIED
# WITH CHRIST

In the legends of Francis of Assisi there is no greater pinnacle
of spiritual imitation than in his encounter with Christ in the
form of a six-winged angel. This happened while he was
meditating alone on Mt. Alverno in the Apennine mountains
of central Italy. It was September 1224, probably sometime between
the Feast of the Exaltation of the Holy Cross (the 14th) and the
Feast of St. Michael the Archangel (the 29th), as two of the early
texts mention each and its proximity to the event. Francis's closest
companions were nearby. They had arrived at the mountain about
one month earlier to have a Lenten experience, according to Francis,
despite the fact that it would have been closer to Advent than to Lent
at that time of year. The Feast of the Assumption, on August 15,
is probably when they began their stay on Alverno, and Francis
intended to stay and pray for forty days (a *Lent*), until the Feast of St.
Michael.

As their stay went on, Francis gradually desired to be more and
more alone. A bridge separated Francis's little hut from those of his
brothers, and the texts tell us that on one occasion, when Francis did
not answer his call, Brother Leo came to see that he was all right.
There, Leo saw Francis kneeling in the woods in a mystical ecstasy.

*111*

Leo later recalled having seen a flaming torch above the saint's head, and a bright light. On one of the following days, the same sort of experience happened to Francis again, but this time while he was completely alone. No friars or friends saw what happened. Francis later told a select few of them that he had had a vision of a six-winged angel, known as a seraph, looking down at him.

The seraph was a symbol of profound holiness and purification that Christians know from the Hebrew prophet Isaiah:

> In the year that King Uzziah died, I saw the Lord sitting on a throne, high and lofty; and the hem of his robe filled the temple. Seraphs were in attendance above him; each had six wings: with two they covered their faces, and with two they covered their feet, and with two they flew. And one called to another and said:
>
> "Holy, holy, holy is the Lord of hosts;
> the whole earth is full of his glory."
>
> The pivots on the thresholds shook at the voices of those who called, and the house filled with smoke. And I said: "Woe is me! I am lost, for I am a man of unclean lips, and I live among a people of unclean lips; yet my eyes have seen the King, the Lord of hosts!"
>
> Then one of the seraphs flew to me, holding a live coal that had been taken from the altar with a pair of tongs.[92]

This wasn't the first occasion that an image of Christ had communicated with Francis; the encounter with the crucifix of San Damiano had happened some fifteen or sixteen years earlier. But in contrast to the crucifix, the seraph on the mountainside did not speak; there was no voice of God this time. Overwhelming light is part of the description that dominates all of the early narratives of what happened, all of which must surely stem from Brother Leo, the only friar close to Francis during that retreat on Alverno.

As we have noted, Francis was nearly blind by this time in his life. His eyes were crying all the time and his vision was seriously impaired. Only in the last one hundred years have scholars begun to suggest scientific reasons for why Francis cried so often in his last decade. Alban Butler (of the old-school hagiographers) wrote about 250 years ago, echoing a tale from *The Little Flowers*: "He was endowed with an extraordinary gift of tears. His eyes seemed two fountains of tears, which were almost continually falling from them, insomuch that at length he almost lost his sight." Butler goes on to explain that Francis's physicians implored him to cry less, because it was the tears that were deepening his eye problem and pain. It is as if Francis's holiness caused his physical suffering to deepen. We know today that the opposite was most likely true. We can now suppose that Francis suffered from an eye disease such as glaucoma. Medieval physicians often confused symptoms with maladies. Their age was one that spiritualized physical realities, making them into spiritual evidences.

For Francis to see anything with clarity at this time would have itself been a miracle. The six-winged seraph was not a product of his imagination—I am not suggesting that—but if sense perceptions are determined by the abilities of our senses in addition to our beliefs about what we think we have seen, then the seraph that Francis saw is not the seraph that Leo would have seen, had Leo seen it!

William of Auvergne and Robert Grosseteste, two contemporaries of Francis, were teaching theories of perception at the University of Paris at the precise time that Francis was on the mountain.[93] Both William and Robert studied light from philosophical and mathematical perspectives. They immersed themselves in Plato's, Aristotle's, and Galen's writings on these subjects, articulating what they called a metaphysics of light. Roger Bacon did the same, following in their footsteps thirty years later, and then, after teaching for twenty years in Paris, became a Franciscan in 1256. Are thoughts dependent on sight? How does the human eye *grasp* what it sees? In Genesis 1:3 when God created the first light (before sun and moon), how did that act relate to Christ the Light of the World ( John 1)? These were the sorts of questions that occupied scholars during Francis's day.

Scholarship was wedded to religious instruction and understanding in the early centuries of university life. Both William of Auvergne and Robert Grosseteste, in fact, later became bishops. All their work was aimed at explaining how God works in and through natural phenomena. Robert Grosseteste even offers an explanation that would rationalize, or perhaps just spiritualize, visions such as the one that resulted in Francis's stigmata, the implanting of the wounds of Christ on his flesh:

> I therefore say that there is a spiritual light that floods over intelligible objects and over the mind's eye—that is related to the interior eye and to intelligible objects just as the corporeal sun relates to the bodily eye and to corporeal visible objects.[94]

All of this was of no interest to people like Francis and Clare. Theirs was a simplicity of mind that follows from a certain kind of obedience that comes from an experience of presence. When mystics feel that God is with them, or within them, why would speculation still be necessary? Questions of perception never dogged Francis, even when children were throwing mud at him in the streets of Assisi.

The seraph itself exhibited the five wounds. *The Legend of the Three Companions* explains that "within its wings was the form of a beautiful, crucified man, with hands and feet extended as if on a cross, and whose features were just as those of Jesus Christ."[95] Both Bonaventure and *The Little Flowers* add detail to compare the wings of the seraph with the wings of the seraph from the passage in Isaiah quoted above, saying, "Two of the wings were raised above his head, two were spread out in flight, and the other two covered the whole body." Francis stood there and adored the seraph. He marveled at it, and also sorrowed for Christ crucified, who was looking down upon him. *The Little Flowers* says beautifully that "Francis was so afraid, but yet filled with sweetness and sorrow mingled with wonder." This must have gone on for quite some time, as Francis gazed at the seraph and the Crucified One gazed back at him.

Somehow at that moment, Christ, in the form of that seraph, transmitted the wounds of stigmata to Francis. There was a brilliant light similar to the one that Leo had overseen on the earlier occasion. Two years later, after Francis died and the announcement was made to the world about his stigmata, there were numerous stories in Umbria about that light, of people saying that they had seen it, too.

*St. Francis Receiving the Stigmata*

The stigmata wounds were seared into his flesh—one in each palm, one in each foot, and a piercing in his right side. They were painful and bloody—both of which phenomena Francis tried desperately to cover up for the last two years of his life. The wound in Francis's side always appeared "unhealed, enflamed, and bleeding," according to *The Little Flowers*. The early chroniclers tell us of friars and cardinals and others trying to sneak glimpses of them, and Francis wearing shoes, extra garments, and so on, to conceal them.

Francis did not tell a soul at first, although eventually he did. Bonaventure says, "Eventually, he understood from this . . . ," and *The Little Flowers* similarly says, "Later, he marveled at what an amazing and undeserved vision he had had." Most likely, the friars came to know about the wounds by accident, when they had to wash Francis's clothes. It is probably then that the courageous ones—those who knew him best—asked, and were told. At some point, Leo was allowed to help Francis care for the wounds with washing and dressings.

Francis's stigmata wounds were the first recorded instance of this miracle in history. It is easy to forget that fact these days, when the miracle has been reasonably claimed dozens of times over the last several centuries. Most recently and prominently, the Capuchin friar St. Padre Pio is said to have experienced the wounds in the middle of the twentieth century and, since he lived in the age of television and photography, we have hundreds of photographs showing Padre Pio wearing bloody coverings for the wounds in his hands so as to hide the sanctity as best he could.[96] Francis also covered up his wounds, and only those closest to him came to know of them prior to his death.

## LETTING THE WORLD KNOW

Scholars believe that it was most likely within days (or perhaps, the very evening) of Francis's death that Elias, the minister-general of the Order, wrote his letter announcing the death of Francis, mentioning for the first time the wounds of Christ found on his body. Elias was in the immediate stages of grief when he wrote his letter. He begins by writing, "Before I begin to speak, I sigh," and "my groans gush forth," speaking of fears and dreads being fulfilled in the events that have just happened. He acknowledges the immense loss to the world and to the Order and also to himself, saying, "he has left me in the midst of darkness." But after the sadness is past (Elias warns everyone not to mourn for long), he explains that a miracle has happened: "Not long before his death, our brother and father appeared crucified, bearing in his body the five wounds which are truly the marks of Christ."[97] Elias's notice sounds almost startled, as if he has just been brought into the circle of those who knew this miracle two years earlier. He records that the wounds were known to emit blood, a sign that he had spoken to those who were closest to Francis and had seen the same, firsthand. This is the first recorded word of what had happened.

In 1262, more than thirty-five years after Francis's death, Friar Jordan of Giano, best known for his work on behalf of the Order in Germany, recounted: "After the death of Blessed Francis, Brother Elias, who was his vicar, addressed a letter of consolation to the brothers throughout the Order who were dismayed over the death of so great a father. He announced to one and all, as Blessed Francis had commanded him, that he blessed them all on his behalf and absolved them from every fault. Furthermore, he made known to them the stigmata and the other miracles which the Most High God had deigned to perform through Blessed Francis after his death."[98]

However, one of the early texts also tells us of some other people, perhaps including friars, who doubted the stigmata and its authenticity. *The Legend of the Three Companions*, written about the same time as Thomas of Celano's *Second Life* of Francis, mentions "many people who looked unkindly on the man of God and doubted the stigmata," leaving us without details, intrigued to know more.[99] We also have evidence that Pope Gregory IX did not accept calling the wounds stigmata at the time of canonizing Francis. It took Gregory IX ten years, in fact, to call them that.[100]

## PRECEDENTS AND MEANINGS

Thomas of Celano sounds downright philosophical in his *Second Life* when he summarizes: "Perhaps the cross of our Lord had to appear in the flesh [to Francis], since it could never be explained in words. Therefore, let silence speak where words are empty."[101] But we should try to say a little something more.

Francis was not the first person to embrace Christ on the cross in a way that achieved some sort of identity or unity with his object. Christian tradition is replete with examples of men and women practicing a devotion to the crucifix that results in some sort of physical identification with the Crucified. St. Paul said in Galatians, chapter two: "I have been crucified with Christ; and it is no longer I who live, but it is Christ who lives in me. And the life I now live in the flesh I live by faith in the Son of God, who loved me and gave himself for me." Francis would also have known the story of St. Bernard of Clairvaux, who was once praying alone in church, lying prostrate on the floor, when Christ separated his arms from the crossbar of the cross in order to embrace him. I once saw a statue of St. Ludmilla, as well (it was for sale on eBay), showing Christ unfixing himself from the cross in order to embrace her.

Many a mystic has stood or kneeled before the Crucified Christ, adoring him and imagining embracing him. And then, after Francis's experience, there were many others to come. After Clare's death, Bonaventure wrote a letter to a Poor Clare sister, saying:

> Draw near . . . with loving feet to Jesus wounded, to Jesus crowned with thorns, to Jesus fastened to the gibbet of the cross; and be not content, as the blessed apostle Thomas was, merely to see in his hands the print of the nails or to thrust your hand into his side; but rather go right in, through the opening in his side, to the very heart of Jesus where, transformed by most burning love for Christ, held by the nails of divine love, pierced by the lance of profound charity . . . you will know no other wish or desire.[102]

It is difficult to tell if this sort of language was a spiritualizing of the meaning of stigmata, or advice on the right approach to replicating it. Salimbene even wrote in the 1280s of a disturbed friar who was led by a voice to partially crucify himself in order to fully identify himself with Christ. They found him fastened by nails, all but one hand.

There are many ways to embrace Christ. Thomas of Celano describes Clare as "drunk on her tears for the Passion of Christ." Particularly during the offices of prayer that were said each afternoon, Thomas says, she felt penitence most deeply, "wishing to sacrifice her life for the One who was sacrificed."[103] In the centuries before Francis and Clare, mystics often meditated on the crucifix; they focused on the eyes of Jesus, the arms held open, the kiss of his mouth, comparing it to Song of Songs 1:2, "Let him kiss me with the kisses of his mouth!" and feeling the wound in his side.

Gazing meditation was common for medieval mystics. Very little of this survives today. A century ago, the Irish poet W. B. Yeats offered this simple "Drinking Song" that communicates something rather profound: "Wine comes in at the mouth / And love comes in at the eye; / That's all we shall know for truth / Before we grow old and die." When Francis and Clare gazed at an object, they absorbed it in ways unrealized even among religious people today; love came in at the eye. We barely pause long enough to consider ourselves, let alone to consider objects outside of our bodies. We will look at a sunset or some other piece of scenery, but we rarely gaze with what might be called the eyes of the soul, as saints once did.

The medieval imagination was geared toward the visual. Seeing the consecrated host of the Eucharist, for example, was a profoundly moving experience for many. It was uncommon to see it in those days, and still less common to receive it; and it was to the medieval imagination the crucified body of Christ made miraculously present. To see the Eucharist was to be transformed in some small way by it. There were cults or followings of the Eucharist just as there were cults of popular saints. Looking simply or disinterestedly at icons was uncommon, while gazing at them and looking into their eyes was quite common. The ancient tradition of covering images in church on solemn occasions, such as Good Friday, stems from the idea that all eyes should be down at these times—including the eyes of the images looking back at us.

When Francis looked at a crucifix, or when Clare looked on a sick man or woman left in her care, they each beheld a reality that is much deeper and more inscrutable than sight alone may determine. Their will was as creative as their vision, both of which combined to see reality in symbols and the stuff before their eyes as the raw material of God. Francis and Clare gazed, not just looked, and they perceived as much as they saw. By today's standards, these qualities make them unusual, the sort of people that most of us wouldn't ever invite for dinner. However, we might remember the instruction of Thomas à Kempis: "There is an incomparable distance between the things people imagine by reason, and those that illuminated people behold by contemplation."

The six-winged seraph in the form of the crucified Christ is rarely understood as the love symbol that it was for Francis and his contemporaries. When the troubadour poets had dramatically praised their lovesickness as "the wounds of love," they were secularizing (and trivializing) an ancient Christian way of describing Christ as both a lover and a seeker of lovers. The Lord who loves us on the cross is also the One who pursues us, and even pierces our hearts with love's arrows. One historian has summarized this tradition as "Christ as Cupid."[104]

The Old Testament Song of Songs showed first to Jews and then Christians that God has always loved with an intensity that *wounds*: "You have ravished my heart, my sister, my bride, you have ravished my heart with a glance of your eyes, with one jewel of your necklace" (4:9). Ideas and images such as the pierced heart, the flaming heart, and the Sacred Heart of Jesus all had their origins in these same traditions. In the fifth century, St. Augustine of Hippo wrote in book nine of his *Confessions*: "Thou hadst pierced our hearts with Thy charity, and we carried Thy words as it were fixed in our entrails."[105] In her autobiography, written more than a millennium later, St. Teresa of Avila describes a mystical encounter with an angel, using words almost verbatim from Augustine:

> In his hands I saw a long golden spear and at the end of the iron tip I seemed to see a point of fire. With this he seemed to pierce my heart several times so that it penetrated to my entrails.

*121*

When he drew it out, I thought he was drawing them out with it and he left me completely afire with a great love for God.[106]

The most passionate love between God and human is bittersweet. A mystic will tell you that is why not everyone wants to love God. In the century before Francis and Clare, the Cistercian Gilbert of Hoyland meditated on the passion of Christ, wishing for himself what later happened to Francis: "Would that [Christ] might multiply such wounds in me, from the sole of my foot to the crown of my head, that there might be no health in me! For health is evil without the wounds that Christ's gracious gaze inflicts."[107] That is just what occurred on the quiet mountainside when Francis met the seraph, alone.

For two years, Francis kept this incredible secret from all but those closest to him. All that was left for him was to keep pleading with the brothers to follow the original intentions of the *Rule*. In his final writing, the *Testament*, Francis pledged his eternal obedience to the ministers-general of the Order, but also said to all future ministers-general that they were bound by obedience (to Francis, perhaps, and to God) "not to add to or take away from" those original ideals in the *Rule*, reiterated in the *Testament*. As he lay dying, he asked his brothers to sing his beloved *Canticle of the Creatures* in Italian, rather than the usual prayers and songs in ecclesiastical Latin. They probably also sang the Ave Maria, in honor of the Virgin Mary, to whom Francis was always dearly devoted.

Hail Mary, full of grace,
the Lord is with you.
Blessed are you among women,
and blessed is the fruit of your womb, Jesus.
Holy Mary, Mother of God,
pray for us sinners
now and at the hour of our death.
Amen.

He died late on Saturday, October 4, 1226. The friars carried the body from Portiuncula, where he breathed his last, back into Assisi on Sunday morning. Bonaventure says that people from all around joined them in procession carrying tree branches and flaming candles. They began the journey early in the morning at the break of dawn, as the birds were rousing the city.

CHAPTER

11

# THE CANTICLE OF THE CREATURES

A
ll of the sources tell us that Francis insisted on feeling the earth on his body just before his death. The medieval assumption was that every Christian should want to die in a holy place—in other words, in a church—if possible. If salvation was possible only in the Church, then the church was the place that all wished to be at the moment of passing. A good life made possible a good and appropriate death, which would include solemn Masses, general confession, and last rites from the hands of a priest. In these ways, the Church was brought to the dying, even if the dying couldn't make it to church.

Remarkably, there is no mention in the poignant fourteen chapters of Bonaventure's *Life* of Francis of Masses, confessions, and last rites. As Francis was dying, he wanted to be taken back to St. Mary of the Angels—Portiuncula. But on the way there he asked to be laid on the bare ground. *The Little Flowers* has Francis saying to the brothers who were carrying him, "Lay me down on the ground. Turn me to face Assisi." Bonaventure added with feeling that Francis laid himself on the ground naked, which usually meant without habit or cowl, but still some sort of undergarment. "He prostrated himself with passion and spirit, naked on the bare earth." And Thomas of

*124*

Celano in his *Second Life* shows Francis doing the same, looking to heaven, and then saying to the friars who were gathered there, "Now, I have done what is mine to do. May Christ teach you what is yours to do!"

## LOVE FOR LIFE AND DEATH

Just as human and animal combined in the worldview of Francis and Clare, so too, life and death were intertwined. "In the midst of life we are in death," says the ancient funeral rite. No era knew this fact as well as the Middle Ages.

When Francis was nearly blind a year before his death, he composed that remarkable hymn *The Canticle of the Creatures*. In the song, he expresses his belief that the wildness and expectancies of nature are part of God's plan for human life. This marked the true dividing point—the first real signpost—for what has become the modern understanding of how earth and heaven join together. As one contemporary author has put it:

> The *Canticle* signifies that the whole creation is a cosmic Incarnation—earth, air, water, sun, moon, stars—all are related to Brother Sun who is the splendor and radiance of the Most High. We might read Francis' *Canticle* as foreshadowing the new creation, when we will find ourselves related to all things in the spirit of reconciliation and peace.[108]

It all began with Francis of Assisi's fear of mice. Two years before his death, Francis was living in a small hut outside the walls of San Damiano in a place that Clare had prepared for him among the gardens. His eyesight was getting so poor at this time that he suffered constant pain from both sunlight and from simply opening his eyes. He was growing blinder by the day. After only sixty days at San Damiano, he was unable to see at all.

The description in the text[109] says that what happened next was a temptation of the devil. It was "by divine permission that for increase of his affliction and his merit"—mice began to infest his hut. "So many mice came into his cell that they were running all over his body and all around him both night and day. They kept him from resting as well as from praying. Even when he tried to eat, the mice swarmed onto his table and infested him by the multitude." It is difficult to read such a description without checking around one's feet!

Francis responded by praying to God: "Look on me and comfort me in my afflictions, so that I may endure them with patience!" He had reason to be upset; first blindness, then an infestation!

Jesus responded to him "in spirit," in other words, through non-verbal communication that is heard in the soul: "If a certain man was given a treasure so great and precious that the whole earth was as nothing compared to it, wouldn't he rejoice despite any infirmities or afflictions he might experience? Be glad, brother, and rejoice in your difficulties. As for the rest, take heed of them no more than you would if you had already entered My kingdom!"

Francis rose the next morning and began to compose his *Canticle*. He began by integrating the natural and the spiritual in a way that deliberately honored those creatures and aspects of Creation that we normally either forget or despise. He said to his brother friars: "I must add to the praise of God, our own consolation, and the edification of our neighbor, a new song of praise for those creatures of God that we use every day and without whom we are unable to live. If we do not praise them, we must terribly offend their Creator. For continually we show ourselves ungrateful for so great grace and so many blessings, not praising the Lord and giver of all."

Most high, almighty, good Lord God,
>to you belong all praise, glory, honor, and blessing!

Praised be you, O my Lord and God, with all your creatures,
>and especially our Brother Sun,
>who brings us the day and who brings us the light.

He is fair and shines with a very great splendor:
>O Lord, he signifies you to us!

Praised be you, O my Lord, for our Brother Wind,
>and for air and cloud, calms and all weather
>through which you uphold life in all creatures.

Praise the Lord for our Sister Water,
>who is very useful to us and humble
>and precious and clean.

Praise the Lord for our Brother Fire,
>through whom you give us light in the darkness.

He is bright and pleasant and very mighty and strong.

Praise the Lord for our Mother Earth,
>who sustains us and keeps us,
>and brings forth the grass and all
>of the fruits and flowers of many colors.

Once the *Canticle* was composed and Francis had taught his companions to sing it, he then saw need to add another verse. The bishop of Assisi was then arguing with the local governor so fiercely that the bishop excommunicated the governor and the governor forbade any citizen to enter into any contract with the bishop. The text[110] tells us that Francis was grieved when he heard of their bickering, but "most of all he was grieved that no one had gotten between them to try and make peace." And so, Francis wrote this verse for his song, which speaks to the need for mediating justice and peace between the powers of the world.

> Praise be you, O my Lord, for all who show forgiveness and
>> pardon one another for your sake,
>> and who endure weakness and tribulation.
> Blessed are they who peaceably endure,
> For you, Most High, shall give them a crown.

He told one of his companions to ask the governor to come to the bishop's house along with the officials of the city. Francis was too sick to go, but he sent instructions with his companions, probably Leo, Angelo, and Rufinus, that they were to sing the *Canticle* before the gathering and "have trust in the Lord that he will humble their hearts." This is how it happened: the governor was the first to apologize, asking for the bishop's forgiveness, and the bishop accepted and embraced him once again as a brother.

And last, Francis made room for death in his great song.[111] He could hardly open his eyes, and any sunlight was painful to him. "Brother Ass," he had once called his own body, comparing it to the beast of burden that never does all that its master requires of it. But Francis transformed his discomfort into praise for those parts of earthly existence that most challenged him. Once he was told by his doctors and companions that his infirmities were beyond healing, the time had come to look forward to death, and he did.

He asked for Leo and Angelo to come to his side and sing to him of Sister Death. Francis had written the last verse:

> Praise to you, O my Lord, for our Sister Death
> and the death of the body from whom no one may escape.
> Woe to those who die in mortal sin.
> but blessed are they who are found walking by your most holy will,

For the second death
> shall have no power to do them any harm.
Praise to you, O my Lord, and all blessing.
We give you thanks and serve you with great humility.

This vernacular song has been sung ever since, by Franciscans and others. The attention paid by Francis to the creatures has led many scholars to draw fascinating connections between his emphasis on looking with fresh eyes on the created world with the renaissance of interest in geometry and the study of light and visual perspective that followed. The Byzantine era of painting was dark, featuring idealized figures, but what emerged from the Italian painters Cimabue and Giotto in the thirteenth and fourteenth centuries was a renewed attention to real life, details of the human figure and all manner of creatures, and a perspective of light that hadn't been seen since the classical era. Many of those famous paintings are reproduced in black and white throughout this book. The generation that was Francis's and Clare's represented the one before Scholasticism was born in Paris; before Bonaventure and Thomas Aquinas (both d. 1274) lovingly combined a scholar's mind with a mystic's heart; before architecture soared with new expression for God's splendor in Gothic forms; and before Cimabue (d. ca. 1302) and Giotto (d. 1337) brought realism and light back to painting.

*Detail of "Pilate and the Priests"*

129

# THE SEPULCHER OF
## ST. FRANCIS

In the last years before his death, Francis visited Clare and the sisters at San Damiano after being pestered to do so by the friars and by Clare, and he responded with one of his most dramatic gestures. Instead of preaching as he was expected to do, Francis sat down before the gathering and had ashes poured all around him in a circle. Then he took an additional container of ashes and poured them over his head. After a short time, he stood and began to recite Psalm 51, his favorite prayer of confession. It goes, in part, like this:

> Have mercy on me, O God, according to your loving-kindness; in your great compassion blot out my offenses.
>
> Wash me through and through from my wickedness and cleanse me from my sin.
>
> ...
>
> Create in me a clean heart, O God, and renew a right spirit within me.
>
> Cast me not away from your presence and take not your holy Spirit from me.
>
> Give me the joy of your saving help again and sustain me with your bountiful Spirit.

I shall teach your ways to the wicked, and sinners shall return to you.

Deliver me from death, O God, and my tongue shall sing of your righteousness, O God of my salvation.[112]

Some have seen a kind of stubbornness in this *sermon* of Francis. It is regarded by some scholars of the last century as something akin to the "anti-sermon"—and that may be true inasmuch as Francis emphasized a different sort of preaching. This was a dramatic example of preaching with one's life. To live a life according to Psalm 51 is not to speak about it but to do it, as Francis demonstrated. One of the messages of the ashes sermon was undoubtedly that there is an essence to the Christian life that can easily become lost among traditions of formal learning and formal practices of worship (such as preaching and listening), and that this essence is experienced in contrition, the most basic response to Christ.

But there is another, deeper way of understanding the ashes sermon. All great spiritual teachers, both Christian and not, have used silence to communicate the essence of faith. At the end of his life, the prolific Indian poet Rabindranath Tagore said that "languagelessness" was more important than poetry, and he then tried (ironically) to capture the spirit of silence in his final verses. Sometimes, it is what is *not* said that is of the utmost importance. Regardless of the medium, there is something utterly basic about silence as we relate to the divine, and yet we so easily miss it.

Francis's ashes sermon should remind us of when Jesus was confronted by a group of scribes and Pharisees in the temple. They brought to him a woman caught having sex with a man other than her husband. They asked Jesus, who had previously angered many Jewish leaders by teaching amendments to the law of Moses, saying that the law orders them to stone the woman: "What have you got to say?" they asked him (John 8:5). Jesus responded with silence. The next verse reads, "But Jesus bent down and started writing on the ground with his finger."

The ashes sermon may also remind us of what, in Buddhist tradition, is regarded as the Buddha's most important sermon. This is known as the flower sermon. In the fifth and sixth centuries BC, the Buddha was born in India and later died in China. Toward the end of his life, he gathered his followers together and delivered this memorable *talk*; but instead of speaking, he held up a flower. He held a lotus for many minutes without saying a word. The Buddha's followers were all confused and looked at each other. Some of them began to speak, trying to explain the purpose of the flower, its origins, its relationship to the tenets of religion. But it was only when one of them smiled, looking back at Buddha with understanding and obvious acceptance of this simple but dramatic gesture of serenity and peace and silence, that Buddha knew who would be the one to carry on his teachings. The tradition says that Buddha responded to that one, saying, "What can be said I have said to the others, but what cannot be said, I have given to you." I think that we need to understand Francis's ashes sermon in that same context: it was the occasion of Francis's passing on his teachings to Clare, who must have understood perfectly.[113]

Throughout her religious life, Clare lived behind the walls and iron grille of San Damiano that separated the first Franciscan women from the outside world. It was through that grille of intersecting iron bars that the women would receive the Eucharist from the hands of the brothers. We often get the sense that she wanted to be out and about more often with Francis and the friars, doing things that Sisters of St. Clare sometimes do today, but that were not really possible for religious women in the thirteenth century. The cloister remained her only home for more than forty years. But the world came to Clare. Bishops, cardinals, and popes were known to visit her in person at San Damiano in order to listen to her heavenly conversation. And since the early days of her ministry with Francis, when he and the friars would daily send the sick to San Damiano to be blessed by Clare and the sisters, the Poor Clares had been recognized for the heavenly power of their prayers.

The body of Francis came to Clare just after his death. Clare and the sisters could not be there when he died, as they stayed behind their iron grille, but the procession into Assisi brought Francis's body to them. Bonaventure tells us that the friars set down the body and stayed at San Damiano for quite a while, and the sisters both saw it and embraced it. The grille was removed. Biographer Paul Sabatier wrote: "In one of the frescos of the Upper Church in Assisi, Giotto has represented St. Clare and her companions coming out from San Damiano all in tears to kiss their spiritual father's corpse as it is being carried to its last home. With an artist's liberty he has made the chapel a rich church built of precious marbles."[114]

When Clare cried over the body of her good friend, her grief was probably increased by worry for what was happening to the movement they had founded. Elias and Cardinal Ugolino, who had been appointed by the pope to look after the young Franciscan Order, were slowly and deliberately steering things away from Francis's original *Rule*. And then, Cardinal Ugolino was elected Pope Gregory IX less than six months after the death of Francis. Clare's struggles to keep to the ideals deepened. "Almost everything that was done in the Order after 1221 was done either without Francis's knowledge or against his will," explains Sabatier.[115] And the same was true for Clare in those final years.

On the third of October, 1226, St. Francis began his final agony, and after having the *Canticle of the Creatures* chanted to him once more he breathed his last. It is the great privilege of saints and poets that death opens for them even on earth a new life, for before the time of mourning is past, the glorious dead begin to excite the world, their words and example serving to incite generation to generation of disciples to interpret and imitate them. So, in order to be just to them, one must not only credit their lives and the works that they have left to us, but also with the followers they have inspired.

The poetic mission of St. Francis, eclipsed by other cares during his lifetime, never shone more brightly than in the century after his death. He had chosen for himself a burial-place on a hill to the east of Assisi called the Hill of Hell, where criminals were executed. But they had no sooner laid him in the tomb than an irresistible thrill stirred the world and

The friars then left San Damiano en route to the church of San Giorgio (now a chapel within the Basilica of St. Clare in Assisi,) where Brother Elias had arranged for the funeral and burial. But the body would not rest at San Giorgio for long. On April 29, 1228, Pope Gregory IX issued a papal decree, or bull, announcing his intention to build a *specialis ecclesia*, "special church," to honor Francis. Less than eighteen months after the body was buried at San Giorgio, Elias acquired the land on the northwestern edge of Assisi known as the Hill of Hell, where thieves and murderers were often executed and then buried, and plans were underway to transform the land to the glory of St. Francis.

The unrepentant and the heretic could not, according to medieval laws, be buried in holy ground. That is why a place such as the Hill of Hell existed in most medieval towns. Bodies of those who were outside the Church needed to be buried somewhere. Ironically, there was no corresponding law against burying a good Christian in an unclean place. The Hill of Hell was unknown by firsthand experience to most Assisans, and was a place of frightening legends to the children of the town. That Francis would choose such a location for his burial was perfectly in keeping with his desire to be regarded as the lowliest of all before God. It was also a final act of solidarity with Christ, who died among thieves.

During the medieval era, many peasants, saints, and even kings would give much thought to how they should appear before the judgment seat of Christ after death. The belief was that a dead person, body and soul, would go directly to judgment, to face the question of one's eternal destiny. It was important to make the right impression. Once a fate was announced, he or she would go to heaven or hell, or perhaps, purgatory. Even the sixteenth-

became the inspiration of many minds. Pope Gregory IX placed him among the saints and decreed that his resting-place should be called the Hill of Paradise. From that time no honors were too great for this humble saint. People remembered his love for them, and wished to reward him richly for all the sacrifices he had made on their behalf.

Although he had had neither shelter nor servant, they built for him a magnificent resting-place like the palace he had dreamed of in his youth, where all types of artists might soon enter into his service. The rock had to be hollowed out to an unusual depth in order to protect the body from the risk of those thefts of relics which were so frequent in medieval times. Immediately over the tomb they erected a basilica to receive the crowd of pilgrims, and over that again they erected a second one from which prayers might ascend more quickly to heaven.

A northern architect, Jacopo Tedesco, came to build this double edifice, and applied to it all of the resources of Gothic art, all the traditions of Christian symbolism. He designed the lower basilica in the form of a solid nave without ornament, with arcades and openings that admit only a dim light, as if to recall the life of penitence of St. Francis on earth. He built the upper church with thinner walls, with bold arches, and with long windows through which the light streams in, as if to represent the glorious life of St. Francis in heaven.

*—Frederick Ozanam*

century Emperor Maximilian I, who was no great saint, left instructions that his body should be burned, his teeth smashed in, and his head shaved upon death. Despite what his earthly record might show, he wanted to at least seem physically penitent when he appeared before God.[116]

Gregory and Elias would honor Francis's request of burial site, but not according to the spirit of Francis's wishes. Elias was named the architect of the new basilica. Three months later, the same week that Francis was solemnly canonized by Gregory IX in a ceremony at San Giorgio, the first stone was ceremonially laid for the Lower Church of the new basilica. Gregory IX himself laid the stone, and the Hill of Hell was renamed the Hill of Paradise.

A new church building of the magnitude of the Basilica of Saint Francis in Assisi was never undertaken lightly. This solemn place was seen as a new tabernacle of Moses, a divine place where God would dwell in a special way with his people. It was a symbol of the New Jerusalem but, more literally, also as a gate to heaven. And it was built on the foundation of Francis of Assisi. Within two years, the Lower Church was completed and Francis's body moved there, and then within six additional years, the Upper Church was constructed, later to be adorned with priceless frescos by Giotto and others depicting the lives of Francis and his brothers, including an image of Elias himself kneeling before a crucifix.

The building of the basilica was one of the greatest architectural and artistic achievements of the Middle Ages. There is no denying the tremendous gifts that Elias possessed for architecture and organization. Gregory IX honored him by declaring through a papal bull that the basilica was now the mother church for all Franciscans, a title that had previously been used by the Poverello for the "little portion," Portiuncula, according to the *Mirror of Perfection*. All of this disgusted that handful of Franciscans who had been closest to Francis.

In the General Chapter meetings of 1230, the year that Elias completed the Lower Church, he maneuvered himself into position to be elected minister-general of the Order. But he failed, and another friar, John Parenti, was elected instead. For the next two years, Elias dedicated himself to constructing a shrine for Francis and turning Assisi into a place of pilgrimage that would rival Jerusalem and Compostela.

The body was buried in the Lower Church deep into the stone wall of its foundation. One writer has described the immense piece of rock that had stood in the middle of the Hill of Hell before the basilica was built—"an isolated rock surrounded on three sides by sharply falling precipices, and only joined to the city by a narrow neck of land almost cut through by a ravine which at the present day is filled up and built over by the upper and lower piazzas of San Francesco"—and it is probably into this foundation that the relic was securely entombed.[117]

A ceremony was planned, and guests invited, for the transferal of the body from San Giorgio to San Francesco. It requires about fifteen minutes to walk this distance today, and a procession would have taken well over an hour. But as the friars, honored guests, and townspeople all realized upon arriving at the basilica, the body was not there. Elias had arranged to have it secretly buried a few days earlier for fear that the crowd would tear it apart for relics.

The absence of a grave marker was not in itself unusual. Grave markers were uncommon in the thirteenth century, as the purpose of burial was not to commemorate a person as much as it was to add one to the community of believers. Anonymous burials in a common place of consecrated ground such as a chapel or parish were the norm. Even those clergy and religious who were buried inside a church were usually done so in unmarked spaces.[118] But still, Elias and the friars were afraid of the body being stolen by relic hunters. They hid it. The body was entombed into rock in such a way that exactly where it was remained a mystery for nearly six hundred years. Only in 1818 would a pope give permission to find the body and rebury it in the crypt of the basilica.

## RESCUING THE SEPULCHER

As Elias and Pope Gregory were transforming the landscape of Assisi and organizing the Franciscan Order, Clare continued to play a leadership role on the spiritual side of the movement, but from a distance and from her cloister. It is believed that certain of the brothers—those who saw themselves in a direct line from Francis's earliest spiritual intentions—came to visit Clare and the sisters often, hearing confessions and administering the Eucharist, among other things. While he was still alive, Francis had actually warned the friars from visiting the sisters too often, but after his death they needed to reconnect with what united them.

These friars came to be known as "Spirituals," because they felt a strong connection to the original *Rule* of St. Francis and its emphasis on living strictly according to the Gospels. They would later fight bitterly, sometimes with deadly consequences, with the leaders of the Order and with the papacy in ways that would have saddened Francis and Clare. Brothers such as Leo, Angelo, Rufinus, Giles, Juniper, Bernard, and Masseo all lived to grieve for Brother Francis, and also for the integrity of their life. Elias and the others were replacing dancing with processions. They turned simplicity and humility into grandeur for the newly canonized. In their hands, the wildness of evangelical poverty and preaching was becoming tame and organized.

The friars surrounding Clare, and many of those scattered about, probably wanted to rescue Francis's sepulcher from Elias, and from those who would use pomp and riches to honor a saint who would have wanted nothing of it. The Spirituals would rather have been fools than churchmen. The ministers who followed Elias co-opted Francis's life and legacy for their causes, which included fundraising, building cathedrals, and devising intellectual systems that would endanger the Poverello's single-minded passion for firsthand experience. Elias and others were sincere in their reasons for building upon the foundation that had been laid by Francis and Clare, but there is no question that gone with Francis was the original movement he had founded.

# BURNING BOOKS

T he story of Brother Francis and Sister Clare is replete with books and their reactions to books. Francis loved to use them for prayer, as we know from the early texts. He took books with him while traveling so that he could read the prayer offices while on the road. He began his religious life by turning to ornate books of Gospels and other texts from the bishop's library, but then later fought with friars who wanted to possess books of their own.

As the First and Second Orders filled rapidly with men and women of promising potential, many of them were ambitious, smart, and thoughtful. They heard Francis preach that learning and study and books were possessions no less dangerous to a holy life than were money and pride. He told them again and again that a friar or a sister needed simplicity and poverty more than books, but many of them didn't quite believe it. How could a preacher preach well without study, they wondered. Why must a joy-filled life exclude books and learning? The problems were very practical ones. In order to study, one needs books and leisure time. Stability also becomes important for a student, requiring ongoing access to libraries and teachers. All of these things were beside the point of faithfulness to Christ in the worldview of Francis and Clare.

On one memorable occasion, Francis pleaded with a young friar who wanted to own his own breviary. Francis was trying to teach the friars that prayer books were for changing one's life, not for owning, but by the time of this encounter, he was no longer the minister-general. Nevertheless, the young friar persisted in asking for Francis's blessing to own one. Francis wouldn't give it, but instead, pleaded with the boy to become a passionate follower of Christ who doesn't need to own anything. He shouted, "*I* am a breviary! *I* am a breviary!"

Some of the most beloved books of the first Franciscans were actually about Francis. Thomas of Celano's *First Life* was circulated the year after canonization (in 1229), and his *Second Life* about eighteen years later (in 1246 or 1247). These volumes looked little like our books of today, except that they were usually taller than they were wide, and similar in size to today's books. They were hand copied, as this was the era before the printing press, and usually made of vellum, a prepared animal skin. This made some books very sturdy and rigid, while others could become greasy. Few books in those days were of one text only. There was no such thing as copyright law, and books were all custom-made. A biography of St. Francis might also include a litany of the saints, the little Office of the Virgin, a collection of penitential psalms, an anonymous treatise on the Apocalypse, and a prayer to the patron saint of the book's owner.

We also know that Thomas's two biographies of Francis circulated outside of the friaries and were among the most popular books of the day. Since Francis was believed to be a saint even before his death and his canonization was decisively swift, the stories about him were quickly assumed into the already popular genre of devotional literature known as the lives of the saints. Numerous First, Second, and Third Order Franciscans joined because of having read Thomas of Celano's accounts. The same has happened in subsequent eras: Carmelite convents were flooded with young women in the decades after Therese of Lisieux's *Story of a Soul* was first published at the end of the nineteenth century, and Thomas Merton's Abbey of Gethsemani was bursting at the seams in the late 1940s and early 1950s as young men came back from World War II and read Merton's autobiography *The Seven Storey Mountain*, finding the meaning to their lives.

Given all of this, it must have been especially difficult for the friars to obey an order in 1266 to destroy all copies of Thomas of Celano's biographies of Francis.

Bonaventure wrote his *Life* of Francis at the commission of the General Chapter meeting of 1260. He wanted to bring peace to the factions that were tearing apart the Order. Details were added that enhanced the legend of Francis as the founder of a brilliant new movement. Bonaventure's book represented no new research or insight, but rather a beautiful retelling of Thomas of Celano's stories without references to the loss of spiritual ideals. It is simply a redaction, which is why it is unfortunate that today Bonaventure's is by far the most read of the early biographies of Francis.

At the General Chapter of 1266, Bonaventure and the Franciscans declared that all earlier biographies of St. Francis were to be destroyed. The resolution reads:

> The General Chapter commands likewise in the name of obedience, that all legends that have been written about St. Francis shall be destroyed, and where they are found outside the Order, the Brothers will seek to dispose of them, because the legend which was written by the General is made up of what he heard from their mouths, who were with St. Francis nearly all the time and knew everything with certainty.[119]

No stories have come down to us of massive book burnings in the friaries or convents, but no doubt, there were some strident friars and sisters who stoked fires in places like Siena, Bologna, and Florence. We know very little about how books were destroyed and how many. We can imagine that many copies were buried rather than burned, as it was the medieval tradition to bury a holy book in order to dispose of it, as a show of respect. Still other copies were hidden away from the eyes of those who desired them destroyed. Meanwhile, the Spirituals were soon to begin collecting and writing down the stories of Francis and Clare that became *The Little Flowers*. The loss of Thomas of Celano's accounts made pulling together other texts all the more important.

A battle was not just brewing; it was already underway for the heart of the movement. Nowhere do we see this tension as clearly as we do in *The Mirror of Perfection*. In the tenth tale, for example, Francis is depicted as counseling his brothers how to build a house and church upon settling in a new city. It is impossible to read this tale today without seeing the hand of a later editor at work, using comments of Francis to dispute the leaders of his Order after his death. Francis's comments about the building of churches must have been intended to counter the extravagance of the new Basilica of St. Francis just built in Assisi by Brother Elias:

> And let them make little churches, for they ought not to have great churches built, neither for the sake of preaching to the people nor upon another occasion, for the humility is greater and the example better when they go to other churches to preach. . . . Many a time do the brethren have great buildings made, breaking thereby our holy poverty, giving occasion of mischievous whispers, and setting a bad example unto many.

*143*

Similarly, as we mentioned above, the editors of *The Mirror* quote Francis as saying that Portiuncula, "as the smallest and poorest church," should always remain "the head and mother of the poor Friars Minor." The fifty-fifth tale even quotes Francis as saying, "The Lord wishes that no other church should be given to the friars, and that the friars should not build a new church."

Despite the Spirituals' best efforts to change things back to where they had been, the movement was formalizing in ways that were supported by the majority of the friars and sisters and by Rome. Bonaventure understood that changes had to be made in order for the Franciscans to enter a new, post-Francis era of productivity and growth. Never mind that those were not virtues in the mind of their founder, and the Franciscans of the generation after Francis believed that what had begun simply and with purity should naturally develop into something more defined and sustainable. At one point, Bonaventure makes this clear, as he defends the lack of book learning among the first followers of Francis:

> It should not disturb you that the first brothers were simple and illiterate. On the contrary, that should confirm your faith in the Order. I confess before God that this is what most made me love the life of Blessed Francis—that it was like the beginning and perfection of the church itself, which began first among simple fishermen and later progressed into the most renowned and learned doctors. . . . That this was a divine work is demonstrated by the fact that the learned did not refuse to join the company of such simple men.[120]

With Bonaventure's rule as minister-general, and the changes that were happening in step with it, Francis and Clare became saints to revere more than life examples to imitate. Many of the principles of

Francis's original *Rule* faded away or were taken far less literally, and those who dissented from these majority opinions were marginalized.

## THE INFLUENCE OF BROTHER ELIAS

Francis loved Elias, that we know. Three years after Francis's death, Thomas of Celano recorded that Elias was "the one he chose to be as a mother to himself, and also as a father to the other brothers." Elias was the only one able to insist that Francis take medicine to alleviate pain, when others had failed. Francis appointed him as minister to the all-important province of the Holy Land, and then later visited him there just after abdicating his leadership of the Order. Elias was one of the privileged few to have seen up close and firsthand the wounds of Christ imprinted on the saint's body, two years before his death. And Thomas wrote of Francis's deathbed, saying, "There was a brother there whom Francis loved with the greatest affection," which was most likely Elias.[121] Clare also praised Elias in her second letter to Blessed Agnes of Prague. Clare urged Agnes to "follow the advice of our honorable father, Brother Elias, the minister-general, so that you will walk safely in the way of the Lord."

In the election of 1232, Elias succeeded John Parenti and was elected to the post of minister-general. His work of protecting the body of Francis and building Assisi into a palace of pilgrimage was largely over. But by 1239, after Clare's letter was written to Agnes, Elias had been deposed by the pope at the overwhelming demand of the friars. Salimbene tells us that Elias, once one of Francis's trusted advisors and friends, turned against his own brothers after the founder's death. Elias was the leader of those who would expand the role of the friars in the world, welcoming the ownership of property, the cultivation of learning, and the building of splendid churches and monuments—including the Basilica of St. Francis in Assisi. Salimbene no doubt felt betrayed by Elias as well, as it was Elias who received young Salimbene as a postulant and sheltered him from his angry father (who wanted to thwart the conversion) while Elias was minister-general.[122] But Elias's independence was combined with excessive pride and a lust for increasing influence.

When he was finally deposed as minister-general, Elias rebelled by joining up with the excommunicated Holy Roman Emperor Frederick II, who was at war with the pope. He took some friars with him in this fight, and the reputation of the Order was seriously damaged. Salimbene recounts that "I myself have heard a hundred times" the singing of a little ditty by the Umbrian peasants whenever a friar would pass by during this time, "Frater Elias is gone astray / And hath taken the evil way." Salimbene says: "At the sound of this song, the good brothers were cut to the heart." By the time Thomas of Celano wrote his *Second Life* of Francis in 1246–1247, Elias had been disgraced and is not mentioned by name.

# CHAPTER 14

# THE RISE AND FALL
# OF THE SPIRITUALS

P rophets are supposed to make religious leaders nervous. They challenge the status quo and attempt to incite people to change their ways. When Francis and Clare insisted on absolute poverty for themselves and their followers, this always rankled the popes and cardinals who were assigned to look after them. The situation may remind us of what it was like in Jesus' last week in Jerusalem before the Passion, when religious fervor was everywhere and was stimulated easily by passing prophets and teachers. Like the church in Francis's time, the synagogue in Christ's time was interested in settling matters of doctrine and practices of faith and organizing religious activities and tithes under the umbrella of those good teachings and works. In other words, organized religion has always preferred to remain organized, and the Catholic Church in the days of Francis and Clare was no different from organized faith anytime, anywhere. Preaching lives of voluntary poverty was subversive to these ends. How would the people tithe to the church if they had no money? Would they even come to services if they were following an itinerant preacher? Francis practiced a peripatetic faith that did not lend itself easily to settled communities of faithful churchgoers.

Francis experienced skepticism about his unorganized band of followers from the very beginning, when they visited Pope Innocent III in Rome. Innocent III hesitated before granting approval to Francis for his young movement. He wanted to be sure that they were properly organized and that they took on characteristics of a true religious order. To that end, he made sure that the twelve of them were tonsured, marked as religious at least by their visible haircuts, before leaving Rome. And he deliberated long before sanctioning the sort of poverty that the Poverello insisted upon, trying first to persuade him otherwise.

Pope Honorius III later hesitated as well before approving Francis's revised *Rule*. Honorius, in fact, persuaded the saint to remove a clause that would permit friars to follow a literal interpretation of the *Rule*, even if their future ministers objected.[123] A few years later, Pope Gregory IX had brought about additional changes to the original vision, revising Francis's teachings on poverty even further. Two or three years before Francis died, the quotation from Luke's Gospel—"Take nothing for the journey: neither staff, nor haversack, nor bread, nor money; and do not have a spare tunic"—was removed from the *Rule* despite Francis's objections. It was no longer deemed prudent to expect that all friars would or could follow such an instruction to the letter. The *Rule* of 1223 is, in fact, changed from the original vision in many ways. The overall effect was the slowing of the gospel of Franciscanism. Brothers were no longer called "Friars Minor," which literally means "Lesser Brothers," a name instituted by Francis as a description of their poverty; they were permitted to ride rather than walk; and poverty began to take on spiritual rather than literal meanings. The idealism of Francis and Clare was giving way to something much more familiar.

Francis's body was already falling apart at this time, in 1223. The next year, he made his monthlong retreat on Alverno, which really sapped his energies and by which time he was almost blind and crippled. When he finally left the mountain, Francis was forced to ride a donkey rather than walk. It is on this occasion, as they traveled through various towns en route back to Assisi, that Francis was recognized as a living saint in the eyes of the people. "*Santo, santo,*" they called him, in those last years of his life. They touched him, snatched pieces of his clothing, and followed him, sensing the vanishing presence of a unique man.

His detractors said nothing out loud at this time; it was clear to all that Francis was dying. He would spend more time preaching, the familiar voice but without the usual vitality, and he would be for a while at San Damiano in Clare's care. The time to continue *normalizing* the Order was close at hand for Gregory IX and Elias.

The opponents of Francis and Clare thought that he and his most energetic followers were reckless. Imagine a group of reforming Christians who refuse to own anything, decline opportunities for comfort or schooling, and who refuse to plan for the future or even to take good physical care of themselves. Established communities have persecuted groups that fit one or more of these characterizations for centuries. According to the Franciscan Spirituals, Christians without such a literal commitment to the teachings of Jesus were consumed instead by a "worldly prudence and caution."[124] Meanwhile, their detractors called the Spirituals fools, and they didn't mean this as a compliment. The conflict was between order and chaos, and the Spirituals preferred chaos. Miguel de Unamuno was accused of a similar sort of foolishness in the last century, and he responded sarcastically: "No—nothing that is regulated and contained and channeled and directed by graduates, curates, barbers, canons, and dukes is fanaticism. Nothing that flies a banner proclaiming log-ical formulas, nothing that has a program, nothing that offers a plan for tomorrow which an orator can expound in a methodical fashion, is fanaticism."[125]

Which excess would you prefer? For the Spirituals, the choice was an easy one: an excess of faithfulness to Francis and Clare and to Christ.

The name *Spirituals* is actually a misnomer when applied to the beliefs of any Franciscan before the fourteenth century, for it appears that the term did not exist until about that time. But to understand the name, it is necessary to travel back in time to an earlier prophet who inspired Francis, Joachim of Fiore. Paul Sabatier summarizes the life of the enigmatic, traveling ascetic:

> Converted after a life of dissipation, Joachim of Fiore traveled extensively in the Holy Land, Greece, and Constantinople. Returning to Italy he began, though a layman, to preach in the outskirts of Rende and Cosenza. Later on he joined the Cistercians . . . and there took vows. Shortly after being elected abbot of the monastery in spite of refusal and even flight, he was seized after a few years with the nostalgia of solitude, and sought from Pope Lucius III a discharge from his functions (1181). . . . Then began for Joachim a life of wandering from monastery to monastery that carried him even as far as Lombardy. . . . When he returned to the south, a group of disciples gathered around him to hear his explanations of the most obscure passages of the Bible . . . in the very heart of the Sila, the Black Forest of Italy. . . . This new Athos received the name of Fiore (flower), trans-parent symbol of the hopes of its founder.[126]

Joachim's interpretation of history prevailed in the minds of the early Franciscans. He divided the history of humanity into three periods. The first period he called the reign of God the Father; this was a time when people lived under the law and the threat of punishment for failing to keep the law. The second period was the reign of God the Son, when grace was brought to troubled humanity and humanity was taught to be obedient in a new way, as kin or family. And the third period—believed by the Spirituals to be the period into which they were presently entering—was the reign of God the Spirit. This third era was to be characterized by love and freedom triumphing over fear and law.

With this prophetic understanding, the true spirit of what became known as the Spirituals began way back when Francis and his first followers were staying in the caves of Carceri, tending to lepers, and during the time that they lived loosely around Portiuncula, working in the fields during the day, preaching in the churches, begging for their bread, and sleeping under the stars at night. In those very things was the essence of the movement, according to Francis. He wrote in his *Testament*, his last and greatest work, that the friars should always be "strangers and pilgrims" in their observance of poverty without property and possessions.

At the same time, it is easy to understand why some of the followers who came soon after this golden period wanted much more, and believed that God wanted more for the Franciscans, too. Ironically, Francis's idealism drew not only thousands of men to the First Order, but also some of the most talented and intellectual men of the day. More ironic, still: these men would not remain satisfied with humility and mendicancy. They would become influential scholars and powerful clerics, and would build grand churches such as the basilica in Assisi and Santa Croce in Florence. They built churches; they built schools; they developed massive libraries; they sent the smarter friars off to university in Paris and Rome and elsewhere;

they sent emissaries—not just on mission trips—but to visit with cardinals and popes and protectors throughout the civilized world. The Spirituals wanted none of this. They wanted things to remain as they were in the early days with Francis and Clare. To them, there was little difference between the *Rule* of St. Francis and the Gospels themselves; that is, in fact, how Francis intended it.

Beginning at about the time of Francis's death, the ministers of the Order began to take firmer control. The dissension that eventually led to the separation of Conventuals from Spirituals began even in Francis's own lifetime. He resigned as leader of the Order and changes began to take place. The Order was growing into something that was too large for him to lead simply by the force of his charismatic teaching and personality. We even see scenes in which Francis, at the end of his life, was pleading for permission to speak to gathered assemblies of Franciscans.

After Francis's death, it was the papacy of Gregory IX that really heated up the debates. Gregory listened carefully to those ministers who wanted to make changes. On the other side were Brother Leo and his followers, who insisted that the words of Francis's *Testament* be enforced. In the *Testament*, Francis wrote very clearly that there should be no other rule for Franciscan life than the *Rule* that he wrote, and also that his *Testament* would provide any commentary on the *Rule* that was necessary. Gregory IX ruled controversially after Francis's death that the *Testament* did not have any legal authority on the Order because it had never been formally approved by the ministers.

Prominent among the Spirituals after the deaths of Francis and Clare were the friars Leo, Angelo, and Giles, but the minister-general at that time, John of Parma, was also sympathetic. A priest and professor of theology, he was the sort of Franciscan that the Conventuals could easily understand, but yet the texts tell us that he aided the Spirituals' cause by removing restrictions that had been put upon them. John of Parma held office from 1247 until 1257, when it is most likely that he was urged to resign by Pope Alexander IV. Bonaventure was then elected minister-general, and he tried John of Parma in a doctrinal court for heretically adhering to the teachings of Joachim of Fiore. Eventually, John was acquitted and retired to a hermitage.

Ubertino of Casale (d. 1329) led the embattled Spirituals into the fourteenth century. He is the monk made famous by Umberto Eco in his novel *The Name of the Rose*. Late in life, he became known as a grizzled veteran of spiritual and political battles within the Order. There is a touching scene from 1285 when Ubertino visited the aging John of Parma at his hermitage in Greccio, the place memorable for the reenacted Nativity that Francis created with real people and animals. Like John, Ubertino became a champion of the ideas of Joachim of Fiore and wrote a lengthy work applying Joachim's historiography to his present situation.

*The Nativity of St. Francis*

The Spirituals did not always stand on solid, reasonable ground in their disputes with the leaders of their order, and the papal schism of the early fourteenth century (when two or three competing popes were ruling simultaneously, sometimes excommunicating each other) only confused the situation further. Like Joachim of Fiore, Ubertino strove to demonstrate how then–current events fit God's prophetic plans. He believed that Elijah prefigured Christ, and that Christ prefigured Francis of Assisi. He was enthralled with the Apocalypse of St. John. We shouldn't trust this sort of enthusiasm. We have good reasons, in fact, to be suspicious of any Christian who has a strong attachment to the book of Revelation. Nothing good has ever come of such speculation. Instead, wars have begun, passions enflamed that run counter to the teachings of Christ, and endless theological debates. We shouldn't trust Ubertino's prophetic comparisons of the anti-Christ in Revelation 13 to Pope Boniface VIII any more than we trust such comparisons to figures in our own day.

The first effort of the Spirituals to really organize came in the days just after the death of Bonaventure, in 1274, at the Council of Lyon that year. Their leadership came from that area of Italy known as the Marches of Ancona, a region where many of them were living in relative seclusion, safe from the Conventuals, who occasionally wanted to do them harm. It was in the Marches that the Spirituals preserved the oral tradition of the tales of Francis's life known as the *Fioretti*: "The province of the Marches of Ancona was once full of holy men shining like lights from heaven. Their holy, resplendent example filled the skies as stars illuminate the world on a dark night."[127] In fact, there were not only holy *men* in the Marches— there were holy *women*, as well. Most scholars believe that the first convent of Poor Clares outside of Assisi was founded there when an entire convent of Benedictine women asked for permission to join the movement founded at San Damiano.

It would not be long, however, before the Conventuals would tolerate the Spirituals no longer. Religious truth was taken very seriously in the late Middle Ages in ways that are difficult to understand today, and monastic obedience was an equally serious matter. The Conventuals believed that obedience was more important than any other virtue in a friar, and the Spirituals were disobedient sons who needed to be punished in order to learn the truth. Obedience could even be beaten into someone, if necessary.

# AFTER CLARE'S DEATH

C lare had been alluding to her impending death for months by the time she lay dying in a small corner of San Damiano. Thomas of Celano tells us that she was looking forward to death so that she could meet the poor Christ whom she loved so much. It was the summer of 1253, exactly twenty-seven years after her friend, Francis, had gone through his own preparations for death.

Clare knew that she would die. In the days before modern science and medicine, it was far more common to wither away slowly from disease than it was to die of a massive coronary or be trampled by an oxcart. Clare called for one of the friars to come and hear her confession and give her Communion, and it appears that it was Brother Reginald who came first. Other friars came too, and she asked them to recite various passages from Scripture, probably the penitential psalms, and then the psalm that Francis had prayed just before his own death, number 142:

> I cry to the LORD with my voice;
>> to the LORD I make loud supplication.
> I pour out my complaint before him
>> and tell him all my trouble.

# After Clare's Death

When my spirit languishes within me, you know my path;
>
> in the way wherein I walk they have hidden a trap for me.

I look to my right hand and find no one who knows me;

> I have no place to flee to, and no one cares for me.

I cry out to you, O LORD;

> I say, "You are my refuge,
>
> my portion in the land of the living."

Listen to my cry for help, for I have been brought very low;

> save me from those who pursue me,
>
> for they are too strong for me.

Bring me out of prison, that I may give thanks to your Name;

> when you have dealt bountifully with me,
>
> the righteous will gather around me.[128]

Thomas tells us that when Clare saw Brother Juniper among the friars, she asked him to speak his eloquent parables and witty sayings, teaching her again with reminders of Franciscan beauty, joy, and foolishness. His words so moved her that she turned to the sisters and reminded them of their vows and the promises of their calling. Medieval deathbed penitents were often advised by their clergy to look at a cross on the wall, or to simply lie on their backs and look up to heaven, and to fear death. But Clare was not afraid; she wanted death to come, and Juniper had reminded her why.

Clare was mindful of the young but troubled movement she would be leaving behind. We also know that Angelo and Leo were there at her deathbed, along with many of the sisters. They were Spirituals, and of one mind with Clare about the future of their way of living. She was the most important disciple of the one who first inspired her—and all of Italy—to joy and faith and a renewal of the bond between humanity and creation. Francis had burst onto the parched religious scene half a century before, and after two decades of meteoric spiritual growth and enlightenment, his movement had been waylaid by controversy, dissension, and scandal. And now, there lay Clare. Together with only a handful of others, she represented another ending of an era of faithfulness to the original ideals.

An Austrian artist known to history as the Master of Heiligenkreuz painted a scene of Clare's deathbed in about 1400 that accentuated the mystical. The remarkable painting hangs now in The National Gallery of Art in Washington, D.C., and depicts the vision of Sister Benvenuta, one of Clare's original followers, as she testified at the hearings for Clare's canonization. Benvenuta saw her spiritual mother surrounded on her deathbed by the Virgin Mary and various virgin martyrs. In the vision and in the painting, St. Mary supports Clare's head, comforting her, while St. Barbara, St. Margaret of Antioch, St. Catherine of Alexandria, and St. Agnes of Rome stand all around.[129] In addition to psalms, it would be surprising if Clare's sisters had not sung the Salve Regina to honor the Virgin Mary at the death of this virgin soon-to-be saint:

Hail, holy Queen, mother of Mercy!
Our life, our sweetness, and our hope!
To thee do we cry, poor banished
children of Eve, to thee do we send
up our sighs, mourning and weeping
    in this valley of tears.
Turn, then, most gracious advocate,
thine eyes of mercy toward us; and
after this our exile show unto us the
blessed fruit of thy womb, Jesus;
O clement, O loving, O sweet Virgin Mary.

Pray for us, O holy Mother of God
that we may be made worthy of the
promises of Christ.

Just before passing away, Clare began speaking quietly to herself, saying, "Go forth, go forth, you are blessed and created by God." One of the sisters asked her who she was talking to, and Clare replied, "I am talking to my own happy soul!"

Clare had always wanted to stick to the ideals. Nothing else would do—for either the Poor Clares or for the other Franciscans who insisted on faithfulness to the original *Rule* of Francis. It is somewhat unfortunate that she took to calling herself Francis's *pianticella*, or "little plant," because she was much more than that. Bonaventure later built on Clare's self-declaration and referred to her as "the first flower in Francis' garden," which couldn't have meant the chronological first, but rather, the superlative first. Even so, I believe that these images diminish more than flatter her.

She had been given a great gift on her deathbed. Clare was the first woman in history to write her own *Rule* for religious life, and it was approved only two days before she died. The story of Clare composing her *Rule* is a story of tremendous courage and a testimony to the strength of her will. Before Clare, men wrote all of the rules for women. But she campaigned for the opportunity to compose her own for much of her religious life, and especially after the death of Francis. Preserving voluntary poverty in all areas was her goal. She wanted to be sure that the Poor Clares would own nothing, including the houses that they lived in, and rely entirely on the graciousness of the brothers to bring them what was necessary. In 1253, Pope Innocent IV granted approval for Clare's *Rule* that included these provisions. A few years earlier, he himself had insisted that the women relax their commitments, just as Pope Gregory IX had done in the years immediately following Francis's death. She kissed her *Rule* before she died, beside the place where the pope had signed it with his approval.

Clare's *Rule* would prove a disappointment to the true disciplinarians, however. The Dominican sisters, who were closest to the Poor Clares in many respects, had rules against laughing or making someone else laugh, eating without permission, and any subtle rebellion in word or deed. Penalties for breaking the rules were spelled out in detail. Flogging was a common form of discipline, and humiliating oneself by eating bread and water while kneeling before the rest of the community, a common penance. With its themes and emphases, Clare sent the message to her sisters and to the authorities who approve monastic rules not that Franciscans were not serious or strict—because Francis and Clare could be both—but that to be a Franciscan was a decision made each day, voluntarily, for Christ. The spiritual life is not a path of renunciations.

She died on August 11, 1253, and her body was buried, as Francis's had been, at San Giorgio. Two years later, on September 26, 1255, Clare was canonized by Pope Alexander IV, who had once been Clare's cardinal-protector but then succeeded Innocent IV as pope. In 1260, again like Francis, her body was transferred to the crypt of a great church built for her, the Basilica of St. Clare. The two basilicas face each other, one on either end of Assisi.

After Clare's death, the spirit of the age seems to have turned more and more away from the joy and freedom and charity that had defined the previous fifty years. Ominous events showed the waning of their spirit on the religious scene. There was, for instance, the rise of self-flagellation and the use of self-inflicted pain as a tool for spiritual understanding and commitment. The theologian Peter

Damian had defended self-flagellation in the eleventh century but the practice did not become widespread until the middle of the thirteenth. Flagellants and others used pain as a vivid way of remembering what Christ did on the cross—and, more aptly—in the scourging he received on the way to the Cross.

The Flagellants became a group of like-minded and penitent laypeople in about 1260. Led by a hermit from Perugia, neighbor town to Assisi, they felt that they were atoning for their sins through public whippings, and their emotion seemed to match the era, which was full of war and conflict, plague and death. These groups of people appeared from town to town throughout what is now Italy, France, and Germany, and became especially prominent a century later when the plague, or Black Death, was at its height.

Franciscans also began to discriminate narrowly as to who would be admitted and who would not in the decades after Clare's death. Contrary to Francis's original vision of inclusiveness, Salimbene tells of the friaries judging on the basis of parentage, literacy, and seriousness—none of which were important in the early days. Some of those who were ultimately rejected by the Order on grounds such as these would periodically form their own makeshift groups in attempts to model themselves after the *real* Francis. The response of the Franciscans to these groups was to condemn them and to appeal to Rome to take measures toward the same. We actually see some of the first instances of what would later become known as litigating to prevent trademark infringement, as the ministers appealed to the pope to forbid any other organizations from copying the traditional Franciscan habit, sandals, and cord.

Theology took on greater importance as well. Within one year of Clare's death, the task of fighting heresy—known as the Inquisition— was transferred from the Dominicans to the Franciscans. The

Dominicans were founded for the express purpose of fighting heresy, which is why the pope so quickly granted permission to young Dominic of Guzman's new order. The name Dominican (*Domini canes* in Latin) means literally "Hounds of the Lord." The early Dominicans commonly used force, fierce argument, and religious courts in order to combat those who held heretical beliefs within Christianity, and occasionally, non-Christians. Supported by the brilliant theological method of Thomas Aquinas and Albertus Magnus, two great Dominican theologians, they sought to solidify their theological system as the official one of the Church, and to argue its infallibility to those who might disagree.

Francis and Clare had had no stomach for these sorts of militant, theological arguments over orthodoxy; but after their passing, many of the Franciscans did. The transferring of Inquisition responsibilities was a way for Rome to place its support firmly against the Spirituals, who only wanted to continue the focus of Francis and Clare: Love over the sword, orthopraxy over orthodoxy. The hope of Dante's *Paradiso* would have made sense to them, but not the intimate characterizations of divine punishments and sentences of judgment in the *Inferno*. Dante wrote fifty-five years after Clare's death. A generation later, when the plague reached Umbria with terrifying force in 1348, many called it God's judgment. Francis and Clare never would have had such an idea, even though they came into contact with a tremendous amount of sickness and death. Essential evil was not a subject that they ever chose to think about. Until the end, their sole vocation remained loving rather than identifying or discussing what might be the opposite of love. Dante's final couplet from *Paradiso* fits perfectly as the voice of Francis and Clare:

My will and my desire were turned by love,
The love that moves the sun and other stars.[130]

## KILLING THE SPIRITUALS

The series of events that brought an end to the breakaway movement of the Spirituals is one of the darkest in the history of Christianity. After Clare's death, the aim of the Spirituals was to obtain authorization for a separation from the Order. They insisted that they must have the right to practice their faith as they believed Francis himself would have them to do. Many of them, in fact, by this time in history had never once resided in a Conventual, or approved, Franciscan monastery. They were living completely outside the boundaries of the accepted Order. They wandered from town to town and preached, begged, and prayed, as Francis had done. They flourished—more in vehemence and emotion than in numbers—primarily in the Umbrian and Marches regions of Italy and also in southern France. But the divisions grew deeper and deeper. The Spirituals were more separated from the Conventuals than ever before, both geographically and religiously, and the Conventuals seemed to them to be completely lost. By 1292, for instance, a rule actually had to be passed that told friars to stop carrying knives and purses in their belts.[131]

For less than a year, from July to December of 1294, the Spirituals found a friend in Pope Celestine V. Celestine gave them permission to live in separated, small hermitages, similar to those that once surrounded the Portiuncula, and to practice Francis's *Rule* apart from any outside interpretations, from the papacy or elsewhere—a right that Francis himself had foreseen would likely be infringed upon as he wrote: "I, Brother Francis, firmly command and decree that no one delete or add to what has been written in this life. The brothers may have no other Rule."[132] These particular Spirituals formed another breakaway group from the larger, more disorganized Spirituals, and for a time took the name Celestine Friars, in honor of their champion pope, or Poor Hermits, a phrase of which Francis would only have approved the first half. There were splinter groups everywhere at this time, and Church authorities were becoming more and more impatient.

Celestine V had a hermit's disposition and a saintly personality. He was completely unsuited for the late medieval papacy and resigned in less than a year, the first man ever to do so. Within three days of his election in December of that year, the new Pope Boniface VIII rescinded every favor of leniency that Celestine had granted in his year in the chair of St. Peter. Many Spirituals fled to faraway places such as Greece and Sicily to both "withdraw from the brothers' wrath and . . . that they should retreat to . . . freely serve the Lord," according to Angelo Clareno, who took over the leadership of the Celestine Spirituals in 1305 and later wrote the history of the period.[133] The Spirituals then rejected Boniface VIII as pope, and were promptly (and understandably) excommunicated by him.

Boniface, meanwhile, chased down and imprisoned Celestine—employing soldiers to hunt him on foot through the woods of Apulia (Celestine simply wanted to find a quiet hermitage) and then by sea as the monk fled across the Adriatic in a boat—because Boniface was afraid that Celestine's sweetness and sympathies for the Spirituals could gain the appearance of ecclesiastical authority. A pope had never abdicated the throne before, and Boniface's paranoid mind feared that the people might not accept his resignation as easily as the College of Cardinals had done. In truth, Boniface—a skilled jurist and diplomat—had maneuvered and manipulated for the resignation and removal of the recluse Celestine. Eventually, the poor ex-pope washed ashore in the middle of the night as a result of a violent storm and landed back in Italy, at the village of Vieste on the tip of the Gargano peninsula, a beautiful place that is mostly national park today. Celestine would have liked to remain there in quiet, but instead was captured by Boniface's men and returned to Rome. He was brought before Boniface and then sentenced to exile in a castle near Rome, where he died less than a year later.

After Boniface, Clement V was elected to the chair of St. Peter in 1305. Like Celestine before him, Clement was at times lenient with the Spirituals and pleaded with them in France to find monasteries in which to reside, wanting to bring a peaceful end to the controversies surrounding observance. As a result of Clement's peacemaking efforts, three Franciscan monasteries saw an influx of Spirituals return: at Beziers, Narbonne, and Carcassonne, all in the Languedoc region of France. But within a few years, when both Clement and a sympathetic Franciscan minister-general (Alexander of Alexandria) had died, Conventual superiors were again appointed at these convents, and the conflict really heated up. The Spirituals were booted from the three monasteries, and they responded by attempting to take two of them, Beziers and Narbonne, by force. This won them quick, fresh excommunications, but the Spirituals persisted, this time by peaceful means, taking their appeal to yet another General Chapter meeting of the Order, in Naples, Italy, in 1316. In the year following, then Pope John XXII, at the urging of minister-general Michael of Cesena, brought a number of the Spirituals' leaders, including Angelo Clareno and Ubertino of Casale, to appear before him in Avignon for a doctrinal trial. They were ordered to submit to authority or be excommunicated and burned at the stake. "Great is poverty, but greater is obedience," Pope John infamously said.

Twenty-five of these men were given over to an Inquisitor, who, according to the euphemistic language of the *Catholic Encyclopedia*, "succeeded in converting twenty-one of them," which means that they were threatened and tortured. The remaining four refused to acknowledge a religious authority higher than the original *Rule* of St. Francis, which they believed to be equivalent to the very gospel of Christ. These four were burned at the stake in Marseilles on May 7, 1318, a horrific day in the history of the Church and the Franciscan movement.

The two most prominent Spirituals were spared death at the hands of John XXII: Ubertino of Casale, because he was defended in Avignon before the papal court by a sympathetic cardinal, and Angelo Clareno, because he fled for his life. Any remaining Spirituals were further marginalized and resided with Angelo in one of the most remote and arid regions of Italy, Basilicata. It is there that lonely mountain peaks slide down into the Ionian Sea. These men were soon known as *Clareni*, because the Spirituals had been officially suppressed, and after Angelo himself died in 1337, we hear very little more of them.

# 16

# LIGHT IN
# THE DARK AGES

The most famous scene of Francis and Clare together must be the occasion of their "Holy Conversation." The occasion was alluded to in chapter 1 in the discussion of St. Benedict and St. Scholastica, and an image of that day can be seen on page iv of this book.

Francis had to be persuaded by his brothers to eat this special meal with Clare. For some reason, even though the texts say that Francis would often visit Clare at San Damiano, he was hesitant to sit down at table with her there. Perhaps he felt that the formality of it, or the preparations that would be made for it, were unnecessary. Nevertheless, this is one occasion when we see the friars chiding their founder. According to *The Little Flowers*, his companions said to him, "Father, it seems to us that you are being too strict in this instance, and not living according to the love that you preach. You should grant this simple request of Sister Clare, in so little a thing as having a meal with you."

He was persuaded and replied, "Since it seems so to you, I agree. But, let's make the meal even more enjoyable for Sister Clare, and have it at St. Mary of the Angels [Portiuncula], for she has been cloistered for a long time. Besides, she will enjoy seeing that special place once again where she first became the spouse of Christ."

When Clare arrived that day, she first paid respect to the statue of the Blessed Virgin above the altar, and then the friars showed her around the place until dinner was ready. It had been several years since she had seen Portiuncula and the small compound of huts that had grown up around it. They all ate together on the bare ground, as Francis always preferred to do. During the first course, it is said that Francis began to speak about God in such a way that the whole place was filled with light. Clare listened, and spoke, and together the two of them became so caught up in the presence of God that a miraculous light shone brighter and brighter all around their humble table. As would happen later on Mt. Alverno, people would remember that day as one when an inexplicable light shone brightly in the distance. In fact, it is even said that some men from Assisi ran to Portiuncula in order to put out a blazing fire, but saw only Francis, Clare, and the others with a beautiful meal placed before them, beside themselves in contemplation of God.

In the life to come, we may imagine the Poverello and Pianticella still together, enjoying each other's company at that humble but elaborate banquet. The image of a sumptuous meal is an appealing metaphor for heaven. Who wouldn't want to sit at that table, even if just for a few minutes!

Long before that meal and holy conversation in Assisi, a Pharisee named Simon invited Jesus to a meal. When Jesus arrived at Simon's house and took his place at the table, Luke says that a woman came in who had a bad reputation in town. She had heard that Jesus was dining with the Pharisee and brought with her an alabaster jar of ointment. As she was waiting behind Jesus, weeping, her tears fell freely on his feet and she wiped them with her hair. Then she covered his feet with kisses and anointed them again. The Pharisee doubted that Jesus could be a true prophet, since he knew that the woman was disreputable and since he allowed her to touch him. But Jesus said to Simon: "I tell you that her sins, many as they are, have been forgiven her, because she has shown such great love. It is some-one who is forgiven little who shows little love." And then he said to the woman, "Your sins are forgiven."[134]

This story of Jesus and the woman with the alabaster jar speaks to why we may feel drawn to Francis and Clare. Jesus forgave the woman's sins not because of her *beliefs*, or even because of her repentance (she does not, in fact, repent using any words), but simply because she *loved*. This is very much how Francis and Clare lived. They did not accumulate many beliefs, and they were not famous for their penitence. They were lovers.

There will always be skeptics on the relevance of living a life in the way of Francis and Clare today. Skeptics will argue that the radical nature of their commitments make for a nice story, but not for a plan of life. If we take evolution at face value, people will say, then humankind originated as a species struggling to survive over other species. We are intended to struggle with each other; unconditional charity for strangers is out-of-date. Families and communities and nations must be protected, and this often means that loving all people seems impossible. Francis and Clare's radical love for their neighbor may have once been possible for friars and sisters, but for the rest of us in the secular world, it simply doesn't work.

Voluntary poverty is unrealistic, they will argue. God wants us to have our hearts' desires. Besides, successful economic systems and social structures are built upon the premise that there will be winners and there will be losers. Hard work is justly rewarded.

Skeptics will argue that redefining *family*—so that we develop attachments with a wide range of people, even strangers and the unwanted, as our brothers, sisters, mothers, and fathers—does not work in our world. We need to care for and provide for and protect our families, first and foremost. What helps my family may directly or indirectly hurt others, but that is just the way it is in a fallen world.

Some of those values praised by Jesus in the Sermon on the Mount—meekness, poverty of spirit, peacemaking, purity of heart—were for a past era. Today, we have to look out for ourselves.

We still live in the Dark Ages when we think or live as if we believe these things. If we live today in a golden age of learning and moral enlightenment as compared to the late Middle Ages, we'd better understand that our vice and inhumanity still rival or exceed what was happening in those centuries that we often label as "dark." Our religious sophistication has not cured us of irreligion, which is as common now as it was then. And for all of the progress we have made against superstition, for medicine and education, these enlightenments have not made the famines, misery, ferocity, or ignorance any less.

Francis and Clare turned dark thinking upside down. According to their way of life, winners become losers and losers become winners. This can be done dramatically, as in the example of St. Maximilian Kolbe, who offered to die in a Nazi concentration camp in place of another man because the other man had children to care for. By giving up what little power he had left, Maximilian Kolbe gained everything that matters most. But it happens most often in very subtle, less dramatic, unseen ways. What would happen if Christians were to begin to follow Jesus in some of the ways of Francis and Clare? The world as we know it would change slowly but surely into something resembling the kingdom of God that we yearn for.

In the Sermon on the Mount, Jesus asked us to be perfect. Remove from your mind the images created by others as to what "perfect" means. When we love, we are remembering Christ's love for us, but more important, we are literally re-membering the broken Christ. That's perfect. Much more than recalling what Christ once did, to be the body of Christ is to literally put him back together in that new formation that Jesus hinted about and Francis and Clare remind us of. That's perfect. When we accept that Christ has given us the power to forgive sins—"not seven times, seventy times seven"—we realize that we are called to become like God. That's perfect. When we begin to become who we are supposed to become indwelled by Christ, that is perfect.

His biographers tell us that Francis was profoundly affected by the words "The Word was made flesh" from the beginning of John's Gospel. Francis felt a great tenderness toward the incarnate Christ lying in a stable manger; and he felt passionately driven to make sense out of the responsibility of having the same stuff on his bones and in his heart as Christ had.

Both Francis and Clare lived an incarnational life, seeing themselves as more fully human the more that they became like Christ. They showed God's presence not by argument or even by teaching so much as by the way they embodied it. According to Francis and Clare, the purpose of faith is to follow Christ, and the purpose of following Christ is salvation for others. Salvation is not only for the soul; it is not, in fact, primarily about the soul. Following Christ means saving the world in each situation presented to us: that's the goal of perfection. It means bringing about the kingdom of God, which, as Jesus said, is right here and now. When Francis and Clare burst on the scene at the beginning of the thirteenth century, they were faced with enormous corruption in the Church, war between cities and religions, and malaise from those who had grown tired of what wasn't true about faith. Theirs may remind us of earlier eras, or even our own.

Think back to when Jesus cleared the temple in John's Gospel, chapter two. Worship at that time was based on money (the ability to pay) and the slaughter of animals. John tells us that in the temple Jesus found those who were selling everything from pigeons to oxen. The pigeons were for those with little money and the oxen for those with much. The money-changers were the men who would exchange your Roman coins with images of Caesar on them for currency that was allowed in the temple, without such images. The money-changers of course added a surcharge onto each of those transactions, which were necessary before you could buy your animal for sacrifice in the temple. Jesus came to save his people from religion—this sort of religion. Francis and Clare did the same.

We must continually overcome what happened on the Milvian Bridge in AD 312. It was there and then that the Emperor Constantine saw a vision of a cross in the sky "above the sun"—according to the story he later told to Eusebius of Caesarea—along with the words "Conquer by this." The night after his vision of the cross in the noon-day sun, Constantine said that Christ appeared to him in a dream and commanded him to use the Chi-Rho sign, a symbol that features the first two Greek letters of the name Christ, "as a safeguard" in battle. So he outfitted his soldiers with the symbol and they marched on Rome and conquered Constantine's rival, Maxentius, saying that their victory was thanks to the true god of Christianity. Within a few years, Christianity was treated as the favored faith in the empire, and Christians went from a persecuted minority to the state religion within a decade. What had been protected, nurtured, brilliant, and passionate in small communities of committed

believers and the catacombs became *official*. What the Christians of
antiquity and the Middle Ages believed to have been God's providence and greatest miracle may have, in fact, created a big obstacle to
true faith.

Francis and Clare made clear by their lives that being a follower of
Christ can sometimes get lost amid the details of being a cultural
Christian. Many Christian observers in India eighty years ago thought
that they saw St. Francis of Assisi in Mohandas Gandhi. Gandhi never
renounced his Hinduism, but he often declared himself a follower of
Jesus Christ. There were times during the 1920s and 1930s when
Gandhi would arrive to give a lecture and would simply quote from
the New Testament, usually from the Sermon on the Mount and the
Beatitudes. On one occasion he did this and said: "That is my address
to you. Act upon that." A Hindu intellectual of the 1920s said about
Gandhi: "What the missionaries have not been able to do in fifty years
Gandhi by his life and trial and incarceration has done, namely, he has
turned the eyes of India toward the cross."[135]

It is ironic but true that Gandhi may have been a more faithful
follower of Christ than many Christians have been. Francis and Clare
return us to the essentials of following the Poor Crucified: Give to
the poor; preach good news in your life and with words; worry
little about tomorrow; care for creation and its creatures; always show
humility; and love your neighbor to the point of sacrificing your life
for him. They indeed transformed the darkness of the Middle Ages—
and of all ages—by their lives and teachings. What the Crusades could
not do, burgeoning papal power did not accomplish, and the threat
or promise of hell or heaven would never do, Francis and Clare
accomplished with the help of the Holy Spirit. They transformed
thousands, and then, over time, millions of lives with their way of life.
To live in the spirit of Francis and Clare today is to model Christ in

ways that will cause you to be dismissed as a fool, forgotten like the poor, reviled for your optimism, and yet, somehow, remain enormously attractive to the rest of the world who are seeking peace and meaning. Perhaps that is the sort of revolution we need today.

# CAST OF CHARACTERS

*(by order of their appearance in the book)*

**Clare of Assisi** called herself Francis's *pianticella*, or "little plant," who grew to show God's beauty and provide sustenance for the movement he started. By all accounts, she was a woman of great physical beauty and charm. The document known to history as Clare's *Acts*, written to support her canonization, mentions several marriage proposals. She left domestic life behind at the age of eighteen to become the first woman to follow Francis and was the founder of the Second Order of Franciscans, the Poor Clares. She was a woman of wisdom, sensitivity, and strength. She died on August 11, 1253.

**Francis of Assisi** called himself the *Poverello*, "little poor man," who unwittingly started a massive movement toward Gospel living, receiving thousands of men and women in the first decade alone, following his own conversion from a life of youthful luxury and uselessness. He died on October 4, 1226.

*And the first three to join Francis…*

**Bernard of Quintavalle** remained a lay brother (not a priest), as did all but one of the first twelve followers of Francis. Also like many of the first followers, Bernard came from a prominent and wealthy family in Assisi and was the first person to become a full-time companion of Francis. Tradition holds that this happened on April 16, 1209, when Francis, Bernard, and Peter Catani opened the Scriptures together. He later recruited the first friars in Bologna, in 1211. Bernard died in the early 1240s in Assisi.

**Peter Catani** joined Francis and Bernard to open the Gospels together at the home of the bishop of Assisi on April 16, 1209. They read Matthew 19:21, Luke 9:3, and Matthew 16:24 in turn, and decided then and there that those words of Christ to the first disciples would also be their rule of life. A well-educated man, Peter was appointed the first minister-general of the Friars Minor in the fall of 1220, when Francis resigned his leadership in the Order. Peter died only a year later, in 1221, at the Portiuncula, where he is also buried.

**Giles** left the city of Assisi from the east gate that leads down to San Damiano one week after Bernard and Peter had joined Francis, seeking to join him, too. When Francis met Giles on the road, he led him down to the plain to the chapel at Portiuncula and declared him the fourth brother. One of the most legendary and important of the first friars, he traveled the world on early missions, sought martyrdom during the Crusades, as did Francis, and was with Francis when he died. After Francis's death, Giles was a leader among those who deplored the relaxations of the original ideals. He was visited by popes, cardinals, and Bonaventure, and died an old man in 1262 in Assisi's neighboring town of Perugia, where Francis had assigned him and where Giles lived much of his life.

*The three known as "the three companions," and others...*

**Leo** was, with Angelo, the closest friend of Francis among the early friars. He was ordained a priest at some early point in the history of the movement, and seems to have become Francis's confessor, traveling with him all over Italy and listening to both his teachings and his troubles. Leo was present at the saint's death, and along with Angelo (and Juniper), was also present at the death of Clare. Leo and

Angelo form a vital bridge between the first, best, and most difficult moments of the early Franciscan movement. He died an old man in 1271, and his burial place in the Basilica of St. Francis may be seen today in the crypt below the Lower Church.

**Rufinus** was a cousin of Clare and called a saint by Francis himself. With Leo and Angelo Tancredi, he joined Francis in 1210, one year after the first disciples. He was with Francis during the important early days in the caves of the Carceri when the friars were spending time each day caring for lepers. And he was with Francis on Mt. Alverno when Francis received the stigmata. There are many stories of Rufinus's having dark visions and temptations from the devil, sometimes aimed at getting him to believe that Francis himself was evil, and Francis was known to counsel Rufinus through these trials. He lived to be very old, dying later than all of the other, original twelve, probably in about 1280. He is also buried in the Basilica of St. Francis.

**Angelo Tancredi** was a knight before joining Francis, and his bearing always remained noble, despite voluntary poverty. He was the fortunate friar to accompany Francis on the walk that became the first sermon to the birds. He kept vigil at Clare's deathbed and testified at her canonization hearings. Angelo died in 1258 and is the third friar to be buried in the crypt of the basilica. Some scholars have found evidence to suggest that Angelo and Francis may have been biological brothers.

**Elias** was two years older than Francis. He grew up in and around Assisi and knew Francis from their childhood. A shadow hangs over Elias, as he appears to have had ulterior motives for sanctity from early on. He enjoyed power but lacked the creativity that marked most of the other early followers. He became minister–general after Peter Catani, but his rule was controversial. He was seen as despotic to some, even essentially evil, especially to those who rejected any changes made to Francis's original intentions. Pope Gregory IX dismissed Elias in 1239, and one year later, Elias joined Emperor Frederick II, a violent enemy of the Catholic Church, as an advisor. After a decade of serving Frederick II (whose mercenaries were famously repelled by Clare in their attempt to besiege San Damiano), Elias repented his sins to a priest and the excommunication placed on him was lifted. He died in 1253.

**Juniper** was a close friend of Clare's, and was among those present at her death. He was a terrific fool, and one of the strictest imitators of the life of Christ that the world has ever seen. Francis of Assisi praised him, believed that he probably possessed the greatest degree of self-knowledge of any of the brothers, and trusted him with various missions and responsibilities. He died in 1258.

*Other important friars and Poor Clares listed alphabetically…*

**Agnes**, Clare's sister, joined her in religious life approximately two weeks after Clare's conversion. Agnes was the second member of what came to be known as the Second Order of Franciscans, the Poor Clares. A decade later, Francis and Clare sent Agnes to Monticelli, near Florence, where she served as abbess for more than thirty years. She died in 1253, only a couple of months after her sister Clare.

**Agnes of Prague** was Clare's contemporary and also the daughter of the king of Bohemia. With Clare's encouragement, Agnes of Prague refused arranged marriages to both Emperor Frederick II and

King Henry III of England in order to become a Poor Clare in the Bohemian capital.

**Angelo Clareno** entered the Order in the decade after Clare's death and knew brothers Leo and Giles. He became the leader of the Spirituals in 1305 and fought in vain to return the Franciscans to Francis's ideals of poverty, work, simplicity, cheerfulness, and preaching. Paul Sabatier wrote:"With him we see the true Franciscan live again, one of those men who, while desiring to remain the obedient son of the Church, cannot reconcile themselves to permit the dream to slip away from them, the ideal to which they have pledged. They often teeter on the borders of heresy; in their speaking against corrupt priests and unworthy popes there is a bitterness which the sectarians of the sixteenth century never exceeded. They seem to renounce all authority and make final appeal to the inward witness of the Holy Spirit, and yet, Protestants would be mistaken to seek their ancestors among such men. No, these Franciscans desired to die as they lived: in the communion of the Church which they loved."[136] Angelo Clareno wrote a book, *Chronicle of the Seven Tribulations*, and claimed that the problems between Conventuals and Spirituals began very early in Francis's ministry. He died in a remote region of Italy, leading the few remaining Spirituals, in 1337.

**Anthony of Padua** was born around 1195 and was a priest and monk of St. Augustine before joining the Franciscans in 1220. We know that Anthony was present at the General Chapter of 1221 when Francis presented the second edition of his *Rule*. He was known as a great thinker, a theologian, and one of the early followers to turn to learning more than Francis would have liked. He was canonized by the same Gregory IX who canonized Francis, and even more quickly (only one year after his death in 1231).

**Bonaventure** never actually met Francis, for he was born just as Francis was dying. Bonaventure became minister-general at a contentious time. He wrote a *Life* of the founder that was intended to unify two competing factions: those who were gladly obedient to the pope and cardinals who modified Francis's *Rule*, and the Spirituals who insisted on the original ideals of poverty and humility even when it meant disobedience to their leaders. Soon after Bonaventure's *Life* of Francis was published, all of the previous biographies of Francis were ordered destroyed. He was known as the "Seraphic Doctor," for his combination of personal holiness and brilliant intellect. Bonaventure died in 1274.

**Innocent III**, one of the most influential and powerful popes of the Middle Ages, strengthened the role of the bishop of Rome in ways that have continued to today. He was pope from 1198–1216, and gave the first, verbal permission to Francis for his new movement.

**John of Parma** was minister-general before Bonaventure, from 1247–1257. He was minister-general of the Order at the time of Clare's death. John was sympathetic to the cause of the Spirituals and eased restrictions that had been placed on them. He was also an admirer of the teachings of Joachim of Fiore and was tried for heresy related to those teachings after he resigned as minister-general. He was eventually acquitted and retired to a hermitage in Greccio.

**John XXII** was the pope who effectively brought a swift end to what is called the Spiritual–Conventual controversy, or the fight between those who separated from the Franciscan Order in an attempt to purify it and live according to Francis's original precepts and those who remained within the Order, living according to papal guidelines for it. John called the Spiritual leaders before his court and demanded that they submit to papal authority. "Great is poverty, but greater is obedience," he famously told them. John died in 1334.

**Ortolana** was the devout mother of Clare who later joined her at San Damiano, becoming a cloistered Poor Clare after the death of her husband. Ortolana died before Clare, but her remains were later buried in the Basilica of St. Clare in Assisi.

**Salimbene of Parma** wrote "the most remarkable autobiography of the Middle Ages," according to medievalist G. G. Coulton. He was born in 1221 and joined the Franciscans in 1238. He traveled widely in Italy and France and wrote about the corrupt state of the Church in the thirteenth century as well as about the ways that the Friars Minor were changing things for the better.

**Cardinal Ugolino (later Pope Gregory IX)** took his papal name upon election as an honor to the great reforming pope before him, Gregory VII (1073–1085).[137] As Cardinal Ugolino, appointed in 1217 by Pope Innocent III's successor, Honorius III, to oversee Francis's enthusiastic young movement, he later became pope just before Francis's death, oversaw his canonization, and brought great changes to his Order.

# CHRONOLOGY AND CALENDAR OF IMPORTANT REMEMBRANCES

These dates are taken from a variety of sources, including Raphael Brown's standard edition of *The Little Flowers*, as well as Brown's second appendix to the second English language edition of Omer Englebert's *Saint Francis of Assisi: A Biography*,[138] and various other studies. Dates without days, and even some of those with days, are best estimates only.

## CHRONOLOGICAL OUTLINE OF THE EARLY FRANCISCAN MOVEMENT

**1181** Francesco Bernardone is born in Assisi. In the absence of his father, Pietro (Peter), his mother gives him the name Giovanni, or John, which is later changed by his father to Francesco, or Francis.

**1194** Chiara Favarone is born in Assisi. Her mother, Ortolana, named her Chiara, or Clare, meaning "clear" or "illumined one."

**1206** Francis is twenty-four when his conversion begins in earnest. He renounces his earthly father in front of the bishop. Bonaventure writes in his *Life of St. Francis* that Francis's conversion began twenty years before his death (in October 1226). Pope Benedict XVI paid tribute to the eighth centenary of the conversion of Francis in an August 2006 letter written to the Bishop of Assisi.[139]

1209   (February 24) God reveals the way of life to Francis through verses read during Mass from Matthew, chapter ten: "As you go, proclaim that the kingdom of Heaven is close at hand. Cure the sick, raise the dead, cleanse those suffering from virulent skin-diseases, drive out devils. . . . Provide yourselves with no gold or silver, not even with coppers for your purses, with no haversack for the journey or spare tunic or footwear or a staff, for the labourer deserves his keep."

———    (April 16) Bernard of Quintavalle and Peter Catani become the first and second people to formally join Francis. The movement is founded. Soon afterwards, the three of them settle in the abandoned church of St. Mary of the Angels, known as Portiuncula, or "little place."

———    (April 23) Giles becomes the third person to formally join Francis. Soon afterwards, Francis and Giles travel to the Marches of Ancona region of Italy, which would later become identified with the friars who resisted changes to the Order. By the end of the year, Francis and eleven followers walk to Rome to try to see the pope.

1210   Clare hears Francis preach at the Cathedral of San Rufinus in Assisi. Her conversion begins in earnest.

1212   (March 18) Clare shows her renunciation of worldly affairs to the bishop and townspeople of Assisi during the San Rufinus Palm Sunday service. The following evening, she formally joins Francis in his movement, taking the habit as the first sister friar.

**1216** (October) A letter of Bishop Jacques of Vitry indicates that there are many communities of "Lesser Brothers" and "Lesser Sisters" in Italy living "according to the form of the primitive Church, about whom it was written: 'The community of believers were of one heart and one mind.'"[140]

**1217** or **18** Francis loses control of his Order, abdicates the leadership role, and appoints Peter Catani the first minister-general. Francis struggles to get his friars to adhere to his original values.

**1219** A General Chapter of the Order is held at Portiuncula. Five thousand friars attend, signaling the rapid growth of the first decade.

**1221** (March 10) Peter Catani dies while Francis is away, and Brother Elias is elected the second minister-general.

**1221–1226** Brother Elias is minister-general. Francis calls him his "mother."

**1223** (November 29) Pope Honorius III gives the first written papal approval of a *Rule* of Francis.

—— (December 24) Francis creates the first live Nativity while staying at Greccio.

**1224** (September 14) Francis receives the stigmata on the Feast of the Holy Cross on Mt. Alverno.

**1225** (Spring) Francis composes his hymn, *Canticle of the Creatures*.

**1226** (October 3) **Francis dies and is reborn to heaven.**

**1227** (March 19) Cardinal Hugolino is elected pope and takes the name Gregory IX.

**1228** (July 16) Pope Gregory IX canonizes St. Francis of Assisi.

**1229** (February 25) Thomas of Celano presents the first biography of Francis to the pope.

**1230** (May 25) The relics of Francis are brought to the Lower Church of the new basilica in Assisi, constructed with walls seven feet thick by design of Brother Elias in order to safeguard the body from intruders. Elias conceals the burial of the body in a wall of solid rock.

**1232** Brother Elias begins his reign as minister-general of the Order. He will be dismissed finally by Pope Gregory IX seven years later.

**1240** (September) Clare confronts the Saracen mercenaries hired by Emperor Frederick II as they attempt to attack San Damiano.

**1253** (August 9) Pope Innocent IV visits Clare on her deathbed and Clare kisses the papal bull, *Solet annuere,* a final approval of her *Rule.*

—— (August 11) **Clare dies and is reborn to heaven.**

**1255** (September 26) Pope Alexander IV canonizes St. Clare of Assisi.

—— Thomas of Celano writes the first biography of Clare.

**1257** Bonaventure, the Seraphic Doctor, is elected minister-general of the Franciscan order at the age of thirty-six.

**1266** All Franciscans are ordered to destroy Thomas of Celano's two biographies of St. Francis.

**1288** Former Franciscan minister-general Girolamo da Ascoli Piceno is elected the first Franciscan pope, Nicholas IV.

**1318** (May 7) Four friars, known as "Spirituals," are burned at the stake in Marseilles at the urging of their minister-general and Pope John XXII.

**1318** The *Mirror of Perfection*, written by Brother Leo and others, is written.

**1320s** *The Little Flowers* (*Fioretti* in Italian) is compiled by Brother Ugolino and other members of the Spirituals.

## CALENDAR OF IMPORTANT REMEMBRANCES

*For those who may want to remember these important early Franciscan events in their cycle of daily prayer and worship, what follows is organized by calendar (month/day).*

**February 24** (1209)  God reveals the way of life to Francis through verses read during Mass from Matthew, chapter ten: "As you go, proclaim that the kingdom of Heaven is close at hand. Cure the sick, raise the dead, cleanse those suffering from virulent skin-diseases, drive out devils. . . . Provide yourselves with no gold or silver, not even with coppers for your purses, with no haversack for the journey or spare tunic or footwear or a staff, for the labourer deserves his keep."

**March 18** (1212)  Clare formally joins Francis in his movement, taking the habit as the first sister friar.

**April 16** (1209)  Bernard of Quintavalle and Peter Catani become the first and second persons to formally join Francis.

**April 23** (1209)  Giles becomes the third person to formally join Francis.

| | |
|---|---|
| **May 25** (1230) | The relics of Francis are brought to the Lower Church of the new basilica in Assisi, constructed with seven-foot-thick walls by design of Brother Elias in order to safeguard the body from intruders. Elias also conceals the burial of the body in a wall of solid rock. |
| **July 16** (1228) | Pope Gregory IX canonizes St. Francis of Assisi. |
| **August 9** (1253) | Pope Innocent IV visits Clare on her deathbed and finally approves her *Rule*. |
| **August 11** (1253) | **Clare dies and is reborn to heaven.** One hundred fifty monasteries of Poor Clares exist throughout Europe at that time. |
| **September 14** (1224) | Francis receives the stigmata on the Feast of the Holy Cross during a Lenten retreat on Mount Alverno. |
| **September 26** (1255) | Pope Alexander IV canonizes St. Clare of Assisi. |
| **October 3** (1226) | **Francis dies and is reborn to heaven.** |
| **December 24** (1223) | Francis creates the first live Nativity while staying at Greccio. |

# NOTES

1. Thomas of Celano uses a metaphorical sentence for Francis that explains what I mean by not having to take the hair-shirt description of Clare as fact. He writes in chapter 5 of his *Second Life*: "He wore a religious spirit under his worldly clothing," describing the saint in the midst of conversion.

2. *Francis of Assisi: Early Documents,* vol. 1, ed. Regis J. Armstrong, J. A. Wayne Hellmann, and William J. Short (New York: New City Press, 1999), 579.

3. *The Road to Assisi: The Essential Biography of St. Francis,* ed. Jon M. Sweeney (Brewster, MA: Paraclete, 2004), 81.

4. The authorship of the first *Life of Clare,* dated to 1253–1255, has been debated for centuries. It has variously been attributed to St. Bonaventure and others, but there is still strong evidence to support Thomas of Celano as its author. See *Clare of Assisi: Early Documents*, trans. Regis J. Armstrong (New York: New City Press, 2006), 272–75.

5. Now available as *The Road to Assisi: The Essential Biography of St. Francis* (Brewster, MA: Paraclete Press, 2004).

6. All quotes are taken from the first edition edited by Paul Sabatier (see note below for complete biographical information). These lines appear on the last page of the Sabatier edition, followed by "Done in the most holy place of S. Mary of the Little Portion, and completed this fifth of the Ides of May in the year of Our Lord 1228."

7. Sabatier's *Speculum Perfectionis seu S. Francisci Assisiensis legenda antiquissima* appeared in Paris in 1898. The first English translation appeared that same year, published in London. The title page read: "*S. Francis of Assisi the Mirror of Perfection*, written by Brother Leo of Assisi, edited by Paul Sabatier, translated by Sabastian Evans, published by David Nutt."

8. John Moorman, *A History of the Franciscan Order: From Its Origins to the Year 1517* (Oxford: Clarendon Press, 1968), 295.

9. Ozanam was born into a French family living in Milan, Italy. Initially

trained as a lawyer, he became a judge in the French city of Lyons. At age twenty, he and some friends began what became known as The Society of St. Vincent de Paul, a ministry aimed at helping the poor of all faith backgrounds during the Industrial Revolution. The Society was named for a Paris priest who had lived more than two hundred years before Ozanam and had spent a lifetime serving the needs of the poor. Ozanam himself never tired of his youthful zeal to put his words into practice and to live the gospel. The Society soon spread throughout the world and was established in the United States by 1845.

10. Robert H. Hopcke and Paul A. Schwartz, *Little Flowers of Francis of Assisi: A New Translation* (Boston: New Seeds, 2006), xiv–xv.

11. Unless otherwise noted, quotations from medieval sources are the author's own translations.

12. *Dialogues II*, chapters 33–34.

13. Just to name two: St. Wilgefort asked God for (and was granted) a beard in order to disgust her male suitors. Similarly, Catherine of Siena sheared her long, blond hair for the same reasons, wanting to simply spend time in seclusion and prayer.

14. As we have seen in recent years, works of fiction—such as Dan Brown's *The Da Vinci Code*—can greatly influence public opinion about religious history and spiritual thought. This is nothing new, as Kazantzakis was doing the same a generation ago.

15. Nikos Kazantzakis, *Saint Francis*, trans. P. A. Bien (New York: Simon and Schuster, 1962), 21. Kazantzakis refers to Clare's father as Count Scifi, taking his cue from the great French biographer Paul Sabatier, who made the same mistake in his classic life of the saint. Clare's family name was actually Offreduccio.

16. Ibid., 226.

17. Ibid., 228.

18. Kazantzakis was Orthodox, and some bishops of the Orthodox Church in America have also regretted his romantic notions of the life and faith of St. Francis, but for very different reasons from my own. Responding to a sympathetic letter about Francis written to an Orthodox magazine, the editors recently responded: "For several centuries, various Orthodox intellectuals . . . have succumbed to the lure of a theatrical and romantic

Western vision of sanctity largely unknown in the pre-Schism East or West (except as a symptom of spiritual delusion), but perfectly captured in the cultus of Francis of Assisi. . . . He was a fanatic Papist, lived after the separation of the Roman Catholic Church from Orthodoxy, and practiced a romantic and emotional spirituality foreign to genuine Orthodox spiritual traditions." *Orthodox Tradition* 12, no. 2, 41–42.

19. A film version of the life of Francis of Assisi that is more faithful to reality, yet still full of emotion and beauty, is Roberto Rossellini's *The Flowers of St. Francis*: 1950, 87 minutes, cowritten by Roberto Rossellini and Federico Fellini. It was filmed in black and white, in Italian with English subtitles, and is currently available on DVD from The Criterion Collection.

20. Gloria Hutchinson, *Clare of Assisi: The Anchored Soul* (Cincinnati: St. Anthony Messenger Press, 1982), 1. (This is a pamphlet taken from the larger book *Six Ways to Pray from Six Great Saints*, by the same author.)

21. Adrian House, *Francis of Assisi: A Revolutionary Life* (Mahwah, NJ: Hiddenspring, 2001), 135.

22. Murray Bodo, *Clare: A Light in the Garden* (Cincinnati: St. Anthony Messenger Press, 1992), 13.

23. Miguel de Unamuno, *Our Lord Don Quixote*, trans. Anthony Kerrigan (Princeton: Princeton University Press, 1967), 77.

24. The following stories had their origin in Thomas of Celano's *Second Life* of St. Francis. They were curiously excluded from Thomas's *First Life*.

25. Matthew 5:40–41.

26. Quoted in Norman Davies, *Europe: A History* (New York: Oxford University Press, 1998), 279–80.

27. Luke 16:19–20.

28. *The Legend of the Three Companions*, ch. 4.

29. Umberto Eco, *Art and Beauty in the Middle Ages*, trans. Hugh Bredin (New Haven: Yale University Press, 1986), 55.

30. Søren Kierkegaard, *Training in Christianity*, trans. Walter Lowrie (Princeton: Princeton University Press, 1944), 108.

31. Shusaku Endo, *Silence*, trans. William Johnston (Rutland, VT: Tuttle, 1970), 219.

32. Ilia Delio, OSF, *Franciscan Prayer* (Cincinnati: St. Anthony Messenger Press, 2004), 6.

33. The kissing the leper scene is chapter 5 of Thomas of Celano's *Second Life*. This phrase is from chapter 6, at the beginning of the story that is to follow.

34. Translated by Thomas Lentes in "'As far as the eye can see…': Rituals of Gazing in the Late Middle Ages," in *The Mind's Eye: Art and Theological Argument in the Middle Ages*, ed. Jeffrey F. Hamburger and Anne-Marie Bouche (Princeton: Princeton University Press, 2006), 360.

35. Quote from Salimbene taken from G. G. Coulton's *From St. Francis to Dante: Translations from the Chronicle of the Franciscan Salimbene (1221–88)*, 2nd ed. (Philadelphia: University of Pennsylvania Press, 1972), 297. Slight changes to punctuation and spelling are made throughout in an effort to bring the translations up to date.

36. Ibid., 49.

37. Augustine Thompson, OP, *Cities of God: The Religion of the Italian Communes, 1125–1325* (University Park: Pennsylvania State University Press, 2005), 381. Salimbene joined the Friars Minor in 1238 and traveled widely, writing about what he saw in the Church and in the Franciscan Order.

38. Quoted in Eamon Duffy, *Saints and Sinners: A History of the Popes,* 2nd ed. (New Haven: Yale University Press, 2001), 128.

39. *The Legend of the Three Companions*, ch. 7, 21.

40. G. K. Chesterton, *St. Francis of Assisi* (London: Hodder & Stoughton, 1946), 67–68.

41. *The Mirror of Perfection*, chs. 56–57.

42. Bonaventure, *Life*, ch. 2, 4.

43. *The Legend of the Three Companions*, ch. 6, 17.

44. Bonaventure, *Life*, ch. 2, 3.

45. Thomas of Celano, *First Life*, 98.

46. See Gerald B. Guest, "The Prodigal's Journey: Ideologies of Self and City in the Gothic Cathedral," *Speculum* 81 (2006): 35–75.

47. Luke 2:48–50.

48. *The Rule of St. Benedict*, trans. Anthony C. Meisel and M. L. del Mastro (Garden City, NY: Image Books, 1975), ch. 58, 93, 95.

49. Johannes Jorgensen, *Saint Francis of Assisi*, trans. T. O'Conor Sloane (New York: Longmans, Green, and Company, 1913), 127.

50. *The Little Flowers*, ch. 26.

51. Quoted from Chesterton's essay that began as a review of a devotional book about St. Francis and was then collected into the book *Twelve Types*, and again as *Varied Types*.

52. Moorman, *A History of the Franciscan Order*, 10.

53. Thomas of Celano, *Second Life*, ch. 9.

54. Eve Borsook, *The Companion Guide to Florence* (London: Fontana Books, 1973), 114–15.

55. *The Mirror of Perfection*, ch. 15.

56. David Burr, *The Spiritual Franciscans: From Protest to Persecution in the Century after Saint Francis* (University Park: University of Pennsylvania Press, 2001), 6.

57. *The Mirror of Perfection*, chs. 39 and 41.

58. Unamuno, *Our Lord Don Quixote*, 11.

59. The following descriptions derive, in part, from Augustine Thompson, OP, *Cities of God*, 314–19.

60. 1 Corinthians 11:1.

61. The chapter numbers and Scripture quotations are taken from Paul Sabatier's classic edition of *The Mirror of Perfection*, 1898.

62. Christian Bobin, *The Very Lowly: A Meditation on Francis of Assisi*, trans. Michael H. Kohn (Boston: New Seeds, 2006), 83.

63. Rosalind B. Brooke, *Early Franciscan Government* (Cambridge: Cambridge University Press, 1959), 85.

64. Simone Weil, *Letter to a Priest*, trans. Arthur Wills (New York: G. P. Putnam's Sons, 1954), 36–37.

65. Bernard of Clairvaux, *On the Song of Songs,* vol. 1, trans. Kilian Walsh (Kalamazoo, MI: Cistercian Publications, 1981), 6. The first sentence of the quote is from the Walsh translation; the rest is my own.

66. *The Little Flowers*, xxvii.

67. Thomas of Celano, *Second Life*, ch. 146.

68. Boyd Taylor Coolman, *Knowing God by Experience: The Spiritual Senses in the Theology of William of Auxerre* (Washington, D.C.: Catholic University of America Press, 2004), 9.

69. In keeping with his commitment not to own anything, not to touch money, and yet not to be beholden to any other religious organization, Francis sent

a basket of fresh fish to the abbot of the Benedictines once a year as payment of rent.

70. Since Holy Week of 1957, the San Damiano crucifix—which is known throughout the world—has hung over the altar in San Giorgio's Chapel in the Basilica of St. Clare in Assisi. This is the oldest part of the church, apart from the crypt.

71. Thompson, *Cities of God*, 141–42.

72. 1 Timothy 5:5.

73. Chesterton, *St. Francis of Assisi*, 85–6.

74. Jorgensen, *Saint Francis of Assisi*, 340.

75. Thompson, *Cities of God*, 339.

76. Hopcke and Schwartz, *Little Flowers of Francis of Assisi*, 20.

77. Ibid., 22.

78. *The Mirror of Perfection*, ch. 48.

79. Chapter 2, par. 7. All quotes from the writings of Clare are the present author's translations, based on comparisons with several existing translations. The most authoritative resource for the writings of Clare is currently *Clare of Assisi: Early Documents,* rev. ed., trans. Regis J. Armstrong, OFM Cap. (New York: New City Press, 2006). For the sake of easy reference, each quote from the writings of Clare will reference the paragraph of the letter, *Rule*, or *Testament* from Armstrong's edition.

80. Beatrice of Nazareth, in *Mediaeval Netherlands Religious Literature*, trans. E. Colledge (New York: London House and Maxwell, 1965), 27.

81. Jacobus de Voragine, *The Golden Legend: Readings on the Saints*, vol. 2, trans. William Granger Ryan (Princeton: Princeton University Press, 1993), 225–26.

82. But it does help to be pre-Copernican in order to believe these things. Physicist James Trefil wrote in *The Dark Side of the Universe*: "It's hard to imagine a more gloomy ending to the Copernican odyssey, particularly if you want to believe in your heart of hearts that the earth and its occupants occupy a special place in the universe." The sixteenth-century English poet and preacher John Donne said: "Man, now displaced from the center of the universe, not only sustained a loss of dignity, purpose and direction, but also he was tragically and psychologically divorced from God, the all-unifying center."

83. Thompson, *Cities of God*, 348–49, 378.

84. These stories would never be published as a children's book today; they are best read by older readers. They read like additions to *The Little Flowers,* which was obviously the intention of the anonymous creator. *The Chronicles of Brother Wolf written by Tertius*, illustrated by Sylvia Green (London: A. R. Mowbray and Company, 1939 and 1952), 99, 102. I have modernized the language of the text only slightly.

85. These tales of birds come from Thomas of Celano, *Second Life,* chs. 126, 127, 129. Some are shared in Bonaventure's *Life*.

86. Luke 15:3–7. The quotation of John the Baptist comes from John 1:29.

87. Bonaventure, *Life*, ch. 8, 6.

88. Jacques Dalarun, "Francis and Clare: Differing Perspectives on Gender and Power," *Franciscan Studies* 63 (2005): 16.

89. See *The Assisi Compilation*, ch. 110.

90. Quotes from this text are all taken from *Clare of Assisi: Early Documents* (New York: New City Press, 2006), 259.

91. Thomas of Celano, *Second Life*, ch. 151.

92. Isaiah 6:1–6.

93. Katherine H. Tachau, "Seeing as Action and Passion in the Thirteenth and Fourteenth Centuries," in *The Mind's Eye*, 336–59.

94. Translation by Katherine H. Tachau, "Seeing as Action and Passion in the Thirteenth and Fourteenth Centuries," in *The Mind's Eye*, 343.

95. *The Legend of the Three Companions*, ch. 17, 69.

96. The story of Padre Pio is a fascinating one. His superiors were consistently suspicious of his wounds, questioning their validity for most of the friar's life, but there is no doubt that the mystery of the inexplicable surrounded Padre Pio all his life, making him perhaps the most popular Catholic religious figure of the last century.

97. *Francis of Assisi: Early Documents,* vol. 2, ed. Regis J. Armstrong, J. A. Wayne Hellmann, and William J. Short (New York: New City Press, 2000), 489–90.

98. *13th Century Chronicles*, trans. Placid Herman (Chicago: Franciscan Herald Press, 1961), 57.

99. *The Legend of the Three Companions*, ch. 17.

100. Jacques Dalarun, "The Great Secret of Francis," in *The Stigmata of Francis*

*of Assisi: New Studies, New Perspectives* (St. Bonaventure, NY: Franciscan Institute Publications, 2006), 19.

101. Thomas of Celano, *Second Life*, ch. 154.

102. Bonaventure, as quoted in Moorman, *A History of the Franciscan Order*, 260.

103. Thomas of Celano, *Life of Clare*, 30.

104. Barbara Newman, "Love's Arrows: Christ as Cupid in Late Medieval Art and Devotion," in *The Mind's Eye*, 263–86.

105. E. B. Pusey translation.

106. Teresa of Avila, *The Complete Works of St. Teresa of Avila*, vol. 1, trans. E. Allison Peers (London: Sheed & Ward, 1946), 192–93.

107. Quoted in Newman, "Love's Arrows," in *The Mind's Eye*, 271.

108. Ilia Delio, OSF, *Franciscan Prayer* (Cincinnati, OH: St. Anthony Messenger Press, 2004), 136.

109. *The Mirror of Perfection*, tale 100.

110. Ibid., tale 101.

111. Ibid., tale 123.

112. From The Book of Common Prayer 1979, Episcopal Church USA.

113. When Francis was faced with the horrific effects of leprosy, his story also reminds us of the Buddha's, who saw death and suffering for the first time as a young man and learned there and then that the world was not as his father had led him to believe. But, unlike Buddha, but like a true follower of Christ, Francis returned to face the leprosy-afflicted beggar, and he kissed him.

114. Paul Sabatier, *Life of St. Francis of Assisi*, trans. Louise Seymour Houghton (New York: Charles Scribner's Sons, 1938), xxxiii. In quoting from Sabatier's biography, I use the same principles in modifying the translation as I used in *The Road to Assisi: The Essential Biography of St. Francis*; see 171–72 of the latter work.

115. Sabatier, *Life of St. Francis of Assisi*, 275.

116. Heiko A. Oberman, *Luther: Man Between God and the Devil* (New Haven, CT: Yale University Press, 2006), 26.

117. Harold Elsdale Goad, *Franciscan Italy* (New York: Methuen and Company, 1926), 70.

118. Thompson, *Cities of God*, 409–11.

119. Translation of Johannes Jorgensen, *St. Francis of Assisi*, 380.

120. Translation is my own, modifying slightly that of David Burr, *The Spiritual Franciscans*, 36–37.

121. Thomas of Celano, *First Life*, 98, 109 (these are the sections of the work as divided by scholars).

122. But some commentators have argued the reverse: that Salimbene betrayed Elias by becoming such a critical and one-sided detractor, despite all the good that Elias obviously did for him as a young man. See Brooke, *Early Franciscan Government*, 45–55.

123. John Moorman, *A History of the Franciscan Order*, 57.

124. *Saint Francis of Assisi: The Legends and Lauds*, ed. Otto Karrer (New York: Sheed & Ward, 1948), 152.

125. Unamuno, *Our Lord Don Quixote*, 14.

126. Paul Sabatier, *The Road to Assisi*, 28.

127. These are the often-quoted opening lines from chapter 42.

128. From The Book of Common Prayer 1979, Episcopal Church USA.

129. An image of this painting can be seen on The National Gallery's Web site: http://www.nga.gov/cgi-bin/pinfo?Object=41425+0+none.

130. *Paradiso*, xxxiii, trans. Dorothy L. Sayers.

131. Moorman, *A History of the Franciscan Order*, 185.

132. *Francis of Assisi: Early Documents,* vol. 1, ed. Regis J. Armstrong et al., 86.

133. *Angelo Clareno: A Chronicle or History of the Seven Tribulations of the Order of Brothers Minor*, trans. David Burr and Emmett Randolph Daniel (St. Bonaventure, NY: Franciscan Institute Publications, 2005), 157.

134. Luke 7:36–38, 47–48.

135. Quoted in the Methodist missionary E. Stanley Jones's *The Christ of the Indian Road* (New York: Abingdon Press, 1925), 78. The Anglican missionary to India C. F. Andrews also compared Gandhi to St. Francis in several places in his books, including *Mahatma Gandhi's Ideas Including Selections from His Writings* (London: George Allen & Unwin, 1929).

136. Sabatier, *Life of St. Francis of Assisi*, 1938, 410–11.

137. Pope Gregory VIII—Gregory IX's immediate predecessor in name—was pope for only two months in 1187.

138. Omer Englebert, *Saint Francis of Assisi: A Biography,* 2nd English ed., trans. Eve Marie Cooper, revised and augmented by Ignatius Brady, OFM, and Raphael Brown (Chicago: Franciscan Herald Press, 1965).

139. The letter was read to the attendees of a conference in Assisi. Robert Mickens, "Pope re-evaluates 'spirit of Assisi,'" *The Tablet*, September 9, 2006, 30.

140. *Francis of Assisi: Early Documents,* vol. 1, ed. Regis J. Armstrong et al., 579.

# ACKNOWLEDGMENTS

Many thanks go to the people who have read and commented on the manuscript, as well as to my insightful editors, Patricia Nakamura and Robert J. Edmonson. Many thanks, too, to Marek Czarnecki, the talented Connecticut-based iconographer who has graciously granted permission to reproduce his icon of Francis and Clare in this book. All but one of the other illustrations are reproductions of the photographic images of Giotto paintings in Basil de Selincourt's classic, *Giotto* (New York, Charles Scribner's Sons, 1905); "The medieval St. Peter's Basilica in Rome" comes from *Medieval Italy* by H. B. Cotterhill (London: George G. Harrap & Company, 1915)

Two of my sources deserve special mention. Each has been recently published and, as any reader of the notes portion of the present work will testify, I am indebted to both of them for many of my ideas. These are *The Mind's Eye: Art and Theological Argument in the Middle Ages*, edited by Jeffrey F. Hamburger and Anne-Marie Bouche, from Princeton University Press, 2006, and Augustine Thompson's masterful *Cities of God: The Religion of the Italian Communes, 1125–1325*, published in 2005 by Penn State University Press.

I dedicate this book to Christina Brannock-Wanter, who has taught me much that is in here. Nevertheless, to paraphrase G. K. Chesterton's introductory note to his classic book on Thomas Aquinas, the aim of the present work will be achieved if it leads those who have reflected a little on the lives of Francis and Clare of Assisi to now read more about them in better books.

# INDEX OF NAMES,
# SUBJECTS, AND SCRIPTURES

# ABOUT PARACLETE PRESS

## *Who We Are*

Paraclete Press is an ecumenical publisher of books and recordings on Christian spirituality. Our publishing represents a full expression of Christian belief and practice—from Catholic to Evangelical, from Protestant to Orthodox.

Paraclete Press is the publishing arm of the Community of Jesus, an ecumenical monastic community in the Benedictine tradition. As such, we are uniquely positioned in the marketplace without connection to a large corporation and with informal relationships to many branches and denominations of faith.

We like it best when people buy our books from booksellers, our partners in successfully reaching as wide an audience as possible.

## *What We Are Doing*

### Books

Paraclete Press publishes books that show the richness and depth of what it means to be Christian. Although Benedictine spirituality is at the heart of all that we do, we publish books that reflect the Christian experience across many cultures, time periods, and houses of worship.

We publish books that nourish the vibrant life of the church and its people— books about spiritual practice, formation, history, ideas, and customs.

We have several different series of books within Paraclete Press, including the best-selling Living Library series of modernized classic texts; A Voice from the Monastery— giving voice to men and women monastics about what it means to live a spiritual life today; award-winning literary faith fiction; and books that explore Judaism and Islam and discover how these faiths inform Christian thought and practice.

### Recordings

From Gregorian chant to contemporary American choral works, our music recordings celebrate the richness of sacred choral music through the centuries. Paraclete is proud to distribute the recordings of the internationally acclaimed choir Gloriæ Dei Cantores, who have been praised for their "rapt and fathomless spiritual intensity" by *American Record Guide,* and the Gloriæ Dei Cantores Schola, which specializes in the study and performance of Gregorian chant. Paraclete is also the exclusive North American distributor of the recordings of the Monastic Choir of St. Peter's Abbey in Solesmes, France, long considered to be a leading authority on Gregorian chant performance.

Learn more about us at our Web site:
## www.paracletepress.com,
or call us toll-free at
1-800-451-5006.

# Also by Jon M. Sweeney

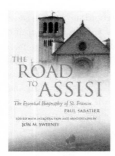

## The Road to Assisi
### *The Essential Biography of St. Francis*
Paul Sabatier

Edited with Introduction and annotations by Jon M. Sweeney

204 pages
ISBN: 978-1-55725-401-6
$14.95, Trade Paper

*A Selection of:*
Book of the Month Club
History Book Club
Crossings Book Club
The Literary Guild

In his 1894 biography, Sabatier, a French Protestant, portrayed a fully human Francis, with insecurities and fear, but also a gentle mystic and passionate reformer who desired to live as Jesus taught his disciples. This modern edition features maps and illustrations, helpful sidebars, explanatory notes, and a complete bibliography.

"Sweeney achieves a fine balance between excellent scholarship and sweet accessibility for every average reader. To learn the life of Francis, to learn to love that life, and at the same time to experience the time in which he lived, this is the book to read."
—Walter Wangerin, Jr., author of *St. Julian* and *The Book of God*

# Also by Jon M. Sweeney

## Strange Heaven
### *The Virgin Mary as Woman, Mother, Disciple and Advocate*
### Jon M. Sweeney

220 pages; b&w illustrations
ISBN: 978-1-55725-432-0
$23.95, Hardcover

"A rich resource of information, insights and beauty . . .
Both critical and reverential, Sweeney offers tribute to a young woman of
courage who became Mother of the Lord and then herself an icon for unending prayers of intercession, consolation and thanksgiving."
—Bishop Frederick Borsch, Professor of New Testament
and Chair of Anglican Studies, Lutheran Theological Seminary

"One imagines Popes John XXIII and John Paul II,
both deeply devoted to Mary and to Christian unity, reading *Strange Heaven*
with glad smiles and prayers of thanksgiving."
—*Crisis Magazine*

# Also by Jon M. Sweeney

 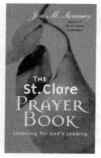

## The St. Francis Prayer Book
*A Guide to Deepen Your Spiritual Life*

## The St. Clare Prayer Book
*Listening for God's Leading*

These warm-hearted little books are a window into the souls of St. Francis and St. Clare, two of the most passionate and inspiring followers of Jesus. "Prayer was to Francis as play is to a child—natural, easy, creative, and joyful," and "Clare was a well to Francis's river," author Jon Sweeney tells us.

*With these guides, you will:*

- Pray the words that Francis and Clare taught their spiritual brothers and sisters to pray.
- Explore the time and place and feel the joy and earnestness of the first Franciscans.
- Pray in classic Franciscan themes of embracing Christ, purity, walking the path of conversion, listening with the heart, adoring Christ, true discipleship, and redefining family.
- Experience how it is possible to live a contemplative and active life, at the same time.

*St. Francis Prayer Book*
164 pages
ISBN 10: 1-55725-352-8
ISBN 13: 978-1-55725-352-1
$14.95, Deluxe paperback

*St. Clare Prayer Book*
192 pages
ISBN 10: 1-55725-513-X
ISBN 13: 978-1-55725-513-6
$15.95, Deluxe paperback

Available from most booksellers or through Paraclete Press:
www.paracletepress.com; 1-800-451-5006
Try your local bookstore first.